TRANSFORMATION SPACE

A strong, sweet, familiar smell pervaded the air. Scraping sounds rasped along the floor.

Jo-Jo fought a compulsion to raise his head and look. As if sensing his desire, Randall pressed harder on his head.

He concentrated on his breathing, keeping it light and quiet. On Dowl station he, Bethany and Petalu Mau had escaped the notice of the Saqr for a few minutes by keeping low, crawling until they'd reached a service lift.

Quiet. Still. Pray. Jo-Jo imagined Randall spitting the words out in that order.

Maybe not pray. She hadn't shown belief in anything much, other than her own ability. Even when things were bad in the Extro ship, he'd never heard Randall call for any god's help.

The sweet scent grew stronger; the scraping sounded right above them. A single Saqr? More? *Don't move. Don't!*

BY MARIANNE DE PIERRES

TRANSFORMATION
SPACE

Book **4** of *THE SENTIENTS OF ORION*

marianne de pierres

www.orbitbooks.net

ORBIT

First published in Great Britain in 2010 by Orbit

A CIP catalogue record for this book
is available from the British Library.

ISBN 978-1-84149-759-4

Typeset in Caslon 540 by Palimpsest Book Production Limited,
Falkirk, Stirlingshire

Printed and bound in Great Britain by CPI Mackays, Chatham ME5 8TD

Papers used by Orbit are natural, renewable and recyclable
products sourced from well-managed forests and certified
in accordance with the rules of the Forest Stewardship Council.

 Mixed Sources
Product group from well-managed
forests and other controlled sources
www.fsc.org Cert no. SGS-COC-004081
© 1996 Forest Stewardship Council
FSC

Orbit
An imprint of
Little, Brown Book Group
100 Victoria Embankment
London EC4Y 0DY

An Hachette UK Company
www.hachette.co.uk

www.orbitbooks.net

For Darren Nash

Sole

Close'm now
Pretty pretty
Know you-all
Eat you-up

Belle-Monde chief of station Astronomein Balbao poured over his daily analysis data flow of the gas entity known to them all as Sole. Something was wrong. Wave readings showed a disturbance in Sole's near space. In the months that the OLOSS scientific community had been studying the Entity, nothing like this had shown in their sweeps.

The Balol scientist pondered whether to discuss this with the tyros. For the most part he found the Godheads – as they liked to think of themselves – a most self-serving and conceited bunch. There'd been a marginal improvement in their attitude these recent weeks, with the absence of the Lostolian Tekton. Of all the tyros, the chief found Tekton the most unreasonable. The pompous archiTect had even tried to foist an unqualified noblewoman upon him as an intern. The very thought of it made the chief's neck frill stiffen.

Tekton always acted as if he had influence, when the chief suspected that he had little. His cousin Ra, however, was a different matter. It had come to the chief's attention that Ra had been seen in the company of Commander Lasper Farr, veteran of the Stain Wars and Defender of Peace. Though the chief wasn't terribly interested in the specific nature of the tyros' projects, like all station masters (and for all intents and purposes, that is what he was – signing damn recreation passes and maintenance schedules all day when he should be addressing more important things), he liked to know the state of play on his station. Belle-Monde may have once been a pleasure palace, but the gigatonne, spinning superficial world was now his observatory.

Mine!

And he found ArchiTect Ra truly the oddest of creatures – unfriendly and jewel-eyed since his most recent transformation by Sole Entity. The chief admitted he'd felt a tang of jealousy knowing that the tight-skinned bastard from the Tadao Ando studium could now see all the waves of the light spectrum. What an amazing gift!

And terrible. Having one's humanesque thought architecture so profoundly changed *must* have flow-on effects, not all of them positive. But then the whole mindshafting process that Sole insisted upon so that he could better communicate with his tyros was as profoundly altering as a thing could be – and no great asset to the already profoundly selfish natures of these professionals.

Take Dicter Miranda Seeward and Lawmon Jise. When they weren't indulging in unashamed sex games in the rooms and corridors of the pseudo-world, the pair were most concertedly trying to upset the research projects of the others. Labile Connit had gone quite insane over Miranda's constant prying into his affairs. Connit had come to the chief, begging protection from the woman, citing that she was stalking him.

The only effect his begging had was to irritate the chief. Why should Balol's pre-eminent scientist have to deal with such petty doings when there was an unparalleled scientific discovery in front of his nose, excreting screeds of empirical data?

And now that data was telling him something had changed.

With more reluctance than he cared to acknowledge, Chief Balbao instructed his moud to call an immediate meeting of the tyros. Decision made, he ordered a hearty roast beffer. The least thing he could do was face the glory-seeking parasites on an empty stomach.

MIRA

Mira lay in the Primo vein, struggling to deal with her dread. Even the soothing nano-replenishers swimming through her blood couldn't calm her emotion. She had begun to lose her pregnancy waters in the conference room on Intel station. Only a trickle at first, but increasing by the time she reached her ship, *Insignia*.

Will my baby die?

The biozoon did not respond through their mental link immediately, and she hoped it was weighing alternatives, not ignoring her.

There is a facility on Scolar that is trialling cell acceleration. They may be able to help us, Insignia said finally.

Cell acceleration?

Your foetus is too immature to survive. It's only weeks old. Cell acceleration may save it. The Pod knows of them and approves.

But Thales believes Scolar society to be affected by the virus. We could be at risk if we go there.

The facility is quite isolated. I don't believe it to be a problem.

You think that is the best option?

Yes. Insignia sounded patient, but Mira knew the creature was fretting to leave Intel station. The normal quiet hum of its biologics roared through her body.

How is shift space? Mira asked.

Insignia relayed an image to Mira's visual receptors. The rings of the Intel shift sphere flared with activity. Queues had already begun to form. Craft jostled each other to gain advantage.

Word is spreading quickly that the Dowl sphere has reopened. 'Esques and aliens are scared. We must leave now, or they may disengage the sphere.

I've caused mass panic, Mira thought.

We don't have time to absolve you of your mistakes. All pretence of patience had left the biozoon's mind tone. It sounded preoccupied. Its anger would come later. *You have shared the truth. The Post-Species have amassed significant weaponry, and some of it is thought to be located on Araldis. OLOSS's existence is under threat. Now is the time to concern ourselves with* our *survival.*

The biozoon was right. *Can you shift early?*

Imperfect shift again?

Si.

Of course. The Omniline are already preparing for it them-selves.

They will return to the Pod?

Yes. Are you able to make a decision as to where to go? Or is your mind impaired by your hormones? If so, then I will choose.

Insignia's last question held no trace of humour.

Mira hesitated, floundering. Where should they go? With the Dowl sphere open, they could try shifting to Araldis and attempt to rescue the survivors on their own, but that would be dangerous, and her baby would surely die.

The Geni-carriers she'd seen leaving Extro space had been headed there, she was sure of it. The Post-

Species had sent a formidable force to her home world. But why Araldis? And when would they loose their arsenal on the rest of Orion? Was that why the Dowl shift sphere had reopened? An attack?

The two 'esques to whom she would have looked for counsel, Rast Randall and Josef Rasterovich, were captives of the Extros. She could not help them. They could not help her.

And yet it felt cowardly to retreat and abandon the survivors on Araldis. Cowardly to run to a distant world and hide and hope that the Post-Species did not go there. But where could she hide? Which planets would the Extros choose to destroy first?

She broke from her inward reverie and glanced at the Secondo vein. The scholar Thales Berniere was enveloped by the vein-sink; only his face and the tips of his fingers were visible where he grasped the edges. A tall broad female soldier in plain garb bent solicitously over him. What was her name again? Fariss. Fariss O'Dea.

'Thales?' said Mira.

'Yes, Baronessa?' he croaked, lifting his head above the cocoon so that they could see each other.

'My baby will be born prematurely. *Insignia* tells me that there is a facility on Scolar that could save my child.'

'Mount Clement,' he said. 'It is ... I'm told ... the best of its kind. But it's foremost an experimental facility – not available to the public, as far as I know. They focus on in-vitro genetics. Bethany spoke of it. She has expertise in that area.'

Bethany. Mira felt a pang of loss for Bethany Ionil's brief friendship. A woman's company right now would reassure her. Fariss O'Dea was not one, Mira guessed, to concern herself with affairs of childbirth. 'Where is Beth?'

The soldier straightened. 'Bethany Ionil travelled to Intel with us.'

'Bethany? On Lasper's ship? You didn't say,' said Thales, looking up at her in surprise.

Fariss laughed. 'You didn't ask. Figured it was best left at that.'

'Bethany may know someone at Mount Clement, Mira.'

'Can we contact her?'

'Yeah, sure, if you want to attract the Commander's attention to us,' said Fariss in dry tones.

Mira, we do not have time to wait. Do you comprehend this? Insignia's urgency sent a skewer of energy through her.

She wavered for another moment. Wait and try and contact Bethany, or leave now? The memory of the Geni-carriers blossomed in her mind. Waiting could mean death for all of them.

'Soldier Fariss, seat yourself in the Autonomy nub. It will protect you through imperfect shift,' Mira said.

'Imperfect shift? Shit! Always wanted to do that.' Fariss gave Thales's shoulder a squeeze and stepped across to the command seat mounted in a tubercle.

Protect her, Mira told *Insignia*.

Res-cushioning flowed around the large body from the tubercle's pores.

'Don't touch any of the functions,' Mira added.

Fariss crossed her arms. 'Wouldn't think of it.'

Insignia, *we should leave.*

Yes. I will manage shift. It is better that you rest.

Mira hesitated. *Insignia* had sedated her twice

without her permission. And yet now fear and fatigue made her almost welcome the idea of oblivion. How long since she had truly rested? How long since she'd had a moment of peace? How long since worry had not gnawed its way through her bones? *Will it help slow down the loss of fluid if I am . . . sedated?*

Yes.

Very well.

Insignia's reply was relaxation stealing across her neural pathways, a drowsy warmth and sense of security. She felt all her muscles loosen and her churning stomach settle. Insignia? *Can you do the same for Thales?*

Yes, Mira.

She drifted, then returned to say one more thing. *I had to warn them. You understand?*

Yes, she heard *Insignia* say before she succumbed. *And no.*

TRIN

They stumbled across the caves in the grey light of predawn. Exhaustion would have stopped them anyway. Most had used up the stimulant pods which had helped them climb up through the tangled undergrowth that cloaked the mountain. There were pods left, but Trin wanted to conserve them until Djes could harvest more and they could build a store.

'Wait! Stay here in the bushes,' Trin told his band of survivors. 'We'll search the caves just before sunrise.'

Djes moved closer to him as the others sank gratefully to the ground.

'Are these the caves you saw when you came here before?' Trin asked her.

She sat down on the moist ground, legs curled out to one side, and waited for him to join her.

His stimulants had worn off as well, and a stale aftermath crept over him. He reached for her as he settled, and she leaned into his arms. Around them, others were doing the same, squatting or lying in the undergrowth close to each other, staring at the dark shadows that signalled cavities in the mountainside.

'Not sure. I think the ones I saw might have been lower down. Perhaps we missed some. We're so close to the summit here. I don't think I climbed this high; I didn't have time. It was dark . . . I'm not sure.'

He stroked her arm. Her skin still had an odd texture from spending so much time in saltwater – slippery, like an eel's, and yet wrinkled. How did he find her even remotely attractive? he wondered. She was not familia, *and* she was part alien.

Yet, her part-Miolaquan heritage – her ability to swim like a fish – had saved their lives. And he'd watched as she'd changed a little more with each passing day she'd spent at sea. The webbing between her fingers and toes had become thicker, her hair thinner, even her eyes; the aqueous membrane showing as she blinked and adjusted to the bare sunlight.

She ventured no further comment now, and Trin found himself drifting to sleep, one arm around her and his back wedged against the trunk of a stunted tree.

He woke like that a short time later, his arm cramping. The lightening sky showed the caves as gaping holes in the pale rock. The mountain is soft, he thought. No wonder the wind has eaten at it.

Around him, others stirred. For so long now they had slept in short grabs, through the daylight, as they sought to escape the invading Saqr. It was impossible to imagine a full night's sleep.

Juno Genarro, Trin's most trusted carabinere, crawled from the arms of his cousin Josefia and over to them. 'Principe? What are your orders?'

'We should eat, Juno. Then take Tivi and look inside the caves. Joe will stay in command of the group. If the caves are not safe, we'll need to find thicker cover before the sun rises.'

Juno nodded. 'And you?'

'Djes and I will walk to the top. It is only a short distance now, and it is important that I see how the land lies from above.'

'You'll have to hurry, or you will be caught without shade, Principe.'

Trin touched the carabinere's arm briefly. 'Tell Tina to bring us some food. And be careful in the caves. The checclia that we saw at the base of the mountain might not be the only mutations on the island. The vegetation is lush by Araldis standards; other creatures could survive here.'

Juno nodded and crawled away.

'Djes?' Trin shook the sleeping girl.

She woke quickly and fearfully, her webbed fingers grasping at the air and her eyes flickering open, revealing her secondary lids.

Trin still experienced a shock when he saw them, yet he'd grown to depend on her devotion; her belief gave him confidence even though his feelings for her see-sawed.

Recently, when it had seemed that she knew more than him, he'd resented her. Trin wondered whether his attachment to her would survive her growing assertiveness and his men's tacit approval of her decisions. There was a place for only one leader among them, and it was not the bitter and gaunt Cass Mulravey, nor the dour Kristo, nor Djeserit, nor any of the others. This was his world, his birthright, and he would do anything to see that it remained so.

'Trinder?'

Djes's gentle question broke him from his trance. He held out his hand and pulled her to her feet, smoothing away his guilt with action.

'We should go to the summit before Leah rises,' he said.

She glanced upward and nodded, seeing no need to question him this time. On many things they were of one mind.

Not all, though, he reminded himself, as they accepted a breakfast of dried fish from the hands of Tina Galiotto. Djes had discovered and used the stimulant pods herself, without telling him about them. She had done it to ensure they were safe, she'd said, a foolish and bold risk. In their flight from the mainland, they'd depended on her to lead their boats across the islands. Without her abilities to swim and fish, they would have perished.

She followed closely behind him as he dragged his weary body up the short but steep distance of bush-covered rock to the mountain peak.

At any other time, the view from the peak would have lifted his mood: sheets of brown sea broken up by the irregular shapes of tiny white islands, and the roaring stretch of the Galgos Strait that they had just navigated and, by Crux's blessing, survived.

To the west he saw larger islands, separated from each other by greater distances and then eventually becoming lost in the Southern Sea. Their yachts would not have made it to any of them, he thought. This island was their only hope.

He swivelled east, to look again in the direction that they'd come. Beyond the strait and the delta of tiny islands nestled against the coastline, the central continent of Araldis was a slim snaking line tinted red by the rising haze of blown sand.

Trin looked back across their track and felt a pang

of loneliness. He was cut off from all the places he knew, forced now to find a way to survive on this island mountainside.

'We've travelled so far. It's hard to believe,' said Djes.

'Si, bella. Surely the Saqr will not bother to pursue us here.'

She nodded. 'I hope not. I suppose, though . . . it depends on why they're here.'

He dragged his gaze from the wide vista to Djes. Why were the Saqr here? Every one of the survivors pondered that question endlessly, he was sure, but there had been no time for discussion, no energy for anything other than keeping the will to survive. 'You have ideas on that?'

She shrugged. In the growing light she looked so tired and jaundiced that he pulled her into his arms. For all his concerns about her growing independence from him and her natural leadership qualities, he could not bear to lose her.

She leaned closer and slid her own arms around his waist, reaching beneath his fellalo to stroke his bare skin.

Trin felt a spark of desire but knew he did not have the vigour to pursue it.

She sensed that almost immediately and withdrew her hand. Locking her grip behind his back, she stayed close to him. 'It's good to be away from them. They watch us together.' She sighed.

'We can't stay much longer,' said Trin. The light was gaining potency.

'Just a few moments. Please.'

He held her tightly. How was it possible to know a person so well, and yet barely have talked to them of anything other than the most practical things?

'Trinder?'

'Si.'

'What is that?' She drew away from him a little and pointed.

High above them, he saw a circular object like a wheel spinning free across the sky. They watched its trajectory to the east in silence.

'Mira?' asked Djeserit finally, hope lifting her voice.

Was it? Had the eccentric Baronessa returned with help for them? Trin's heart contracted for a single beat, and then settled. As far as he knew, OLOSS did not have craft of such a shape and size. 'That is not an OLOSS ship. It would be hasty to think it signifies our rescue. Perhaps it transports more Saqr.'

'No!' Djes turned her face to his. 'Please, let it be Mira. Can't it be her?' Tears squeezed out onto the taut skin of her cheeks.

He trailed a fingertip in their wake. Djes was not given to quick emotion. He did not recall her crying before, other than when the Saqr had attacked her and torn her leg. 'Don't raise your hopes.'

She sniffed and nodded. 'You're right. We are not that lucky, I think.'

He grimaced at that and at the way she straightened her shoulders, and it made him think about her parents. What had driven them to abandon such a pragmatic and resourceful child? Or had that strength grown from her abandonment? When he'd found her outside Villa Fedor, she had seemed needy and weak. Back then his thoughts for her had been purely carnal. Now, though, he found himself relying on her calm, her belief in him.

And perhaps it was not only Djes that had changed.

Though Trin had hated his papa, Franco, for sending him to the carabinere station at Loisa, it had forced him to assume a leadership mantle, or be demeaned. 'We must go back now. I doubt the others could see the craft from below the mountain's lip. Perhaps we should not mention it yet. We can come back here again, the two of us, and watch.'

She nodded. 'I would like that. Lead the way, my Principe.'

They returned to find the group sitting close together under the bushes, listening to Juno Genarro.

'Principe!' Juno sounded excited. 'The caves are deep and cool. I think we've found a safe place.'

A small cheer went up from the group.

'How many?' asked Trin.

'Two larger caves, and several shallow ones. Some rockfall needs to be cleared in one of the bigger ones, but there is room enough beside it for the moment.'

'They are empty?'

Juno nodded. 'Some small droppings, little else. And the floor is clean gravel.'

Trin glanced at the bright sky. Leah was rising. The cave mouths were only a short distance away, but that distance was unshaded. They must move now or spend another day under the bushes.

The thought of lying in a cool darkened place was irresistible. 'We move now. Split numbers equally between the two large caves for today. When we've searched them more closely, we'll decide who shall sleep where.' It was a popular decision, he could see from their expressions. 'Cass Mulravey?'

Mira Fedor's gaunt friend lifted her head and stared at him. 'Yes?'

'Tivi and Joe will go with you. They'll carry Thomaas.'

She didn't argue. Her man lay with his head on her lap.

Trin stepped out from the bushes and ascended the rocky path to the caves, ignoring Joe Scali's look of reluctance at being separated from him.

From me? he wondered. Or Djes?

Trin knew that he was deliberately keeping Joe Scali apart from Djeserit. The moment of physical closeness he'd seen between the two on the beach was chewing at the edges of his mind. They'd been bringing fish back for the others and had guiltily moved apart at the sound of his voice.

He reached for Djeserit's hand. She gripped him back, but the webbing between her fingers prevented him from interlacing Trin's through hers. *Not her. Not Djes. She would never betray me.*

It was a short climb, and only Thomaas had to be carried. Even his madre, Jilda – the oldest and most feeble – managed it, assisted only by her servant Tina Galiotto.

The group divided naturally. Mulravey was followed by her women, her brother and his friends, and Joe, Thomaas and Tivi. The surviving carabinere and the miners who'd joined them in the Pablo mines followed Trin. The korm tagged behind him also.

That surprised Trin, as the outsized alien child had spent most of the journey with the women. Though he knew its devotion to Djeserit, it had stayed shy of him since Loisa, and to be honest the creature made him uncomfortable. He sensed judgement in the strange beaked blue-skinned face. When not shadowing Djes, the korm often paired with Cass Mulravey's ragazzo. Though the ragazzo was much younger – maybe only six or seven Araldis years of age – the two were often together at meals, or as they'd trudged the desert. Right now Trin resisted ordering the korm back to the others. Djes would protest.

He looked ahead. The entrances to both of the larger caves were smooth and oval, one larger than the other. Trin took his party into the large one.

'Why so perfectly formed?' he asked Juno Genarro.

'Lava tubes, Principe. Made by hot gases, I would guess, not erosion.'

Inside, even the walls were smooth. Trin ran his hands along them, feeling the thick grain of the long-ago-cooled rock. As his eyes adjusted, he saw the wider, deeper cave beyond, and the thick back wall of a rock-fall. He glanced at the roof. It seemed safe enough, but it was hard to tell.

'Spread out and find spaces close to the sides. Leave a path free through the middle of the cave. Juno, set watch at the mouth. Then we shall eat and sleep.'

He heard more murmurs of approval as the carabinere surged past him to find resting places in the cooler dark. Juno and Josefia stayed closer to the light, sorting the remaining food from Djeserit's last fishing trip.

A short time later they called everyone to them and handed out the last portions of the xoc. Several days old now, the sea creature tasted bitter. Yet its dry flesh filled the gnawing emptiness in his belly. Trin had ceased to think of food as a pleasure; it was merely a necessity, of which there was never enough.

'I'll fish again tonight,' said Djes to the group.

'And we will begin our search for other foods, and bring more water back,' Trin added.

Despite the bitterness of the xoc and the discomfort of the gravelled cave floor on which they sat, people began to contribute ideas. Optimism sparked into a flame.

A few nights without constant wearing travel, dehydration and exposure would return even more of their confidence. And Trin would be there to steer them. He had been right not to mention the craft he and Djeserit saw from the mountaintop. His people were too fragile for false hope.

JO-JO RASTEROVICH

There had been very few instances in his life when Jo-Jo Rasterovich hadn't been able think of a reply to a question. But this was one of them.

As he knelt beside the mercenaries Randall and Catchut, clawing at the inside wall of the Post-Species ship that held them captive, he had nothing to offer.

'Rasterovich!' Randall's imperative was sharp and unhappy. 'At the risk of repeating myself, how are we going to get us out of this fucking thing?'

Jo stared at the ridging on the ship's smooth inner skin where Mira Fedor's biozoon had torn itself away from the *Medium*. He shook his head. 'I'm the one who had the idea that we should get out. Your turn to come up with how.'

Rast shot him a frantic intense stare. The mercenary looked worse than shit, Jo-Jo thought. Her hair was messed stiff with dry Extro goo, her skin was whiter than anything that had blood running beneath it should be, and her eyes . . . They reminded Jo-Jo of a trapped and vicious animal, one that would gnaw its arm off to get free. He had to think of a way to get out of the Extro ship, or Randall would likely kill herself, and possibly him, trying.

He sympathised with that feeling. His iniquitous confinement on Dowl station and then a recent stint paralysed beneath Extro goo with only his own thoughts for company were enough to convince Jo-Jo that death was preferable to further entrapment.

No doubt the stare he bestowed back on Randall matched hers for lunacy. But thanks to the interference of the newly discovered, and infinitely obtuse, Sole Entity he found he could still think, as well as panic. Randall's unfocused terror suggested that she couldn't.

Whatever Sole had done to Jo-Jo's mind had given him the ability to think in two entirely different ways. It wasn't like that all the time, but under pressure he felt the division like two slices of fruit sliding apart. Emotion and logic – clearly separated, not messily and inextricably interwoven as it was for most sentients.

He glanced at Catchut. The 'esque nursed a broken wrist and a groggy expression that ruled him out as a source of ideas.

'If it's anything like human tissue, the scar is always the strongest part. Like a broken bone. Let's concentrate on an area close to the edge of the scar.'

Randall nodded. 'Sounds right.'

No, it didn't. Jo-Jo knew it as he said it. The *Medium* had travelled though space and res-shift; there would be no weakness. But he needed to keep Randall distracted and working on something while he thought of a solution.

He picked a spot near the corner of the scar and began pinching at it. It was surprisingly malleable. 'Help me.'

Randall immediately began gouging with her fingers. Catchut leaned a hand on the wall but didn't have enough strength to do anything more.

Jo-Jo pinched and pulled the area in front of him while he sought an idea. He couldn't go back inside the *Medium* data flow now that the substance beneath them had solidified. Not that he wanted to. Being suspended within the Post-Species auditory space, deprived of most of his senses, had been the second worst experience of his life. The first was being shot out into space in an EVA suit with little air and no certainty of being rescued.

Perhaps he should just confess to Randall that he was out of ideas and—

'Rasterovich!' Randall shouted.

Jo-Jo couldn't wrap his tongue around a reply because the floor buckled up underneath his feet and propelled him towards the wall. He tried to brace himself, but the momentum drove him head first into the area he'd been prodding.

Instead of the impact he expected to feel, though, his head was suddenly encased by the wall substance, and a smothering sensation overpowered him. He fought to pull back, to breathe, paddling his hands, pushing frantically. But the wall tightened around his head and began to suck him forward, encasing his shoulders and then his waist.

Again. The *Medium* was devouring him again.

But this time, as he let go of his spent breath, his head crowned into clear air and space. He blinked and gasped in sweet painfully pure oxygen. Dizziness came and went. His eyes cleared, then blurred, then cleared again. He felt wind on his skin, heat, and then he was falling.

This time the expected impact occurred, jarring every last piece of him, robbing him of breath again. And yet, miraculously, he was still alive. His brain began to organise images and sounds – moans of pain and garbled words.

He rolled over and spat out a mouthful of sand. Suddenly he was hot. Hotter than he'd ever been. His fingers moved convulsively, scraping at whatever coated his body. More sand. Warm grains stuck to his skin.

'Jo-Jo!'

'Yeah.' It took a while, but he got the word out, spitting more sand with it.

Someone he knew had said his name. *Mira?* He'd been thinking about her, seemed to always be thinking of her. He wanted to look at her face, but sand stung his eyes, so he forced himself up onto his elbows. A haze hovered over his thoughts, his senses only working roughly, but the leverage gave him something to work with.

Darkness. Grades of it. Above him was an expansive gloom littered with sparkling beads. In front of him there was something denser and more . . . sinister. It struck him as funny that he could come up with that word just now. He wanted to laugh, but a stinging slap snatched that thought away.

'RASTEROVICH!'

Abruptly his vision cleared. He was outside, under stars, with the Post-Species ship encroaching on the greater part of his vision. Rast Randall was talking to him, not Mira Fedor, and the mercenary was as belligerent as he'd ever heard her.

'For fuck sakes, get with it! We're out! We're fucking out!'

'How?'

'We got spat out, maybe? You stink like shit. I dunno.

Let's get Catchut moving before they change their minds and suck us back in. Or the Saqr find us.'

Saqr. He crawled over to Catchut, positioning himself alongside so that he could hook Catchut's arm over his shoulder.

'So far – I've had – all – the ideas. Now you – tell me – which – damn direction,' he told Randall, thick-tongued.

The merc pointed without hesitation to rows of scant dotted lights, high above and beyond the dark shape of the spacecraft. 'That's gotta be Mount Pell over there. Which means we're close to the landing port. Can't see it till we get round the other side of this thing.'

Jo-Jo shouldered Catchut's weight, his feet sinking into the sand and his legs trembling. He wouldn't be able to walk far. 'You're sure we're on Araldis?'

'Smells and feels like the same dry piece of crap to me. Sure hot enough to be. Now shut up until we're further away,' said Rast.

Jo-Jo saved his breath for the effort needed to get past the *Medium*'s never-ending girth and over the dunes to the mountain.

He felt better as they walked, buoyed by the blood flow returning to his body. The euphoria of movement wouldn't last long, though. He'd been inactive for too long, nourished only on Sole-knows-what. This burst of energy would fade.

Activity seemed to help Catchut as well, and he began to take more and more of his own weight until he eventually shrugged them off.

Jo-Jo relinquished his hold on the wiry merc with relief.

'I'm figuring the port'll be crawling with Saqr still,' said

Rast, when she deemed it a safe enough distance from the Extro craft to speak. 'Maybe that's why they spat us out. They think we won't stand a chance out here.'

'Coulda spat us into the vac, Capo.'

'I doubt it'd be able to thin its skin in space to junk us.'

'Yeah,' said Jo-Jo. 'Or maybe it'd learned what it needed?'

'Like what?' Randall's voice was sharp and clear, even though she was a few paces ahead of him.

'Dunno,' said Jo-Jo. 'Just a thought.'

'Yeah, well here's – what – I – got,' Randall puffed as she floundered doggedly up the next dune.

Jo-Jo had to force his legs along harder to keep up with her. Randall had her weaknesses, but stamina wasn't one of them.

Catchut did the same, habit more than anything else.

Randall stopped at the top and caught her breath before saying more.

'I'm reckonin' the Extros are here cos they need somethin'. More'n likely a mineral that Araldis has, but not necessarily. Could be somethin' else as well. Thing is, between that motherfuckin' big drum of weirdness and the Saqr, they don't need much to survive here. The *Medium* appears self-sufficient, and the Saqr are primitive as fuck. Jancz and Ilke might be the only other 'esques here apart from any survivors.' She stared towards the darker outline of the mountain. 'I'm bettin' that whatever hasn't burned up there is still how the Latinos left it. There's got to be an AiV in one of those fancy places that works, or that we can get to work. We do that, then we can go scout for anyone left alive. Mira said she told Pellegrini to head for the islands. If they've made it, that's where they'll be.'

It was a long speech for someone not long out of a puddle of Extro goo, and her voice got hoarser with each word. Jo-Jo took some time to digest it all. 'So we've just got to dodge Saqr till we find something that can fly?'

Randall started down the dune and they automatically followed her. 'You got it. More important though . . .'

'Yeah?' As they reached the bottom, Jo-Jo felt firmer ground under his feet and the sting of pebbles.

'Look,' she said.

Jo-Jo could see her pointing to the sky. Sunrise was coming.

'We've got to get to shade before Leah's up, or we'll be mummified before you can think jack shit.'

TEKTON

Tekton's legs didn't seem to want to hold him upright. Fortunately, the nanosuit he'd borrowed from Samuelle lent him stability. A glance across Commander Farr's cabin told him that the old Stain Wars veteran Jelly Hob was feeling much the same.

The pair had been arguing over Tekton's wild demands – that Hob fly him back to Belle-Monde – when Farr's com-sole had activated to record the summit meeting on Intel station. At first they'd paid only scant attention to it, too busy with their own exchange, and the fact that Hob had discovered Tekton trying to access the Commander's Dynamic System Device.

But since Baronessa Fedor's sudden and unvarnished announcement to the summit that the Post-Species were mobilising mass weapons, neither had spoken a word.

Hob broke silence first. 'Only one place this ship'll be going now, Tekkie, and that's to war.' Alarms started up, as if to lend weight to his words. 'I be thinking that you'd best get off now 'less you wanna be flying inta a dogfight with the Extros. Catch a civilian ride; there's enough of them here. Best to hurry though. Things'll get messy, I warrant.'

Tekton nodded, thinking Hob made good sense.

'Yes. Best. What ships are available? And how do I get to them?'

Hob took a step closer to Lasper Farr's com-sole and ran gnarled but surprisingly deft fingers down the pad, calling up reports. Images of the shift sphere formed in the air between them. The rings glittered with activity as ship icons changed positions and jostled for queue ranking.

'Ship's moud says there's around three thousand civvies in-system,' said Hob, reading from the display. Not sure how much longer, though. Dowl res station in the Leah system's been reported as open agin. Couldna' be a good sign. Not if them Extros are there like she said.'

The Baronessa had told the summit that a primitive species, the Saqr, had invaded the planet Araldis and the Dowl station. Now she feared a huge Post-Species force had based itself in the same place – her home world.

Mira Fedor. Such an unimposing figure to be delivering such profound news, thought Tekton. His abdomen tightened with apprehension. Though his academic life had been coloured with devious and sometimes murky politics and the pursuit of personal aspirations, he had never suffered physical threat.

Since venturing into the wider worlds, though, as part of his endeavour to construct an edifice that would impress the Sole Entity back on Belle-Monde, his life had taken a sinister and terrifying turn.

Not quite recovered from Lasper Farr's failed attempt to murder him on the planet Edo, he'd been coerced into hiding aboard the same lunatic's ship as the only way to escape.

Now, it seemed, he'd found himself in the last place

in the galaxy he could wish to be. If the Dowl shift station had reactivated, and Mira Fedor was truthful in her pronouncements, it could mean only one thing: the Post-Species were preparing to invade the OLOSS worlds. And Intel station – where he was now berthed – with its concentration of OLOSS leaders and dignitaries, was a most plump and juicy target.

A trap! yelped Tekton's free-mind. *This whole summit meeting was designed to bring OLOSS leaders into one place. It could be the Post-Species' first target.*

After a few extra moments of consideration, his logic-mind was in complete agreement. *Dastardly simple and effective.*

'They're coming here,' Tekton told Hob. 'The Extros are coming here first.'

Hob stared at him unhappily. The sirens had settled into a high-alert pattern. 'I'm thinkin' you be right, Tekkie,' said the old Stain Wars veteran. 'I gotta get to the bridge.'

Tekton gave Hob's shoulder a light squeeze. He was not inclined to friendly physical displays, but the occasion seemed to call for it. Though their acquaintance had been brief, the grubby pilot genius had saved his life and extended him compassion and kindness. Tekton had never needed those things before; never cared for them nor offered them to others. The halls of the Tadao Ando studium and the corridors of the Belle-Monde pseudo-world had not been places for such things.

To say that the scales of selfishness had fallen from Tekton's eyes was perhaps overly dramatic, but his perspective had altered, he allowed, on some counts.

And now he wanted an opportunity to explore his newfound compassion, see how it affected his decision-making and the outcomes of events in his life.

These arrogant and infuriating Extros, who were planning to annihilate every sentient species in Orion, did not serve his new frame of reference at all.

'Lead on, good fellow. Show me the way off this ship,' he said, gently pushing Hob out of the cabin door. 'But just let me pee first. I'll be but a step behind you.'

The pilot nodded and stepped outside.

In a trice Tekton had snapped up the small black box on Lasper Farr's com-sole and stuffed it inside the seal of his nanosuit. Sammy would be furious to loose her spare combat gear, but there was no time for bargains or explanations. The suit adjusted around the DSD, leaving only the faintest telltale bulge over his belly.

Let's see how Lasper Farr goes without his Dynamic System Device, thought Tekton. And let's see what I can do with it.

He hurried out of the door to join Hob. They moved quickly along the corridor to the lifts.

'Ship'll be in lockdown soon. You c'n use the Commander's uplift to get down ta cargo. Should be able ta still get out through the hold. They'll be loadin'. In that suit they'll think you're Sammy. Shouldn'a be too many questions. Jus' look like you know where you're going. Good luck, Tekkie. We're gonna need it – all of us.'

Hob used his ident to open the door to the private lift and ushered Tekton in. Then the door slid across, and Hob's battered old face was gone.

A ridiculous pang of loss stung Tekton as the lift plummeted to the cargo area of the ship. He might never see the old fellow again, depending how things panned out.

For Crux sakes, suck it up, free-mind barked with passionate concern. *We've got to get out of here. No time for blubbing.*

Concentrate, proffered logic-mind more moderately.

With his Sole-altered minds badgering him, he had no time to dwell on loss. The doors at the other end opened, and he stepped into the ship's large and gloomy cargo bay. No one took any notice of him; automatons and crew hastened around the hold, shifting and securing payload.

Tekton slipped into a gap between crates and crouched down, Sammy's suit making slight wheezing noises with his movements. The loading ramp was still open, but not for much longer, he guessed. He must leave now or face being stuck on Lasper Farr's ship.

That realisation brought an unfamiliar surge of adrenaline-fuelled determination, and Tekton ran with suit-enhanced speed towards the ramp. One of the crewmen saw him and shouted. The ramp light flashed its closing sequence, and the connecting section began to retract.

Heart pounding painfully, legs burning with the effort, Tekton sprinted up the inclining ramp and leapt the distance to the Intel loading facility. He landed heavily, jarring his legs and falling forward onto his hands and knees.

He looked back. Relief lessened the pain. The ramp was almost closed now, and the disorder out on the docks meant that no one would chase him.

Disorder? More like an apocalypse! Free-mind was aghast.

Like an anthill that's been kicked over, thought Tekton. Scramble and scurry.

But logic-mind gave only questions and warnings.

Don't fall in front of that loader! Look for the exit! Which ship is leaving next? Check the signage.

Tekton scanned the leader boards for each dock, but the ship names and codes meant nothing to him. *Something commercial. A captain who'll accept money and ask few questions*, logic-mind instructed.

He walked purposefully through the crowd, his suit lending him agility and speed, praying to avoid an accidental meeting with Commander Farr or Samuelle. Soldiers in a host of differing uniforms swarmed, waiting to be let aboard their ships. Tugs descended to pull the bigger ships to the launch bays. As soon as one left, another replaced it, and the loading continued at a frenetic pace. Tekton could barely make sense of the endless broadcast announcements.

To avoid Farr's soldiers, he headed to the furthest dock, stopping only to ask random 'esques where they were going, hoping to find a non-military ship. His enquiries were met with either garbled panic or ignored.

'I'll pay double your normal fare,' he begged one harried ship's bursar.

'I told you there's no room, mate. I don't give a crap about how much you can pay. We've got the entire Matamon government aboard, and not enough res buffers to fit them. You come on here, and you'll likely rattle to death. That's if we even get out of this damned system in time.'

'What do you mean?'

'The fucking Extros are coming, mate. That's what I mean.'

Tekton stepped back from the bursar's sweaty vehemence. The man was almost harassed enough to pull his holstered pistol and shoot the next person who asked to be taken aboard.

With a growing panic fingering his insides, Tekton watched as the bursar shouted closing instructions for the hold and headed up the ramp.

What will I do? he asked his minds. Wild and dangerous options danced across his thoughts.

Then, unexpectedly, the bursar stopped and ran back down.

'Look, there's a 'zoon hybrid scheduled for berth as soon as we pull out. It's one of the last coming in. Everyone else is in the shift queue or gone in-sys. Hang around this berth and you might get luckier with them.' He checked his hand-com. 'Ship's name is *Salacious*.'

Tekton nodded his appreciation.

'Good luck, mate,' said the bursar and hurried onto his ship.

Tekton's minds considered options while he waited for the trader ship to slip dock. He could go to the station master and request assistance, but with the station in utter chaos it was unlikely he'd be heard. That option also meant he risked an encounter with Farr.

Or he could pay his way onto this hybrid and take what fate brought him. If the Extros were indeed coming, a biozoon might be a safer option than an OLOSS military ship or a mercenary vessel. Biozoons were rumoured to trade with the Post-Species.

All he needed was to get himself, and the DSD that pressed so uncomfortably against his ribs, out of this system. He could make different travel arrangements from the next place he docked. He would wait. Yes. That was best.

Stepping back near the frame of a loader, he grasped its hydraulic arm and held on. The structure shook as ships peeled from their moorings in quick succession, hurrying from the station.

In an absurdly short amount of time, Tekton was alone on the dock and the vibrations had stopped. It was eerie and surreal; just him and the rows of automated loaders.

He wondered, irrationally, if he was the last left here.

Ridiculous, snapped logic-mind. *Not enough ships to get them all off.*

How can you be sure? challenged free-mind.

Tekton let them bicker while he concentrated on his breath and attempted a meditative manner.

At inhalation three hundred or so, he heard a noise. Glancing up, he saw the scarred grey belly of a biozoon descending through one of the docking channels. It set down heavily into the mooring, as though worn out with the effort.

For the briefest flicker Tekton thought it was the Baronessa Fedor's biozoon, the one he'd seen docked at Rho Junction, but upon inspection it was smaller and less impressive. The restrained cephalic fins and generally degraded appearance confirmed the bursar's statement that it was a hybrid. From what Tekton knew of biozoons, hybrids tended to lose their condition, especially those who fell into the hands of less considerate operators.

Tekton quickly reached inside his suit and shifted the DSD so that the telltale bulge lay at his back.

The egress scale peeled open, and an 'esque climbed out onto a set of rungs crudely pegged to the biozoon's skin.

Wait, both minds warned him simultaneously. *Don't approach him.*

He listened to them. Samuelle's combat suit could be interpreted as threatening, and he noted that the 'esque carried a weapon. Tekton didn't wish to test the suit's weapon resistance ability. It was, after all, Samuelle's spare.

The 'esque stopped just short of him, giving him a slow appraisal. At the same time a grey-skinned Balol emerged from the egress scale and began to climb down.

'You the welcoming party?' asked the 'esque.

Tekton slid back the suit hood and showed his face. He and the 'esque were of similar height and both lightly built. Tekton, of course, had the advantage of wearing combat protection but even so the man's casual demeanour unnerved him; his pale eyes were not unlike Lasper Farr's.

'Of a sort, sir,' Tekton said. 'It's been recommended that I seek passage on your ship. I'd be happy to pay a generous fee, of course.'

The man scowled. His skin was as pale as his eyes, giving him the look of one of the nocturnal races or that of a perennial space traveller.

'Recommended by whom?'

'The last ship leaving,' said Tekton a little ruefully. 'My decision to leave my own billet was rather last-moment. It seems that passage has become rather hard to acquire, due to . . . circumstances.'

'Circumstances!' The 'esque snorted out a laugh. 'Ilke, you hear that? These are *circumstances*.'

The Balol sauntered up and stopped alongside her

companion. Unlike him, she was stocky and muscular, and wore no clothing other than her natural grey skin plating to cover the fact that she was female.

Tekton couldn't help but examine her with interest. He had heard that Balol females made energetic, though often violent, lovers, if you could ignore their odour.

The 'esque noticed Tekton's scrutiny and laughed again. 'What's yer name?'

'Tekton,' said Tekton. 'From Lostol.'

'Well Tekton-from-Lostol, I'm called Jancz, and we're picking up some urgent payload. If yer credit checks out, then maybe we can offer you a ride. Where would ye be heading?'

'Primarily, away from here, but if the reports of imminent invasion are true then I would be seeking transportation to Mintaka. Or thereabouts.'

The 'esque nodded as if giving the request serious consideration. 'That's a fine combat suit you're sportin' there, Tekton. Only seen one like it before.'

'I . . . err . . . borrowed it from a friend. She was concerned for my protection in these uncertain times.'

The 'esque exchanged smirks with the Balol.

Tekton didn't mind if they danced naked together as long as they took him off this doomed station.

'Got some things to attend to,' said Jancz when he'd gotten through being amused. 'Ilke will check yer credit and take ye aboard.'

Tekton stifled his misgivings as Jancz moved on. After all, lowbrow types like this wouldn't have enough imagination for anything sinister.

MIRA

Mira?

Sì?

We are close to Scolar.

Mira worked to get her eyelids open. She'd slept the entire sub-light leg from the shift station to Scolar orbit, and her body craved more. Still.

Baby? She moved her hands through the viscous protection of vein-sink and touched her stomach.

Our baby will be born soon. Its survival is now dependent on the humanesque medics, Insignia commented.

Mira shifted, and Primo responded by buoying her up and withdrawing its receptors from her skin. She swung unsteady legs onto the floor of the buccal, wiping a layer of goo from her face and blinking rapidly.

As her hand fell back to cup the small curve of her belly, she watched Thales, sedated in Secondo, his face relaxed in sleep. Less ravaged.

She felt a flowering of tenderness for him. He wasn't the person she'd first imagined him to be, but he had his own strengths, his own sense of honour. She was glad to have seen to the true heart of the man.

Thales?

He is recovering. But diverting attention to his medical needs has been . . . distracting.

Mira wanted to smile at *Insignia*'s annoyed tone.

The biozoon didn't welcome relationships with ordinary humanesques. It cared only for itself, her and her baby. *Thank you for caring for him. Where is the soldier?*

Eating. The humanesque female has an insatiable appetite. There is only a small stock of food left. My stores have not been replenished for some time. Nor has my nutrient supply. My own health is at risk.

Insignia's last statement brought Mira fully awake. The biozoon had not received an amino acid boost since visiting Akou. *I will negotiate for refugee aid on Scolar.*

It is possible that you will not be well received on that score.

Why so?

Planets have begun stockpiling supplies.

What do you mean? Mira waited in silence. Insignia? *Please answer me.*

The biozoon gave its grunting equivalent of a sigh. *It is best you see the farcasts for yourself. It will no doubt affect how you negotiate with Scolar.*

Because she was no longer deep in vein-sink, *Insignia* broadcast the images in the space above her. For a moment she couldn't make sense of the images blinking in and out of existence.

What is it?

A sampling from the OLOSS 'casts from Dowl and Intel stations.

Mira studied the images again. At Intel, craft fled the system in panicked disorder. Dowl was a different matter. The station space was studded with traffic and the unmistakable signatures of Geni-carriers.

OLOSS is trying to close shift stations across Orion, but that means a halt to all trade. Some worlds won't survive without it and are objecting. It's maybe too late for many, anyway. Geni-carriers have already been reported in dozens of systems. The Pod has been informed that the Melal, Sharmet and Keoskie systems have been attacked.

Mira wasn't familiar with the places that *Insignia* listed. *Are there casualties?*

The Pod estimates several billion lives lost between the three.

Billions! Mira found it almost impossible to comprehend that kind of devastation. *What about Scolar?*

The bulletins report that the Scolar Sophos are advising OLOSS. There has been no change to the status of the system.

Advising? Isn't it too late for that?

Not entirely. Your pre-emptive warning has allowed many of the OLOSS leaders to escape. Another few hours, and they would have all been trapped at Intel.

Has station master Landhurst been mentioned? He drew all the leaders to Intel. He wasn't surprised when I told the summit what I knew. I think that—

He has been connected to the Post-Species?

Si.

The Pod has been suspicious of that, also.

The tiny consolation Mira felt that she might have averted the deaths of some OLOSS leaders was overwhelmed by the knowledge that so many souls had already been extinguished. She should have done more. *What can OLOSS do?*

Insignia took another pause before replying. *I'm not experienced in aspects of war but if res stations are being disabled then the Post-Species have already divided us. Farcast will be our only communication outside our worlds. The Pod believes if this situation persists then, in*

*time, the sentient species on the isolated OLOSS worlds
will die.*

No!

Many are not self-sustaining, Mira. It is the simple truth.

Insignia's prophecy galvanised her. *I'll wake Thales.*

*You must move slowly, or the amniotic fluid will flow
again.*

Mira left Primo and shuffled across the buccal to
sit on the edge of the Secondo vein. Her clothes
were sodden with *Insignia*'s secretions, her hair
matted, and she felt a rivulet of warm fluid leak onto
her thighs.

'Thales.' She touched his shoulder lightly.

His eyes opened wide in fear, then relaxed when he
saw her face. He licked his lips before speaking.
'Baronessa. We are alive?'

'Si,' said Mira. 'Although dead people have felt
better, I'm sure.'

He smiled weakly.

'*Insignia* has healed your face,' Mira added. 'There
is scarring still, but the colour is better. The necrosis
has gone.'

He lifted his hand to his cheek and felt along the
contour. This time his smile was wider, more animated.
'Truly I am grateful.'

Mira nodded.

'Where are we?' he asked.

'Scolar.'

'Home? I am home?' Gladness crept into his voice,
colour to his skin.

Mira let herself enjoy his pleasure. 'There are people
I'm sure that you wish to see. I would only ask that

you support my request to be treated at the Mount Clement clinic.'

Thales jerked up a little. The vein responded by buoying him upright. 'Of course. Baronessa, forgive me. How is your baby?'

'*Insignia* has slowed my fluid loss, but I risk infection without proper care. I would ask your advice on how to contact the clinic quickly.'

The colour deserted his face as he climbed to sit on the side next to her, the effort taxing him. 'I must contact my wife.'

Mira stared at him steadily. 'Sophos Mianos's daughter, the one you spoke of in front of the summit meeting? Will she help you?'

'I – I'm not sure.' He stared back at her just as intently. 'But we have been through much together, you and I. I will do my best for you.'

'Give *Insignia* the details and she will attempt contact. Do you wish to bathe first?'

'That would be preferable, or my wife may not recognise me.' Mira heard the tinge of bitterness in his humour.

'I would bathe also.' She rubbed her hand across the small hard lump in her belly. It felt lower, as though it pressed on her bones. 'But I don't have much time, Thales.'

He nodded. 'I will hasten.'

They helped each other as far as the cucina, where Fariss appeared. The tall soldier's face softened when she saw Thales. 'You're awake.'

'Could you help him to a cabin?' Mira asked her.

Fariss stuffed the biscuits she held into her mouth,

and scooped up Thales in her arms as if he weighed nothing. The young scholar sank against her with complete trust.

As Mira watched them disappear along the stratum, her heart tugged a little, not from jealousy but envy. She hadn't experienced comfort in another's company since her sister Faja had died. Even *Insignia* and the nurturing of the Primo vein did not fill her need for humanesque intimacy.

She continued on to her cabin, where she bathed and brushed her hair, taking care to keep her movements slow and steady. When she was finished, she located an absorbent wad in the cabin cupboard and inserted it into her fresh underwear.

Feeling more ready to cope with what would come next, she sat on the bed.

'Wanton?'

The Post-Species individual was where she had left it, resting on her bed covers against the tiny blisters of mycose. The pile had dwindled since her last visit to her cabin, indicating that Wanton was still in trouble.

'Mira-fedor. Wanton is most pleased to hear your voice.'

'H-how are you?'

'The mycose has preserved my life. It is not an inexhaustible supply though. I would hope to heal the fracture in my casing before it has depleted much further.'

Mira leaned closer to the small gelatinous object. Its voice sounded plaintive, but she was never sure if attributing humanesque characteristics and emotions to it was appropriate. Did Wanton have feelings in the way she understood them? The Extro had helped her to escape her Post-Species gaol, and had displayed a very humanesque sense of self-preservation throughout their escape from the Hub world, but something was intrinsically different between them. Something she couldn't qualify.

'We are in Scolar space,' she said.

'Yes,' said Wanton. 'The biozoon has been exchanging information with me.'

'*Insignia?*' said Mira with surprise. 'And you?'

'We have shared our knowledge of humanesques. It is surprising to see what information we both lacked.'

Mira sat back, annoyed and amused. Wanton and *Insignia* had been talking about her. 'And what did you learn?'

'Contradictory would seem the most appropriate word.'

Mira couldn't control her defensive reflex. 'I wouldn't specify that as a solely humanesque trait. I have known you to be evasive, and *Insignia* to be contrary.'

'It is true that both biozoons and Post-Species Hosts display minor idiosyncrasies, but with humanesques it seems to be . . . quintessential.'

'What do you need to heal yourself?' Mira changed the subject quickly. Together Wanton and *Insignia*, it seemed, would be impossibly superior.

'I am not permitted to disclose the required healing substance.'

'Then how can I help you?'

'I will tell you when and how.'

Mira let out an exasperated breath. 'Now who is being obtuse?'

Mira, interrupted *Insignia*, *Thales is ready to contact Scolar.*

Mira pressed her hand down into the bed to ensure that the mycose blisters rolled as close to Wanton as possible.

I'm coming.

BELLE-MONDE

The tyros filled the ménage lounge with chatter and the smell of fruit cocktails. Chief Balbao seated himself, stiff-backed, in a lounge chair in the centre of the small bar and waited for them to assemble around him: Miranda Seeward, Javid Javiddat, Labile Connit, Lawmon Jise, Ra of Lostol and the uuli pair whose names he could never remember.

'What is so important, Chief, that you would brave us in our den?' warbled Miranda Seeward.

The eminent dicter was perhaps the most irritating and repulsive of all the tyros, her rolls of loose flesh and superior attitude a counterpoint to each other, as though one gave the other credence. Unfortunately, she was thick with Lawmon Jise, who Chief Balbao had a great and wary respect for – the man who had sculpted the new OLOSS charter and was known for his diamond-cut intellect. Labile Connit was the other one that made the chief nervous. Rumours had risen around Belle-Monde that the geneer had dubious and powerful connections. Jividdat was less of a concern and kept to himself, and Ra was simply weird. Tekton, thank Sole, had gone on practical absence leave – something about overseeing the manufacturing of a construction – and not returned. On the one hand, the chief hoped that something terrible had befallen the tight-skinned hairless fop. On the other, he wished the greedy back-biter was here. He had one enormous problem, and these idiot Godheads were his best hope of a solution.

'I have an announcement to make. Something unsettling and perplexing. I have . . .' his Balol pride made it a struggle to get the words out '. . . need of your expertise and opinion.'

That set off another round of chatter and calls for more drinks.

By the time the bartender arrived with another tray of deadly concoctions, the chief's neck frill was stiff with anger. All the years of scientific training and devotion to perpetuating the betterment and longevity of the sentients of Orion, all that learning and civility, began to disappear underneath an unholy rush of pure Balol aggression.

'Sit down and shut up,' he roared, 'before I rip your heads off!' He bared his teeth for good measure.

The open-mouthed Godheads switched to playing meek children in a trice, each sipping their drink as carefully as if it were their last.

The chief opened his mouth to explain his terrible dilemma, but shut it again as the holo-field near the bar flared into life. They all swivelled their attention towards it. What was so important as to cause an impromptu feed?

'It's the OLOSS summit,' groaned Miranda almost immediately. 'How tedious. Turn it off!'

'Quiet, Miranda,' said Jise, picking up on something that the rest hadn't. 'Switch to maximum function,' he told the station moud.

Suddenly it was as if they were all at the summit

meeting, albeit off to one side, seated behind the untidy skieran contingent.

The chief recognised a number of highly important dignitaries, including Warrior Butnik, President Gan, JiHaigh the OLOSS all prime, and the most infamous of all 'esques, Commander Lasper Farr.

A thin young woman stood at the open end of the U-shaped meeting table. Her head was bent, eyes to the floor, shoulders tense as though she bore the greatest of weights upon them.

All attention seemed to be directed her way.

'I know her!' said Connit. 'At least I've seen her. She's the Latino woman who escaped from that horrible little backward planet when it was invaded.'

'Oh yes,' said Miranda Seeward. 'Some type of coup there by those ghastly primitive Saqr. Tekton knew of it. And I think . . . maybe, that I had relatives in the area.'

'Shh!' hissed Jise again. 'We're missing it. Listen.'

The tyros fell silent again.

'All very fascinating, Baronessa,' said President Gan to the Latino woman. 'And it would seem that the Post-Species are responsible for the Saqr adaptation. But what is the significance?'

'Goodness!' Miranda Seeward exclaimed. 'Those damnable Extros.'

The Baronessa replied. 'I have sought to build a picture, President Gan, so that you understand the gravity of what I am about to tell you next. As *Insignia* approached the shift sphere leaving Post-Species space, we came across a terrifying sight. Millions of Geni-carriers. Shifting.'

At the summit meeting a buzz of reaction broke out

from the attendees, but in the mélange lounge the silence was exquisite, and uncharacteristic.

The chief did not like the anxious expressions on the tyros' faces.

'Millions, Baronessa?' Commander Farr finally spoke up, quieting the chatter in the Summit room. 'An exaggeration surely? There were only three in the Stain Wars. Manufacturing on such a large scale in the time that's elapsed since then is impossible.'

'My biozoon can verify this,' said the thin woman.

'Then instruct it to do so,' ordered the OLOSS prime, JiHaigh.

'I do not instruct my biozoon,' she said quietly. 'But I will request.'

After a protracted silence in which nothing happened, the convener of the summit began shouting accusations.

Chief Balbao didn't recognise him, but one of the tyros did.

'Landhurst,' said Labile Connit. 'He's the station master at Intel.'

A guard stepped forward and seized the Latino woman and a commotion started, Commander Farr among the many voicing their displeasure. It was the Commander, in the end, who drowned the others out.

'Wait!' he bellowed.

His imperative caught everyone's attention, including the tyros of Belle-Monde, who gravitated closer together, as if proximity to each other would help them digest the situation better.

Focus in the summit room altered as a projection appeared on the hub-screen. It became difficult to see over the skierans, who almost doubled their size as they swelled with concentration, blocking the lower edge of the images.

Even so, there was no mistaking what was happening at the top half of the projection.

'Geni-carriers,' gasped Javid. It was the first time he'd spoken since entering the room.

'How many?' moaned Labile Connit. 'How goddamned many?'

The chief continued to stare at the images, his mind processing what he'd just seen. What did that mean? Why was it happening? And did it bear any relation to . . . 'Kill the feed,' he subvocalised to the station moud.

The tyros blinked at each other, and then at him.

'There is something else you should know,' he said without further pause. 'The Entity has gone.'

Sole

Time to get'm
Soak'm up
Let'm burn all
Push push push
Make all change
Luscious

'You took the blame for me,' said Thales.

Fariss had lounged on the bed while he bathed, and now she watched him while he searched among the shelves for a robe that would fit. He found a plain fellalo and slipped it over his head, pressing the seals together with weak fingers. Though the biozoon had healed the worst of his facial scars, Thales felt his strength was a long way from returning.

Fariss whistled with disappointment at his vanishing nakedness. 'You getting dressed already?' she teased, ignoring his question.

Thales's body warmed as she leered. He couldn't quite explain his feelings for this semi-literate Consilience soldier. She'd broken a man's neck on Edo to save him, and risked much to bring him aboard Lasper Farr's ship as her consort – booty, she'd called him. Then, when he'd stabbed the mercenary Macken who was trying to rape him, she'd broken this man's neck too and smuggled Thales off the ship. Taken a murder charge for him.

They'd only known each other a few weeks, but her impact on his life was beyond measure. On the trip to Intel station for the summit meeting she'd instructed him on when and how she would like sex, and slapped him if he offended her. Her behaviour made a mockery of the way he'd been socialised – sensibilities, etiquette, appetites all turned inside out. And yet as he stood before her, as shy as a young boy, a deep-seated longing beset him. He was in love with Fariss O'Dea in a way he hadn't known to be possible.

His time with Bethany Ionil – Lasper Farr's sister – had been comforting and educational, but never once had he experienced such powerful, overwhelming emotions.

Only one woman had made him ache with longing before, and he had to speak to her soon, tell her what had befallen him in the months since he had fled his home. His wife.

'I have to speak to . . . someone who may be able to help the Baronessa. The biozoon hasn't been able to stop the birthing process that has begun, only slow it down. She will have the baby soon – a day, or maybe even hours.'

'Well, I'm all for getting her off here then. Pregnant women make me angry.' She laughed, then squeezed one of her breasts into a lewd shape. 'Might give us some alone time. I've been pretty bored while you've been sleeping. Time you entertained me.'

Thales's skin heated with desire, but he shook his head. 'Farris, there are things I want to do here. Would – would you help me?'

Fariss had come with him of her own free will. Her time and interest was not his to command.

'Like?'

'When I left Scolar, I was running away from the Sophos. The things that have happened to me since then have been ugly . . . sordid. I'm not sure what I've

learned exactly, other than to know that this is important. Truly. I must warn the Sophos of the virus that
has been loosed on our people. I cannot let our society
lose the one thing that gives it meaning – its intellect.
Gutnee Paraburd must be brought to account for what
he has done, and so must the ones who devised such
an insidious agent.'

'Brought to account,' repeated Fariss. 'I like the
sound of that.' She grinned. 'I'm with you as long as I
get to play with you first.'

Thales moved over to her and sat down. Her big
muscular body took up most of the bunk. He stared at
her fingers, which were laced together across her
stomach. He would never forget her choking the life
from Lasper's man. 'Farris, the person I would speak
to shortly, to help Mira Fedor, is my wife.'

He stole a glance at her face.

Her expression didn't change. 'And that would
mean?'

He felt relief and disappointment. What had he
hoped for? Jealousy? Possessiveness?

Fariss saw his expression and laughed. 'My rules are
simple, pretty one. When I want your attention, I get
it. And don't you *ever* lie to me. Lying gets people
dead.' She poked him with her toe. 'Got it?'

He nodded slowly. 'So you don't mind that I'm
married.'

She shrugged and pressed her foot against his groin.
'Nope. Do what you have to do, Thales. If it gets to
the stage where we need to be exclusive, you'll know.'
She grinned, and her face lit with magnificent energy.
'I'll make sure you do.'

Mixed reactions caught him again. He didn't know how he felt about his wife any more, yet he knew he didn't want to share Fariss with anyone. 'Does the same apply for me?'

His question threw her off balance for the merest blink. Then she laughed again. 'Make your own rules, but be sure to tell me what they are. I'd like to know when I'm breaking them.'

He smiled at her. 'I have to go to the buccal and talk to Rene. I'll come back here then.'

Fariss pushed him playfully off the bunk. 'Hurry up. I'll be waiting.'

Mira Fedor was in Primo vein when he reached the buccal. 'Give *Insignia* the contact protocols,' she instructed.

The pair sat in silence while the biozoon attempted to make contact with Rene Mianos.

'Would you prefer privacy?' Mira asked eventually.

Thales hesitated. 'Perhaps, at the end. If you would be so kind.'

'Of course. *Insignia* tells me that Rene Mianos has accepted your 'cast request.'

Thales sat straighter and touched his scarred face. Would his wife even recognise him? 'Visual display, please.'

The space above Primo resolved into the head and shoulders of a beautiful but languid woman.

'Rene?'

She stared so long at him without recognition that Thales feared she would cancel the 'cast.

'Rene, it's Thales.'

'You don't look much like my husband,' she said carefully. Quietly. 'How would I know it's you?'

'So much has happened to me since I left Scolar. I would be pleased to tell you all of it, if you were disposed to meet me. But first, I have a matter of urgency. I'm travelling with a woman who has gone into premature labour and needs urgent medical attention.'

Rene seemed distant. 'Even if you are my husband, why would you come to me with such a problem? Take the woman to a medic. Is the child yours?'

'No.' He struggled to keep the agitation from his voice. This subdued almost dull woman was not his sharp-minded wife. 'Her circumstance . . . her condition . . . is complex and unusual. I believe she needs to go to the Mount Clement clinic.'

Rene frowned as if the conversation was an effort. 'But the clinic is for specialised genetic research. It is not an antenatal facility.'

'I know, Rene. You did some of your post-doctoral research there. You told me that they can accelerate cell growth. I believe they are the only ones who can save this woman's baby.'

His knowledge of her past seemed to make her more alert. 'Thales? Is it really you?' The clarity of *Insignia*'s 'cast-imaging showed that her lips trembled.

Tears burned the back of his eyes. 'Yes, dearest. Did you not see me speak at the summit meeting on Intel?'

'I – I've been on retreat. I've heard things about the Post-Species and Consilience. But so much is rumour. The Sophos have instructed us not to heed the farcasts.'

'Rene, please watch the feeds from the summit

meeting. Verify that I spoke to the assembled leaders, including your father. We believe that a Post-Species invasion of OLOSS territories is imminent. Scolar must disengage its shift spheres soon or face annihilation. I must speak to the Sophos.'

She frowned. 'But they will arrest you if you land.'

'Will you help me convince them to give me an audience?'

Her pale fingers strayed to her lips in a familiar absent-minded mannerism. 'I will review the summit feed. Please wait.'

Thales did not look at the Baronessa when the 'cast winked out.

'Your wife is beautiful,' said Mira.

'Yes,' agreed Thales, 'and clever. But her loyalties are tied, above everything, to the Sophos. I learned that the hardest of ways. Yet today she did not seem herself.'

'Perhaps she too has been affected by the virus.'

Thales stared at the Baronessa. 'No.' His denial was soft and unsure.

'If your leaders are also tainted by it, you may have difficulty convincing them of any danger.'

'You don't think that I should meet them?'

Mira gave the slightest shrug. 'What are the consequences of this virus?'

'In truth, I don't know. I saw signs of apathy among both the young thinkers and the Sophos before I left. I was frustrated but not alarmed, thinking it merely a passing thing, something that would rectify itself with a new crop of free thinkers. I was resolved to fight alone, to continue to ask hard questions when questions seemed passé. It was not until I met Villon that

I considered it could be more than a mindset. Now I see that Scolar has fallen ill.'

'Then will the Sophos believe you? Are they capable of truly grasping or caring about the threat?'

The 'cast display shimmered alive before he could reply.

'Thales?'

'I'm here, Rene.'

His wife's voice seemed sharper. 'Is the woman you seek to help the fugitive Baronessa from Araldis?'

'Yes.'

'On what grounds do you believe Mount Clement can help her?'

Mira left Primo to stand near Thales in the broadcast space.

'I am Mira Fedor, Rene Mianos.'

Rene inclined her head, eyes narrowing slightly. 'Baronessa.'

'I would plead for your help. My baby, conceived on Araldis, has been subject to experiments in the Post-Species worlds. It is only a short time in the womb, and yet it wants to be born. My biozoon is of the belief that the child is not properly humanesque.'

'The father is alien?'

Thales saw the faint wrinkle of distaste in Rene's expression, and felt embarrassed by her prejudice.

'No. We fear it may be a Post-Species hybrid.'

'That sounds far-fetched, Baronessa.'

The scant colour in Mira's face drained away, and she suddenly looked so tired that Thales thought she might faint.

He took her arm. 'Rene, please. I know her, and

have travelled with her. The things she says are true. She needs help, or the baby will die. The cell accelerator may save her child.'

Rene looked away from them, as if to someone out of their view. 'Very well, Thales. I'll make contact with the clinic.'

'Thank you.' Mira steadied herself and nodded to Thales. She left the buccal.

Thales watched her leave, and then looked at his wife.

'We are alone now,' he told her.

'Strange company you keep these days, my husband.'

'Fortune has taken me in unexplainable directions.'

'Is it fortune? Your appearance . . .'

'The scarring will soften,' said Thales. 'And the cause of it is not a story to be told in brief. I had hoped to see you again. I've thought of you often.'

'I'm afraid that your fate is out of my hands, Thales. I would wish you well.'

'That is all, Rene? That is all you would wish me?' He couldn't stop his voice from rising.

She gave him her look of practised patience. 'That sounds more like you, Thales.'

'What sounds like me?'

'You were always so easily hurt.'

Thales faltered for a moment. 'Is that how you remember me? As weak?'

Her expression softened. 'Not weak, Thales. But someone with a deep sense of entitlement.'

Suddenly all the nervousness and the expectation of speaking to Rene again drained away in the face of her criticism. 'I'm not the person you remember, or think you know, Rene,' he said stiffly. 'And I'll manage my own fate. But I would ask one thing for what has happened between us. One boon for a marriage lost.'

She waited.

'Whatever happens to me in the coming days, please take care of the Baronessa Fedor. So many things depend on her.'

JO-JO RASTEROVICH

'That's it!' Randall called down to them.

Jo-Jo crawled up the crest of a dune and peered over. The Araldis landing port might have looked like any other outer-world docking arrangement if over half of it hadn't been burned beyond recognition. There was movement in the ruins too: Saqr, crawling lethargically around the twisted remains of docking tubes and hydraulic platforms.

'Shit,' said Jo-Jo. 'What now?' The sky was lightening, with sunrise imminent. Already the air felt like it was blistering his skin.

Randall pointed to a low-set catoplasma building still intact, on the near side of the port, at the base of a bare red-rock mountain. 'Pellegrini buildings. For a bunch of nobles, they were big on bureaucracy. Been in a couple of their offices when we first arrived here. Franco liked to show off his stuff. I say we head there. Should be coolers and water, might even be some food left.' She looked at Catchut. 'You make it, Cat?'

'Sure, Capo,' the mercenary rasped. 'Not dyin' out here.'

Rast nodded. 'Let's move then. Keep low.'

Dropping down behind the last line of dunes, they skirted the breadth of the landing port until the sand became the rocky underlay of the mountain.

A faint hot breeze prickled against Jo-Jo's sweat-drenched skin. The relief wouldn't last long. One ray of direct sunlight, and every drop of moisture in his body would evaporate in the blink of an eye.

'Rest, Capo?' pleaded Catchut.

Randall glanced to the horizon. 'Not unless you wanna change your mind about dyin' out here.'

Jo-Jo glanced up. About a hundred metres of climb to the building, and only precious minutes before sunrise. He reached for Catchut's arm again and hooked it around his neck. Randall did the same on the other side.

Between them, they clawed their way up the already burning red rock. Their time trapped in the *Medium* had atrophied their muscles, and Jo-Jo struggled to make headway, each movement the result of willpower, nothing else.

One more step.

One more step.

One more.

One.

By the time his hand touched the base of the cato-plasma wall, Catchut was moaning with distress, and even Randall didn't have the energy to tell him to shut up. She pointed to the far side. 'Should – be – stairs.'

The two of them crawled along to the edge, dragging Catchut behind them. To Jo-Jo's relief, stairs jutted from the side.

As Leah burst above the horizon, they crawled up the stairs, clinging to the shade of the building overhang.

Randall made the top first, turning around to pull

Catchut up behind her. The injured mercenary rolled into the doorway. By the time Jo-Jo joined them, Randall had popped the door seal and dragged Catchut inside.

Jo-Jo resealed the door after them and fell back onto the floor, alongside the others. The cool wash of air was like a fever breaking, allowing him to sweat. The environmentals were still working. *Thank fucking Crux!*

But after a few desperate lungfuls of cooler air, Jo-Jo gagged. The place stank of death.

None of them spoke, though Catchut retched as well.

Jo-Jo rolled away from the other two and fell into an immediate exhausted sleep. Cramps woke him at some stage and then he fell back to sleep, dreaming that his legs were trapped in the hardening Extro gel. He started awake again, thrashing.

A sharp kick to his thigh stopped him. He scrubbed his face and coughed out watery vomit.

'Get up. I've found some food,' said Randall. 'You been out for hours.'

She was standing an arm's length away, leaning on the railing of a stairwell. Closer to him, Catchut was sitting up, eating something that looked like dry dough and drinking from a bucket.

'Hope you don' mind,' Randall drawled sarcastically, nodding at the bucket. 'They're a bit short on cups.'

Jo-Jo took the container from Catchut and gulped down some tepid liquid. 'Cheers.'

Catchut broke off some stale dough and gave it to him.

While Jo-Jo ground a piece between his teeth, he marvelled again at Randall's resilience. Hair caked with dirt and clothes ragged with filth, her lean face still looked alive and determined.

'Most stuff's intact here,' she said. 'Even a place to wash. Haven't found an AiV yet, but a coupla days holed up here should give us some recovery time. Might even be able to listen in to the 'casts if we can get the comms working.' She glanced at the ceiling. 'That's if anything's goin' on up there that we can follow.'

'Can't believe we're still fuckin' alive, Capo,' said Catchut, weakly. 'Any chance we could find some boots somewhere?' His feet were blistered and bleeding from the rock climb.

'Sure thing. Plenty of bodies. Could have you dressed like an aristo, Cat. What you say?'

'Never said no to a dead man's clothes, Capo. He got no use for them.'

Randall gave a screwy grin. 'Life's been kind to us, fellas. We'd ended up in here a few weeks ago, we'd be spewing our guts up at the stink.' She sniffed the foul air. 'They're mostly dried out – just a little bit of dead left now. Rest is dust.'

Jo-Jo wondered if Randall had ever felt any reverence for the dead, or whether that part got lobotomised along the way. 'You think the Saqr are likely to come up here? There was plenty of 'em down at the port.'

'Can't see no sign that they've been back here since the first attack. They've eaten and left. We just need to keep real quiet until we work out what to do.'

Jo-Jo nodded. With stiff shaky movements, he got to his feet. First things first: he needed to take a piss, real bad. 'Where can I wash?'

'Up the stairs, next floor, other end. Few bags of bones along the way.'

Jo-Jo followed her directions to the bathroom, stepping over several robed bodies showing signs of mummification. Randall was right – a few weeks ago the stench would have been unbearable. As it was, Jo-Jo still wanted to heave up his newly ingested stale dough.

He relieved himself, sparing a moment to wonder whether being suspended in Extro goo had any lasting repercussions for his body. So far everything seemed to be working as usual, although he hadn't had a crap since leaving *Insignia*, and that couldn't be a good thing. The *Medium* had nourished them during travel, but how well, and with what consequences, he couldn't tell.

He stripped off his clothes and activated the water flow in the handbasin. Then he washed as much of himself as he could fit under the spray. Not bothering to dry, he took clothing from one of the bodies outside in the corridor, and was tying the waist cord on the robe when Randall and Catchut joined him.

'A pretty fit, if it was made for a scarecrow,' said Randall.

Jo-Jo stepped back into the bathroom and looked in the mirror. His face was so gaunt underneath his beard that he barely recognised himself.

They were all bone-thin, and paler than a living person should be. He stuck his chin out. 'You could do with change of clothes yourself. I'm gonna look around.'

'Just make sure you don't set off any alarms. Don't want something pinging down the port to the Saqr.'

He nodded. 'Where will you be?'

'We'll get cleaned up and meet you in the kitchen on the third floor. There's some dried food left in the cupboards.'

Jo-Jo searched the first two levels before fatigue ambushed him again. The lifts weren't working, and he took care not to turn on any lights. That meant stumbling into overturned furniture, and having to feel his way through offices. The absence of bodies other than the ones in the corridor outside the bathroom made him curious. Had everyone evacuated before the Saqr came?

He made his way to the third-floor kitchen and found Randall cooking up a pot of pasta.

Jo-Jo stared at her with mild surprise. 'You can cook?'

'As needs,' she said tersely, 'and don't get used to it. I'm powerful hungry; feels like I haven't eaten in a year.'

Jo-Jo was feeling the same. Now that he'd moved around a bit, hunger gnawed like a bitch.

Randall strained the pasta and dumped it onto three disposable plates. 'One thing you can say about these Latinos: they know how to stock a storeroom with food. Every building has a dining hall. Guess there's no running out for quick food in this stinkin' climate.'

Jo-Jo sat himself down at the table next to Catchut. Randall had bandaged and braced his ankle, and they both looked cleaner.

'No dead down below, other than the ones near the piss room,' said Jo-Jo.

Randall forked some steaming farfalle into her mouth and took a moment to savour the taste before she answered. She gestured up with her thumb. 'Go look in the meeting room up there.' Then she added, 'Might wanna let your food go down first.'

Jo-Jo wasn't sure if she was serious, or just provoking him. Either way, he'd finish his exploration after he'd eaten.

Between them, they ate the entire pot and drank another bucket of water. Meal finished, Catchut stretched out on the floor and fell straight asleep.

Randall, though, got down on her hands and knees to search the bottom shelves of the cupboards. 'Gotta be some . . . Knew it!' She slid out two big flasks. 'The other good thing about Latinos. Araldisian red.' She unscrewed the plug and drank deeply. Her satisfied glugging made Jo-Jo's mouth water. How long since he'd had a drink?

She belched, plugged the flask and threw it to him. 'A few hours ago I figured never to taste this again.' Her bloodshot eyes sparkled as she watched Jo-Jo twist the cap off. 'Been in plenny of tight spots over the years, but never come so close to losin' it as I did in that Extro ship.'

Jo-Jo took a swallow and nodded. 'Weird stuff, all right.'

'I said I'd never forget the fact you got me out of there, and I won't.' She opened the other flask and sucked in some more. 'Can't think of a much worse place to die than in that goo. Even the vac'd be better. You did all right in there, Rasterovich.' She tapped her temple.

Jo-Jo shrugged, not wanting her to make something out of it. 'More to do with how the Entity fucked my head over back when I discovered it than anything else. Made it easier for me than for you to think.'

They sat in silence for a while, drinking.

'You think she's still alive?' Randall asked him.

'Mira?'

'No, the fuckin' Extro queen.'

She was baiting him, but he laughed. It felt good to be alive. 'Yeah. I do. Might just be wishful,' he said truthfully, 'but she's a survivor.'

'Like us?'

'No. She's smarter than that.'

They both laughed this time.

Then Randall's expression sobered. 'I shouldn't have left her alone on Rho Junction,' she said. 'Thought she'd be OK. We were so damn close to the ship. Didn't expect anything to happen. Bethany was with her too. Beth's got smarts.'

'No. You shouldn't have,' said Jo-Jo. 'And I won't fuckin' forget it till we find her alive.' It was the first time the mercenary had admitted guilt at Mira Fedor's kidnapping.

Randall stared at him. 'Figured as much. I don't give a fuck about your forgiveness, though.'

Jo-Jo didn't like the direction of the conversation, so he hauled himself to his feet, then bent down and rubbed his shins. 'Gonna find somewhere to sleep. I'll finish looking around in the daylight.'

Randall nodded. 'Thinkin' the same way. Don't change the shade settings on the windows, and stay away from them once it's light. Might be that the Extros in that big ol' flying drum were happy to get rid of us, but the Saqr might fancy a bit of fresh brain juice.'

'Hear you,' said Jo-Jo. 'Where da ya think we'll find a flyer?'

'There're buildings all over the mountain. If we go out at night, we should be able to cover most of them. Could be, we get lucky and find one that hasn't been damaged.'

'Or?'

'Could be, we spend the rest of our days eating pasta, right here. Until it runs out.'

'I think we're gonna get lucky,' said Jo-Jo with a certainty he didn't feel.

'Sure,' said Randall. 'And OLOSS is gonna fly right in here and take Araldis back. Mira Fedor will be with them. She and I'll fly off into the black together and get rich.'

Jo-Jo gave her his best scowl. He didn't like that scenario much better than the first.

Mira

'Your placenta is breaking down. We must take the baby from you soon, or it will starve.'

Mira felt vulnerable lying on her back, covered by a translucent membrane and under the scrutiny of an array of sensors. The clinician – Dolin, he introduced himself as – was like all the others who had come to examine the odd Latino woman carrying a child of inde-terminate biology: curious but nursing a hint of faint repulsion beneath his spill-resistant research whites.

Rene Mianos had been true to her word, arranging for Mira's transfer to the Mount Clement facility as soon as the biozoon docked. It had come at a price, though. Thales Berniere had been escorted off the ship, straight to the Sophos, by red-robed police. The Consilience soldier, Fariss O'Dea, on the other hand, had easily disarmed her would-be captors and simply disappeared.

Mira wondered if Fariss and Thales had worked out a plan for this eventuality, or whether the soldier had simply decided to cut her losses and leave. Either way, Mira went to Mount Clement alone.

As she and Thales had been escorted away from the egress scale – Mira on a hospital float and Thales in restraints – she had seen a fine-looking, slim woman standing in the background of the down-lift area. She'd wanted to tell Thales his wife was there, but the Scolar authorities had allowed them no time to speak or say goodbye.

'Will my baby survive?' she asked Dolin.

'We're unsure, Baronessa. We're not a neonatal facility as such, though our cellular accelerator may be just what you need. If you agree to its use, then we should be able to mature your infant's development enough for it to survive. You should know, however, that to date we have only used it on test clones.'

'What could happen to my baby?'

'The accelerator has been seen to trigger Werner syndrome in a small percentage of recipients.'

'What is that?'

'Werner syndrome causes accelerated aging. The process goes ... too far, if you like to look at it that way.'

Mira closed her eyes as he continued to speak.

'The good news is that despite its short gestation the baby in your womb appears unusually well-formed for its biological age. It should only need a short exposure time. More worryingly, our scans show that the baby has some unusual physical characteristics. You say the father was humanesque?'

Mira had been over this so many times in the past few hours that her tongue refused to cooperate again. She stared at the clinician in frustration. They'd all wanted endless details from her but were prepared to give only generalisations in return.

Dolin saw her expression and relented. 'Do you consent?'

'What will happen without it?'

'We predict the baby will only survive a few minutes. Its lungs are too immature, as are some of its other organs.'

Mira levered herself up onto one elbow to stare at the scientist. He was tall, with a narrow face and a furrowed expression. Not an unkind fellow, but one with deep preoccupations.

'Use the accelerator to save my child,' she said, cupping her stomach. 'She's all I've got.'

'She?' The clinician looked interested. 'You believe the child is a girl? Our scans were inconclusive.'

'Si. At least, I'm n-not sure. My biozoon symbiote couldn't tell me. Biozoons have different sexual references to humanesques.'

'I know,' said the clinician. 'I studied among the Pod for a time.'

Mira stared harder at him. 'You were permitted into the Pod?'

He nodded. 'I met Designate Ley-al at a conference on Mintaka, many years ago. Ley-al showed much interest in my research and was able to convince the Pod to allow me a short sabbatical among them.'

'Where did you live?'

'Aboard Ley-al. It was a remarkable experience, and somewhat frightening.'

Mira relaxed a little, knowing Dolin had been with Ley-al. The leader of the biozoon's first diplomatic family would not let an unethical 'esque near the Pod.

'We should proceed with preparation,' said Dolin gently. 'Your consent, please.' He held out a disclaimer.

She pressed her finger against the film and waited for it to copy her DNA.

As she felt the tingle of identification being completed, Dolin's technicians moved in around her, pressing adhesives on her skin, spreading absorbent sheets around her body. Mira listened as Dolin described living among the Pod. He was still talking, distracting her, as a transparent crib was wheeled in, and lights shone directly at her face so that she couldn't see past the end of the bed. She felt a cold sensation against her thigh.

'Dolin!'

He leaned past the bank of brightness until his face was close to hers. 'The accelerant has been administered.'

'How long will it take?' She felt short of breath, as though the infusion had robbed her of oxygen.

'The biozoon slowed down the fluid loss with a synthesised hormone that will now be nullified by the accelerant. Soon you will feel contraction pains. The baby is small, so we do not anticipate difficulty with the birth. However, we think the accelerant will have more time to work if the baby is born through the birth canal – not by the normal procedure.'

Mira tried to sit up. 'You mean an uncontrolled birth?'

'The accepted term is natural birth. Afterwards, though, we may have to take the baby away quickly. Try not to be alarmed.' Dolin smiled reassuringly, but Mira could see the concern in his eyes. 'Our tests show us that the baby's physical characteristics are primarily humanesque, Latino origins, but there would appear to be some anomalies in its blood work. We will know more soon.'

He withdrew behind the lights.

Within moments Mira felt the first twinge – milder than the gripping pain she'd felt on Intel station. She lay back on the bed, suddenly wishing that her sister, Faja, or her friend Estelle were with her. Even Bethany Ionil.

A different kind of fear struck her. Only women caught in dire circumstances went through uncontrolled childbirth. Even on Araldis, natural birth was a rare thing.

'What will happen?' she asked after another contraction.

'Your body will know what to do. Just accept what happens as part of a normal process. We are monitoring your progress.' Dolin's voice echoed past the lights. 'Don't be afraid.'

The next contraction squeezed her abdomen into a tight ball, and she gasped aloud.

'We can't administer pain relief with the accelerant, Baronessa.'

She nodded and felt another contraction. This one started in the small of her back and radiated to her side and down into her pelvis, finishing in a fierce cramp that made her draw her knees up. She grabbed the edges of the bed and rolled to one side.

Gloved hands reached through the bank of lights. 'Stay on your back. We must feel inside the birth canal.'

'No!' Mira jerked upright. 'Where are the women?'

'Baronessa?' said Dolin's voice.

'I want women in attendance.'

'There are no women on this shift.'

Mira lashed out with her foot, knocking over a bank

of lights. She slid off the bed to her feet and blinked into the dark side of the room. It was filled with male 'esques.

She gritted her teeth through the next wave of pain, waiting for it to pass before she could speak again. When she could, she straightened. 'Dolin . . .'

He righted the lights and moved them further back. Then he stepped to her side.

'Yes, Baronessa?'

'Find a woman to help me, then do not come back in here until the baby is born. None of you!'

'But we must—'

'As soon as the baby is born, you may do what is necessary to save it.' She was quiet but emphatic, using the most commanding manner she could muster.

In the silence that followed something unspoken passed between the observers. They quietly disappeared, leaving only Dolin. He helped Mira back onto the bed.

'Your customs don't allow males present at the birth?'

She nodded. 'Latino women are modest. I have adapted to . . . many things since leaving Araldis, but not this.'

The furrows in Dolin's forehead grew deeper. 'I'll see what can be done.'

He disappeared.

She lived in the narrow world of managing pain until the door finally opened again, and a stocky woman dressed in food-smeared overalls entered. The dark hair escaping a white cap marked her as a domestic of some kind. She marched straight over to Mira's side.

'What're all these harsh lights for? For Scolar's sake

'. . . men!' She straightened the cover and put her hand to Mira's brow. 'What's yer name, love?'

'Mira Fedor.'

'Well, Mira Fedor. I'm Linnea, the galley supervisor in this place. Come from just down the mountain in Clementvale. Only ever delivered one baby the old way. Me own. Got caught out in the protein fields on Argamon. Had me son right there in the clod. Used me pocket knife to cut the cord.'

Her reassurances were thin, but her voice was strong and centred, like Faja's. Mira became calmer – until the pain piled in again. She gasped for air.

'Little breaths, love. Above it. Ride above it.' Linnea left her to search through some drawers. She returned with a wad of absorbent pads and a white overall. She stripped out of her kitchen garb and donned the clean overall right then and there, unconcerned about modesty.

The sight of her bare chest made Mira gasp – not the nudity, but the myriad of finely inked lines spreading across her naked breasts. 'Pensare!'

'What?' Linnea pulled the overall up and sealed the seam.

But Mira was caught in another contraction and couldn't speak. When the wave of pain passed, she reached out for Linnea's hand.

The woman stepped closer, surprised. 'What is it, love?'

'You belong to the Pensare.' She traced her fingers across her own breast with her other hand.

Linnea nodded, understanding, and smiled. 'Aaah. I'd heard it called different things, but never that. Here we are the Swestr – sisters. The women's lobby. Even on famous Scolar, things are not always equal. Do you bear the marks?'

Mira shook her head; another contraction was coming. 'Mia sorella . . . sister . . . mine,' she panted.

'Roll on yer side. Let me rub your back, little Swestr.'

But Mira barely heard her. The individual stab of her contractions turned into one long excruciating pain that shifted to her back. Then a strange sensation overtook her body, as though her pelvis might split apart. Her focus fell to it, and the sense of movement within her.

'It's coming.' She thought she'd spoken aloud. Had she?

Linnea began helping her onto the floor, into a squatting position. Her sturdy body bore Mira's weight easily.

'Better than on yer back, love. Use gravity to help you get yer little 'un out.'

Mira's legs trembled with the exertion.

'It's crowning. Now lean on me back,' instructed Linnea. 'I'm goin' to get down low and make sure yer baby doesn't slip.'

Mira collapsed across Linnea's broad back, fingers spasming into the folds of the cook's overalls.

'Just one little push. Now. Not too hard. This one's slipperier than an eel.'

Mira felt disembodied, seperate from her skin. Not able to think.

'Mira! Swestr! Push!' said Linnea, sharply. 'Bear down.'

Mira's mind began to slip away somewhere, to a place that she'd been before. But then *Insignia* drew her back from that blissful oblivion, insisted she return.

Mira?

Insignia had been silent in her mind until now.

Our baby is about to be born, said the biozoon. *You must help her.*

Mira felt something. Her eyes flickered open.

Linnea had gripped her shoulder with one hand, reaching up, her other hand still cupped between Mira's parted legs. The thick fingers bit into her flesh with no apology.

'You must push now. This baby needs to be free of yer.' Bright eyes and a sweat-glistening face. 'This is yer important job, Mira,' Linnea told her. 'The one you were born for. Don't fail yerself. Or yer baby.'

The woman's intensity grounded her. Suddenly it wasn't Linnea, a stranger, delivering her baby, but her beloved sister Faja. The same look, the same voice, the same determination.

Fa!

Mira let the sensations back in – the pain, the sense of her own body being torn – and pushed down.

She felt her baby's head move.

'Babe's here!' cried Linnea. 'It's here. Once more.'

Mira pushed again, and with the sliding sensation came a release from the pain.

'Here, I've got yer babe in my hands.' Linnea lifted a bloody bundle up so Mira could see.

With trembling fingers, Mira reached for the tiny body. 'It's a girl,' she said.

'Guess so. Can't see no man's tackle down there. Now lie yerself down on the bed while we deal with the afters.'

'A girl,' repeated Mira, as she weakly levered herself onto the bed. 'Thank Crux!'

Linnea smiled, but continued to hold the infant. 'Yer babe looks good an all to me, love. A tad undersized, as you'd expect, but its lungs seem to be working fine.'

'I wish to hold her,' said Mira.

Linnea shook her head and laid the bloody babe in the transparent crib. 'Promised Dolin I'd put her straight in here, soon as I cut the cord. It's the only reason he let me in. Once the scan's done, yer can have her back. How are yer planning to feed her?'

'Feed?' Mira hadn't even thought of it.

'Yeah. They do need it, yer know,' Linnea said with gentle sarcasm. 'And what name have yer picked?'

Mira felt her face warm with embarrassment at her exposed ignorance. Estelle wouldn't have been so ill prepared. Nor Faja. Both would have picked their child's name before the birth.

She spent some precious moments thinking about her sister and her best friend, wishing they were with her, longing for their company and advice. Then she let her self-pity go and looked to her child.

Our child, *Insignia* corrected.

THALES

'Villon?' The detention room was so achingly familiar that Thales felt compelled to say the old philosopher's name aloud.

But no aged and gentle person emerged from one of the bedrooms; no refined and thoughtful voice replied. Villon was dead, and Thales found himself back in the exact room he had shared with the great man.

Rene had been in the docking bay when the politic guards led him away. He'd seen her there, pressed back against the wall, a slim almost ethereal figure with her fingers clasped tight. He didn't call out to her or plead for her help. He hadn't endured the last months to return home like a boy needing protection.

In the furore of their arrival, and Mira's transfer to Mount Clement, Fariss had eluded the guards. Even though she hadn't really understood all the reasons for him risking detention again, she'd happily acknowledged his determination. If she'd forbidden him, he didn't know what he would have done. His urge to obey her was so strong, and yet his desire to preserve the integrity of his world was equally so.

Fariss had supported him through her nonchalance, and he'd seen the sparkle in her eye at the promise of trouble. She relished conflict and battle.

'Do what you must,' she'd told him before they

berthed on Scolar. 'And I'll do the same. Right now, that means not surrendering to your police. I'll be there for you, watching from the sidelines.' Her beautiful big eyes widened in thoughtful surprise. 'And to tell you the truth, I'm not sure why, except that your skin feels good against mine, and your voice is like a song to me, and my guts tell me to protect you at all cost.'

Her unexpected declaration almost liquefied his resolve. Tears had burned his eyelids, and he'd knelt before her.

She'd cuffed him gently and pulled him to his feet. 'Pleasure me now, before what will be.'

And they'd rolled together in their bunk with a passion that had left Thales weak again.

'Msr Berniere?'

Thales blinked from his reverie. A guard was standing at the door of what had been Villon's bedroom. How long had he been there while Thales was lost in thought?

The red-robed guard gave him a curious look. 'Follow me.'

Thales walked between two Robes, along the familiar marble-grand corridors, until they ushered him into an opulent meeting room. This time, though, Thales viewed the whole Pre-Eminence building through fresh eyes, marvelling at the smooth polished flooring, intricately carved window frames and rich textured furnishings.

How luxurious these surroundings were, compared to the oddity of Rho Junction architecture, or Lasper Farr's world of parasite-clean refuse. Now that he was home, he found the aesthetics of the building both soothing and unsettling. *We have such wealth, but have lost our wisdom.*

'Thales Berniere.'

This time it was a member of the Sophos who spoke his name. A dozen of them sat along one side of a long table, as if keeping a deliberate physical distance from him.

Thales recognised most of them: Lauda and Kantos, Averro-ji and Juan Alermo. Sophos Mianos was the notable omission, but in his place sat his daughter.

'Rene,' whispered Thales.

His wife's delicate complexion lacked colour, and she moved one hand repeatedly, back and forth, between her lap and her mouth. Thales remembered this agitated mannerism as clearly as if they had never been apart.

His heart contracted for an instant, but then the image of a broad face with thick lascivious lips entered his mind, and the pain eased. *Fariss. Where are you?*

'Rene Mianos will represent her father on the Sophos until his return.'

Thales looked at her, sitting there among the aged male 'esques. Rene had coveted a seat on the Pre-Eminence, and he'd worried that she'd thought his immaturity would hold her back. To see that she'd finally realised her ambition through her father's misfortune – a misfortune precipitated by Thales – seemed more than ironic. Bitter amusement ate into his composure. Would his wife side against him?

Sophos Lauda began to speak. 'The Sophos has reviewed both the recent farcast from the OLOSS summit on Intel station, and the recordings from the

OLOSS ship which connected with the Baronessa Fedor's biozoon companion.

'You've made grave accusations and bold statements, Thales Berniere. You secreted yourself aboard an OLOSS ship in order to escape questioning for an incident in a kaffe klatsch, in the Kant quarter. During Sophos Mianos's interrogation of the Latino noble Mira Fedor you chose to assist her escape by attacking Mianos, and accused him of murdering our greatest philosopher, Amaury Villon. An offence, I might add, that amounts to treason.

'Having absconded on the Baronessa Fedor's ship, and having been absent for some months, you now return to our notice, accusing Sophos Mianos of barbarity. You have also declared that members of the Pre-Eminence, and others in our world, have been infected by a virus that alters our ability to think critically. How would you defend yourself against the charge of insanity?'

Thales locked his knees to stop his legs from buckling. He was not afraid of the Sophos, but his wife's presence made this more difficult. He would hurt her when he spoke of his encounters with her father, and then she would choose not to believe him. Whatever . . . friendship might have endured beyond their separation would surely be destroyed.

'I will not even address the charge of insanity, Sophos Lauda. My mental health is not relevant, as I will repeat my story *in my own words*, and then offer proof of it.'

He looked along the row of faces. Age had blurred their features, as well as something else – disinterest, perhaps. It was as if they were merely going through the motions of a hearing that would never amount to anything. These people would be impossible to convince or move to action; the motivation did not lie within them. They were too comfortable. Diseased.

Amaury? Give me guidance. But Amaury Villon was gone. Mixed emotions swirled within him. He would let them see what it was to question. Remind them of the nature of passion.

'After leaving Scolar, circumstances saw me in the company of the Baronessa Fedor. Though the decision to break away from the OLOSS ship that transported Sophos Mianos out to question her was the Baronessa's, I would have supported her action. I regret the injury caused to my father-in-law, but he ... intended to impound her ship and hold her in detention. The Baronessa was desperate and frightened.'

He told them of Mira's story and the invasion of Araldis, but throughout his tale the faces remained unmoved, almost bored.

'How did the Baronessa become pregnant in this untenable situation?' asked Rene.

Thales looked directly at her for the first time. Her eyes seemed dull to him, her sharp intellect hidden behind cloudiness. 'That is her story to tell, if she so wishes, and in truth I did not know of her pregnancy until our paths crossed again more recently.'

'Where did you leave the Baronessa's company?'

'On Rho Junction. She was abducted by a Post-Species sect, and I met a tyro from Belle-Monde who offered me quick passage back to Edo.'

'Belle-Monde?' It was Kantos who spoke, but they

all adopted a similar disdainful expression. 'What would one of the famous Belle-Monde tyros be doing on Rho Junction?'

Thales told them about Lasper Farr and the DNA.

'You expect us to believe that we've been infected with a virus that affects our desire to question, that softens our intellect.' Kantos burst into laughter. 'Of all the preposterous accusations! This one borders on hallucinatory.'

Thales expected the others to share this open scepticism. 'The virus affects the orbitofrontal cortex, where decision-making occurs. Have you noticed a change in each other? A reluctance to make decisions? A tendency to maintain equilibrium? A fatigue that takes you when deep thought is required?'

The Sophos members exchanged eyebrow-raised glances.

'There is something else you can check. Fortunately, I chose not to carry the DNA in my bloodstream, as Commander Farr wanted me to. That, coupled with the virus the Commander administered to force me to comply with his wishes, would surely have killed me. As it was, it left its legacy.' He touched his cheek. 'Necrosis. The Baronessa's biozoon has helped the healing.'

'But surely your HealthWatch would have protected you?' said Rene.

He stared at her intently. 'It had been tampered with. Commander Farr scanned me when I returned to Edo. He told me that my most recent update had been sabotaged.'

Rene's pale face flushed. Her hands flew to her cheeks. 'Impossible. You used the Sophos clinic.'

'Someone deliberately interfered with my renewal, Rene Mianos. Scan my immunity and match it to the batch I received.'

A murmur spread along the table. One to the other, they whispered and conferred.

'Gutnee Paraburd's premises were in the port terminal. Search his office and question him,' Thales continued. 'You shall soon see the veracity of my story.'

'Who would have created such a virus, and why, Msr Berniere?' asked Rene. She seemed to struggle to form the simple question.

'I met the tyro Tekton of Lostol. He was able to trace the chain of business from the laboratory on Rho Junction to the original supplier.'

'Which was who?' demanded Lauda. Of all the Sophos, he seemed the sharpest, the most energised.

'Her name is Miranda Seeward, a dicter of some note and also a tyro on Belle-Monde.'

The Sophos began to murmur among themselves again. Clearly many of them knew of Dicter Seeward.

Finally, Lauda stood up. 'We shall consider your claims. Withdraw to the anteroom until you are called.'

Thales nodded and followed the Robe out. Was the Baronessa right? Were the Sophos beyond making intelligent or balanced decisions? Were they beyond hope? And how did she fare right now? Had the baby been born? Had it survived? Thales felt weighed down by concerns.

The bond between him and Mira was not romantic, as his feelings had been for Rene. Nor did it resemble the deeply passionate way Fariss moved him. It was more a genuine warmth, and a desire to see things go well for her. Friendship, he thought, one that would grow and endure, given a chance.

He sighed and turned his attention to the two Robes waiting with him. Had the virus affected all walks of Scolar life or merely the philosophers? The politic guards seemed as composed and expressionless as he was accustomed to seeing them, but were they as committed to upholding the law of the Sophos as they had always been? Or had the ennui crept in among them too?

'You heard my story,' said Thales. 'What's your opinion?'

The guards showed no indication of hearing him.

'Have you seen a change in the people you serve and protect? Do you see that your world is different?'

This time the guards exchanged glances but didn't reply.

'Our Sophos is no longer reliable. Their decision-making has been compromised by a virus. Are you still prepared to blindly follow their edicts, knowing that?'

His statements were inflammatory, treasonous. He knew that and cared not. A sense of urgency had taken hold of him. There was little time to preserve his world.

One of the guards looked as though he might speak, but then he stopped and nodded at an instruction unheard by Thales. He walked to the inner door and opened it. 'Enter,' he instructed.

The Robes followed closely behind him as he returned to the Sophos meeting room and stood in front of the polished table.

'You are fortunate, Thales Berniere, that one of our

caucus has seen fit to support an investigation into your story,' said Sophos Lauda.

Thales eyes flicked to Rene. Had it been his wife?

Her expression remained as serene and detached as that of the politic guard.

'You will show the Robes and myself to the offices of this man you call Gutnee Paraburd. If he can be located and questioned, we will review our decision.'

Thales nodded. 'I th-thank you, for this much at least. However, it is possible that Paraburd has moved premises. I would imagine that a man of such criminal inclinations does not stay in one place for long. You may have to extend your search.'

'You learned much about criminals on your travels?' asked Kantos.

Thales heard the superior, mocking tone. 'It is logical that he would do that, Sophos Kantos. That is all,' Thales answered firmly.

'Let's hope not, Msr Berniere. For your sake.'

But Thales had not finished. 'While you pursue your investigation of my claims, I would beg you to take steps to disable the shift sphere. The Post-Species are an imminent threat to our world.'

'You believe we should cut ourselves off from Orion,' said Rene.

He turned to his wife, imploring her. 'If we don't, we'll lose everything.'

'But if we disable our shift sphere, we lose our influence. OLOSS cannot function without our counsel,' said Kantos.

Fury blazed through Thales's body, overcoming his intention of remaining calm. 'You speak of *my* insanity,

Sophos Kantos. OLOSS forces will act with or without our counsel, to protect sentient life. We can offer them nothing else now. What *we* should have done is seen the possibility of this happening, and guarded against it. *We* should have been able to predict, or at least theorise that the Post-Species would return with a greater force after the Stain Wars. Instead, we have been isolationist and self-concerned. You – all of you – would do your job too late.' His gaze roamed the line of preeminent thinkers. 'All that is left for us now is to survive.'

Sole

Scurry scurry
Little'n's go
Follow, follow
Drink'm up
Eat'm up
See'm truth

Tekton

Tekton sat in a once luxurious, now filthy, lounge on board the hybrid biozoon. From his brief inspection, the craft appeared to have been beautifully and comfortably outfitted, but without regular cleaning or maintenance it now resembled a place for squatters – or at least what he imagined a place like that might be like.

He tried not to show his revulsion for the discarded food containers and empty flasks of alcohol. The stench was harder to ignore, though, a mixture of something sickly sweet and well percolated, probably musky Balol body odours.

He closed his hood and set his suit to filter the scents. He wasn't filled with confidence by his rescuers' attitudes, but his situation had called for decisive thinking and compromise. If they took the money for his passage and delivered him to Mintaka, then he could put up with certain deprivations. A filthy ship was nothing, after all, compared to free-falling from an airborne taxi into the grips of detrivore, which had happened to him on Edo. He was, he told himself, able to take this eventuation in his stride.

Only a matter of months ago he would not have dealt with this change in fortune nearly as well.

Finally! said logic-mind. *Rationalism.*

Lowering your standards, you mean, sniffed free-mind.

Both minds were correct, he thought, and it didn't bother him that they were. For a while he stared at the brown biozoon secretions on the ceiling, contemplating this until the 'esque Jancz slipped into the room with the surreptitious manner of a crook.

'We're out of Intel space,' he said quietly.

Tekton smoothed back his hood and nodded appreciatively. 'Msr Jancz, has my credit for the trip to Mintaka been transferred into your accounts?'

Jancz's eyes narrowed a little, and a small smile played about his lips. His face was so long and thin that it seemed almost deformed. 'With the excitement about the Extros and all, the lenders are off-cast. Too much demand has bogged their systems. Everyone's trying to move their credit somewhere else. We'll try again in a day or so, when things've calmed. Meantime, we got a few errands of our own to run. Not in any rush, are yer?'

Of course I am, you filthy imbecile. 'No,' said Tekton blithely. 'Whenever you deem it safe and appropriate is fine by me. Though I might, if I could, request a cabin.'

Tekton knew he was being ridiculously polite to this low-life, but while the semblance of civility remained between them, he would hold up his end.

Don't trust him, free-mind urged.

He's done nothing to suggest untrustworthiness, logic-mind countered.

'Sure,' said Jancz, stepping back towards the door. 'This way.'

Tekton followed Jancz to a small cabin not far from

the galley. It was neat enough, if sparse, with the appearance of not having being used for a long while.

'Help yourself to whatever's in the galley. We aren't ones for makin' meals. Eat as yer go on this beauty.'

Beauty? That absurd notion stayed with Tekton as he closed the door and locked it.

Little was beautiful about this hybrid 'zoon. What luxury it had once entertained had now faded in the wake of abuse. Its corridors were acrid with astringent scents, and its walls the pale pink of poor circulation. Rubbish was piled in every corner, and sticky secretions layered surfaces. *The poor sad creature is sick.*

Tekton pared open the seal of his suit and fished around for Lasper Farr's DSD. With relief, he pulled the box free and set it on the bed. Then he stretched out alongside it without bothering to remove the rest of the suit. His back was raw from rubbing against the device's sharp corners, and suddenly, now that he was safely away from Commander Farr and Intel, he felt exhausted.

He slept for a while, woke, peeled off the suit, drank, and washed in the tiny san. He found some lotion in one of the cabinets and spread it over his body. Despite having to put on the suit again, he felt refreshed and more able to think.

His stomach complained of hunger, but Tekton ignored it. He did not want to venture out of his cabin into the galley just yet. Instead, he checked the door lock again, then sat himself down before the DSD.

Taking a deep breath, he settled into a comfortable position, leaning against the bulkhead.

'Balance,' he said.

The undulating 3D image of a Lorenz Attractor sprang into being above the box. Tekton watched the fluctuating brilliance of the fractal structure for a moment before speaking the next password.

Was Cousin Ra really responsible for creating this magnificent device? What gifts did Sole bless my arrogant cousin with, to enable him to do this?

Tekton had a sudden and overwhelming craving for his life to be as it was – before Sole, even. Back at Tadao Ando studium he'd been mired in politics and a certain level of intrigue, but nothing there had been beyond his experience or imagination. Since leaving Belle-Monde on his quest to win the Entity's favour, his life had become nothing if not chaotic and dangerous. Tekton longed for safety – and regular sex.

His akula swelled a little and then deflated again. On an insalubrious hybrid biozoon, in a location that could well be in the teeth of an impending galactic war, and with only two obnoxious mercenaries for companionship, thoughts of carnal pleasure were neither easy to sustain nor really practical.

With a deep and heartfelt sigh, Tekton spoke the next password. 'Shame.'

A beam shot from the centre of the Attractor and he was swallowed up by the device's stimulation of his visual cortex. Images appeared and spun quickly through his mind, coloured lights with no form or substance.

He let himself adjust to the speed and glitter of the data, then focused on a recurring speck. The spin slowed and his reality shifted as if he was sucked forward into it. He found himself in the buccal of another biozoon, watching Mira Fedor lying in the pilot vein, her hands resting on her swollen belly.

She's been busy, his free-mind sneered.

Logic-mind urged Tekton to experiment further, to learn control of the device's quirks.

Tekton let his focus withdraw from the Baronessa and slip back among the coloured lights. He tried concentrating in different places, and quickly became adept at controlling the speed and flow of the images.

It's an instinctive system, logic-mind mused. *Designed for humanesque minds. Even uneducated ones.*

Bit like a recognition game, observed free-mind.

No. It employs simple logic, logic-mind said. *Like this . . . and this . . .*

Tekton began to group images to form rough linear timelines, and practised the knack of viewing concurrent events.

The device itself was a pure delight, responding to a variety of physical and neurological cues from its user. Tekton knew he could lose himself for days, dipping into the affairs of the galaxy and the permutations of the elegant arrangement of information – if, that is, the news out there had been better.

As it was, what Tekton saw shook his composure. The galactic war which Mira Fedor had prophesied to the summit just hours earlier had already begun.

Tekton flipped between terrifying spectacles. Entire systems were being swarmed by Geni-carriers. Thousands upon thousands of incendiaries descended into the atmospheres of habited worlds.

Many of the DSD's recorder eyes had been damaged, transmitting barely discernible images of dense dust clouds where populated moons should be. Others showed the partial obliteration of colonies, and still more sent footage of suffering and carnage.

Worse than that, the Geni-carriers had targeted the galaxy's grandest architectural achievements – structures and designs which attracted billions of tourists. The bridges between the Latour moons now hung rent and broken, like tentacles torn free from the body of a huge sea creature. Who knew how many had perished during their destruction? There were over a million tourists inside the Great Diorama Well of Mapoor, helplessly trapped within sightseeing gondolas as the kaleidoscopic walls around them began to implode.

Outrage, horror and despair consumed Tekton, drowning out any rationale that his logic-mind could offer. How could anyone ... any *thing*... perpetrate such ruin ... such *sacrilege*?

All our greatest achievements, free-mind wailed. *Everything that we are. Everything we strive for. All our beauty.*

The only tiny sliver of hope the DSD afforded him was that his home world, Lostol, had been one of those who'd heeded the Baronessa's warning. The Lostolians had disabled their shift spheres, preventing the Geni-carriers from entering their system. Tekton could not detect their shift signatures, which meant that the Post-Species had likely bypassed Lostol.

Relief was replaced by more anxiety. He was cut off from his family, which pained him despite the fact that he seldom communed with them. Doris Mueller, his mother Alaman, uncle Tolos, the Tadao Ando studium ... All were beyond his reach.

Unreasonable sentimentality! Logic-mind had to bellow at him to be heard over his worrying. *When was the last time you spoke to Alaman or Tolos? Or even wondered what they were doing?*

Tekton nodded to himself. Logic-mind was right. To weep over lost familial connections was asinine, but this mass destruction of the galaxy's architectural monuments, that was completely deplorable. Unacceptable.

In addition to his marrow-deep outrage and grief, Tekton was besieged by a wave of momentous guilt. From his glimpses into the chaos propagating throughout Orion, Tekton deduced that OLOSS was gathering in multiple locations, planning reciprocation. But its forces were fractured, blinded by the breakdown of res-shift and without a clear leader. Lasper Farr's ship appeared to be stranded in the vicinity of Bellatrix, apart from the rest of its fleet, and Farr was without the device that had clearly allowed him to stay one step ahead.

I've stolen his prescience, and the OLOSS worlds will pay.

The Godhead closed his eyes and his mind to the device, and fell back onto the bed, curling into a tight ball. Tears leaked from his narrow seldom-used tear ducts, and he didn't bother to wipe them away.

What have I done?

There, there, free-mind soothed.

All is not lost, said logic-mind with uncharacteristic sympathy, as it worked for a solution.

Tekton and his minds lay in a huddle of mutual despair for some time until logic-mind came up trumps.

Well, we have the device, don't we?

Yes, agreed free-mind and Tekton.

Then let's use it!

BELLE-MONDE

'Gone where?' demanded Miranda Seeward. She was the first to recover and demand an answer.

Chief Balbao surveyed the group of agitated tyros. To his disappointment, each one of them seemed as surprised as the next. 'I'd hoped you might have that answer for me.'

'But that's t-terrible,' spluttered Javid.

The rest nodded, each seeing their generous study grant vanishing.

'Terrible, but true. I suggest we take a few hours to digest this news and study the newscasts on the purported invasion. We should meet back here then and devise a strategy. I would request that none of you contact your institutions or benefactors about this until we have had time to assess and evaluate. It could be that the Entity will reappear in a short time, in which case we would look most foolish for panicking. OLOSS has enough to concern itself with at the present.'

A group nod. Even the uulis flared their agreement colour.

'Your mouds will inform you of the meeting time. Thank you.'

Balbao made a quick departure before any of them could attach themselves to him. The one thing he'd learned about the tyros was that, like children, they could ask endless questions.

His office offered no solace. A deluge of enquiries and requests for instruction awaited him on his moud. Most imperative of them all was the 'cast query from the OLOSS steering committee, asking why they hadn't received the most recent data.

Inform them that changes in the Entity's electromagnetic field are interfering with our data collection. There'll be a delay of some days, he told his moud. *And contact Balol on my private account.*

Balbao paced the circumference of his office while he waited. Belle-Monde, while unwholesome in terms of its decor, had afforded him the most important research assignment he'd ever had. Success here meant the opening of doors all over the scientific worlds. If there were worlds left.

Balbao was not given to moments of anxiety – it wasn't in his Balol make-up to be jittery – but the current state of his affairs was less than desirable. And he hated being at the beck and call of the tyros. Though they were learned beings of his ilk, their selection on this programme and their subsequent shafting had made them less than trustworthy, and more than unpredictable. It was as though they were at the whim of the Entity, not studying it.

In his next meeting with them he would find out more about their projects. He would demand to know more. The time for secrecy was over.

Chief Balbao, farcasts are disintegrating. There is no reply from Balol.

No reply.

No, sir.

And generally?

It is varied. Mintaka and the near systems are still responding, as are Scolar and a small cluster near them. Lostol and most of that sector are rimming.

What news of the supposed invasion?

Common cast is resonating with disinformation. Many channels say it is a hoax, and as many again report it to be true. May I suggest using the emergency frequency on the evacuation ship?

Excellent idea, moud. I'll head there now. Inform security.

Balbao collected a water tube and some meat gnarls from his office cooler, and walked the distance to the EVAC ship. He needed the thinking time. His route took him past the labs and munitions lock-ups and onto the perimeter walkway. This particular boardwalk ran the circumference of the pseudo-world, the equivalent of a fire exit on a real building. On Belle-Monde though, all exits led to the EVAC ships – four of them, though one was undergoing maintenance.

Gravity was much lighter out here, and he managed the endless stairs without any real effort. Eating the gnarls was another thing entirely; he had to slide them into his mouth straight from the packet to stop them floating off.

Eating and walking always calmed Balbao. Doing them together was almost like meditation. By the time he reached EVAC #1, he'd reached a decision. If the invasion threat was real, he must take action. The survival of Sole's chosen sentients – not to mention his own skin – could depend on his decisions.

The Balol guards on duty saluted and opened the outer hatch. He nodded at them to stand at ease as he disappeared inside. EVAC sentry duty was the most boring rotation on the security roster.

Ahhh. The smell of slightly stale air, catoplasma and titanium residues summoned sharp memories of his early years, which he'd spent on cramped ships in distant systems, dropping payload and studying data flow. He felt a sudden longing for the past, but brushed it away. Sentimentality would not help him sort out this mess.

He settled in front of the com-sole and activated the 'cast. First he tried to contact his immediate reportage, Commander Lars Unthak at the Group of Higher Intelligence Affairs, which was based in the Alnitak system. The 'cast faded, so he switched to the Balol coding. It took some time to get a reply on the emergency line, and then it was only a harried junior officer at the Balol trans-cast relay station.

'This is Chief Astronomein Balbao, from Psuedoworld 9176, Class 18. Transmitting OLOSS ident.' He waited for the pingback before speaking again. 'I'm unable to make contact with my direct reportage at GHIA. I require a risk analysis of our situation.'

'Chief Balbao, I can't help you,' said the young officer. 'All the senior personnel are in conference. Stand by for instruction.'

'Stand by? For how long?' spluttered Balbao.

'I can't be exact. Within six hours.'

The chief grunted and pushed away from the com-sole to swallow some more gnarls. Sometimes he felt the meat concentrate was the only thing that kept him going.

Moud, inform the tyros that the meeting has been trans-ferred to this location.

At what time, Chief Balbao?

Now.

Now translated into much longer.

Balbao counted the group as they squeezed into the comm-cabin. *Moud, where are Javid Jividdat and the uulis?*

Uuli Ummman and Nummun are in commune, and couldn't be disturbed. Godhead Jividdat is nowhere to be found.

'Javid's probably off with that piece of skin and bone from the service crew. And as for Um and Nu ... of all the ridiculous times to be off with the Humm,' said Miranda Seeward sourly. She was squashed uncomfortably into the second comm-seat, her dimpled flesh overflowing like a spilled jelly.

'What's the idea of this?' Lawmon Jise demanded.

'What does GHIA say?' asked Labile Connit.

'Calm down, please, and listen.' Balbao took a long swill of his water tube. 'The station comm is rimming, as you may have gathered. I've had to use the emergency 'cast.'

'To Balol?'

'To the relay station, to be precise. I am waiting for an answer, hence the location of our meeting.'

'Are things so dire, Balbao, that you must wait here on their whim?' warbled Miranda.

Jise pinched her arm to quiet her, and she squealed.

Balbao glowered at them both. To think they were considered the greatest minds in their fields. *In their fields. Remember that*, he told himself. *And you are the greatest in yours.*

'Having had time to reflect and possibly confer with each other, do you have any theories on the Entity's sudden disappearance?'

'Isn't it obvious?' said Miranda. 'The Entity is unimpressed with this ridiculous war and has decided to avoid it.'

'Nonsense,' said Connit. 'The war could not touch Sole. It is beyond such things.'

'Is it?' This came from Ra. The strange jewel-eyed Lostolian had not spoken since taking a seat in the cramped comm-cabin. He sat stiffly, legs crossed, wary of damaging his skin on the lifeship's surfaces.

Thin-skinned weirdo, thought Balbao. 'What are you saying, G-Godhead Ra?' He stumbled over the pretentious title.

'I'm saying that I have seen glimpses of Sole's inner world, and the Entity is not without purpose.'

'None of us are without purpose, Ra,' said Jise impatiently. 'Is there something you wish to share?'

'There are things we should *all* share, if we are to understand where the Entity has gone.'

'Are you suggesting we disclose the nature of our projects?' Miranda Seeward spat with indignation.

Balbao steeled himself for another round of their ridiculous bickering, but found himself physically gripping his seat as a muffled explosion sounded station-side, and the whole ship shook with the impact.

The tyros all started out of their seats.

'Sit down,' Balbao barked. *Moud, what in the—*

'My moud is offline,' screeched Miranda Seeward.

'Mine too,' said Jise.

Moud! Moud!

Another explosion, this one louder and closer.

Balbao's fingers stumbled over the com-sole, trying to pull up status reports, but the station mayer-domo didn't respond. He asked for external views of Belle-Monde, but again nothing.

'Balbao!' said Ra. 'Launch this ship immediately. We're in the direst of predicaments.'

Balbao set the manual override on the EVAC ship's cameras and rotated them in an arc. Belle-Monde's near space was dominated by floating debris, bodies among the flotsam and jetsam. One drifted up close to the camera, its appearance so distorted by trauma that Labile Connit gagged.

'Strap into something,' barked Balbao. Without his moud, he'd need help to pilot. He set the ship's controller to automatic launch and tried to recall how to programme trajectory. It had been more than a decade since he'd been in a ship without a moud, and even then it had only been a training run.

A moment of weightlessness before the stabilisers cut in, and they shot at full propulsion away from Belle-Monde.

The quick gravity change sent the tyros moaning.

'Heavens,' gasped Miranda. 'What in Sole's—'

Her terrified exclamation broke Balbao's concentration. He jerked his head so he could see the screens running the external views. Breaks in the floating debris gave them a glimpse of an object as big as Belle-Monde, which was shedding flecks of light.

'What is it?' whispered Jise. 'It's like rain.'

'Incendiaries.' Labile Connit pointed uselessly, as if

they could follow by line of sight. 'A Geni-carrier.'

'The Extros are here,' said Miranda in a hoarse soprano. 'We'll die.'

Balbao was gripped by an emotion he'd never experienced before: a warrior's focus funnelling a brilliant mind. He turned back to the pilot com-sole with a fierce determination to survive. 'No, we will not!'

Jo-Jo Rasterovich

Jo-Jo watched every dawn and dusk with new appreciation. Right now it was the dusk: violent reds, browns and bruised purples that bled into each other.

In fact, being trapped inside the Extro drum had made him much more acutely aware of . . . everything. Despite malnutrition and screwed-up biorhythms, it was good just to be able to feel again. And smell. And see. Hell, it was incredible! He felt like he could sit for long periods of time just bathing in the feedback from his senses.

Randall had other ideas.

'Get your carcass away from the window. Don't want the Saqr seeing movement or shadow.'

'The windows are tinted,' he argued.

'Yeah, but we don't know how their eyes work. Could be they can see straight through it.'

Randall had a point. Jo-Jo didn't know much about tardigrade micro-organisms, let alone these mutated macro counterparts. 'What's up?'

Randall had donned the boots and coat she'd taken from the dead Latino. 'Time to take a little look-see outside.'

Jo-Jo nodded. 'You got a plan?'

She shrugged. 'Can't see much from here. Wish we had a 'scope of some kind.'

The view out over the plains was clear and vast even in the dying light, but looking back to the mountain it was hard to distinguish the buildings from the boulders.

'Seeing as we're at the bottom of the mountain, I say we divide it into sections. Go all the way to the top, each time. Couldn't take more than a few hours each way.'

'What if we see trouble when we're up top?'

'Take some water with us. Hole up in one of the other buildings until the next night.' She threw a canister and shoulder strap at his feet. 'Standard issue for visitors. They're all over the place.'

Jo-Jo picked it up and peeled the lid back. The stale water stank of sulphur. 'We could just start close. Do the whole near perimeter. Might be we don't have to go to the top to find what we need.'

Randall inclined her head, thinking about what he'd said. 'Could do that, if you're too weak to go all the way.'

He ignored her goading. Something told him it was better to rest now, not exhaust themselves again, hiking the mountain in the blistering night winds. 'I am,' he said, and met her gaze. 'And I'm bettin' you are too. You're just too dogged to say so.'

Her eyes narrowed with mistrust. She was as mentally sharp as always, despite exhaustion and starvation. 'Your way this time. But don't get used to it.'

He nodded, and followed her upstairs and along to the end of the building, to the door through which they'd first entered. Just the two of them. They left Catchut up a level, near the san, with a couple of water canisters and a plate of two-day-old polenta.

'I'll be shittin' bricks by the time you get back, Capo,' he'd said to his boss.

'Long as it's in the right place, Cat. Not cleaning up after you.'

Catchut had barely smiled. He'd been subdued since escaping the Extro ship. The toll he'd paid hadn't just been an injured foot. Something had deeply shaken his confidence. His eyes constantly followed Randall, as though he was seeking reassurance. When they were leaving him, his face showed fear and a little desperation.

Jo-Jo hadn't said anything to him. Catchut wouldn't appreciate it.

Now, as they stepped outside into the dark, Jo-Jo concentrated on following Randall's back. He'd stopped short of suggesting that they strap themselves together so they didn't get separated.

As if reading his mind, Randall stopped and glanced back over her shoulder. 'Take a good look where the building is in relation to everything else. If we end up being split, you'll have to find your own way back.'

'I spent thirty years scouting minerals in the unchartered territories,' he told her abruptly.

'Yeah, but did you ever do it without your gear? Your instruments?'

He didn't answer. She was right about that. Dead reckoning wasn't something he'd ever had to use.

'Just take a good look,' she said. 'It's always different in the dark.'

He did as she suggested without further protest, mapping points of reference: the angle of the landing port in the distance, the shape of the building, the approximate distance to the shadowy peak of Mount Pell.

He signalled that he was ready, and she began to climb.

Randall had already told him what she knew of the area: that many of the larger buildings – villas, she'd called them – had been owned by the wealthy upper-caste Latinos. The dwellings were scattered around the impressive sprawling studium compound, the Principe's palazzo and other official structures.

'I'm figuring the Saqr will've been through all the important places – anywhere there might've been a concentration of 'esques or resources. Could be we'll have more luck in houses of the lesser nobles, and the smaller offices.'

Jo-Jo liked her reckoning and settled in to let her lead the way. Randall had been here before. The closest he'd gotten to planetside before now was the detention block in the Dowl station, and then . . .

Helpless. Drifting in the black alongside Dowl. Bethany Jonil had dragged him back to safety when they'd escaped the station by shooting themselves into space. He owed her.

He spared a moment to wonder if she'd found happiness with that idiot scholar. Though used badly by life, Beth had determination – like her brother, Lasper Farr. She'd made Jo-Jo promise to find her daughter. He'd agreed, never imagining he'd be back here.

Now that he was, the idea gave him purpose. He'd seek Beth's daughter out, if she'd survived. What was her name? 'Jess?'

'What?' hissed Randall.

'Nothin',' he replied.

'Then stop talking to yourself. You're creepin' me out.'

He refocused on the climb through the darkness. Much of the mountainside was smooth, bare rock, or scree slopes of slippery gravel. Randall did her best to stay on the harder surfaces, but several times they found themselves slipping back in tiny rockfalls.

'At this rate, we'll have them all over us,' she said as they stopped to rest.

Jo-Jo pointed through the dark to the solid shadow above them. 'Something there.'

He heard her suck in a deep breath, even though her hood was up. 'Okay, let's back up a bit and try climbing a bit further out. Even if we have to go higher and come back. We need to stay on the hard rock.'

She climbed off sideways for a while, and then began to ascend again.

Jo-Jo worked on keeping her feet in sight, as the sweat poured from him and his muscles began to tire. The night winds burned the exposed skin on his cheeks. He wanted to close the hood, but he wouldn't be able to see Randall clearly if he did.

By the time they reached the footings of the closest building, the mere act of breathing hurt his dry lips and swollen throat.

He grabbed Randall's ankle. 'Water. Stop,' he rasped.

Randall slid down close to him. 'What?'

He mimed drinking.

Randall glanced up. 'Better in there. Night winds – bad tonight. Mebbe – storm – brewing. Drink up – let's move.'

Jo-Jo poured fluid past his stinging lips and forced himself to climb on until they reached the side of the building. Thankfully, the door unsealed without a protest, and they found themselves in a building with a very similar configuration to the one they'd left.

'More offices,' pronounced Rast, after they'd caught their breath. She sounded disappointed. 'Need to get to the villas. Better chance of finding an AiV in one of them.'

Jo-Jo gulped water as he leaned against the wall, and wished his body would cool down. Randall didn't seem bothered by the same discomfort.

Jo-Jo felt another wave of begrudging respect for the woman. Resilient didn't even begin to describe Rast Randall. The only chink he'd seen in her armour was a psychological one. Trapped inside the Extro ship, unsure whether they were actually alive or just an aggregation of sound bytes, Randall had nearly lost it.

Whatever the Entity had done to Jo-Jo's mind when he'd first stumbled across it, it had somehow enabled him to survive and function in the Post-Species environment. Better than Randall had, anyway.

Maybe he owed Sole something for that.

He hadn't felt the pull of the Entity since Edo, and he hadn't missed its presence. The way it had drawn him to Belle-Monde and into Tekton's clutches, and then his irresistible impulse to accept Lasper Farr's deal and travel to Rho Junction with Mira Fedor . . . it was like having strings attached to his limbs.

'I'll take the top levels. You do the basement,' said Randall. And she was gone before he could argue.

Jo-Jo made his way down the stairwell. Like the one they'd just left, the building was a catoplasma structure, with some of the quirks and problems that came with spontaneous gro-materials. The basement ceiling bulged so low in one spot that he had to bend over, and as he ran his hand down the wall alongside the stairs, he felt how it had buckled inward.

With his eyes well accustomed to the dark, he was able to make out shapes. The basement looked like a storage area. Jo-Jo moved among the shelves, feeling along them where he could reach. Some familiar objects, some unidentifiable.

He was fingering a narrow and compact case when Randall called down the stairs to him. 'Trouble. Move.'

Jo-Jo stuffed the object in the pocket of his fellalo and scrambled up the stairs.

Randall was already at the exit door, a bundle of shadow, crouched low. She grabbed his arm and squeezed, a signal that he took meant to keep quiet.

Without warning, she turned and shoved him back down the stairs. Sliding alongside him, she flattened herself against the pinched catoplasma steps. Her hand found the back of his neck and pushed his head down.

At the same time he heard the pop of the door seal. A strong, sweet, familiar smell pervaded the air. Scraping sounds rasped along the floor.

Jo-Jo fought a compulsion to raise his head and look. As if sensing his desire, Randall pressed harder on his head.

He concentrated on his breathing, keeping it light and quiet. On Dowl station he, Bethany and Petalu Mau had escaped the notice of the Saqr for a few minutes by keeping low, crawling until they'd reached a service lift.

Quiet. Still. Pray. Jo-Jo imagined Randall spitting the words out in that order.

Maybe not pray. She hadn't shown belief in anything much, other than her own ability. Even when things were bad in the Extro ship, he'd never heard Randall call for any god's help.

The sweet scent grew stronger; the scraping sounded right above them. A single Saqr? More? *Don't move. Don't!*

Jo-Jo's muscles twitched with an uncontrollable desire to spring up at the creature. Attack it before it could find him, surprise and aggression as his weapon. Not crouch here, shitting his pants, waiting for its maw to open and the bone-piercing stamen to extend down and skewer his skull.

Jo-Jo remembered how it was: 'esque bodies flung across the floor of the food court on Dowl, Saqr gorging on their body fluids. The adrenaline that had poured through him then now threatened to overcome his self-control, but Randall kept steady pressure on his head, pressing so hard that the pain across the bridge of his nose began to overshadow his fear.

She's breakin' my nose!

How long did they stay in that position? The only thing Jo-Jo registered clearly was when the pressure suddenly eased and the acute pain across the bridge of his nose faded. He turned his head sideways. Randall's breath was warm and slightly rancid in his face.

'We go quiet and quick,' she whispered. 'Straight home while they're inside here.'

'What if there're more out there?' he whispered back.

'We're fucked.' Then she added, 'But we're fucked if we stay in here. If there's more, split up. They're slow to make decisions. But once they have, they move real quick.'

He heard her quiet intake of breath as she bunched up and leapt lightly up the stairs. He followed, his movements as quick and agile as he could make them, controlling his breath so that he didn't gasp.

Outside, he could see better. One of the moons was beginning to rise, its soft glow bringing form and feature to the dark. But the wind was a buffeting torrent of heat.

Randall sped off, sure-footed, to the bare rock, then dropped to her arse and began to slide. He copied her movements, shuffling over the hot dry surface as fast as his limbs would allow.

He didn't look back until they were once more under the overhang of their own building.

Randall barrelled inside, but Jo-Jo paused to look back. As he did, the moon cracked the horizon and bathed the whole of Mount Pell in bright light. It was a harsh and eerie sight.

'Get in here!' Randall whispered fiercely.

Jo-Jo dropped to his hands and knees and backed up. When the door was closed, Randall hauled him to his feet.

'What the fuck do you think you're doing? Sightseeing? Who told you to stop?'

Jo-Jo stared at her. He couldn't see much in the gloom, just the outline of her figure and the blunt edge of her features.

'I—'

'You just wanted to bring them right here. Fuckin' Crux!'

'What is it, Capo?' Catchut limped down the stairs.

'This fuckin' idiot decided to stand in the moonlight and wave to the Saqr,' said Randall. She grabbed his arm. 'Give me a single reason not to break your neck.'

Jo-Jo's face burned even hotter than the night winds had made it. He fumbled inside his pocket and pulled out the flat pack he'd found in the basement. Shaking off her grip, he thrust it at her.

She snatched it from him without a word and snapped the cover open. Inside were a pair of field binoculars, a nav aid and a friction light.

Her grin showed pale teeth. 'Well, that's a start,' she said.

'Might be we can scope out the right place. Save us stumbling around all over the mountain,' said Jo-Jo.

She nodded. 'Next time, though, you don't stop anywhere unless I tell you to. Got it?'

He could have argued, but she was right. He'd made a mistake that could've gotten them killed. Could still get them killed. He glanced back at the door.

'Go get some sleep,' Randall said to them both. 'I'll watch the door for a while. Do some figuring as well.' She patted the binoculars. 'With these little babies, we can work out where the islands are, and how long it'll take to fly there.'

'Yeah,' said Jo-Jo with feeling. 'Now all we need is a way to get there.'

THALES

A rush of memories assailed Thales as he entered the port terminal and led the guards and Sophos Lauda to the kaffe where he'd first met Paraburd.

He explained to Lauda how the owner had become furious when he didn't have lucre, only credit. 'That's how Paraburd and I made our acquaintance. I was out of cash, and he offered to pay for my drink. We got to talking. After a while he offered me a job. I saw no reason not to take the opportunity. I was desperate.'

'Accepting a courier job from a complete stranger seems more than little naive, Msr Berniere.'

Thales flushed. 'I know that now. But at the time I was distraught and lost. Both my marriage and my future had been derailed.'

Lauda nodded, as if vaguely satisfied. 'And where did you go then?'

Thales walked past the kaffe and looked around. This section of Scolar's main terminal had not seen refurbishment for some time, and the scent of fried foods mingled with mould. Thales found the door into the service ways easily enough, but then became confused. Months had passed since his brief walk through them, and so much had happened in that time.

He closed his eyes, trying to block out Lauda's impatience and the guards' silent scepticism. He drew the memory to the top of his consciousness by reconnecting with his feelings of betrayal and anger. Rene hadn't stood by him, and Villon ... the Sophos had taken Villon.

He remembered how grateful he'd felt towards Gutnee Paraburd, and his surprise that the warren of service corridors even existed. A lesson, perhaps, that life wasn't always the way that it seemed, or the first blow to his naivety.

Gutnee had led him inside and turned left.

Thales began to walk that way, replaying their conversation in his mind, hearing his innocent questions and Paraburd's slippery evasions. His foolishness embarrassed him now, and yet in another way he mourned his lost innocence.

He walked until he found himself standing in front of a featureless grime-smudged door.

'Here, I think,' he said.

The four Robes pushed him aside and drew weapons. They burst into the office, and their curt observations floated back out to him almost immediately. It was empty.

Thales and Sophos Lauda followed them inside.

It was the right room, Thales thought; he recognised the damp, the desk at which Paraburd's Balol assistant had sat and the remnants of the shelves that had contained a mess of medical supplies.

Thales knelt down and retrieved the plastic end of a syringe. 'This is it. His interior office was there.' He pointed to the marks on the wall that showed a screen had been attached there. 'He gave me the uniform and then took me almost straight to the ship.'

Lauda's lip curled in disgust at both the premises and Thales's feeble explanation. 'You may be convinced, but I am not. Escort Msr Berniere back to detention.'

Thales's heart sank. Mira Fedor had been right: nothing would persuade the Sophos to believe him. They were too comfortable to be aware of the insidious mediocrity creeping up on them.

As one of the Robes grasped his elbow and pulled him to his feet, Thales protested, 'I am hardly a risk of any kind, Sophos Lauda. What is there to be gained by holding me captive?'

'You are a dissident, Thales Berniere. That is patently apparent. You spread lies and falsehoods. You even claim that Villon was murdered by the Sophos—'

'Not *all* the Sophos! I think that Mianos—'

'And now these wild accusations of biological warfare being waged on Scolar. What is not apparent is for whom you are working. Is it the warmonger Lasper Farr? Or even the Post-Species that you pretend to abhor? Who pays you to cause dissent on our peaceful world?'

Thales mouth fell open. 'Who pays *me*? I could well ask the question of you, Sophos Lauda.'

Lauda flushed. 'Take him back.'

'Please . . . at least believe me about the Post-Species threat. You must close the shift sphere!'

But Lauda left without answering him.

With the Sophos gone, the Robes handled him roughly, shoving him between them. One of them punched him below his ribs. He doubled over, gagging for air.

But they gave him no time for recovery, dragging him along.

For some reason his thoughts flashed to Mira Fedor. He prayed that her circumstances were better than his, that her good fortune had held.

Let her babe survive.

He didn't know who he prayed to. The concept of God had always been problematic to Thales. Now, having seen some of the wider galaxy, he felt even further from belief than before. *Right* now, he felt further away from a god than he ever had. Justice had never seemed more irrelevant. He'd failed.

But as they reached the door to the terminal, a large body hurtled through, slamming it shut and smashing the lock mechanism down with an implement.

The Robes grabbed for their swords, but giant fists wielding a large iron bar dealt with the four of them in a few short breaths.

Fariss stepped away from their fallen bodies and lifted Thales up by the shoulders. 'I don't mind you doin' your thing here, trying to save your world and all. But I ain't about to let ya rot in some gaol.' She leered happily. 'I got plans for you.'

Thales stepped into the big woman's embrace, burying his face into her chest. 'Fariss.'

She hugged him tight, then set him on his feet so he could see her face. 'We need to get out of here till these Sophos fuckers have forgotten about you. You got any ideas?'

TEKTON

Thankfully, Jancz and Ilke left Tekton well alone while the hybrid 'zoon navigated away from Intel. Hybrids required much more command attention than unfettered biozoons – they were less inclined to think for themselves and had to be watched for neuroses. Or so he'd heard.

This one, he guessed, would be in deep in neuroses; any creature as unhealthy and abused would be.

So Tekton used the time getting the DSD to propagate outcomes from the Post-Species threat. The device, he knew, could be utilised to change things – to alter history before it became so. But how to identify at what point change should be introduced to the system? With so many potential transformations, Tekton felt lost in a sea of possibilities.

Even logic-mind floundered.

In desperation, Tekton focused on Lasper Farr, tracking the Commander's movements and wishing he could somehow glean an idea of what to do from mere observation. He spent hours and hours on this pursuit, stopping only to steal the short distance to the galley, procure something edible and hasten back to his locked cabin.

Of all the thousands of scenes that he viewed, one image cache particularly caught his attention – Farr and Bethany Ionil on the bridge of his ship, arguing.

Tekton still couldn't fathom how the device captured such extensive visual feed, or how it reliably relayed the information. One of Sole's secrets, no doubt.

If only cousin Ra was here to ask. Not that the obstinate fellow ever gave Tekton a straight answer about anything.

The mystery of the device left logic-mind with grave doubts. How could Tekton even know if what he watched was authentic? The events could be randomly generated imaginings, not real occurrences.

And yet free-mind wanted to trust it. After all, Sole was behind its creation, and Tekton had glimpsed briefly – terrifyingly – the depth and breadth of the Entity's intelligence.

He shuddered, remembering the assault on his senses, the deluge of knowledge and the overwhelming enigma of the universe. It had left him floundering to recover, saturated in the shock of his own limitations.

'Focus on Lasper Farr,' he told the device. 'Closer.'

The star-verse of glittering motes brightened, and he fell forward again, using facial movements to direct and slow his focus. Bethany was there with Lasper, in the place he fell to, and so was a bulky round-faced 'esque who towered over the pair. The three stood in a large cabin aboard a ship. Lasper's ship, Tekton thought, recognising the stark lack of decoration in the Commander's cabin.

Tekton stepped closer to Bethany, assessing her mood and state of mind, all the while wondering how it could feel so completely and utterly real. Did they . . . Could they know he was there? Was this the present, or had this already played out? A thousand questions tugged at logic-mind, while free-mind let go and immersed itself in the surroundings.

'Where is it, Beth?' asked Farr quietly.

Tekton had never seen the Commander look so pale or tense. His displeasure would've given Tekton great satisfaction, if the man's wrath hadn't been directed at Bethany. She was smart and sweet, and direct in a way that Tekton had found refreshing. She'd also resisted his advances, which made her even more desirable than she'd originally been.

Stop it! Tekton clamped down on free-mind's akula rush and listened.

'I don't have it, Lasper. You'd do better to question your enemies, not your sister.'

'I'm comforted to hear you say that.' Her brother gave her a small and humourless smile. 'Unfortunately, I don't believe you.'

Bring them in, Farr sub-vocalised so discreetly that only Tekton, in his privileged position of surveillance, could hear.

The cabin door flew open with such force that Tekton stepped back instinctively. Soldiers marched Samuelle into the room.

'Get her out of that thing,' Farr ordered.

At gunpoint, they forced the old 'esque to shed her combat suit.

To Tekton's acute mortification, the woman was naked underneath. Though her wiry physique had been kept well conditioned by the suit's muscle stimulators, she was old, and her skin looked several sizes too big for her skeleton. It hung from her neck and belly and arms like a loose shift.

'Lasper!' cried Bethany. 'This is unnecessary. Why are you doing this?'

Samuelle was the one who answered. 'Cos he's scared, Beth. Someone's stolen his little god machine, and he's shittin' himself.' She put her hands on her hips, refusing to be shamed.

Tekton found himself overcome by a gross fascination. He wanted to touch her old body, feel its age. But his attention shifted back to Bethany, who rounded on her brother with a quick, intense fury.

'You're insane, brother. Orion is being destroyed around us and you're worrying about some ridiculous prescience device. Geni-carriers are being reported in thousands of star systems. Thousands of worlds aren't replying to 'cast signals, meaning that they've either disbanded their shift spheres or been annihilated.'

'And why do you think that's happening, Beth?' said Lasper quietly.

She stared at him.

Samuelle cleared her throat and took a step forward, so that she formed a close triangle with them. Again, Tekton felt an overwhelming desire to touch her.

'He thinks he can run things with it. One of those god-fuckers gave it to him, and he thinks he can make things go his way. Save us or fuck us over, dependin' on what he feels like.'

Farr transferred the focus of his gaze to Samuelle. 'You know nothing, you mouthy old bag of meat.' He flicked one of the guards a look, and the 'esque punched Sammy in the back, below the ribs.

The old woman went down without a sound.

'Lasper!' screamed Bethany. She leapt to Sammy's side.

Tekton found himself clutching his own back in sympathy.

Straighten up, fool, free-mind told him.

You're just an observer, logic-mind reminded him.

But Tekton couldn't separate himself from what was happening. He knew Sammy, after a fashion. He'd shared a cabin with her for a short time, watched her sleep and dream, and worry. She was a good woman despite her flaccid old age.

Good woman! Both minds choked out an exclamation as Sammy regained her feet with Bethany's help.

'He's rattled, Beth. Lost his grip. He's blind without that device, vulnerable as you or me. More so, cos we can live without it. He don't know what to do now. Can't make a decision without it. And everyone's waiting for him to do something grand.'

Bethany let go of Sammy and advanced on her brother. 'I don't have your device, Lasper. And neither does—'

But a pounding at the door stopped her.

Lasper blinked at one of the guards, who opened it.

Jelly Hob ran, out of breath, into the room. His mouth sagged open at the sight of Samuelle's nakedness. 'Aww, Sammy.' He automatically began to remove his filthy tunic.

'Hob? What is it?' Lasper gripped Bethany's arm and shifted her back out of the way. Her face contorted as he held her in a painful grip.

'It's yer device, Commander. I come to tell ya. Weren't Sammy who took it! Or her.' He pointed at Beth.

'How do you know?' said Lasper.

Tekton shifted his invisible presence to stand alongside Hob. *Don't tell him, Jelly. Don't say anything*, he shouted.

Hob draped his tunic around Sammy. 'Commander, let her get dressed.'

'Jeremiah!' rasped out Sammy. 'Think before you speak.'

He smiled at her, a wrinkled, heartfelt movement of his battered face. 'Not lettin' you take me blame, Sammy,' he replied softly, and looked across at Lasper. 'Was me, Commander. Least, not me that took it, but me that was there, and let it be took.'

Farr let go of Bethany. 'Speak plainly, Jelly. Or I'll skin that dry parchment that keeps your organs in place.'

'You'll be doin' that anyways, I'd be thinking, Commander. Was the Godhead, Tekton, that took it! I found 'im in here when youse was stationside. He was wearin' Sammy's other suit, and fetchin' to get off the ship.'

'Tekton of Lostol. On my ship? You're sure it was him?'

No one spoke.

'Beth?'

Tekton recognised the dangerous edge to Lasper's tone.

Bethany did too, but she stood resolute against it. 'I haven't seen Tekton since Edo. I thought he'd returned home.'

She didn't waver or flinch in her reply, and Farr turned back to Hob. 'Are you saying that Tekton of

Lostol ... *Tekton* ... took my device? How ... ? Did you bring him on board?'

Hob shrugged and nodded. Sammy moved closer to him, her scrawny shoulder touching his.

'I picked him up fallin' free in the well on Edo. Not far from yer worshipping place. He wuz in a taxi, bein' savaged by detrivores. Got him out jus' in time. Whole thing disintegrated.' He made an appropriate noise. 'Can't think what he wuz doin' there.'

Farr's eyebrows lifted almost imperceptibly. Surprise. And irritation.

Tekton danced a few restless steps around them all. *Yes, you psychopath!* he shouted. *I'm not dead! And I've got your precious device.*

'And you brought him aboard?'

'Didn't know what else ta do wiv him, sir. He wuz kinda lost. I wuz thinkin' ta drop him off at Intel. Let him be on his way.'

'With my device?' Farr's tone had lost its quiet control, a note of wildness creeping in.

'Din't know he'd nicked it. Found him here all right. Figured he wuz just bein' nosy, you know, seein' how a fancy Commander lives and stuff. I took him down to the cargo bay and let him out. He musta taken yer thing when me back was turned.'

Hob's explanation was so simple and ingenuous that Farr seemed confounded by it. Fists clenched, he stalked to a corner of the room and stood there, processing the situation.

Tekton watched Samuelle take Jelly Hob's hand and squeeze it. She gave him a grateful smile for protecting her part in it.

As Hob grinned at her, Tekton was filled with conflicting emotions yet again. Delight led the field; he'd annoyed and trumped Lasper Farr in no uncertain terms. But worry undermined his pleasure – what had Lasper thought to use the device for? How had he planned to prevent the Extros from taking Orion? What would the repercussions be?

Then another kind of concern began gnawing. What would the insane Commander do to Jelly Hob now?

Of all the 'esques Tekton had ever met, Hob was the only one to have stirred any real sense of gratitude in him. Tekton didn't even hold it against him that he'd told Farr who'd stolen the device. He was right to protect Samuelle. Consilience – their independent political organisation – might be the only group capable of stopping the Extros. And for Consilience to operate, Samuelle and Bethany needed to survive.

As Lasper stepped out of his corner and paced one quick circuit of the cabin, Tekton placed his imagined hand on Hobb's shoulder, willing the old fellow to do something clever to save himself.

Then Tekton saw the Commander become very still, as though shocked into immobility. After a long, uncertain moment, he cleared his throat.

'Kill the pair of them,' Lasper told his men. Then he pointed to Bethany. 'And lock her in her cabin – for now.'

BALBAO

Debris from Belle-Monde battered their lifeship. With each collision, Balbao's desire to survive grew stronger. Chunks of flight instruction broke free of his long-term memory and floated into the present, and he began frantic res-shift preparations: check buffers, trajectory parallels, co-ordinate sequ— His hands shot out of virtual arrangement as the ship shuddered under the impact of something large.

He righted himself, snatched the vessel back into position and began acquiring damage feed. The view outside the ship showed a frightening minefield of flotsam between them and the Geni-carrier.

We must stay unnoticed long enough to make shift. That meant . . . *No!* A sliver of panic crept in. *I – I can't . . . pilot as well as . . .*

A thin-fingered hand touched his knee. His eyes refocused on Ra.

'What is it, Balbao?' asked Ra. 'What do you need?'

'With no moud, I must prepare for shift manually.'

'And?'

'The Geni-carrier will detect us if we don't use the debris to hide.'

'You need someone to pilot while you prep?'

Balbao nodded.

Ra unclipped his safety net and teetered across the

small space. His light frame fell against Balbao's as the internal gravity fluctuated wildly.

'Strap me in with you,' said Ra. 'I am able to pilot without a moud.'

'How so?' asked Balbao, fumbling to secure them both.

Ra's strange segmented eyes rippled as if lit from within. 'Sole's reward. Release the backup.'

Balbao banged a panel to his right, and a sensor piece dropped out. Ra slipped it across his forehead and pressed the interface point to the back of his neck. He lifted his hands above his lap and waited for the virtual field to activate. 'I will keep us as well hidden as I can.'

His fingers began to twitch and twirl. Almost immediately the buffeting stopped.

'Thank Sole!' Miranda exclaimed with relief. 'What can I do?'

'Start thinking,' said Balbao curtly. 'Work out what the hell is going on and, if we survive, what we should do about it.' He didn't bother to look at her. 'And for Crux sakes do it quietly!'

With half an eye on Ra, Balbao fell back to his task. Only a tiny portion of his mind registered Ra's manoeuvres, but enough that he would remember his skill for ever. However long that turned out to be.

His own virtuals showed him that the remains of Belle-Monde were spread in a shining metallic landscape across Mintaka's outer system. The lifeship's EM scanners were giving similar information for the space between them and the shift station. He double-checked his coordinates. Min Minor, the closest planet, wasn't where it should be. Instead, there was a giant expanding dust cloud.

'Fuck,' said Balbao, with full Balol anger intonation.

Ra didn't pause or react.

Labile Connit did. 'Bad news?'

'Min Minor,' said Balbao. 'It's gone.'

'Gone? A planet can't be gone.' Miranda lifted her head from whispering in Jise's ear. Her face was puffy.

Balbao might have been disgusted by her appearance, had he not been distracted with his own fury. He wanted to bellow and break things to vent his upset. 'The fucking planet is fucking gone!'

'It's the Extros ... My God, they've wiped out a planet,' said Connit.

'Fifty million sentients,' said Jise. '*Fifty million.*' He spoke slowly, as if trying to absorb what it meant. 'That can't be. It just can't.' He banged his head back against the seat.

'Fifty million and five, if we don't get out of this system,' said Balbao. 'Ra?'

They waited a long few moments before the Godhead answered. 'I can keep us hidden for a few more hours, but on this trajectory we'll soon encounter the worst of the dust from Min Minor. I'm not sure the ship will withstand it.'

'Can we go around the worst of it, Ra?'

'Not without finding clear space and being noticed.'

'Then what do we do?' asked Miranda.

'There are a number of larger ships in the area. Most are hastening to the shift station,' said Ra.

Miranda's bottom lip dropped. 'Can we contact some

of them? They would take us aboard, surely? We're refugees!'

'Our signal will pinpoint our position,' said Balbao. 'And it's unlikely they'll come for us. Everyone with any sense will be leaving as quickly as they can. They're *all* refugees.'

A glum silence fell over the cabin as Ra and Balbao went back to concentrating on their tasks.

Miranda laid her head on Jise's shoulder. 'I wonder where Tekton is?' she said softly.

'Being carnal somewhere, no doubt. Why?'

'He always was lucky,' she sighed. A tear trickled down her nose and plopped onto her hand.

Jise squashed it with his thumb and squeezed her wrist. They hunched together in mutual support.

Opposite them, Labile Connit closed his eyes and mouthed something prayer-like.

Who'd have imagined this? Balbao mused as the ship's computer ran shift-algorithms. *Though someone should have. The Extros fled quickly from the Stain Wars. OLOSS should have guessed they were rebuilding. No wonder Sole has disappeared.*

Disappointment stabbed him. The entity had not bothered to warn the tyros of the danger. Whatever the nature of its sentience, compassion surely did not feature. Or perhaps the timing was mere coincidence. Perhaps Sole had no foreknowledge.

He considered that notion for a while, then discarded it. Sole knew all right. 'Your god abandoned you,' he said aloud.

Jise lifted his head. 'Pardon me?'

'Sole. He didn't warn you, and he left you to die.'

'What evidence leads you to believe Sole knew what was about to happen?' demanded Connit.

'What evidence is there that Sole didn't?'

Any answer was stalled by a sudden vibration.

Miranda sucked in a noisy breath. 'What's that?'

'Rock showers from the dust,' said Ra. 'We should activate the buffers.'

'But they won't protect the ship enough,' said Connit.

'Do you have any useful comments to make?' snapped Balbao.

Connit glared at him. 'Do you understand the forces at work, Balbao? Ra can't dodge the remains of an entire planet.'

'I don't have to be a geneer to know that.'

'Then change direction and head away from the dust cloud.'

'It will catch us anyway, Labile,' said Ra.

'For Crux sakes, ask for help,' pleaded Miranda. 'It has to be better than disintegration.'

They all stared at each other. Doubt laced their moment of mutual agreement. *Was it?*

Ra sighed. 'I'll 'cast a distress signal and buffer the cabin. At least the planet fallout will make it harder for the Geni-carrier to notice us.'

Within moments of his words the vibration stilled.

'How long will the ship hold together?' asked Jise.

Balbao shrugged. He'd done everything he could, and it hadn't been enough. It seemed so unfair that his brilliance should be wasted on such an untimely death. 'Impossible to say.'

Miranda grasped Jise's hand and then reached out for Connit's. 'Then I think it's time we prayed.'

'Who to?' asked Ra.

'The Entity,' said Miranda. 'Surely if we concentrate our thoughts, it will hear us.'

'And you truly think it would care?' Ra again.

Miranda rebuked him with a stare. 'You, of all of us, should be the closest to Sole. You could at least try.'

Ra sucked his thin lips inside his mouth and nodded. He removed the pilot interface, loosed the safety web around him and twisted around so that he could reach the others' hands.

Balbao watched them with despair. What nonsense were they on about in the face of their own demise? He bared his teeth and let loose a small growl. His frill stiffened in agitation. If only they would use their supposed intellects for something helpful.

Alarms dragged his attention back to the ship information flow. The scanners told him that they were heavily mired in the fallout from both Belle-Monde and Min Minor now; data was escalating; stress limits approaching. Among the confusing accretion of information, he nearly missed the response to their SOS.

Breath on hold, he sent a pingback before alerting the others. When it confirmed itself as an OLOSS ship, sweat oozed out from under Balbao's scaly skinplates. He sent their coordinates immediately, and was rewarded with an estimated rendezvous of less than an hour.

Balbao opened his mouth to share the joyous news with the others, then promptly shut it again. The four tyros were still communing silently.

He leaned back in his seat and took a deep relieved breath. *Let them keep working for it. Let the annoying bastards work for it.*

TRIN

'Do you see them, Principe?'

'Si.' Trin struggled to keep irritation from his reply. Of course he did; the night sky was filled with them, yet Joe Scali had still deemed it necessary to ask, like a child repeating unnecessary things to a parent.

Trin's patience with his friend had been short since he had seen him standing so close – so intimately close – to Djeserit on the darkened beach.

'What do you think, Principe?' asked Juno Genarro. 'OLOSS, perhaps?'

Trin stared at the hundreds of lights floating across the night sky, high enough, it seemed, to be in outer orbit. 'I would like to say they are our salvation, but something tells me not.'

The three men stood on the peak of the mountain. From the same vantage point he and Djes had seen the circular-shaped ship descend several days before. He had not told his people about it, but the appearance of thousands of satellites changed things.

Now a deeply troubled feeling beset him. 'Juno, go down and call everyone together. I will follow soon.'

As he had since the early days of the invasion, Juno complied without argument or question. In many ways, aside from Djeserit, he had been Trin's best ally and aide. Trin felt Juno's respect and their common desire to keep the old ways alive.

'What concerns you, Trinder?' asked Joe Scali, when Juno had left.

Trin meant to dismiss the question. Instead, he found other words coming out of his mouth. 'You have developed strong feelings for Djes.'

Under the glow of the thousands of satellites he saw Joe shrink a little, as if punched. The man had never really regained his equanimity since the Saqr had killed Rantha and her unborn child. Nowadays, Scali wore his emotions openly, and with less control than a young girl. Trin saw him weeping often.

'I . . . we all . . . have great regard for her.' He stumbled over his reply. 'Djeserit has saved us. Kept us fed. Brought us here.'

'That is true,' Trin allowed. 'But it would be foolish to mistake your feelings of gratitude for anything else. Wouldn't it?'

Joe Scali bowed his head. He shifted away from Trinder in obvious discomfort.

'I am clear, signor?' asked Trin softly.

'Si, Principe.'

Trin had expected meekness and embarrassment, but Scali's tone held a trickle of stubbornness.

Should he say more?

No. He would speak with Djes. At the moment there were more important things to address. 'We should join the others.'

He turned his back on his friend and made his way back down the shoulder of the peak to the caves.

The group was assembled outside. Over the previous days the women had swept and moved rocks to make a space that would accommodate them all, while the men had begun fashioning beds and tables from the small bushes that cloaked the mountainside.

Trin had instructed them to take the brush selectively, so as not to plainly show their presence. Djeserit had returned to the sea, taking Tivi Scali to wait on the beach and help her carry her catch. For several meals now they'd dined on white fish and roots that Cass Mulravey had identified as safe to eat. The food was still raw, but their bellies were almost full, and many of them had brush cots to sleep upon. Given time, they could make themselves even more comfortable.

Trin glanced into the night sky. But would they have that time? He stepped into the circle of bodies and crouched in the middle. The division between Mulravey's women and the rest had lessened since their encounter with the giant ligs – as though Trin's warnings of imminent danger had finally brought real acknowledgement of his authority to lead their group.

The women sat interspersed among his men, and already he could see pairings beginning to develop. Juno Genarro and his cousin Josefia, Tivi Scali and Tina Galiotto. Cass Mulravey's brother Innis kept close to his sister and the tall outspoken woman Liesl. His surly expression rarely changed, and of all of the survivors Innis Mulravey made Trin the most uneasy.

They quietened as one, waiting for him to speak, but their excitement was unmistakable. He wanted to reach out and take Djeserit's hand for reassurance, but she was next to the korm, and now wasn't the time for a physical display of need.

He took a breath. 'You would all be hoping that the lights that we can see are the precursor to an OLOSS rescue.' He glanced up. 'I would too . . . but you must know that it's not so.'

Everyone spoke at once, a clamour of questions and protests.

'Quiet!' he cut across them sharply. 'On the day of our arrival at the caves, Djeserit and I climbed to the peak. From there, while you rested, we saw a craft enter the atmosphere and land. It was alien in shape to anything in OLOSS.'

'Could it be an ally still, Principe?' asked Tivi Scali.

Trin regarded Joe's younger cousin. He had a quick resourceful mind, and had not been affected – disturbed – by the Saqr invasion in the way that Joe had. 'It is possible, Tivi. But unlikely. The look of the craft – it was round like a disc, but deep as well.'

'How would we know what's out there, stuck on this backwater planet? Could be OLOSS has a whole fleet of ships shaped like that. What makes you so sure it's not them? I say we start a fire on the beach. Let 'em know we're here,' said Innis Mulravey.

Trin shot him a quelling look, but its impact was lost in the moonlight.

'I saw the ship as well,' said Djeserit. 'And I agree with the Principe.'

'Yeah, but you would.' Innis's laugh was deprecating, almost dirty.

'Innis!' Cass Mulravey placed a warning hand on her brother's shoulder.

'There will be no fires lit. It is more imperative than before that our presence goes unnoticed,' said Trin. 'If the ship that landed is part of the Saqr invasion, then it is only logical that the lights we can see in the sky are more of the same.'

Innis pushed Cass away and stood up. 'You just wanna keep us here, so you can play lord. Well, I'm sick of takin' orders from Your Highness of Nuthin' and your half-breed missus.'

Trin's body went rigid at the insult, his mind narrowing to a single point of fury. He stood up slowly and took a step towards Innis.

Tivi, Juno and Joe all jumped to their feet as well, but Kristo, Mulravey's man, beat them all. He threw a quick hard punch at Innis, which sent him sprawling backwards.

'Shut yer stupid mouth,' said Kristo. 'If it hadn't been fer the both of them, you'd be dead. Like as much, we'd all be. I don't hold to their royalty, or whatever it is, but like it or not he's made good decisions. I'd listen to him and quit yer mouthin'.' He kicked Innis in the thigh for good measure. 'And don't badmouth women. Last time you treated a woman bad, you nearly got yourself killed. That merc was gonna rip yer guts out. Woulda thought you'd learned from that.'

After his long and vehement speech, Kristo turned and stalked back into the mouth of the closest cave. He stood there staring at the sky, arms folded and legs apart.

Innis climbed groggily to his feet and backed away into the darkness.

Cass Mulravey didn't move from where she sat, nursing Mira Fedor's adopted baby Vito. Trin couldn't see her expression clearly, but her inaction was enough for him. She did not support her brother. And what did Kristo mean by 'last time'? What had Innis done to a woman? He would tell Juno Genarro to find out. His trusted carabinere had become friendlier with Kristo over the last few days.

Trin shifted back to the centre of the circle and executed a slow turn. 'We must take great care to be sure nothing of our presence can be seen from the air. Hide the entrance of the caves and keep water and food supplies inside. We need be able to survive several days without leaving the caves, in case the island is searched.'

'How do we hide the caves? That's impossible!' said one of the miners.

'Then we must make it possible,' said Josefia Genarro. She sat at Juno's side, her hand resting on his leg. They were a good couple, Trin thought, resilient and clever and not easily defeated. It didn't matter that they were cousins, not now that their numbers were so few.

'We could hide the openings with boulders,' suggested Cass Mulravey. 'Make it look as though there's been a rockfall. We'll need to stop treading the same route outside, though. Our feet are flattening the ground and making a path.'

'It would be cumbersome, but we could make a rope entry from the rocks above,' suggested Juno.

'Not all of us would be able to negotiate such a thing.' This came from Jilda Pellegrini. Trin's mother had spoken little at group gatherings so far, her energies spent on keeping up with the others and watching her son. It seemed hardly believable that his fragile madre had survived the Saqr invasion when his powerful vigorous padre had not. It was true that her servant Tina Galiotto had cared for her, yet even so Jilda had showed an ability to endure.

Trin had always thought of her as weak, in mind and in deed. Perhaps he'd been wrong. Or perhaps her suffering had made her stronger in some way. It had done that to many of them.

'The principessa is right,' said Djeserit. 'Not all of us could do that. It would be better if we scatter small rocks around the boulders to hide the entrance, and simply climb over them.'

'We need weapons,' said Kristo from behind them. 'Hidin' won't be enough. And what if there're other things on the island – like them giant lig? We got to be able to protect ourselves.'

A murmur of agreement went up from most.

The enormous ligs that had attacked them down on the flat of the island had been chasing the nectar of the night flowers. They had not ventured further up the mountain. But Kristo was right – hiding wasn't enough. They had stopped running, and now they must secure their position.

'Juno, pick a group to find the strongest branches, to sharpen and make into spears. Joe Scali will take the rest and begin placing the rocks around the entrance to hide our footprints. Those that aren't strong enough for either will see to the food.' Trin turned to where Djes sat, near the korm. 'Tivi and the korm will carry your catch from the beach to the caves. Make sure some fish is dried, for storage.'

'Anything else?' said Cass Mulravey.

'Collect more roots. And we need more receptacles. Some for drinking water and others to store the energy pods. They are more potent when they are kept wet.'

'That means more trips back to the spring,' said Juno.

Trin nodded. 'It's the only place we've seen fresh water. Once you've made some spears or clubs, take two others down there with you. Bring as much water as you can carry.'

'There's a rock hollow in the back of our cave,' said Cass. 'We can store water there while we're making more containers.'

'Buono,' said Trin. Semantic had risen, casting more light on the faces watching him. 'I will look for another spring, closer. Now, let's eat and work.'

Trin ate his share of the remaining xoc and chewed a small piece of seaweed. Although salty and unpalatable, Djes assured him it was high in nutrients. When his hunger had eased enough for him to move, he got up and left the circle, walking to the large flat rock that served as the group's evening table.

Juno hastened after him.

'Principe, is it wise to go searching for water alone?' he said quietly. 'In the dark you might trip and fall.'

Trin put a reassuring hand on his lieutenant's arm. 'As we all might, Juno. Everyone is needed for a task. I will walk around the summit at approximately this level, returning from the west side. I would estimate only a few hours. If I am not back by early light, do not attempt to come for me until the next night. I'll take pods and roots.' He reached across the slab and took a collection of edibles, including several pods, slipping them into the pockets of his ragged fellalo. He filled the robe's water-sleeve and checked the drinking tube. Its end was damaged, allowing precious water to leak out if he did not hold it upright. He pinched the valve between his fingertips.

'You need both hands to climb,' said Juno.

Trin tied the tube in a knot to make his carabinere happy. 'I will see you before light.'

Djeserit walked with him until they were out of sight of the caves.

'Take care, love,' she said. It was the first time she had used an endearment.

He peered into her face. Her tight skin, a tribute to her mixed heritage, had aged in the harsh environment. She looked more mature than the girl he had first lain with, in the dry-gardens of Villa Fedor. He touched her hair. Despite spending less time in the water, it still felt stiff, as though the sea didn't want to relinquish its effect on her.

At least she was cleaner than the rest of them. How long since he'd washed with a cleanser? How long until he would? 'And you, Djes. Let the korm and Tivi carry what you catch. Don't tire yourself by doing too much. Or overuse the pods.'

Her thin lips parted in a smile. 'You, also.' She slipped her hand into his pocket and shook the pods.

Her touch near his groin sent a shot of pleasure through his body. Though they lay together every day when she returned from fishing, neither had the energy for more than the comfort of being close. In addition,

Trin found the proximity of the others inhibiting in a way that did not seem to bother some of the other men.

He took her hand from his pocket and drew her further away from the caves. Above them was the sheer rock of the summit; below, the line of brush clinging to the dirt.

'Trinder?' she whispered.

Without answering, her steered her to a spot among the bushes and then pulled her close. His lips tasted of her briny skin and his hands felt the taut lean warmth of her muscled body.

She responded by pulling away and slipping her robe off, to stand naked before him. She pointed at the ground, but he shook his head and turned her from him, bending her over. The ground was too rough for her bare skin. He would not risk injuring her, so he pressed himself inside her this way.

She stiffened at first but he stroked her back and murmured gentle reassurances. Her body began to soften in his grip. Instinctively, she started to move in rhythm, arriving at her climax before him.

His success in pleasuring her quickly fuelled his own fervour, and he reached release almost straight away. He stood, hugging her to him, his hands cupping her narrow waist.

'Trinder, there is—'

'Hush,' he said. 'Do you hear something?' A crackling sound, at odds with the island's night noises.

Djes slipped from his embrace and pulled her robe on. 'No. But I must go and fish now.'

'Si,' he agreed.

They pressed their lips together, and then she cupped his face. 'I'll think of you.'

He smiled, turning his lips to the palm of her hand, feeling the webbing between her fingers scraping his cheek. Perhaps he had not lost her to the sea yet.

They climbed up from the brush to the rock line, where she left him to return to the caves. Trin stood for a moment, savouring the solitude and the physical release from their moment of intimacy. He and Djeserit had paired under the worst of circumstances, yet their regard for each other sustained itself. And now the passion had returned. For a moment he felt content, a ridiculously impossible feeling under their circumstances but real enough.

Another noise in the brush behind him shattered his moment of peace. He scanned the shadows but could see nothing other than the shapes of stunted trees. Perhaps there was an animal in there.

A sense of uneasiness crawled into his stomach.

Keep moving.

MIRA

Mira stared at Linnea. 'It's a girl. It must be. There is no—'

'Not according to this thing.' Linnea had placed the baby in a bubble crib by the bed and was watching the diagnostic display.

Another cramping pain struck Mira before she could reply. Not as intense as the birthing contractions, but deep even so.

'Afterbirth,' pronounced Linnea. She left the crib and slid more absorbent film underneath Mira's thighs. 'One more push now,' she said, as she pushed down on Mira's stomach.

With the final effort, the pain left her.

'Good 'n' healthy one, far as I can see, but small. Mine was all threaded. Too long in the womb.'

Mira heard the door open.

Linnea deftly wrapped the baby leftovers up and transferred them to a large receptacle. Then she pulled a sheet up over Mira's lower body.

Dolin was first to enter the room, hurrying to the crib. He pored over the readouts before, finally, lifting his gaze to Mira.

She sipped on a sweet juice Linnea had produced for her and wondered at the expression on his face. He seemed confused.

'I want to hold my baby, Dolin,' she said.

'Of course,' he said. 'Just a moment.'

More clinicians arrived, crowding around the crib.

'What? What is it?' Mira demanded.

Finally Dolin lifted the baby from the observation bubble and passed her to Mira.

As she took her child in her arms, an overwhelming swell of emotion and responsibility surged through her. She had brought this child to life, and now she must ensure her survival.

Mira pressed her lips to the baby's tiny wrinkled forehead and studied her features. Fine dark hair covered her peeling scalp, and her lips were pursed in a red slash that gave colour to the palest of little faces. She hadn't cried or uttered a sound, and her eyes were open. She stared back at Mira with open curiosity.

'She can see me,' said Mira, startled. 'Her eyes are focused.' She knew enough of babies, from Villa Fedor, to know that humanesques did not focus their eyes immediately. It could take weeks, sometimes longer.

'Yes,' said Dolin. 'The baby has some unusual characteristics, as we suspected.'

'Please stop saying that and explain.'

'Baronessa, there is no other way to say this than plainly. Your baby doesn't have reproductive organs of either sex.'

'My baby is a eunuch?'

'I'm not sure . . . We need to do further tests to determine exactly.'

'What sort of tests?'

'Genotyping, and more . . . neurological and body scans.'

Mira took a deep breath. She could deal with anomalies in the baby's reproductive organs. But neurological anomalies . . . What had the Post-Species done to her child? 'I will be present during the tests,' she said decisively. She did not trust even Dolin to take the baby from her sight.

'The tests will take time, and you must be tired. We can take the child and feed—'

'No!' Mira held the baby close. Something told her not to trust the seemingly benign scientist. 'I will feed her myself. And I will be present at the tests.'

Dolin glanced at the others. 'Very well.'

'Is my baby sick?'

'No.'

'Is she in danger of dying from her prematurity?'

Dolin scratched his head. 'Remarkably, no. The gene accelerant seems to have worked better than we could have hoped.'

'Thank you for saving her. But please leave now, while I acquaint myself with my daughter. Your other tests can wait that long, at least.' She stared Dolin down, until he nodded and motioned everyone out of the room again.

Linnea stood at the foot of her bed with her arms crossed. 'You've got a way with you for someone so thin and pale. What'd you do, swallow a whale's backbone?'

Mira wasn't sure that she properly understood the woman's meaning. She shrugged and lifted the baby to a more comfortable position on her lap. 'Please. Could you show me how to feed my baby?'

Linnea's mouth dropped open, and she burst into a loud laugh. When she finally stopped, she shook her head and wiped tears from the corners of her eyes. 'You just stared down a roomful of our most high and mighty scientists, but you don't know how to feed your own baby. Where the hell was it that you said you came from?'

'Araldis,' said Mira, her face warming.

'That the place where those aliens landed and killed everyone?'

'Si.'

'Been all over the 'casts. So you're the one that escaped.'

Mira nodded.

The woman gave a heavy sigh. 'You've been through a lot, love. Here, let's teach you some mothering things, before the fermenters come back.'

'Fermenters?'

'That what we call 'em. Ferment anything in a dish, they would.'

Linnea put the baby back in the crib and helped Mira to wash, finding her some clean lab overalls to put on. She also got some absorbent film from a drawer for the residual bleeding. When she was dressed, Linnea helped her back on the bed.

'Bleeding might go on for a few days yet. Just keep yerself changed and clean, and there should be no problem. Like I said, the placenta looks healthy enough.'

Then she showed Mira how to hold the baby in the crook of her arm and manipulate her breast so that the baby could attach its mouth to her nipple. Mira found it easy to overlook her natural modesty with the woman's practical ways, and after several painful tries the baby began to suck.

'Now, all yer gotta do is relax.' Linnea laughed again. 'Damn easier said than done. Nothing like a hungry babe working its gums to put you through the roof.'

Mira smiled through her discomfort. Something about Linnea soothed her.

'What you gonna call this babe? Can't be going too long without a name. Not good for your bonding. Yer got someone you c'n name her after?'

'My sister Faja. Or her friend Estelle. They died on Araldis.'

'What about the father? I'm assumin' if you're from that planet, you still choose fathers the old fashioned way.'

'They choose you,' she countered abruptly.

Linnea pulled a face, but was smart enough not to pursue it.

Mira stared down at the baby. The infant looked back at her, even though it was feeding, and its tiny fingers curled and uncurled against her breast. How could her child be so alert? It seemed unnatural.

Milk blew in little bubbles from the corner of the baby's lips, and Mira thought of Vito's solemn face and quiet manner. Her heart contracted. Linnea was right: she must name her child.

'I'll call her Nova. Because she is new and fresh.'

Linnea shrugged and nodded. 'Seems to fit. Now, time to swap over.'

The galley supervisor helped her move the child to the other side, and went through the same steps. But Nova fussed, and kept pushing Mira's breast away.

She lifted the baby so that their faces were close. 'What is it, little one?'

The blue-grey eyes blinked with intensity, as if trying to tell her something. Mira stared into them, remembering how active Nova had been in the womb, especially in times of danger.

The next moment the doors swung open and the clinicians returned, led by Dolin. He stopped alongside the bed and held out his hands for Nova. 'It is time.'

Mira refused to hand her over, sliding her feet onto the floor. 'What do you want to do?'

'I would simply paste a little trace substance in her mouth.' He waved at the wall. 'The nanites will transmit their analysis here, and we will be able to verify your daughter's health and many other things.'

Mira hesitated. Did she really want to know those other things?

Nova flailed her small fists in the air, her fingers curling and uncurling again. She seemed irritated, but that was ridiculous. A newborn could not be that way.

'Can the nanites harm her in any way? What will happen to them when they've done their job? Do they remain in her system? What if she is allergic to them?'

'They are completely benign, medical-grade, and will degrade and be excreted within a short time.'

Mira sought Linnea for reassurance, but the scientists had pushed her to the back of the room.

'Very well,' she said. She stood on shaking legs, and pushed determinedly past the observers to stand in front of the screens. 'But I will administer it, and you will explain everything to me as the nanites transmit.'

Dolin hesitated, glancing around the group.

Mira wondered why he'd been appointed spokes-person. Was it because they thought she would relate best to him, because of his biozoon experiences? Had they hoped to make her more sympathetic to them?

Dolin moved closer to her and produced a small tube from the pocket of his coat. Detaching a small applicator from the lid, he squeezed some paste out onto it.

Mira took it from him and held it near Nova's mouth. The blue-grey eyes stared at her again, and the little lips pursed.

'Come, little Nova. Just this once, so that we can better understand you.'

To Mira's astonishment, the baby's lips parted in compliance. She tilted Nova towards her to hide the extraordinary behaviour, and slipped the applicator in her mouth, sweeping the nanite-infused paste across her gums.

Nova screwed up her face and dribbled, poking her tongue out at the taste.

Almost immediately, the walls came alive with a flood of data, and the observers spread out, examining it.

'This section analyses cell integrity. This one examines organ function. Endocrine. Vascular. Musculo-skeletal. Neurological.' Dolin pointed to different displays.

Mira watched the interplay of information and felt more comfortable. It was similar to being in the Autonomy function on *Insignia*. She rocked Nova. The baby settled in her arms, eyes closing, and she relaxed with it, tiredness creeping up.

But an increase in the level of murmuring brought her sharply alert.

'There!' said Dolin with excitement, pointing. 'I was right.'

Mira concentrated on a single screen that showed a complex diagram she recognised as genome markers. Even from her most basic understanding, they seemed wrong.

'That is not possible. Not for a humanesque,' said one of the clinicians.

'There have been instances of humanesques being born with dual sex organs, but your baby has neither.'

'It is a neuter?'

'Not a neuter exactly,' he said. 'Something else . . .'

'Dolin!' one of his colleagues cried. 'Look at the EM scan!'

Dolin's eyes slid to another screen, and Mira followed his gaze.

Mira?

Si, Insignia?

There is important news that impacts our safety.

But Mira was distracted. *My baby . . . they say that sh-she is n-neither male nor female.*

Arbitrary and unimportant. Nova is healthy; that is all that matters.

But you're not humanesque. You don't understand what that means.

I do.

How could you? Your own species is different.

I know because Nova has explained it to me.

Mira stiffened. *You've spoken to Nova.*

Of course. Our communication began while she was still in your womb, but Nova's thoughts were quite unformed then. They become clearer by the moment. And she is in agreement with me that we should leave this planet.

She? But they say she has no gender.

'She' is a pronoun you seem comfortable with, and I'm happy to accommodate your need.

Need! Mira didn't know whether that angered or amused her. *Why must we leave?* She glanced down at Nova's face. The baby's eyes were open again, and staring steadily at her as if trying to convey a thought.

'. . . The baby has a pronounced electromagnetic field around it,' said Dolin finally.

Mira took a moment to react to his statement. Electromagnetic field? She stared at the baby's translucent skin, so thin that she almost seemed blue from the glow of her myriad tiny veins. 'I'm not—'

But the wall screens suddenly blanked, causing her to pause. Then a loud chiming claimed everyone's attention.

The wall reactivated, showing the head and shoulders of a middle-aged humanesque in some type of ceremonial robe. He spoke without preamble.

'You will all know me as Sophos Kantos. For some time there has been rumour about a Post-Species threat to OLOSS territories. We have been sceptical of such stories, believing them to be the propaganda of extremist groups who are opposed to our philosophies and ideals.' Sophos Kantos cleared his throat and blinked several times, as if trying to clear his vision. 'This morning, however, we have farcast evidence that the threats are neither terrorists nor a hoax. In a moment I will broadcast shocking – unbelievable – images from the Mintaka system, captured by a biozoon. I urge you not to panic but to absorb this information. Mintaka is far, far from Scolar, and the Sophos has already dispatched our full politic guard to protect our shift station.'

Cries of surprise broke out in the lab, only to silence again as new images flickered across the screen. At first they were difficult to understand: exterior views of space interspersed with streaming light signatures, and blurred holo-diagrammatics of the Mintaka system. A commentary started, the biozoon's translated version of what was happening.

Mira recognised the Extro Geni-carriers before anyone else did, knew immediately what they meant. But she stayed quiet, listening to the back-and-forth between the scientists as they proffered their theories.

Then the narrator translator began to list details.

More theories bounced between the scientists. What was a Geni-carrier doing in Mintaka? Exploration, thought some. No! Barter? No! An Envoy?

Dolin was less optimistic. 'Geni-carriers do only one thing: transport intelligent sentient incendiaries.'

Mira wanted to leave the room, to get as far away from the farcast feed as she could, but her feet remained fixed to the spot, and the tightness in her throat wouldn't ease enough for her to speak. She hugged Nova, waiting, forcing herself to watch.

The images cut to show incendiaries spraying from the Geni-carriers and plunging straight into the atmosphere of one of the outer worlds. A wave swept across the planet, as if the rocky surface was suddenly composed of water. The wave buckled, and it erupted across the equator like a horizontal volcano. Dust and smoke spewed from the sides, and an instant later the planet blew apart.

The biozoon narrator listed the losses in clipped tones: '5 billion sentient inhabitants, 3,313 industries, 2,025 service providers, all lost, including an advanced genotyping facility.'

'Mount Kent,' said Dolin in shocked tones. He closed his eyes, and the colour drained from his face, leaving him almost as pale as Nova. 'Our companion lab. We have a mirror facility. We . . . had a failsafe . . .'

An 'esque next to him buckled over and fell to his knees, moaning. Some went to give comfort.

But Dolin opened his eyes and looked at Mira. 'My colleague's wife,' he said. 'She was on transfer there.'

Sophos Kantos reappeared on the screen. 'This is an attack but, as I said at the beginning of the 'cast, we are not in any immediate danger. Our entire space contingent has been sent to Scolar station as a precautionary measure. It is vital that our 'casts stay operational, so that we may advise the OLOSS forces.' He cleared his throat again. 'Many of you will have loved ones, friends and family, on other worlds. I cannot guarantee their safety other than to say that we will be advising their governments.' He stopped and took a deep breath. 'There will be regular 'casts from the Sophos over the next few days, to keep you informed.'

Mira. You must leave and bring Nova back to me. I've been in contact with the Pod. They are convinced that Scolar will be the next target for the Post-Species invasion force. The Sophos are deluded, believing themselves immune. Our best option is to leave there soon.

Many others will think the same, Insignia. *It will be chaotic.*

A good reason to be decisive.

How do I get to you from here? They will try to stop me. There will be much distraction in the wake of this announcement. Use it to your advantage.

As *Insignia* finished its thought, 'esques began entering the room. And leaving. Someone helped the stricken scientist to his feet. Dolin then activated a com-sole and began talking.

Mira slipped across to the back of the room, near Linnea. The galley supervisor's lips were pursed, her forehead creased with concern.

'I need to get back to my ship,' Mira said.

'You need to rest.'

Mira shook her head. 'Terrible things are going to happen to the OLOSS worlds. I might be able to do something to stop it. Please . . .'

Linnea's eyes darted around the room. No one was watching them; Dolin was surrounded by anxious colleagues. 'Quick,' she said. 'My transport is on the roof.'

'You have your own?' Mira remembered Thales telling her that Scolar restricted ownership of private transport.

'I'm considered essential services,' she said. 'Nuthin' more essential than getting your baked breakfast on time, or a late supper if you've been workin' through the night. This way!' She jerked her head and walked straight out the door without looking back.

Mira followed her, holding her breath, waiting for Dolin to shout out, or for a hand to close around her arm. But no one noticed, and she joined the stream of traffic hurrying along the corridor. She turned her body against the jostling to protect Nova. Her baby was squirming, eyes bright and alert.

'In here,' said Linnea after they'd descended two levels. She pulled Mira into a room where the floor was streaked with grease marks and half-full of crates. 'Utilities and storage,' she said. 'Most of our food and disposables sit here before they get unpacked. I park outside here. Much quicker to the kitchens this way.' She gave a sly grin. 'Can nip in and out easily, as well.'

She led Mira across the storage room and out onto a large square of plascrete. A bulky rectangular object took up one whole side of the slab, while a little AiV perched alone in the opposite corner.

Linnea glanced into the sky, then ran across to her flyer and threw the hatch-wings open. 'Quick,' she called. ''Fore the next lunkey lands.'

Mira climbed in beside her, but more slowly, careful not to fall with Nova in her arms. She strapped herself in as Linnea brought life to the AiV. They lifted straight up and forward, almost clipping the edge of the Mount Clement building.

'Sorry 'bout that,' Linnea barked. 'Needed to keep out of the lunkey's way.'

As she spoke, a shadow fell across the cabin. A large transporter vehicle descended past them and onto the pad. It hovered, sprouted pads and landed heavily. The shape of it made Mira glance back at the object sitting on the other side of the plascrete. 'That's a lunkey as well?'

Linnea nodded. 'Best food storage containers around. Fly themselves in and out and keep the produce cool and dry. When they're stationary, they fold down into a big box, more or less. Means you can store them as well.' She slipped an audio piece over her ear and listened intently for a moment.

'Where's your ship?' she asked.

'Central landing port,' said Mira.

'There's a helluva traffic jam down there. Sounds like a lot of people are panicking. And those that wanta get in can't get a clearance to land. I'm gonna have to put down on one of the outer pads. You'll have to walk.' She glanced sideways at Nova. 'You up to that?'

Mira set her jaw and nodded. She'd have to be.

'Info booths will tell you which way to go,' Linnea added.

'My symbiote will help me.'

The galley supervisor's eyes widened. 'You mean you talk to it? Thought only men could do that.'

'That's what makes me different,' said Mira honestly. 'It's why I am still alive, and why I am . . . pursued.'

Linnea pursed her lips and didn't say any more. Mira wondered if the woman thought her crazy – a mother who had not even thought of a name for her child, nor knew how to feed it, and yet had been hunted across worlds.

She set Mira down on a pad that looked to be several mesurs from the main port. Even so, it was crowded and chaotic.

Mira unbuckled her harness and twisted in the seat, ready to step down. Their eyes met and held.

'You want some advice? Service corridors run alongside the main buildings. Use them to get to the central port. Be quicker than fighting the crowds in the public areas.'

'Where do I find them? How do I get access?'

'They're not hard to find. Look for blind corners. Find unmarked doors. Getting in, though . . .' She scratched her head. 'You'll have to use your imagination. You've been through a lot, so it seems. You'll think of something.'

Mira nodded. 'How can I—'

'Swestrs don't need thanks. Like the great Villon says, "Unto the universe." There're plenty of us here that have got no time for the way the Sophos are running the place. Used to be that they were smart and fair, but lately it's been different. Sophos don't care for the people any more. Just themselves. Now they're telling us we're safe when we're not. I wish Villon was still here. Rumours say they had him killed.'

Mira's heartbeat quickened. 'You heard that?'

Linnea nodded and pushed Mira gently. 'I'll look for you in the stars, Mira Fedor. Do what you can to help us!'

Mira leaned across and pressed a kiss onto the woman's cheek. They knew nothing of each other, and yet much. Linnea was Pensare, like Faja, like Alba Galiotto, who had helped her escape the carabinere. 'May Villon protect you, Linnea.'

Mira half-slid down to the ground and, clutching Nova, hurried quickly away from the AiV towards the entry of the sprawling port.

JO-JO RASTEROVICH

The next night they went out again. Abandoning Randall's plan of a methodical search pattern, they spent the day using the 'scope to scour the mountain for the smaller villas. Rast identified one on the east side of their building, on a direct line with the studium.

Mira Fedor had spoken of the Araldis studium many times. From overhearing bits of her conversation with Randall and Thales Berniere, Jo-Jo had learned how she had studied geneering and astrography at the same time as her degree in alien genera and literature. Only a determined individual would pursue such a workload. And despite her apparent physical fragility, Mira Fedor was definitely that.

He remembered her frequent stoushes with Randall, and understood her frustration. The mercenary could be so pragmatic and capable, and then with the curl of her lip turn moody and stubborn.

'Shouldn't take too long, there and back,' said Randall, craning to get the 'scope around the edge of the door.

'Me too, this time, Capo?' asked Catchut.

She shook her head. 'Not till you stop getting the sweats, Cat. You'll dehydrate too quick.'

Catchut made a frustrated noise and smacked his

palm against the wall. The merc hadn't taken well to being an invalid.

'What if we run into Saqr?' asked Jo-Jo, ignoring Catchut's tantrum.

'Been thinkin' 'bout that. Need something to even the odds a bit if we do. Normal weapons don't work so well, their exoskel is too tough,' said Randall.

'What did you have in mind?'

'Need to get into the studium. Fedor said she studied alien genera there. Gotta be info about the Saqr in their data films. Something we can use on them. If the data sys in this place was workin', we could access the studium sys from here. But it ain't, so we gotta get up there.' She pointed to the impressive expanse of architecture up near the crest of the mountain.

'Which first, then?'

'We split it. You go to the studium, I look for an AiV.'

Jo-Jo stared at her, not sure what to make of her plan. What did Randall really have in mind? Was she planning to find some transport and fly out to the islands, leaving him behind?

'Get that paranoid look off your face.' She slapped him on the back. 'If I wanted to get rid of you, I would have done it long before this. We need an edge on the Saqr. Think about it. If we find the survivors, what we gonna do? Hide out with them until we all get old and die? We want to get the hell outta here or, failing that, we try and take the place back.'

She handed the 'scope over to Catchut. He was using his leg more, but a fever beset him every evening, as though something foreign from the Extro ship had entered his body, through the broken skin on his ankle. 'And I'm thinkin' that there won't be any help coming for us. OLOSS looks like it's got too many of its own damned problems.'

'What about Farr?'

Randall rubbed her eyes with yellow-stained fingers. Their skin was still carrying the taint of the Extro fluid they'd been trapped in. 'Carnage will do what suits him. And that can change quicker than you and I can spit.'

Jo-Jo grunted. Randall was right on that score. Farr could be counted on not to be counted on, especially if Mira Fedor had disappeared. He'd no longer be tied to their agreement – if Farr could be tied to anything.

Randall was also right about the Saqr. If they managed to find any survivors, then they needed to have a plan. Like the mercenary, Jo-Jo had no intention of seeing out his days on this lonely scorching dust bowl.

'Agreed,' he said.

She almost grinned. Her mouth moved in that configuration, but he hadn't seen any real humour in Randall since they'd escaped the *Medium*. The Extro experience had changed something in her, hardened even her sense of humour.

'You're not too stupid, for a mappie,' she said.

Jo-Jo made a throaty noise at the derogatory term for astro-surveyors. 'Mineral scout,' he corrected. 'We get our hands dirty.'

The tension eased between them a little, and they were back in a place of understanding. Jo-Jo knew it could – would – change at any moment, but he let himself relax. Crux, they'd been through enough together, and Randall owed him. He didn't exactly trust her, but he knew she wouldn't forget what he'd done.

The three walked back to the galley and ate the last of some rehydrated butter beans. Then, by unspoken consensus, they took up seats at the back of one of the bigger offices that faced out onto the plains, to watch the sun go down.

'For a merciless lump of rock and sand, it's a shittin' pretty sunset,' Catchut proffered.

Jo-Jo and Randall stared at him. For Catchut, that was close to poetry.

'Yeah. It also means we should be heading out,' said Randall. She stood up and stretched, overly lean but still taut. Her hair had grown and had begun to curl around her shoulders. In the weeks that Jo-Jo had known her, he'd never once thought of her as a woman. He didn't know what that meant. It just *was*.

'Keep the home fires burning, Cat,' said Randall.

'Don't think so, Capo. Less you want to trash the whole mountainside.'

She nodded. 'Damn good place to breathe decent air. Damn terrible place for fires.' She hooked a water bottle onto her belt and beckoned Jo-Jo. 'Remember that.'

He crawled behind Randall until they reached the rocky scree they'd seen through the 'scope. From there, she split off from him and headed down, towards a modest villa that appeared only partly damaged by fire.

Jo-Jo continued upward in a straightish line, his sights set on the huge shadow of the Araldis studium. The gardens were so immense that he reached them a long while before the buildings.

Before the invasion, Randall said that they had been protected by a climate bubble. Since the Saqr landed, the bubble had been disengaged, and the once-lush gardens were now a series of dead tree trunks and dusty grottos. The water had evaporated from the recycled fountains, and the lawns had returned to their natural state: slippery screes of rock.

He threaded between the fountains, using them as cover to watch for Saqr. Their observations through the 'scope had told them that the creatures seemed to randomly move among the Latino ruins. Not organised patrols, Randall said. There was little enough to do but forage on a planet like this, once the first ready food source was gone. Which meant that any Saqr they encountered would be hungry.

They'd timed their foray to travel before the moons had risen, and it was hard to see any detail on the facade of the main building. There was a portico, he thought, judging by the columns, which meant inside stairs or lifts.

The last stretch of garden seemed to be open space, perhaps even a games pad or informal gathering area. The 'scope didn't reveal any boulders or ditches, so he risked jogging toward the portico, making it to the first arch without incident.

The exertion had him breathing hard though, sweating copiously onto his fellalo's insulation. He stopped to catch his breath, and then felt his way along the wall until he reached a set of narrow stairs. A servants' entry, perhaps. He stepped onto them, and a dull light flared, sending him jumping back.

Sweat poured from him. He could feel it running down his arms and legs as the robe worked to redistribute it and cool his skin. If the Saqr saw the light, they'd be here soon. He turned and hurried back along the portico to the huge main doors. They were slightly ajar and he cursed himself for not trying them first.

He stepped inside and waited for his eyes to adjust. The biggest staircase he'd ever seen dominated the circular entrance hall, and grand carved doorways led away from it. He walked along them, trying to decipher the signs.

BIBLIOTECA. Randall had suggested he try the library ports to access the data banks. 'There might be some life in them yet, if they're not damaged. Most things here are solar powered,' she'd said.

He pushed the door open and found himself in a chamber lit by the dull glow of emergency lights running on their last dregs. It was filled with rows and rows of seats, divided down the middle by an inactive escalator.

He sat down at one and flashed the 'scope's lamp for long enough to see the array of interface options. He chose the simplest audio download, hoping it still worked.

Slotting the audio pad over his ear, he waited, imagining Mira Fedor here, engrossed in learning from the studium interface. He felt strangely exhilarated, knowing she'd sat in one of these seats, maybe even this one.

The overwhelming and ridiculous nature of his sentiment for her had begun to fade; perhaps it had only been a moment of lust for one of the most decent and refined women he'd met in his life. And yet an equally powerful yearning had replaced it, a yearning for something he would never have. Maybe those moments in space, without air, had done more than scare him. Maybe he'd lost part of his mind, then.

Come on, he urged the library, *talk to me.*

'Choose from the menu,' crackled a faint voice in his ear.

Jo-Jo's heart lurched. 'Alien genera,' he said after listening. 'Saqr.'

He asked for the summary overview.

Tardigrada giantus ... relative of arthropods ... segmented bodies ... eight legs ...

Nothing new there. 'Dietary needs. Reproduction. Special qualities,' he asked.

Polyextremophiles that are known to survive in extreme environments.

'More detail.'

'Tardigrada giantus *can withstand maximum temperatures of 151°C (424 K), through to minimums of -200°C (70 K). Dehydration:* Tardigrada giantus *have been shown to survive for decades in a dry state. Radiation:* Tardigrada giantus *can withstand median lethal doses of 5,000 Gy (gamma-rays) and 6,200 Gy (heavy ions) in hydrated animals. Pressure range: vacuum through to more than 1,200 times Cerulean atmospheric pressure. Environmental toxins—'*

'End.'

The audio stopped.

If humanesques could do even half of that . . . 'Main menu.'

The response was sluggish.

'Visual map of Araldis,' he requested.

He studied the dull image on the film that unfolded from his armrest. 'Southern sector. Islands.'

Thousands of tiny dots scattered across the screen. The survivors could be on any one of them. Then again, maybe not, he thought. Some of the islands were little more than dots of sand with scant cover, and the surviving population would need shade and fresh water.

This time Jo-Jo set some search parameters. The library took so long to respond that he became fidgety, thinking at every breath that he could hear the Saqr.

It wasn't until he was standing up preparing to leave that the search result flashed onto the screen. Only four islands fit the criteria he'd set. Two lay close to the southern axis, too far for the survivors to have reached on yachts or small vessels. The others were across the open water of the Galgos Strait, a dangerous crossing but possible.

The name Galgos scratched at his memory. Mira Fedor had mentioned it, he was sure. The two potential islands were large and according to the map key harboured fresh water. Only one, though, was vegetated. It also had species of fauna not found on the mainland.

He committed the map coordinates to memory and told the search to clear and close. As he made his way from desk to door, a scraping noise drifted across the quiet.

He abruptly changed direction, seeking another exit. Though he could see nothing, the sweet Saqr scent was unmistakable. Something fierce and cold gripped his stomach. How many were out there? Did they know he was here?

He found a narrow door and opened it, stepping through and flattening his body along the wall on the other side. A passage led him to a room that stank of spilled chemicals. More dim emergency lights revealed a number of well-worn com-cast modules, and desk-films languishing on real wood tables. He breathed in air thick with dust. The environmentals were barely functioning in here; heat pooled.

He made his away across the room, looking for another door, but something made him stop and look more closely at one of the com-soles. It was an old-fashioned desk variety, probably used by students who needed to interact with the Vreal studium, or other off-world academics. Mira had mentioned how delayed their farcast signals were, how inadequate – they'd only heard of the Stain Wars after they'd ended. Perhaps if he could get one working, they could pick up signals from OLOSS craft?

He felt along the bottom edge of the com-sole and unclipped it from its station. It was light enough, but awkward. How could he get it back without dropping it? He needed his hands free to climb down the more slippery rocks.

A wash of sweet scent wafted in, drowning the smell of the spilled chemicals. The Saqr were close again – outside the room, perhaps. Taking the com-sole, he dropped to the floor and crawled over to the centre of the room, assessing his options.

A rush of air blew on his face as the door opened, and the sweet scent grew chokingly strong. He stifled the instinct to gag and gripped the com-sole tightly. There must be another door, somewhere he could run to.

Scraping sounds on the far side. He held his breath as the noise moved around the perimeter of the room and back. Hard to tell if it was one or more. *Don't look. Don't move at all.*

Silence. Then another shift of air. The door closed.

He sat for a long time, clutching the com-sole, aware only of the sound of his heartbeat and the wetness between his legs. Jo-Jo Rasterovich hadn't pissed his pants since he was a kid, waiting for his mum to get through an evening with her latest beau. He'd been sitting outside the condo door, in the corridor, playing with a set of chrome jacks. He was four years old.

The loss of control didn't make him proud, but he wasn't ashamed either. He'd seen what the Saqr could do. He was no hero.

When he could make his legs function, he got up and quietly searched the room for something to carry the com-sole. It was curiously bereft of incidentals, as if someone had swept through and tidied just before the Saqr invaded.

Instead, he found another door and exited, stealing deeper into the studium until he came upon the kitchens.

Here, things were different. Every pot, pan and sealed storage container had been rifled. Even the rows of cookers down the centre of the room had been damaged, smashed with the force of an axe or hammer.

That didn't make sense, but he didn't stop to examine them. Instead, he searched among the debris until he found a length of kitchen tie that had once hung meat, and threaded it through a notch on the com-sole. Tying the ends together, he looped it over his shoulder.

The kitchen, he knew, would have a service entry for food loading. Leaving the studium from the rear meant a much longer walk back, but it would lessen his chances – he hoped – of running into Saqr.

He found the entrance to the service bay at the bottom of the extensive pantry, a roller door with a mechanism to handle inter-gal freight cartons. Alongside the door was a hatch, larger than the average Balol. He pressed spots around the roller pad, and the hatch sprang open. He stepped through quickly. It took him moments to adjust to the flooding light outside.

He looked for the moons, but neither had risen. The night skies of Araldis, though, were filled with a flotilla of tiny star-bright objects.

Jo-Jo blinked a few times to see if they went away, but the objects remained above him, cruising in a serene orbit. Instinct told him to get back to Randall and Catchut quickly. If they could get the com-sole working, maybe they could find out what the Crux was happening up there.

MIRA

Even this remote arm of the landing port teemed with activity. Mira threaded her way through queues and past kiosks selling credit exchange and transport vouchers. Ahead, she saw the crowds streaming onto four different conveyors. The signs hanging above them confused her, so she stopped at a seedy kaffe, which served pastries swimming in liquid and oversized cups of dark mokka, and asked directions.

The attendant was unobliging and distracted, his eyes flicking between a man at a corner table and a spot on the opposite side of the transit court, where an unmistakable, roughly dressed figure stood towering head and shoulders above the rest.

Fariss O'Dea would stand out in any crowd, on any world, thought Mira. Something the soldier must've found a mixed blessing.

But who was the man at the table? Mira observed his aquiline nose, large ears and smooth complexion. Something about his looks stirred her memory. She'd never seen him before, but . . .

'Excuse me,' she said to the attendant in crisper, more authoritative tones. 'I believe I know the gentleman on the far table. I've forgotten his name. Would you by any chance be able to tell me what it is?'

The attendant blinked at her, taking a moment to

make sense of her words and assimilate them into his thoughts.

'You callin' him a gennelm'n means you can't know him too well, missus.' He began to stack cups into a washer.

'His name, prego!' Mira snapped. *Insignia*'s need for urgency crawled along her skin. She didn't have time to stop for this, but something told her it was important.

The attendant shot her a glowering look. 'It changes all the time. You want somethin' or what? I'm busy.'

Mira glanced behind her. A queue was starting to build. She moderated her tone. 'Please. I think he might owe my husband money. Just tell me his name, and I'll go.'

The attendant glanced at the newborn baby in her arms and relented. 'Gutnee's a common name he uses. But, like I said, it changes. Now move. Please.'

Mira nodded her thanks and stepped away from the counter. Her stomach churned. She knew that name; Thales Berniere had said it to her many times. Gutnee Paraburd was the man who'd duped him.

Nova began to cry, a gentle but insistent hunger noise.

Our child is hungry, Mira.

Si. I am close.

Then why do you stop?

I've seen the man who duped Thales. He is watching the soldier Fariss.

Insignia made a harsh sound in her mind. *You're being distracted again. Bring Nova to me.*

Mira deliberately shut the biozoon's voice out of her

mind and used the cover of passers-by to move closer to Fariss without being seen. The soldier appeared to be loitering, chewing open-mouthed and surveying the patrons from under half-closed lids. She seemed neither threatening nor alert.

Mira glanced at Paraburd. There was no doubt the man was watching Fariss. But where was Thales? Mira had seen him taken by the politic guards. So why was Fariss here?

I should tell her that she's being watched.

Mira swivelled back towards the soldier, but she'd gone. *Impossible!*

Joining the flow of traffic, Mira walked past the spot where Fariss had been standing and could see nothing save a narrow corridor peeling off from the main thoroughfare.

Jiggling Nova against her shoulder, she stepped into the corridor and sagged against the wall. At the other end was a service door. Fariss must have gone through there, but the door appeared firmly locked. Maybe she'd gone elsewhere? Further into the main station?

The nervous energy that had sustained Mira through the birth and the AiV trip down Mount Clement had completely drained away. Her legs and arms trembled. Tears threatened. She needed to feed Nova.

Slipping her overall off one shoulder, she lifted Nova to lie against her. The baby latched on and suckled without fussing. Mira's whole body relaxed with the movement of her tiny mouth, but with the release came an overpowering need to rest.

She set her feet and fought the sensation. There was

no chair or ledge, and she would not sit on the filthy floor. O'Dea had gone. She would feed Nova and continue on to *Insignia*. It was all she could do.

Nova finished quickly and fell straight to sleep. Mira lifted her back up onto her shoulder and wriggled back into the sleeve.

As she pressed the seal on the overall back together, the service door burst open. A red-robed politic guard staggered out holding his head, blood running from a wound on his temple.

Mira pressed against the wall, out of his way, and he barely spared her a glance as he lunged past. Through the doorway, she saw fallen bodies in uniform robes. She glanced back to the guard, but he'd disappeared out of the corridor, probably looking for assistance.

Mira ran to the doorway and peered through in both directions. She glimpsed two figures, one much taller than the other, trying to open a series of locked doors.

'Thales!' she called. 'Fariss!'

O'Dea jerked around, wielding a metal stanchion.

'Mira.' Thales's voice was hoarse and soft. 'Come.'

She climbed over the fallen guards and hurried to join them.

Fariss levered a door open with her weapon and hustled them inside. While she relocked it from the inside, Thales embraced Mira.

'The baby,' he said, stroking Nova's head. Wonder smoothed the worry from his face, and he looked as young and attractive as the first time she's seen him.

'What have you—'

But Mira didn't let him finish. 'The man that you

spoke of to me ... the one who duped you here. Gutnee.'

'Gutnee Paraburd?' Thales gripped her arm. 'What of him?'

'He's outside, sitting at the kaffe across from here.'

'How do you know?'

'I stopped to ask directions. The kaffe attendant was watching Fariss and another 'esque. The man seemed ... familiar. Not someone I knew, but yet I felt as if I did. I asked the attendant who he was. He said his name ... I remembered it. I went to tell Fariss, but she'd come down this corridor.'

Thales let go of Mira and turned to Fariss. 'I must find him. The Sophos will not be able to ignore me if I can show them Paraburd.'

The soldier's broad expressive face creased with mistrust. 'You sure, hon? From what I can see, they're not gonna believe you anyways.'

'Signorina O'Dea is right, Thales.'

'Fariss,' the soldier said to Mira. 'Not Signorina anything. What's going on out there? 'Esques everywhere. Heard some things while I was waitin' around. Seems too busy to be just rumour.'

Mira quickly told them of the Sophos announcement and the broadcast images. 'I'm going back to *Insignia*. We believe it is better to leave now.'

'But you could res-shift straight into trouble,' said Thales.

'The Pod will keep us informed, and I don't wish to be trapped here. I will take my chances. Now Nova has been born, there are things I must try to do. Will you come with me? Unless the shift sphere is disabled, they will come and destroy your world. Your Sophos don't see the threat as real.'

Thales and Fariss looked at each other, an exchange that held meaning she couldn't decipher.

'Then I must make sure that they do,' said Thales.

Mira saw the strength of his resolution, felt his need to accomplish this.

She nodded. 'Then I wish you success. A woman who works in the galley at Mount Clement, named Linnea, helped deliver Nova. She says many are unhappy with the Sophos. If you find her, she might lend you support.'

'What sort of support?'

'She is Pensare.'

Thales raised both eyebrows.

'Women's movement. They're everywhere. Militant, some of them,' said Fariss. 'I thought about joining 'em, then I met Sammy.'

'Mia sorella is – was Pensare.'

'Your sister was one? I would find this woman at the clinic?'

Mira shook her head. 'Don't go there. They are too curious. Linnea lives in the town below the clinic.'

'Clementvale?'

Mira nodded. 'Si, that's it.'

They stared at each other, and Thales touched Nova's head again. 'You have been a true friend, Mira Fedor. I'll never forget that.'

She nodded. 'And you, Thales Berniere.'

He leaned forward and gently kissed her cheek. 'May Villon protect you and Nova.'

'May Villon protect us all,' Mira said.

Fariss cracked the door open and looked out into the corridor. 'Go now and you'll be unnoticed. They're looking for Thales and me. Not you.'

Mira didn't have to ask Fariss what her decision was. The soldier had chosen to come here with Thales, and she would stay with him. Their coupling was unlikely, but their bond seemed strong. She envied them.

As Mira entered the buccal, she felt *Insignia* quiver. It was only something that an innate could sense, a deep frisson of pleasure and anticipation that played along her skin and resonated in her chest.

Our child, Mira.

'Si.' Mira didn't disagree for now was not the time for such discussions. She didn't understand the biozoon's obsession with her baby, but now that Nova had been born, *Insignia*'s ecstasy was plain. *We should leave.*

We have been given a place in the queue. Will we have company?

No. Thales and Fariss aren't joining us.

Mira sank gratefully down into Primo and laid Nova on her chest.

Insignia's sensors reached out, and the vein surrounded them both. A sense of belonging engulfed Mira. She could rest now, for a time. Not long, but enough. Enough to do what would come next.

Mira, the Post-Species creature has been asking for you.

Wanton? Mira had not thought of the little Extro at all over the last days. *What is wrong?*

Its mycose supply is running low. Its need is urgent.

Mira dragged herself to her feet and carried Nova to their cabin. Wanton lay where she had left it, surrounded by the dwindling mycose.

She sank onto the other end of the bed, careful not to sit too close. 'Wanton?'

It took a while for the Extro to answer. When it did, its audio projection was faint. 'Mira-fedor, Wanton is glad to see you.'

'Please tell me how I can help you.'

She waited again. This time its voice seemed strong, as if it was making more effort – a very humanesque notion, she knew, that probably didn't apply.

'I am close to a critical point. Even sealing my protective layer will not keep integrity. I have only one option.'

'What is it?'

'I must meld consciousness with the Non-Corporeals.'

'D-do you wish to do that?'

'Wanton had thought itself unable to experience fear, Mira-fedor, but Wanton was wrong. Wanton does not wish to cease existing.'

'Where are the Non-Corporeals that you would need to meld with?'

'Mira-fedor would know that better than Wanton. I will accept if that is not possible. And thank Mira-fedor for her . . . friendship. I must conserve energy now.' The Extro went quiet again, and Mira noticed another mycose bubble subsume into the casing. There were only a few left.

With a heavier heart, she returned to the buccal.

Where do you wish to go, Mira? The Pod would accept us. Or we could try to make for one of the fringe OLOSS worlds. The Post-Species will not bother with them; they are too poor and inconsequential. The Pod believes they will concentrate on the political worlds. Alnitak, Scolar and, as we already know, Mintaka.

Mira settled back into Primo, sliding Nova to one side so that the baby was tucked against her shoulder. She waited until her breathing steadied and her heartbeat slowed to sync with the pulse of the vein.

The decision had been easier than she thought. The pieces fitted. All she needed was courage. She would be placing Nova and *Insignia* at terrible risk, and yet she was filled with a sureness that she hadn't felt during her pregnancy. This was the right thing, the only thing. This was the point where she must embrace her fears and be the person inside, the person who would not be propelled by circumstance or the whims of others. She had chosen. *We will go to Araldis.*

This is your humour?

No, Tasy-al. It is not. Mira used the biozoon's real name to emphasise her sincerity. *I've been told that the station is functioning again. When we get there, we will find a way to land.*

What is your aim?

To take Wanton to its kind. To help the survivors. To find Djeserit and Vito and Cass Mulravey.

They will be dead.

No. She sent *Insignia* a very firm thought. *And we had an agreement. You will assist me to help those on Araldis, and then I will go where you wish.*

The biozoon didn't reply.

Mira waited patiently while they lifted from the landing port, left Scolar's atmosphere and followed the fraught trajectory that took them to their place in the frantic shift queue.

In the moments before committing to res-shift, Mira spoke again. *Give me your word*, Insignia, *that you will take me to Araldis.*

Functions and data streamed across her consciousness as *Insignia* immersed her. This time, however, something was different: another presence, a brilliant clear orb, moving through the data streams, radiating curiosity and wonder.

Nova, Mira and *Insignia* thought simultaneously.

Mira felt the recognition like a pouring of warm honey. And the orb that represented her child's presence in their mind meld contracted and expanded and flickered as though it was dancing.

Thoughts poured forth from the orb, but Mira couldn't quite grasp them.

She is speaking to you, said *Insignia.*

I c-can't understand it. What is she saying?

Loving things, and . . .

And?

The biozoon paused for a moment, as if deliberating whether to share the information. *She agrees with you. We should go to Araldis.*

Mira struggled to assimilate the fact that her infant child was able to communicate with *Insignia* about such a thing. It should be impossible. It *should.*

She cuddled the baby closer and kissed the top of her soft head. *Th-then let us not waste time.*

BALBAO

The rescue ship's umbilical connected with the life-ship, sending a shudder through the frame. As soon as the vibrations settled, the tyros and Balbao released their restraints and scrambled for the hatch.

With the hiss of pressure change came a sight Balbao hadn't expected – armed soldiers waiting on the other side.

'Is that all of you?' one barked.

Balbao did a quick head count. 'Five. Yes.'

'Through!' the soldier ordered. 'Quick.'

Miranda tripped on the hatch lip as she hurried. The soldier stepped forward and pulled her up roughly, shoving her on through.

'Stop—' Jise began to protest, but the guard grabbed his shirt and pulled the tyro hard against him, so their faces were almost touching.

'We've got minus time to get out of here before we get turned to gas. So get your arse in here or be left behind.'

The rest of them hurried, Balbao pushing Connit along.

The soldier didn't even blink at Ra's strange appearance; he just sealed the hatch and talked into his comm.

'Take them to the buffer in the cargo hold. We're going to res-shift soon.'

Balbao and the others were bundled down several levels and thrust into a containment room already filled with unkempt deckhands wearing standard ship overalls.

'Strap in, we're moving.' The soldiers followed them in and took their places on the fold-downs near the door.

"Bout time,' one of the deckhands replied.

Jise helped Miranda to the one remaining vacant seat, and tried to compress her swelling ankle with his hands. Ra and Connit gravitated towards them, but Balbao stayed near the door, shoulders set. He could feel the antagonism bristling from the deckhands. No one knew if their next breath would be their last, yet the ship had gone out of its way to rescue them. This clearly hadn't been popular. Which captain, Balbao wondered, had made the call?

A tremor ran through the walls, and he heard the whine of the buffers initiating. He squatted down and leaned back against the door. Even the best buffers could get you thrown about if you weren't strapped in.

He clung to the deadlock handle as the cabin began to shudder. A quiet descended on the chamber. Jise grabbed his belly and doubled over.

The vibration got worse, and Connit, who hadn't taken hold of anything, bounced across the chamber to tangle in the feet of one of the deckhands.

The dekkie lifted his feet clear and pushed Connit away, sending him over towards Balbao.

Balbao thrust out his foot for Connit to grab, and gradually pulled him in. There were dry laughs from the deckhands as Connit clambered over him to get a hold on the deadlock. Blood poured from the tyro's nose, spattering about, and his eyes were already blackening.

The soldiers ignored it all, leaning back into their seats, eyes narrowed and faces grim as they listened to their comms. Balbao wanted to ask them what they could hear. Was everything all right? Would they make it? They were stupid, unanswerable questions, and he bit them back.

Instead, he let go with one hand and fished in his pocket, finding a plaskerchief and handing it to Connit. The man nodded gratefully and held it against his nose.

Balbao tried to relax, tried not to think of the hundreds of things that could be happening.

The vibration got even worse, and he was forced to lock his feet under a lever. Miranda moaned as her swollen ankle was wrenched from Jise's grip and smacked into the floor.

The shaking became so intense that Balbao felt his teeth rattle. A terrifying pain shot down his neck and spine, and his desire to piss was overwhelming. He couldn't take much more of this. Nor could the ship. Even the deckhands were gripping their seats.

Then, suddenly, it was over, and everything became still.

The soldiers were out of their seats first, stretching their limbs and rotating their necks.

'What the fuck was that?' asked one of the dekkies.

'That,' replied a soldier, 'was imperfect shift.'

TRIN

Under the light of Araldis's moons and a plethora of shining satellites, Trin laboured around the rocky crest of the mountain. What should they name this island and these landmarks? It was their right to do so now, and it would mean easier communication between them.

Pellegre, he thought, for the island. He would allow his carabinere, and maybe Cass Mulravey, to pick names for the caves, springs and other landmarks. The island was his to christen; his and Djes's, for in truth she had found it.

He stopped and caught his breath, listening in the dark. Something nagged persistently at the edge of his consciousness. Odd little sounds came to him, but he could see nothing despite regular glances over his shoulder. Then he heard a faint rustle of movement coming from below the next expanse of rock. An animal foraging for food?

He slid down the large slab and peered over its edge, hoping to put his mind at ease. This time he held his breath to listen. His heart beat faster; there was something. He stared intently at the terrain below him, wondering which path to the bottom would be easiest.

There. Where the rock folded over itself. A natural step. But getting there required sliding close to the edge, and would he be able to get back up the same way? Unlikely. He shook himself. Of course there'd be another way up, even if it took a little longer.

He glanced into the sky, which teemed with bright orbiting objects. First light was only a few hours away. He must look now or wait another night.

Something urged him to pursue it now. Another night and everything might change. Who knew what the mass arrival of ships meant? There was no time for hesitation.

He slid closer to the edge, his feet dangling over, fingers searching for grooves and crevices in the slab. At full stretch, he thought he could reach the folded rock beneath, which would act as a step. Slowly, he extended one leg. His toe connected with the surface, and he began to ease his weight down onto it. Perspiration leaked into his robe; he felt it pooling in the crevices of his skin, and his heart thundered.

A scuffling noise behind him. He jerked around to look, trying to stay balanced.

Hands planted firmly into his back.

The force of the push sent him over the edge. He paddled his legs and arms for a brief moment as he fell. Then he slammed hard into the ground below.

The sound brought him round, an insistent noise, and irritating warm splashes across his cheek. Trin opened his eyes to nearly full daylight. He lay only a breath away from water running over a rock.

He tried to raise his head to look properly, but his neck muscles refused to comply. Even so, a number of things registered: he'd been pushed from the rock above;

he was injured but alive; and he would die from heat exposure in a matter of minutes if he didn't find cover.

The latter realisation took priority over everything, and he rolled over, looking for options. The water was coming from underneath the overhang of the slab he had fallen from, a strong enough flow to carry it down the hill before it drained through a lattice of rocks.

Crawl under the overhang. Crawl or die.

Bringing his knees up, he used his feet to push him forward. One leg felt odd, numb below the knee but with sensation still in his foot. He didn't stop to look. It wouldn't matter, not if he was still lying in this spot in a few more minutes.

Sharp rocks gouged his stomach underneath his robe, and pebbles scraped his hands. His fellalo was so worn now that it barely cooled or gave protection. And there was blood. His blood, though he was unsure where he was bleeding. And the aching. Back. Head. All over.

Don't think about it. Crawl. Crawl or die.

The first fingers of direct sunlight burned into his legs as he dragged his torso into the shade. He rolled onto his back and jack-knifed his knees into his stomach, then rolled again until his whole body was in shade.

He lay like that, slipping in and out of a consciousness, for a long time.

Concussion, he told himself when some clarity returned. He made an effort to sit up. This time his neck and back obeyed, and he managed to lean himself against the rock. The spring was within arm's reach, so he leaned over and cupped a mouthful. It tasted tepid but clean. After several handfuls he felt a little revived.

Who had pushed him? The hands in his back had been decisive, and large. Not a woman's hands, and not someone who'd had second thoughts.

Innis Mulravey. Had to be.

Anger burned in him. How dare the filthy 'esque attempt to murder him? *I will have him exiled. No. Killed.*

Cass Mulravey would resist, but on this he would not weaken.

Trin opened his eyes. What had he been thinking about? Where was—? He blinked. Water, rocks and blinding, scorching sunlight only just past his feet. His heart pounded and he sat upright.

Calming breaths helped him better observe his surroundings, to think. Leah was on the wane. He'd been asleep most of the day, and his throat felt raw and his skin dry. Dehydration.

He flopped over to the running water and submerged his face, taking deep gulps. Coming up for air, he repeated the action several times until his belly distended with water.

Within a short time be began to sweat profusely, and the robe tried to cool his overheated body. His heat tolerance was much greater now from the constant exposure, but nothing could stand the direct sunlight on Araldis. Nothing except the Saqr.

For the next few hours he stayed under the overhang and practised moving his limbs, testing them to see if he could walk. The numbness below his knee was still there, and would hamper his climbing ability. *I need a crutch.*

He looked out from his rock shelter. Immediately

below him lay another band of rocks, but below that stood an odd cluster of stunted trees. He would crawl to them when it was dark and find something to lean on, then return to the spring and drink his fill before starting back to the caves.

He considered that plan. Would his leg slow him down too much? Would he be caught in the sun again? Perhaps he should wait for Juno Genarro and Djes to come for him? With their help, the trip back would be much easier. And they would come for him. He knew that. But how long until they did? And what trouble would Innis Mulravey have caused with his lie that the Principe had maybe perished?

Options and strategies stacked up in his mind as the day finally darkened and lost some heat. As Leah sank away, he made a decision. The trees not only offered the makings of a walking stick, but the possibility of edible roots. He was hungry now, the rumbling in his belly overtaking even the thumping in his temples and the shooting pain along the leg that wasn't numb.

He fumbled for one of the two pods in his pocket and chewed a piece from it. Within a short time he felt the tingle of stimulant. Levering onto his hands and knees, keeping more weight on the uninjured knee, he crawled down with painstaking care. A slip this time would mean his end.

Without the moonlight, progress was slower than he'd anticipated. He reached the first few bushes just as Semantic cracked the horizon with a sliver of moonshine. Exhaustion forced him to rest a while before he could attempt to find a stick.

He lay, examining the trees, discerning their difference from those on their side of the mountain. These seemed more lush by comparison.

He reached up to a trunk and stripped a section of bark away. Sap leaked freely onto his palm. He sniffed it, tempted to suck its nutrients, but the scent was unappealing, like dead, crushed lig.

Using the bark, he gouged near the tree's base, searching for its roots. They were shallow, and pliable enough for him to break off a piece. He brushed it off and bit into it. It was hard and earthy, but he forced it down, gagging on the taste of dirt.

For a moment his stomach rebelled, the pod's stimulant effects rejecting the notion of food, but he swallowed repeatedly until the sickness faded. Within a short time, he began to focus better, and his limbs gained strength. He was able to stand and reach for a lower branch. Tearing it off, he broke the twigs from it, modelling it to the size he needed. It seemed strong enough to take his weight and balance him against the lack of sensation around his knee.

Satisfied that it would do, he hobbled to the edge of the grove. The moon was high now, and lit the direction he wanted to go. He glanced back to the spring and the rocky overhang, memorising the surrounding landmarks.

Innis Mulravey's ill intent had brought some reward with it. They could have searched for weeks before locating this spring, which was hidden beneath the rock. Now they wouldn't have to descend the mountain to the beach spring and risk encountering the giant ligs.

Trin grimaced. He wouldn't let the discovery count in Innis's favour. Attempted murder of a Principe required a dire penalty. The carabinere would see to it.

Determination settled in his belly, but as he began to limp forward, something glanced against his face. His dashed it away and walked on. Within a few steps, though, it happened again, and again. He caught one of the objects and examined it. *Lig.*

He heard a noise, a kind of crackling accompanied by a hiss. A shadow appeared over the mountain top, obscuring the moon, and then descended in jerky stages. A swarm of normal sized ligs, heading directly for the grove in which he stood.

Instinct drove Trin to the ground. He lay on his stomach and covered his face, but the ligs engulfed him, crawling inside his robe and hood, all over his skin, searching and probing between his closed fingers.

He forced himself to breathe slowly and evenly; they were mere insects, he reasoned. *Nothing dangerous like the giant ligs from the spring at the bottom of the mountain. They will move on.*

And they did, lifting from his body at some unheard signal, leaving him itchy and shivering.

He sat up and peered behind him into the grove. The moonlight was enough to show black clusters of the insects, which covered the branches of the trees like gloves. He groped for his stick to help him stand, only to drop it as ligs moved beneath his fingers. The stick was covered, like the tree trunks in the grove. He poked it with his shoe, and most of them rose and flew off.

He reached for the stick. The sap was gone, leaving only a trace of stickiness.

He wondered if there was there a connection between the giant ligs near the beach and this swarm. He'd never seen so many. It was not normal for them to behave this way.

He levered himself up and began the laborious climb. There was plenty to contemplate on the trip back to the cave.

TEKTON

From the safety of his cabin, Tekton used Lasper Farr's device to run near-future prediction scenarios. The data stream led repeatedly, and almost exclusively, towards the annihilation of the OLOSS worlds and their allies. There were survivors, but the residual pockets of life were gradually snuffed out through loss of contact with the wider worlds; trade was impossible, and the communities lacked the infrastructure to self-sustain.

In nearly all its long-term projections, the device gave a dismal prediction for the longevity of the humanesque species and other alien sentients. Tekton witnessed the end of his kind through Lasper Farr's DSD again and again, and after several days of it, fell into a terrible depression.

As an antidote to his misery, he developed cravings for both a lotion bath and sex. Neither seemed a remote possibility, so instead he lay curled on his bed, moving only to relieve himself and to visit the galley to gather food and drink.

Much of his misery time was spent in reflecting on his life to that point, and on those with whom he'd shared it. No one really, save Doris Mueller and a stream of warmly ridged vaginas to which he could no longer attribute names or faces. Oh, there had been Miranda

Seeward, briefly. But she was now involved with Lawmon Jise, and *not* to be trusted.

Tekton experienced a sudden longing for his own kind – educated politically devious sorts whose rules he understood. Were the other tyros under threat from the Post-Species? Were they still on Belle-Monde? He even thought nostalgically of his room there.

Inevitably his thoughts returned to the Entity. How strange that Sole would give the knowledge for the creation of such a profound device to his cousin Ra. What was it trying to do? Had it known of the Post-Species' plans? Had Sole seen all this coming?

Perhaps Sole was warning us by giving Ra the knowledge to build the DSD, free-mind suggested. *Giving us a chance to change things.*

Somehow, Tekton thought, that did not fit his impression of Sole. He'd been afforded a glimpse into the Entity's mysteries, and he'd not seen anything resembling compassion among the terrifying dizzying universe of knowledge and experiences he'd been plunged into.

And now that he thought more about it, he couldn't fathom why the Entity had given him that glimpse. As far as he knew, the other tyros had not had similar experiences.

Why me? Why share with me? Unless . . .

Tekton jerked bolt upright and engaged with the device. Frantically he searched streams until he located a feed on Belle-Monde. The only eges in place appeared to be on the res-station satellites, broadcasting images of closespace around the pseudo-world; nothing on Belle-Monde itself, no view into the ménage lounge.

Right now, the sight of Miranda Seeward's thighs would be as close to a homecoming as Tekton could imagine. He perused the views of res-station near space with irritation and disappointment. He'd hoped to learn something more about the Entity, but there was nothing . . . just empty, dusty space.

Nothing! shouted logic-mind. *Can't you see? Nothing!*

Tekton toured through the images again, wondering what logic-mind meant.

It's gone, free-mind wailed. *Sole's gone. Belle-Monde is destroyed.*

A light sweat broke out over Tekton's body. His minds were right: the gaseous distortion of space that signalled the Entity's presence had vanished. Empty space.

Another rush of suspicions piled on top of the ones he already had. Tekton began reviewing some of the general feeds of random star systems, looking for Sole. Instructing the device to set a timeline record, he found an emerging pattern. The Entity had not left Orion, but was appearing in different places, each time close to where the Geni-carriers had deployed their incendiaries.

Sole appeared to be tracking the destruction.

Tracking it? *That makes no sense*, said logic mind. *Observing, perhaps.*

Tekton disengaged from the machine and lay back on the bed. He sipped on his reconstituted juice, letting his minds swirl with possibilities and questions.

Why had Sole given Ra the knowledge to create this device? *Why?* Not for the good of the sentients of Orion, he was sure.

Could it be simply a tease? A game?

Yes, screeched free-mind. *A game. Of course, of course! Sole wants us to play.*

Perhaps not a game. Logic-mind sounded sour and peeved. *More likely a challenge. A competition.*

Tekton's akula swelled in a way it had not for some time; shades of Fenralia's statue of homage to him. In fact, he hadn't felt so hard since the time he'd had Miranda Seeward and Doris in bed together on Scolar. Logic-mind was right, he felt sure. The Dynamic System Device was a clue and a tool, and it was he, Tekton of Lostol, whom it had fallen to; he must unravel its meaning, and he must prevent the Post-Species destruction of humanesques and their allies.

Whether by accident or design, Tekton knew he stood a chance of becoming the most famous sentient Orion had ever known. *So why*, he begged his minds, in a sudden plummet to nervousness, *do I feel so inadequate?*

MIRA

According to farcast bulletins, the Dowl res station is still open. Do you wish to shift directly there, Mira?

Sì. This time it was she and Nova who replied simultaneously. Nova's response was less a formed thought, more a sense of agreement.

It is probably best, Insignia conceded. *Many of the stations are disabled, or in the process of disabling. We may be caught somewhere we have no wish to be. There is news of Post-Species presence in Mintaka. And there is something else.*

Sì?

The relevance of this information is dubious, but it has been reported that the Sole Entity has disappeared.

Mira found herself unexpectedly disturbed by the news. Marchella Pellegrini – Trin's rebel aunt – had wanted Mira to become a tyro to the Entity, had seen it as a way to help the women of Araldis escape their repression by learning how to reverse the Latino male control over fertility. To that end, Mira had harboured a wish to secure a place of study among the brightest minds in the galaxy. And now it was too late.

But what had it all been for? she wondered. Why did the Entity make contact with us? And what had it gained, or lost, that it chose to leave now?

Mira wasn't even sure why she thought it looked to

gain anything. Perhaps Josef Rasterovich's conversations with Rast Randall had influenced her thinking.

That thought brought back sharp memories of the pair. Were they alive? *Insignia* had abandoned them aboard the Post-Species ship which had left Extro space along with the Geni-carriers.

I have set shift. Insignia interrupted her musings. *Now tell me, how do we ensure our safety?*

You said that you had a history of trade with the Post-Species.

Yes. That is so. They trust us in that capacity. But we have nothing to trade.

Tell them we have one of their own. One who is ailing, and requires Non-Corporeal healing. Mira pondered for several moments. *And I want you to broadcast our signature as we shift.*

A full identity 'cast?

Perhaps the survivors will hear.

They are on the run.

It is still possible, thought Mira, stubbornly.

And if they do?

I would give them hope.

This is a foolish notion, Mira. Have the pregnancy changes within your body affected your mind? Even more?

Insignia left the latter part unsaid, but implicit.

Mira refused to let the biozoon's opinion discourage her. *I survived outside the Hub in the Bare World. I was there, in a place you could reach me, when you came.*

But we have a telepathic bond. It's quite different.

Vito is down there. And the korm. And Cass Mulravey. I will find them. Her stubbornness rose again.

Those names mean little to me.

Mira flinched at *Insignia*'s deliberate provocation.

Then an infusion of warmth started in Mira's head and flowed through her body, easing the tension between them. A sensation that didn't come from the biozoon.

Nova?

She could hear *Insignia* talking to her child. The one-sidedness of the conversation – *Insignia*'s side – made it hard to follow, but it seemed that Nova was mediating their argument in some way.

Mira sent a wistful thought to her child. *Why can't you talk to me?*

Can – Mira. Take – time – you. Biozoon – simple.

Nova!

Will – better.

Mira dwelt in a moment of sheer pleasure. She and her child could communicate telepathically. It was something that she'd never anticipated. *Nova, please, call me Mama.*

Mama. Nova repeated the thought.

A swell of something powerful swept through Mira. *I would prefer it – for a while, at least.*

Si – Mama.

Insignia joined their conversation. *We will shift soon. Are you ready, Mira? Whatever happens once we are there, Nova's safety is my priority.*

On some level Mira found herself smiling. *Insignia* could be stubborn and sometimes omitted information, but she never flinched from stating the truth. *Never.*

Never, what? Insignia asked.

Nothing. I am ready. Nova's safety comes first, but I will decide my own actions.

The biozoon's resignation to the latter notion was palpable.

As the colours and layers of shift vibration began to engulf her, Mira bathed in a joy and comfort she'd not felt for too long. Had thought she would never feel again. *Family.*

That moment was something she struggled to hold on to as they shifted into a nightmare.

Geni-carriers circled Dowl station and Araldis like predators, their buffers up against the debris from the ships they'd destroyed.

Fewer escaped than I anticipated, Insignia remarked.

If Mira had not been submerged in Primo, she would have been sick. As it was, the biozoon's nano-membrane adjusted her electrolyte balance and released an antispasmodic into her system to counteract the shock. *Had we not had the benefit of imperfect shift, that could have been us. We could be those fragments of . . . of . . .*

She began to sob. Not in any physical way, but in her mind, a completely sorrowful utterance triggered by the sight of the ruined ships and tiny bodies strewn about shift space.

Pitiless. The Post-Species are pitiless. Her mind dwelt on that while *Insignia* adopted a weaving pattern of sublight movement. Much of the debris was caught in the sphere's gravity, making entry and exit trajectories hazardous.

The Post-Species have contacted me. They wish us to cancel our signature broadcast, or they will renege on our arrivals permission.

Apologise to them and cease 'casting.

They wish to know more about Wanton.

Tell them that Wanton held the title Highness Most Capable of Cultivation: Tissue on the Hub world.

Mira—

Please. Mira cut short the biozoon's scolding. *This has been agreed between us. I would come back here and try. After this, you decide.*

Insignia made a disgruntled sound. *If there is an 'after this'.*

Mira left the buccal and took Nova to her cabin. The Primo vein had tended to all the baby's nutritional needs as they'd travelled, and dealt with her wastes, just as it had done with Mira's. Now, while they waited for the Post-Species answer, she had a little time to practise motherhood. She must find something absorbent to wrap Nova in, and feed her. Mira's breasts, though heavy, were not dangerously engorged. Primo had gently massaged and drained milk from her to keep them healthy and functioning.

As she entered, her gaze fell straight on Wanton.

'Wanton?'

Other than the faintest quiver, the Extro gave no response.

She sighed and shifted it gently to make space for Nova, careful not to touch the remaining mycose blisters. Then she laid her baby on the bed and gazed at her.

It was the first time since Nova's birth that she had been able to sit and look at her, and she could see changes already. Her face seemed less wizened, her cheeks plumper and limbs stronger-looking. Her skin, though, was still translucent. Amazingly, in a few days she'd developed some neck control, and was rolling her head from side to side, looking around with bright eyes.

Mira was sure that 'esque babies normally took weeks to develop that kind of strength. She ran her fingers lovingly across Nova's naked stomach, and the baby kicked her legs. Her little mouth opened wide.

You can do things already. More than I expected.

Si – Mama.

I know a little of babies, Nova. But you are different. I will have to learn. Speaking to her child in such a way seemed impossible, and yet perfectly natural. Instinct told her that little about Nova would be like a normal child. Wanton had admitted that in-vitro experimentation had occurred while she'd been captive on the Hub planet. Was her baby in some way like the Post-Species?

Nova's grey-blue eyes watched her with intelligent interest. The level of comprehension in the baby's expression was almost too strange to bear.

Mira – worry?

Mira shook her head and brushed her lips against Nova's stomach, tickling her. Nova kicked her tiny legs again and made an ecstatic noise.

They played for a brief and precious time until a strong thought entered Mira's mind: *Hungry, Mama.*

O-of course. She parted her robe and picked Nova up, lifting her against her chest. The infant latched on with little fuss and began to suck. It hurt for a time, but as if sensing her mother's discomfort, she softened her grip until the milk flowed and the pain had gone, replaced by the hypnotic relaxation of feeding.

Satisfaction and joy filled Mira's mind, pushing aside everything else. For now.

Jo-Jo

Randall was waiting for him in the doorway. In the moonlight he could see her excitement. Catchut was on his feet too, standing close behind her.

'Crux, Rasterovich!' she said. 'You bin on a holiday?'

He pulled a face and slung the cord holding the com-sole off his shoulder. 'I found somethin'.'

'Me too! Bet mine's bigger.' It was a dumb thing to say, and she burst into laughter. 'Whatcha got there?'

'Portable com-sole. Least it will be, when we can get it working.'

'You mean we can hear what's going on up there?'

'Hope so.'

She took it from him and headed back inside.

Jo-Jo followed her, bemused by her quick change of focus. Catchut slapped a tube of something liquid in his hand as he walked past.

'Salut.' Jo-Jo nodded gratefully and put it to his lips. It was sweet and creamy, and tasted like jam.

By the time he'd followed Randall to the window-less room they'd taken to using during the day, he'd finished the tube and felt revived from his climb to and from the studium. Coming back had been easier, but slower; the moons were up, and he'd had to use even greater caution. Just the weight of the com-sole had exhausted his still-weak muscles. They'd spent only a few weeks in *Medium*'s stasis goo, and yet their bodies had withered in it.

'What did you find?' Jo-Jo prompted Randall.

Her head was already bent over the com-sole as she fingered the device. 'Should work. Seems intact.' She stuck her tongue in the corner of her mouth as she concentrated, fitting the device to the room's power adapter and pressing the frequency seek. 'Should be power enough in the solar storage unit for this.'

Jo-Jo watched the icons blinking as the com-sole calibrated and tried again. 'You said you found some-thing too.'

'Mebbe.'

'Don't play games,' he said, not in the mood for it.

She grinned at him again, in a loose unhinged kind of way. Their imprisonment on Medium had fucked up her head, he thought. She'd changed in a way that he couldn't quite pinpoint.

'I found us an AiV,' she said finally. 'Looks to be working. Won't really know till we power up. Powering up means the Saqr will know we're here. Best we go at next nightfall.'

'Capo?' said Catchut. 'You sure?'

'No.' She pressed the seek function again. 'But it's better than starvin' to death sittin' around here.'

'But where'll we go?' Catchut sounded uneasy.

'The islands. Where the refugees went.'

'Where we *think* they went. They might all be dead. Or still down a mine shaft somewhere. I mean, we could starve out there as well.' Catchut glanced at Jo-Jo.

It was the first time the man had looked for his support.

'We might only get one chance in the air. Let's listen to the com-sole for a day or two. See if we can pick up anythin',' said Jo-Jo.

'What if the Saqr come and trash the flyer? What if it's the only one left on the mountain?' she countered.

'If it's intact now, chances are it will be in a few days too.'

Rast began to tap hard on the com-sole, impatient to get something from it.

Jo-Jo pushed her hand away, slowly but deliberately. 'You break it, we won't hear nothin'.'

Randall's fists clenched and her shoulders bunched, as though she might launch herself at him. He tensed for the assault, but her expression changed again.

'I'm going to catch some shut-eye. Wake me if you hear anythin'.'

She got up and left the room.

Catchut stared down at his hands.

'Sleep's a good thing,' said Jo-Jo eventually, and went out.

Jo-Jo woke some time later, stiff from lying on the floor. He was in the room next to the galley – anywhere else had seemed too far to go. Easing up into a crouch, he stretched his back before attempting to stand. He'd been dreaming of Mira Fedor, he realised. A vivid, intense dream in which they were talking; she was so close that he could smell the biozoon secretions on her skin and see the hunted look in her eyes.

He scrubbed at his face, waking himself up more, but the sense of her stuck with him. When would this

stupid obsession fade? Weeks had passed since he'd
seen her. He'd barely known her before that. And yet
here he was, trembling from the dreamed contact, filled
with a compulsion to try the com-sole again.

He listened for sounds of the others. The building
was quiet except for Randall's shallow snores. Jo-Jo
followed the sound to a room down the corridor, where
Randall and Catchut lay with their backs to each other,
clubs fashioned from broken furniture within easy reach.

Jo-Jo backed out and headed down the stairs, to the
basement room where they'd left the com-sole. He
examined the selection options and reset a couple. On
his first scan, he picked up real noise on several channels. Some of it was coded, or at least in a language he
couldn't understand.

He ran the scan again. And again.

Nothing. Whatever had prompted him awake to try
the device had been wrong. No one was there. No
rescue.

Yet he tried several more times, for lack of anything
else to do.

Still nothing comprehensible. On impulse, he
switched to the visual band. If there were OLOSS ships
out there, he might recognise their ident signatures.

The com-sole's small display showed clusters of
unidentifiable craft.

Extros, he figured. Hundreds. More than hundreds.

He stared at the screen. *What are they doing here?* It
couldn't just be for the quixite. Maybe Randall was
right. There was something else here. Someth—

A new signature appeared in the centre of the display,
and resolved into a recognisable OLOSS ident. A

biozoon. He knew the peculiar wave signature, similar to his hybrid ship, *Salacious*.

He left the com-sole, ran up the stairs and woke Randall and Catchut.

Randall was up and heading from the room before he could speak.

'What? What is it?' she demanded.

'There's a 'zoon up there!' Jo-Jo thumbed skyward.

Randall grabbed his arm with strong fingers. 'Who? Fedor?'

He shook her off and turned to hurry back with her. 'Yeah. For what it's worth, I think it's her.'

Randall accelerated past him, beating him to the com-sole by holding the railing and jumping down the stairs. She was peering at the display by the time he joined her.

'That it?' She pointed to the blip, her voice trembling the same way his body had been when he'd woken.

He wanted to tell her about the dream. How close he'd been to Mira. How he could have touched her . . . but it sounded wishful and stupid. And he had no reason to share it with his competitor, other than that it made Mira seem real and alive.

'Crux, I think you're right,' she said. 'It's a 'zoon, all right. Any chance it's yours? The one that was stolen?'

Jo-Jo shrugged. 'Doubt it. The hybrids leave a slightly different sig. This one looks to be pure 'zoon.'

As they watched, the biozoon wave suddenly extinguished.

'She's gone.' Randall's voice went hoarse.

'No.' Jo-Jo jerked his head up, testing the air as if

he could scent something, or feel a vibration. 'The signature's gone, but she's still here.'

'How do you know that? You guessin'?' Randall rounded on him, her face so close that her spit wet his cheek.

'I don't know,' he said with a self-deprecating laugh. 'But I do. The biozoon's there, and Fedor is on board.'

'Loco,' said Randall, fingers to her temple, pulling the trigger on an imaginary pistol. 'Inventin' things.'

Jo-Jo shrugged. 'Yeah. Probably. But we need to find those survivors. When she comes, it's going to be one trip only. She'll be looking for them, not us. We don't want to miss the ride.'

Randall paced a few steps. 'Did you check the maps in the studium?'

'Yeah. Two likely places with enough cover and fresh water. Got the coordinates here.' He tapped his head.

She snorted. 'Couldn't you think of a safer place?'

'Seemed the safest to me. Insurance in these uncertain times.'

'What about the Saqr? Find out anything useful?'

'They can survive in anything, even a vacuum. Can handle extremes in temperature. A decade without water.'

'That tough?'

Jo-Jo nodded. 'Whoever picked them to take over this planet knew what they were doin'. Seems they can go without food too.'

'The ones we saw acted hungry enough.'

'I guess while they're active they need to eat. But in stasis they can go for years without it.'

'Physical weaknesses?'

Jo-Jo screwed his face up in recall. 'They're plated in five sections by an exoskeleton. Then there're the claws. Everything inside them is real basic: pharynx, colon, ventral nervous system. Not much to mess with.'

'Ventral? Whassat mean?'

'Their nervous system runs along their belly instead of their back. Bastards don't even need each other to spawn.'

'Wait! Along the belly. Gotta be something we can work with there.'

'Maybe. But the exoskel – the cuticle – covers everything.'

'Must be somethin' that can dissolve the cuticle.'

'Fedor will know that,' he said.

'You're losin' it, Rasterovich. No way you c'n know if it's her up there.' He heard her frustration.

They fell silent, both watching the display.

'But it could be someone. Someone who can get us off this dead rock. It's nearly daylight,' she said eventually. 'Get some more sleep. We'll go tonight.' She brushed past him and headed upstairs again.

THALES

Fariss's gaze scalded Thales. 'You 'n' *her*?'

He turned from watching Mira Fedor disappear out of the doorway, and tilted his head to stare up at the woman he adored. Her wide eyes were narrow with doubt. At any other time he might have felt some satisfaction, even pleasure, that she was suspicious. Now though it seemed strangely unreal. 'No,' he said with finality. 'Never. I want to find Gutnee Paraburd.'

Fariss accepted his clipped response without insult or comment. She was a pragmatic person, not a sensitive one, and she was shaking her head. 'Best thing now is to get out of here. Sophos won't listen to you, no matter *what* you got as proof. I say we go 'n' hunt down those that don't like the way things are here. Talk to them. Maybe they got some leverage.'

He smiled. 'You sound like a member of Consilience.'

She cracked the door open again and squinted. 'Whatever it is, you better decide, quick.'

A welter of thoughts ran through Thales's mind. He knew that finding Paraburd was not just about proving his innocence to the Sophos. In all honesty he wanted revenge on the devious fellow. An image of Fariss placing her hands around Paraburd's neck . . . *No!* He stopped himself and searched deep within to touch his

Jainist beliefs. Revenge would not serve them at this point. Revenge was not a worthy motive.

'We should go. Find the woman, Linnea. Build a case among those who would listen,' he agreed.

Fariss glanced back at him and grinned approvingly. She pulled a small dagger from her boot and used it to prise an iron leg from a chair. Then she slipped the bar through her belt as a secondary weapon. 'We go straight for the outside pad. Steal a local ride. Once we get out into the transit area again, I'm gonna start some trouble. Keep me in sight, but stay back. It's gonna be untidy for a bit.'

Thales moved alongside her, and stood on his toes to kiss her mouth.

She responded by lifting him to her and sliding her tongue into his mouth – a moist, passionate, dominating kiss that left him weak. He clung to her for a moment or two, savouring her strength and solidity.

She lifted her head and set him on his feet gently, as if he were a child.

'Fariss. Thank you for staying—'

''Nother time, hon. We gotta go.'

Her casual endearment filled him with unbelievable warmth.

Then she was all business. 'Go left down the corridor and take the first door into the main port. I'll be behind you. Once you're out there, blend into the crowd and tail me. When we get close to an exit, go outside and find a taxi.'

'What if I can't get one? The terminal is frantic.'

She looked at him steadily. 'Thales, I want you to steal one.'

'S-steal? But I'm not—'

'Just get the taxi and get it near me. I'll do the rest.' She gave him a confident smile. 'Got it?'

He nodded and looked to the door.

She stepped in front of him and threw it open. 'Go!'

He ran left without looking back. In a few seconds, raised voices echoed from the way he'd come. Fariss was blocking the corridor, stalling until he got out. He heard the groan as her fists made contact with the first guard. A rifle discharged.

Not her. Please, not her!

But he didn't stop. If he stayed, he'd be a hindrance. He would do as she said. She was a soldier. She could take of herself. *She can.* He repeated it to himself as he ran.

The nearest service entrance to the port was blocked by a cleaning trolley and several large containers containing liquid catoplasma. He tried to heave the trolley to one side, but the containers were too heavy. In desperation, he dropped to the floor and used all the strength in his legs to push. The trolley shifted enough to slide the door ajar. He squeezed through into the terminal.

A quick glance told him the biggest crowds stood around the ticketing counters, so he hurried over and joined a queue.

Only moments later, heads began to turn as the door he'd come through was flung open, and a catoplasma drum – minus lid – rolled out. The liquid splashed and spread like an oil spill. It would thicken soon, and then harden.

Fariss followed it, jumping the puddle of liquid with one enormous leap. The pursuing politic guard tried to emulate her athleticism and fell short, slipping in the mess and giving her a precious advantage in the chase.

But more Robes came from other directions. Thales saw that they were hesitant to use their rifles in the crowds. Fariss ducked under the kaffe railing and threaded through tables, pulling them over behind her, knocking over beakers of mokka and plates. Patrons scrambled away, shouting, adding to the furore.

Thales saw his opportunity and walked quickly to an exit. In his rush, he bumped into someone. An apology sprang automatically to his lips until he recognised the man: Gutnee Paraburd, his hair longer, his chin covered with gingerish stubble.

They stared at each other in unhappy recollection, then Gutnee stepped neatly back to allow a group to pass between them; when they'd gone, so had Paraburd.

Thales didn't linger. The lack of surprise in Gutnee's expression told him that the man knew him to be here. He ran out of the building and across the tarmac among the traffic auditors and the AiVs manoeuvring into parking spots. Fariss was ahead of him, weaving in and out of vehicles, ducking around pay stations

He approached the bank of taxis. 'Esques milled around the pay maestro, demanding rides. The maestro shouted at them, trying to force them into some order.

The taxis were all locked automatons. Thales wouldn't be able to get one without the maestro's release command.

Steal one, Thales.

Keeping track of Fariss, he edged over to the private vehicle lot. A family of 'esques were climbing out of a small domestic flyer, simultaneously engaged in a blossoming argument.

Thales waited until they were at the rear luggage compartment, then crawled into the passenger seat from the other side. He lay there for a few moments staring at the controls, breathing heavily. He'd operated similar vehicles as a child, transporting scholars to and from his birth town to the Logic Courts, and then later, a few times, when he and Rene had taken holidays on the Faust Coast. This one was even simpler than those, a luxurious and virtually automated flyer with an updated verbal command function.

The carriage rocked as the luggage compartment slammed shut.

He had to decide. Fariss wouldn't be able evade the Robes much longer.

Voices grew louder, and the door slid open. A hand fumbled along the pilot seat for the activation slide, the 'esque still talking to his family outside the door. The man had only to turn his head to see Thales lying sideways on his seat.

Thales grasped his chance. He grabbed the slide and rotated his body around, reached for the ignition slot. The slide slipped in, and the vehicle issued a guttural start-up sound which sent the man's head swiveling.

'What—'

'Close doors,' Thales told the craft.

The man instinctively withdrew his hand to avoid having it crushed and yelled.

'Proceed north.'

Thales sat upright and slid into the pilot's seat. The flyer began to move forward, out into the designated taxiing lane.

A glance at the proximity viewer told him that the 'esque was chasing him.

'Lock doors.' He scanned the area for Fariss. From the cluster of guards, they had her cornered by the pay station furthest from the terminal. A politic transport with red and gold markings was approaching from the opposite direction.

The sight of it spurred Thales. If the guards captured Fariss, she'd be taken to detention, as he had been. His thoughts flashed to Villon. He wouldn't fail Fariss as he'd failed gentle Amaury.

He told the vehicle to hasten to the farthest pay booth. It showed a location image on the screen and asked for confirmation.

'Yes!' he said. 'Hurry.'

'At what speed do you wish to travel?'

'Maximum limit.' Then he reconsidered. 'No. Maximum speed possible without damage.'

'You wish to ignore speed limits.'

'Yes. Ignore all speed limits.'

'It is legally required that you record your deliberate intention to break the law.'

'I have instructed vehicle –' Thales glanced up at the registration holo '– MAO4O to ignore speed limits.'

'Thank you,' said the flyer. 'Harness securing.' Safety straps snaked around his shoulder and waist. It lifted and accelerated with force.

Thales fell back against the seat. A few moments

later they were hovering above Fariss. There would only be one chance to pick her up; the approaching politic vehicle was already broadcasting threats.

'Descend at maximum speed and hover three mesurs above the ground surface. Stand by for immediate ascent,' said Thales.

'Confirming that speed will be outside safety parameters,' intoned the flyer.

'Confirmed,' said Thales.

It dropped without further warning to a very short distance above Fariss's head. She jumped for the flyer's struts and wrapped her hands around one of them.

'Ascend and accelerate out of the port zone to Clementvale.'

'Confirm location on map,' said the flyer.

Anxiously Thales tapped in confirmation as the Robes closed on Farris, batting her with their swords. She kicked back at them and swung her long powerful legs around the strut.

As the flyer lifted, one of the taller guards managed to seize her ankle. They flew, clinging together for a short distance, before Fariss slammed his face with the heel of her other boot.

With horror, Thales watched his fall from the proximity cams. 'Proceed with maximum speed.'

They soared over the port boundary, gaining height and speed. He worried that Fariss would freeze or fall, but the politic flyer was pursuing them aggressively now, lights and sirens activated.

Thales tried to think above the pounding of his heart and the trembling of his limbs. He'd never acted so decisively before. This was not impulsive, like his attack on Sophos Mianos, or because he was afraid of dying, like his actions on Rho Junction. This was a clear rational choice, and he must see it through.

And Fariss needed him.

She was kneeling on the horizontal strut now, inching her way up.

'Open the passenger door,' he told the vehicle.

'This is a manufacturer warning. Opening the door at current speed will cause instability and changes in cabin pressure,' the vehicle bleated back.

'Proceed!' ordered Thales.

As the door opened, he was slammed back against his seat by the wind that tunnelled through. He reached out a hand, which Fariss grabbed with bone-crunching force. She hauled herself up onto the seat, sprawling over him.

'Close door,' Thales gasped.

The door slid shut quickly, leaving them tangled and breathless.

Fariss lifted her head and dropped a heavy breathless kiss on his face. She slid her legs down and levered into the passenger seat. 'Where are we going?'

'We'll land near Clementvale. Make enquiries for the woman Linnea.'

'But how we gonna shake them first?'

Thales stared out of the window. The city was passing beneath at a terrifying pace as they reached maximum speed. Worse was the vibration.

'You overridden the safety?' shouted Fariss.

He nodded and waited for her reaction.

She slapped him on the back with approval and

squared her shoulders as the harness wrapped around her. 'Make a soldier of ya yet.'

They didn't try to speak again as the flyer strained toward its destination, leaving the slower politic flyer further and further behind. When they began to ascend Mount Clement, the vibration intensified, and a dreadful tearing noise filled the cabin.

'Slow!' Fariss bellowed.

'Reduce speed!' said Thales.

The command came too late. A large piece of fairing peeled off the nose and smashed into the passenger bubble. The bubble cracked under the impact, and a blasting gust of cold air speared through the cabin.

'Engine malfunction alert,' blared the flyer.

The dashboard flashed a sequence of lights that meant nothing to Thales.

'Land!' he shrieked.

Their descent was swift and ragged. For a few desperate moments Thales thought they'd hit nose first, but the vehicle corrected its wing balance in time to drop tail first. The impact was so hard that Fariss's lap restraint snapped, and her lower body was flung forward. Only the shoulder restraint prevented her from smashing her head.

Thales's neck jerked back and then forward. As he gasped for breath, Fariss was already wriggling out of her shoulder harness and kicking the door open.

She released Thales from his restraint and pulled him into her arms as though he was a small child being rescued by its mother.

'Where to?' She didn't put him down as she slid onto the ground.

Through his daze he noticed grease on her face and the spatter of blood that ran from her high broad cheekbone down to her generous mouth. There was no smile on those lips. They were pursed with pain and determination.

He remembered how easily she'd strangled Lasper Farr's soldier on Edo, the one sent to kill him. And then later how she'd shot the mercenary, Macken, when she'd caught him forcing himself on Thales. When Fariss decided to kill, she showed no hesitation. Or remorse.

He shook in her arms.

'Thales!' she demanded. 'We stay here, and they'll be all over us. Where to?'

He raised his head and tried to get his bearings. They'd landed on a commuter siding near the mouth of the quarry. Thales knew the area vaguely. His father had brought him here once, hoping his son might choose a less lofty position than scholar. He still recalled their conversation – his father's resignation and acknowledgement of his mother's genes.

'You must know what it means to work for a living, Thales. Sometimes I think they forget. Those up there, with their ideas.' He stared into the distance towards the city. It was then that Thales had felt the yearning to go there and become one of the untouchables. The pull had been so, so strong.

'Follow the escarpment. Town's over the other side,' he whispered.

Fariss strode on without another word.

He tugged her shoulder and made her look at him. 'I can walk,' he said. 'Put me down.'

She gave a nod and dropped him to his feet. 'Shame. Kinda enjoy doin' that.'

Another warm feeling infused his hurting body. She could still do that to him despite everything.

They headed up the side of the quarry toward the treeline. Thales found himself jogging to keep up with her. The brush at the top was thick, slowing their progress. Halfway along the escarpment, he begged Fariss for a rest. She stood impatiently over him as he sank into the dry grass, panting.

The politic flyer made several passes over the quarry before settling to land near their discarded flyer. Guards poured out.

She grabbed Thales by the arm and pulled him to his feet. 'Get your arse moving, or I'll be carrying you again.'

Staying under the cover of the trees, they crested the quarry. Beneath them, Clementvale spread through the hollow, between the quarry and another heavily wooded mountain on the opposite side, proof of what the area had been like before its excavation.

'Cat-cons – are – down – there,' Thales gasped. He pointed to a discoloured section of the uniformly white catoplasma rooftops. 'If she's a worker, she'll live there.'

'How will we find her?'

'Ask – someone.'

Fariss nodded. 'Come on.' She gripped his hand as they slid and scrambled down the quarry-side, keeping him upright when he might have fallen.

They skidded down the last section as the guards reached the crest. Fariss had the first line of houses in her sights, and her unrelenting grip propelled Thales forward.

They hastened between rows of houses, weaving

through the lanes at Fariss's whim. He wanted to ask her if she knew which direction to go, but he couldn't catch his breath enough to speak.

As they moved through the centre of the town, a cloak of familiarity descended over him. He'd grown up in a town like this, and the sense of familiarity delivered a rush of emotion. Unbidden, tears began to stream down his cheeks.

Fariss cricked her neck to stare down at him. 'You hurt?'

He shook his head and dashed the moisture away. 'How far to the Cat-cons?'

She glanced at the rooftops. 'Nother block, maybe.'

Scolar's sun had started to set; they'd have darkness on their side soon. For the first time in his life Thales was relieved that Scolar had no moons. The street lights were already warming, and quiet had descended. It amplified the shouts of the Robes tracking them.

Fariss pulled him down one more lane and into a small amphitheatre. They skirted around its edge and past the next set of houses. These ones were a different colour: the Cat-Cons.

A group of children were playing in the last light, throwing balls at a wall. They stopped their game and stared at the fugitives. Then the oldest one grabbed the younger ones and shuffled them inside one of the homes.

Sirens were blaring now, alerting the town to an emergency. Inside the houses com-soles would be 'casting images of Thales and Fariss to the occupants.

An 'esque appeared in the doorway through which the children had disappeared. He carried a weapon.

'Get on yer way!' he bellowed.

Fariss squared her shoulders, and Thales felt her tension escalate. Her body became taut, ready to fight.

Thales straightened and limped forward. 'We're looking for a woman named Linnea. A Swestr. A woman – friend of hers – told us she would help.'

The man glanced back into the shadows in the doorway. He inclined his head towards Fariss and Thales. 'Inside. Quick.'

Fariss stepped in front of Thales, her hands loose at her sides, fingers flexing. As they crowded into the small entrance, a woman spoke to them from the shadows of the hall. 'I'll take you to a safe place until Linnea comes. She'll decide.'

Fariss didn't like it, Thales could tell. He placed his hand in the small of her back and stepped round her bulk so he could see the woman. The man shut the door behind them.

'Thank you. The Robes are searching for us. We don't wish to bring you trouble.'

The woman was round and dark, and her Scolar accent was clipped, less cultured than his. She wore soft boots, loose pants and a collared shirt as if she'd just got off work.

'You already did,' she said without preamble. 'Come.'

They followed her through the dully pigmented corridor, straight to the back of the house and into a neatly paved yard. The automated gate swung open at her request, and she hurried along an equally tidy paved laneway.

They could hear the Robes clearly. They were broadcasting a warning message along the streets and banging on doors. Thales glimpsed two of them between houses. They had their weapons raised and were engaged in animated conversation.

The woman began to jog.

Thales tried to keep up with her, but his body was close to collapse. Fariss fell back and linked her arm with his.

'Just a little further,' she whispered. 'Then we can rest.'

He thought of Mira Fedor – how she'd escaped the Post-Species world and the Saqr invasion. From somewhere he dragged up determination. Mira had no one and nothing, and yet she'd survived. He was blessed with Fariss. He would not let her down. He pulled his arm from her support and quickened his pace again.

The dark was upon them when the woman stopped abruptly. She leaned forward, panting into a comm. The gates to another yard opened, and she hurried them through before they closed again.

From what Thales could see they were in an almost identical yard. Soft garden light lit their way towards the house, but the woman deviated from the path and squatted down among some well-pruned bushes. 'Quiet as you can,' she said. 'Don't want those inside knowing you're here.'

Thales opened his mouth to ask where they were going, but he shut it again. The woman was nothing if not decisive. Like Fariss.

'Hold hands,' she ordered. She grasped Thales's fingers, her own cool and dry against his. He reached out for Fariss, and she engulfed his hand with her huge grip. The woman inched into the dark shrubbery along the side of the house.

They stopped and started a few times, bumping into each other. Branches brushed their legs, and the ground became uneven.

Finally, she stopped and let go of Thales's hand to kneel down in front of a large shadowy object.

Thales could hear rather than see her push the bushes aside from it: the soft crack of the breaking twigs, her even softer cursing. And then faint scraping noises as she turned some type of pump handle.

Fariss was still holding his hand. Her grip tightened when lights flooded the yard. She pulled Thales down into the cover of the bushes in the time it took him to comprehend what had happened.

Voices drifted around the side to them, clear and curt. 'We've not seen your runaways here, Politic.' The voice sounded honest and anxious – an older man.

The woman had done the right thing by not taking them into the house.

'Stand aside while we inspect your yard,' said the robe in reply.

'Mind the garden,' said the homeowner. 'We supply the Sophos offices with lilies. Wouldn't do to damage them.'

'Where's your wife?' asked the robe, ignoring the man's warning.

'She's at work. Won't be home till the dinner's cleaned up.'

'Work?'

'The Mount Clement clinic.'

'Scrubber?'

The man didn't answer immediately. 'Galley supervisor,' he said eventually.

Thales felt a tug on his arm, then the woman's mouth close to his ear. 'Get . . . down . . . in here.' Her words were so faint he barely heard them.

He pulled his hand from Fariss's and reached forward. The soil crumbled away and he felt a smooth edge of catoplasma.

'Hurry,' she whispered again.

Thales contorted his body round and slipped his legs over the edge as the Robes left the veranda. His feet dangled for a moment before connecting with a ledge, and beneath it another ledge – a rough stairway of some kind built into the catoplasma, leading to an underground chamber.

He climbed down as quickly as he could, not wanting Fariss to be left in the open. Within moments, her large feet were following him. As soon as her head was below the catoplasma lip, the opening closed, and they lost all light.

They both landed in a tumble on the dry floor. Neither of them spoke as they disentangled their limbs from each other and listened.

Silence from above.

'OK, hon?' whispered Fariss eventually.

Her concern had its usual anaesthetising effect. Somehow, it meant more to him than any of Rene's slightly patronising attentions ever had.

'What is this?' she asked.

'Underground water tank, I think,' he said. 'All the houses had them in my hometown as well. They pipe the catoplasma into the ground and blow it out so it forms a bubble. It sets hard, and then they siphon rain-water in.'

'They safe?'

'I've never been inside one before.' He thought about it for a moment; remembered his father making him wait a distance from the house when theirs had been installed. 'I suppose so. The problem is the displacement. When they expand the catoplasma they run other pipes to suck the soil out. Usually the catoplasma moulds to the terrain. But sometimes there's a fault or a subsidence, and the whole thing shifts. I've heard of them cracking under significant uneven pressure.'

'Significant pressure, eh? Let's hope we don't get none of that.'

'What do we do now?'

Fariss reached for him and pulled him against her. 'Wait, I'd say. At least for a while.'

He moved closer and relaxed against her hard body. She smelled sweaty and stale, and wonderful.

Her hands slipped inside his robe, stroking his skin. He lay passively in her arms. Fear and exhaustion and claustrophobia seeped away.

BALBAO

They were taken to a cabin high in the ship's structure. Despite the residual head and body ache from imperfect shift, Balbao took in as much of the surroundings as he could. This was a battleship, fully serviceable and worn from recent business, not something dragged from retirement because of the invasion. He noticed little signs – the well-lubed hatches and the working shelf locks.

Because of his observations, he had less of a surprise than the tyros when the captain turned out to be Lasper Farr, Commander of the Stain Wars.

Not all the tyros. He amended that thought. Ra of Lostol showed little reaction, and Labile Connit looked unhappy rather than shocked.

Lasper Farr, like all infamous 'esques, was less impressive in person than in myth. Balbao took in the lean, almost gaunt figure. Though he looked unimposing, something about him made Balbao entirely uncomfortable. It would be wrong, he thought, to underestimate him.

Farr looked along the line of them and offered Miranda a seat. His greeting cabin was sparse and functional: a table and attached seats. He did not ask the rest of them to sit.

'Let me guess,' he said. 'Dicter Seeward and Lawmon Jise. But who are you?'

Balbao shifted under the penetrating gaze. 'Belle-Monde's Chief Astronomien. Balbao.'

'Ahh, of course. So pleased you didn't disintegrate with your world, Balbao. Would be a shame to lose such an excellent scientist.'

The Balol didn't believe for a moment that he meant what he said. Commander Farr, he'd already decided, cared little for strangers.

But Balbao would not be intimidated. 'This is Ra of Lostol and Labile—'

'Connit,' finished Farr quietly. 'I know my own son, Chief Balbao. And Ra and I . . . have worked together on projects before.'

Many glances were exchanged in the shocked silence that followed his statement – two revelations that almost made Balbao wish that he'd perished on Belle-Monde. Had he been harbouring a member of Consilience? What mischief had Labile wrought? And Ra? Why had he been conspiring with Farr? His thoughts swirled in a way that made it difficult to extract answers.

Ra spoke first. 'Where is the device, Lasper? We must locate Sole.'

Farr's face grew pinched with irritation. 'No thank you, Ra? No heartfelt gratitude for the risk taken by me and my ship to keep you alive?'

Ra stared at him steadily, his multicoloured insect eyes shining in the cabin light. 'It was not me you came to save, Lasper. It was your son.'

'Don't underestimate your value to me,' replied Farr, letting his lips curl into a small unreadable smile.

Ra relaxed a little.

Labile Connit, on the other hand, looked as Balbao felt: sick and tense, but not about to be trodden on. 'You are not my father,' he insisted.

Farr regarded him steadily. 'You may not like it, Labile, but it's the truth.'

'Good Sole!' exclaimed Miranda. 'What a pretty state of affairs. I'm sure there is much to be caught up on, but firstly ... thank you, Commander Farr. Can you tell us, are we quite safe now? Where are we?'

Her brash interruption diverted Farr's attention.

'We managed to evade the Post-Species by using imperfect shift. We have taken casualties because of it. Not all the buffers withstood the untested vibration.'

'A bold but necessary move, Commander,' said Ra.

Farr was unimpressed by Ra's declaration. 'Our *only* choice. The Post-Species have obliterated the systems they have reached. Those who heeded the alarms have closed their spheres. But I must thank *you*, Dicter Seeward. The virus you created was quite a success on Scolar, I believe. And because of that, their shift sphere is still open. We are on our way there now.'

Every exposed piece of Miranda's flesh turned pink. 'We are going to Scolar?'

All heads turned to her.

'Miranda?' said Jise. 'What does the Commander mean?'

Grim satisfaction settled on Lasper Farr's face. What did he know about Miranda Seeward, Balbao wondered, that even her colleague and lover Lawmon Jise did not?

'I would give you time to discuss your issues privately.' Farr nodded at the guards.

They moved forward to escort Jise, Seeward, Ra and Balbao out of the room, leaving Connit.

Connit baulked, not wanting to be left with his father.

Ra, on the other hand, had no wish to leave the Commander's presence, and jerked from their grasp. 'Where is the device, Lasper?'

Farr's lips pinched tight. 'It's gone. But you will make another for me soon.'

'Gone? But I'd need equipment, and—'

Two simple arm movements from Farr decreed they all leave his presence, and Ra was unable to finish.

Balbao marched between the guards, grateful to be away from Farr, but his relief faded quickly when he saw where they were to be left.

'We are not criminals,' said Lawmon Jise to the guards. 'We are refugees whom your Commander chose to take aboard. How dare you treat us like this?' The tyro was so outraged that he let go of Miranda's arm to push the guard.

A cuff from the soldier sent him sprawling into the containment cell. The rest of the refugees entered in shocked quiet, at gunpoint. Even Miranda was silent as she hurried over to Jise.

The containment field engaged, and they found themselves in a sparse space furnished with narrow fold-down bunks and a fold-down module that served as both washroom and san. There was no privacy, and the cell was already inhabited.

Two of the oldest 'esques Balbao had ever seen sat together on a single bunk. One, a woman with an impossibly lined face and an oddly toned physique, stared openly at them. The other, a man almost as aged, gazed after the guards.

The woman got up and came over, hand outstretched. 'Call me Samuelle. This is Jeremiah Hob. Whatever you've all done to piss Lasper off, I'm real grateful.'

Balbao and the others stared at her.

'See, he's plannin' to kill us. Then he had to go off dodging Extros to catch up with you all. We're bettin' he's had too much else on his mind to think about us,' she explained.

The male 'esque, Hob, slid off his bunk and began unfolding the others. 'Too much tellin', Sammy. Let 'em catch their breath.'

He hobbled over to Jise and offered him a hand. 'Let's get you up on a bed.'

OLOSS's most vaunted lawmon accepted the gnarled hand, and was helped to a bunk. 'Thank you, sir,' said Jise in a shaky voice. 'Please excuse our disarray; we've had rather a rough time of it.'

'When you're ready,' said Hob, 'we'd like to hear about it, and about what's happening out there. Could be our stories might interest you too. Could be we can help each other.'

Balbao was taken with the old fellow's dignified manner, as, he could tell, was Jise.

'Take a bunk,' Balbao suggested to the others.

Everyone did so, except Ra, who paced the length of the containment. The old woman, Sammy, watched him, clearly fascinated by the Godhead's strange appearance.

'Where in the name of Crux did you get those eyes? Thought I'd seen everythin', but I ain't seen nothing like them,' she said.

Her comment was straightforward, bordering on simple, but Balbao didn't think that was a reflection of her mind. Her sharp eyes were busy assessing every-thing. *What in Sole's name*, he wondered, *could this ancient and seemingly harmless couple have done to enrage Lasper Farr?*

He leaned back against the wall and lifted his legs onto the bunk. As if on cue, a dreadful fatigue washed over him. 'Is there anything to drink?'

Hob got up and went to the washing module. He pressed a panel, and a tube filled with water slid out of a slot. He twisted the tube from the dispenser and tossed it to Balbao. 'Don't take too long to drink it. The tube dissolves after a while so it can't be used for anythin'. Anyone else?'

Everyone except Ra murmured their assent. Hob busied himself doling the water out while Balbao drank his. It tasted faintly musty, as though the recycler need recalibrating. By the time he'd finished it, some of his distress had faded.

He got off his bunk and dispensed another. Settling back to drink it, he began to talk. Jise and Miranda still seemed to be too upset, and Labile Connit looked as if he might be in shock. Ra appeared angry above all.

'Commander Farr rescued us from our lifeship in the Mintaka system. We are now, so we are told, on our way to Scolar.'

'Scolar? Why there?' asked old Sammy.

'We went through imperfect shift, didn't we?' said Hob.

'Yes. Imperfect shift. I believe that biozoons use it, but I've never heard of an OLOSS ship managing it.'

'This ain't no OLOSS ship,' said Hob.

Balbao nodded. 'Indeed. As for why we are going to Scolar ...' He shrugged. 'Perhaps it's the only place left with the shift sphere still functioning.'

'What?' they both cried.

'The Extros invaded Mintaka, destroyed our research station and an entire planet.'

'A *planet*?' Hob and Sammy stared at each other, faces crinkled with incredulity.

'Balbao speaks truthfully,' whispered Jise. 'We are only alive because Lasper Farr came looking for his son.' He turned a bewildered stare on Labile Connit. 'Labile?'

'I'm *not* his son,' Connit insisted from where he huddled on his bed.

The eyes upon him were unconvinced.

Balbao thought he had a lean likeness to Farr, though his colouring was darker, his eyes brown, not grey. It was possible the shape of his face resembled the Commander's, but that could have been his imagination.

'This is not a time for lies, Labile,' said Ra.

The geneer straightened and glared back at them. 'Then I shouldn't be the only one to tell. We all have secrets. Especially you, Ra. How do you know Lasper? What have you done? What was the device you asked about? Have you been working with him?'

Ra stepped closer, his paper-thin skin pale and taut.

Balbao noticed the slight peeling around his hairline. He had little enough hair to hide it.

'Are you accusing me of something, Connit?'

'All I know is that any collusion with Lasper Farr would be suspicious.' Without warning, Connit leapt at Ra, his hands grasping the Lostolian's throat. '*What is it?* What did you build for my father?'

Balbao and Hob both intervened. Hob knocked Connit back with a well-placed punch. The old fellow had been around, thought Balbao as he pulled Ra away.

'Enough,' he bellowed with full Balol ferocity. 'If any violence is to occur, it will be from me.' For the first time since any of them had known him, he bared his warrior's teeth. For good measure he let loose a growl.

Neither Sammy nor Hob batted an eyelid, but Miranda shrieked and clung tighter to Jise.

'What is happening to us?' she wailed.

'Miranda!' Balbao growled again.

She curtailed her wail to a whimper.

'Now,' he said, 'it is time we talked. All of us. And quickly. It may be the only – the last – chance we get. Labile?'

The geneer scowled at Ra as he spoke. 'He is my biological father. But he didn't raise me or have anything to do with me. I don't acknowledge him.'

'Have you met him before?' asked Balbao.

Connit closed his eyes and nodded. 'Once. He came to visit my mother when I was younger. To look me over, no doubt. He didn't like what he found, and we never saw him again. Though he did help my mother to pay the studium costs.'

'So it's thanks to him you're a geneer?' said Ra. 'That's hardly uninvolved.'

'The important thing from our perspective is that you aren't one of his people,' said Balbao.

Jise nodded agreement.

'You mean, was I his spy on Belle-Monde? No. And I take offence at anyone who would suggest it,' Connit said hotly.

Ra made a disparaging noise and turned away.

Sole's favoured Godhead was beginning to annoy Balbao beyond comfortable tolerance. 'Ra?'

'What of you two?' Ra asked the cell's original occupants. 'Who are you? Other than old.'

Sammy opened her mouth to retort but Hob put a calming hand on her arm. 'You heard of Consilience?'

'Are you members?' asked Miranda.

Hob smiled, somewhat proudly, thought Balbao. 'Sammy's one of the leaders.'

Ra froze.

'And I,' continued Hob, 'was Commander Farr's pilot during the war. And more recently. Until I happened to let Tekkie sneak off with some real important device that belonged to the Commander.'

'Tekkie?' shrilled Miranda.

'Device?' chimed in Ra.

Hob grinned at them. 'Yeah, Tekkie. Tekton. He pinched the Commander's future-readin' machine.'

Jo-Jo Rasterovich

Jo-Jo set the coordinates for the first of the most likely islands. Randall had taken control of the AiV, and he sat next to her, watching intently in case he needed to fly it. Catchut lay across the back seats, exhausted from the climb to the villa.

They'd encountered no Saqr on the way, which made Jo-Jo uneasy.

'Where are they all?' he'd whispered to Randall as they entered the abandoned villa from a basement door.

Randall didn't reply till they reached the catoplasma landing pad on the top of the building. Then she tilted her head to the sky. 'You noticed anything up there?'

Jo-Jo took a moment to catch his breath and take in the glittering vista. Neither of the moons was up yet, and the sky was studded with the lights of alien craft. Less of them, though, than there had been.

'They're leaving,' said Jo-Jo.

'Yeah,' said Randall. 'Seems so. Gotta real bad feeling about this.'

Jo-Jo had to agree. 'Let's get out of here.'

The AiV lifted into the air without incident. Randall kept the landing lights off, concentrating on the flight panel, watching the altitude and infrared sensors.

Jo-Jo stared out into the darkness, wondering what stretched below them, besides the desert. What a Cruxforsaken world to have been born into. He felt a pang of sympathy for Mira Fedor. Dust and repression had been her life while his had been so free.

'You plannin' your funeral?' said Randall.

'Nope,' he said. 'Shoulda passed the Extro ship by now. Can't see nothin' down there, though. Unless it's sunk into the sand.'

Randall checked her map. 'You're right. No sign. Wonder when that moved?'

Jo-Jo glanced out at the sky. 'Mebbe it's got something to do with things shifting around up there.' He kept staring until his attention was caught by something lower on the horizon.

'Looks like a fire,' he said eventually.

As they drew closer, the glow cast a dim light and moving shadows across sand dunes. 'That a town?'

'Was Loisa,' said Randall, consulting the flyer's map again. 'Fedor's hometown. She had a villa there with her sister. Thought it'd be all burned out by now, But this damn atmosphere's lethal. Keeps stuff smoulderin' for ever.'

Jo-Jo felt Mira's presence keenly again, as though she was in the cabin with them. He clenched his fists.

'Funeral again?' asked Randall.

'How far, Capo?' asked Catchut from the back seat.

'Day and a night, mebbe. Depending on whether we luck upon them. That's all the fuel we got, anyway.'

'Maybe we can pick up some extra fuel cells on the way.'

She nodded. 'If we see anything. If it's safe to put down.'

They fell silent again, Catchut dozing while Jo-Jo

scoured the murky landscape for wreckage or land-marks. Randall set the AiV on auto and sat almost motionless.

Maybe Jo-Jo slept for a while. He must have, because Randall's nudge to his shoulder and curt 'Crux!' jerked him to awareness.

He rolled his tongue over his teeth. They felt coated with neglect. He blinked a few times and stared out into the dark – by now, the not so dark. Far off to Randall's side of the AiV was a fiery glare: not the orange glow of fire but the stark white of electricity.

'Whassat?' he slurred sleepily.

Randall checked her settings and fingered the location map to take them closer. They executed a wide sweep of the area, keeping their distance from the light.

'Saqr there. Plenty of them, by looks,' said Catchut. 'But what're they doing?'

Jo-Jo strained already tired eyes across Randall's shoulder. 'Looks like they're all over the Extro ship.'

'Well, least we know where it went,' said Randall.

'And where *they* went. Where are we?'

'AiV's map says it's a mine called Juanita, between the Pablo tunnels.'

'Means squat to me,' said Jo-Jo.

'Lost two of my original crew in there. Tunnel collapse. Still ain't convinced it was accident. Always had an inklin' I knew who did it.'

'Tough,' said Jo-Jo. 'But so what?'

'Juanita mine had somethin' goin' on. Namely, quixite. The Pablo mine next door has the longest tunnels on the continent. We had a tour down into one of them where there'd been some trouble. Fedor said she left Pellegrini and the survivors inside the Pablo shafts. She thought he'd follow the tunnels south, get as close to the coast as he could.'

Jo-Jo stared at the eerie sight of Saqr crawling all over Extro ship. 'Can we get closer?'

Randall was obligingly conversational for once. 'I'm figurin' they already know we're here. If we keep on movin', chances are they'll be too caught up in what they're doin' to come chasin' us. We go in close, who knows? They might just blow us out of the sky.'

She was probably right. Their curiosity wasn't worth the risk of attracting attention. Yet something itched at Jo-Jo. Something important was happening there. He knew it.

Randall reset their direction, and within a short time *Medium* had faded into the distance and the dark.

Sunrise came a few hours later, a gradual lightening then a blinding raw incision of light into the scorching world. The cabin windows automatically dimmed, and the AiV's environmentals struggled to keep them cool. Despite wearing the fellalo he'd stripped from the dead Latino, Jo-Jo was hot. The flowing robe with the interior webbing of cooling nanites felt like a shroud.

They discussed the water situation and agreed how best to stretch out their supply.

'They reckon these robes can recycle your piss into something palatable, if you need it,' Randall remarked.

'Got none to spare,' said Jo-Jo. 'Haven't pissed since we left.'

She shrugged and stared out across the endless red desert.

By the time they saw the first glint of water, Jo-Jo's tongue felt twice its normal size. None of them had spoken for several hours.

Randall tapped the map, changing direction.

'What you doin'?'

'We left an AiV on the Principe's island. It's how we got to the biozoon. Mebbe the fuel cell's got some life in it.'

Jo-Jo nodded and blinked away the stinging sweat that ran from his hair into his eyes. The AiV turned on a northerly bearing and followed the coast. The islands beyond were dots of grey relief in a brilliant stretch of ocean. Somehow, it soothed Jo-Jo to see so much water.

'Most of them are nuthin' more than spits of sand,' said Randall, nodding towards the islands.

'You think they made it this far, Capo?' asked Catchut.

The mercenary's ankle injury from being stuck in the Extro goo was festering. Jo-Jo could smell it. Hopefully, Catchut's HealthWatch was enough to over-come the infection. He seemed lucid enough, and without fever.

'Here? Yes. But how they'd get over to the islands?' Randall shrugged. 'Maybe the palazzo'll give us some ideas.'

On the back of that statement, she sent the AiV into a descent. Ahead of them and to the left Jo-Jo saw an island marked with wide-arched buildings, incongruous on the scantly vegetated tract of sand.

'They like things to look like home,' commented Randall, as if reading his mind. 'You been to Latino Crux?'

Jo-Jo nodded. 'Once. The women were too quiet for my liking.'

Randall laughed and gave him a sideways glance. 'Funny how things work out, huh?' She stopped short of saying, funny that you fell for one of them anyway, but the implication was loud and clear.

Jo-Jo bit back a retort. Things had been amicable enough between them on the flight, and he didn't need to fan any flames. He craned forward over the dashboard. 'Any life signs?'

'Don't seem so,' said Randall. 'If there were, they're gone now. I'll land as close to the hangar as I can.'

In descent, Jo-Jo got a clear view of the extent of the Pellegrini holiday chalet, a main building with numerous outhouses connected by covered walkways. The largest of the outhouses had a partially open roof. He took this to be the hangar Randall had mentioned. Wide sand beaches were segmented by empty jetties, and paths wound through the low brush. On the beach closest to the chalet sat another AiV, partially covered in sand.

'It's still there,' said Randall with relief. 'There's a half-arsed infirmary in the chalet. Or there was. Lat used it.' She glanced over her shoulder at Catchut, her face grim.

'He knew the risks, Capo. We all do.'

It was the first time Jo-Jo had ever heard Catchut attempt to reassure Randall.

Losing your crew was a disturbing thing – even Jo-

Jo, who'd spent most of his life working alone, scouting for minerals in the far reaches, understood that. And Rast Randall had lost all of them, apart from Catchut.

'Let's check the infirmary out first,' said Randall. 'See if there's somethin' that'll help yer ankle.'

Catchut nodded his appreciation.

They put down close to the hangar on the wide courtyard and got out, pulling up their hoods against the heat. Randall led the way along the path into the chalet.

The doors were open, and sand piled into the hallway. Every room they walked through was coated in it, and Jo-Jo's throat closed over as he began to wheeze.

'Must've been one helluva dust storm,' Randall observed. 'Enviros are dead too.'

'Not quite,' said Jo-Jo. 'If we can get the doors shut, they might kick in a bit stronger.'

'What's the point?' Randall was already marching purposefully through the sandblasted corridors, her boots crunching loudly in the silence.

The infirmary was as basic as she'd said, but it did offer antibiotic sleeves. They propped Catchut against the central dispenser and hooked him up. Randall wiped sand off the readouts.

'Gonna take a while. Rasterovich, you check through the chalet for food. Closer to dark, we'll head down the beach and get the cell out of the other AiV.'

'Sure,' said Jo-Jo. He hated it when she ordered him around, but they did need to eat. His belly ached from hunger, and he could barely swallow for thirst. The boots he'd taken from the dead Latino back on Pell still chafed his skin, and the fellalo weighed heavily on his weak frame. 'We could fish,' he suggested.

'Easy stuff first.'

Jo-Jo left them and wandered through the deserted rooms. The ones near the infirmary looked like they'd been mostly for entertaining: large spaces littered with overturned chairs and faded parchment-dry brocade wall friezes. Someone – the Saqr, he supposed – had been through and ravaged the rooms, leaving nothing usable or unbroken. Deeper inside he found a staircase that led to bedrooms, some of them furnished to sleep ten or more people. Clearly the Principe had liked to entertain in numbers.

Jo-Jo saw nothing they could use, only ruined furniture and fading paintings. The bathrooms, though, harboured more desalinated water tubes. He put his mouth to one and drank deeply. It poured down his sore swollen throat, causing more pain than relief. When it hit his gut, he doubled up in pain.

When the cramp passed, he trekked down the stairs again, following the corridor to the section behind the infirmary. There he found the kitchen and storerooms. He fingered a scattering of dark shrivelled objects stuck to the metallic work surfaces – food that had decayed and lost its moisture. Even if he could pry the food off, it'd be too tough to chew.

He entered the first storeroom. It was empty and coated with dust.

The second one, though, was lined with shelves stacked with crates. He pulled the nearest crate out and looked at the seal. A dull light blinked in one corner. Whatever was in it was still preserved. His spirits lifted a little. Something they could eat?

When he persuaded the lid to open, he was greeted with the smell of preserving liquids. He quickly resealed it and tried another. This one revealed rows of dehydrated dough balls stacked on top of each other. He dug his hand in and scooped out a round knob. It tasted crumbly and dry and wonderful.

He grabbed some more in the fold of his fellalo and hurried back to the infirmary. Randall was sipping a clear liquid from a tube. She toasted him with bleary eyes.

'Sterilising spirits,' she said. 'Nothin' better.'

Jo-Jo held out his robe. 'Found some bread.'

Randall lowered the tube from her mouth, and Catchut opened his eyes and straightened up.

The three of them sat around the infirmary eating the bread and sharing the raw alcohol.

Soon Jo-Jo felt a whole lot better than he had in a while. 'Reckon we should go back and figure out what the Saqr're doin' with the Extros,' he pronounced after a while.

'You're really wishin' that funeral up, ain't ya?' Randall belched and stretched out on the infirmary bed.

For a split second Jo-Jo considered lying down alongside her, but he stopped himself. He lurched to his feet and went in search of somewhere to sleep. He found it in one of the upstairs bedrooms: a sandy bed with collapsed legs. Despite it being on a slant, it was the best thing he'd lain on in a long time.

Randall shook him awake a few hours later. Before

he could form any words, his stomach had something to say. He rolled onto his side and puked near Randall's feet.

She stepped sideways and gave a hollow laugh. 'Thought you could hold yer liquor better 'n' that.'

Jo-Jo wiped his mouth and glowered at her through blurred eyes. 'You poisoned me.'

'Quit whingeing. It's nearly dark. We gotta look for this fuel cell now, otherwise we'll get stuck here another night.'

Jo-Jo thought of the bed and the storeroom full of crated food. 'Could be worse.'

'A lot worse, if the Extros take it into their headless minds to come after us.'

'Why would they, if they haven't already?'

'Might just be they want to see where we're going first.'

Jo-Jo groaned and rolled out of bed. The alcohol felt as if it had eaten through his stomach all the way up his throat to his skull. Right now, his brain was swimming in a preservative.

He stood up, then sat down again as the world spun.

Randall laughed again and headed for the door. 'We could leave you here.'

She said it mildly – jokingly, even – but Jo-Jo didn't like her jokes. He stood up and followed despite the dark tunnel of threatening unconsciousness. Halfway down the stairs, she turned to him and thrust something into his hand.

He squinted at his palm – dried fruit and more crumbled bread.

He sucked on a fig until his mouth made enough

saliva to swallow, then manfully urged his stomach to let the food enter.

By the time they'd left the chalet and were halfway to the beach, he'd eaten the raisins and the bread. At the tide line his stomach stopped lurching and the tunnel of darkness receded.

'Wait here.' Randall approached the AiV stealthily, as if she half-expected an Extro to emerge.

When she was satisfied it was safe, she motioned Jo-Jo over.

'Seems a long time ago,' she murmured, almost to herself, as he got close. 'Never thought I'd set foot in this shittin' place again.'

She sprang up onto the running board with a speed and agility that he couldn't help but admire. Even gripped by starvation and a host of other deprivations, Randall's body still performed for her.

He copied her but more slowly, pulling himself up by holding the struts, his muscles protesting against the effort. He scraped a thick layer of sand away and peered through the plaspex. There was nothing inside that shouldn't be. Following Randall's lead, he pulled open the passenger-side door and climbed in.

Randall was already fiddling with the com-sole. 'Amazing,' she said. 'It's still intact. Cell's good for a trip back.'

'Maybe we should leave it that way.'

She glanced at him sharply. 'What d'you mean?'

'We've got two working AiVs. Seems better to me than one. Leave one here as a backup in case things get sticky. We know it's here. Know it can get us out of trouble.'

She thought about it for a moment or two. While he waited for her answer, Jo-Jo looked around the cabin. There were trails of dry blood across the back seats and a piece of torn cloth. He reached for the cloth and fingered it. He didn't have to ask Randall to know who it'd belonged to.

'She tore off some of her robe for a bandage,' said Randall without being asked. 'Lat was injured bad. He got pretty attached to her after that. Used to follow her around the ship.'

'Never noticed,' said Jo-Jo, surprised at her openness.

'I did. Used to worry me that he was gettin' obsessed. Thought I might have to step in and ... handle it. Turns out I didn't.' Her head dropped a little, and he saw it again, the keen hurt of having lost so many of her crew.

'No harm in knowin' what's going on around you.' What else was there to say?

She stared at him again. 'What's going on here, then? Why did Jancz bring a ship full of dangerous hungry Saqr to this world to wipe out the Latinos? And why has a fuckin' great drum of Extros turned up here?'

Jo-Jo swallowed, his settling stomach beginning to churn again. 'I say we load this AiV up with some of them crates of food and try and find these survivors. Mebbe they're the ones who can answer you. I only came near this planet following that crazy bastard Tekton.'

The intensity and the heat went out of Randall's stare, her mood swinging on a word or a thought. He knew he should be used to it, but it still startled him.

'We'll do it your way. Take one AiV, leave this one here in case. I say we swap the fuel cells though. This one's got more.'

Jo-Jo nodded. He didn't see any reason to object.

Randall belched up the stench of sterilising alcohol. 'Now let's get moving. See if any of these Latinos made it.'

MIRA

We have contact from a humanesque on Araldis.

Insignia's thought woke Mira from a light doze. She lay on the bed with Nova cradled in her arms, and Wanton just a short reach from them both. 'Which 'esque?' she asked, sitting up carefully so as not to disturb Nova. Then she saw that her child was awake, head rolled towards the Extro.

Nova?

Wanton is dying, Mama.

Si, Nova. Do you understand what that means?

Nova's head rolled back, and the tiny face stared at her, the blue-grey eyes serious. *For Wanton it could mean many things. More an extended limbo than death as we know it.*

Mira floundered to find a way to respond. Nova's escalating mental maturity scared her. And how did she know that the Extro was dying?

I've spoken with it.

Y-you've spoken to Wanton? But it wouldn't respond when I tried.

Wanton apologises. It must conserve energy.

But how—

A different way that does not involve base-level cognition. It has reconsidered, and would like to tell you that the substance it needs to repair itself is quixite.

Quixite? Why wouldn't it tell me before?

It didn't want to interfere with your decisions. It thought that you might endanger yourself finding a source. As you have chosen to come to a place where there is a source, Wanton has reconsidered its position.

Oh. Mira thought for moment. *That is very selfless of Wanton.*

Wanton has much respect for you, Mama. It says that you were caring when its own kind were not. It wishes you peace.

Caring? Mira was surprised to see that even among the Post-Species compassion had its place. But had it been true kindness on her part, or had she simply manipulated the situation so that she could escape? She hardly knew what drove her now, only what she must do – find Vito and the korm, and whoever else had survived.

Mira, you are required to respond to the shortcast. They have threatened aggression if you do not. Insignia's interjection held a tinge of frustration. The biozoon was not privy to her conversation with Nova.

I'm coming.

She took Nova to the buccal with her, and sank into Primo with her baby resting on her chest. It felt reassuring to have Nova's heartbeat so close to her own.

Open the 'cast, she told *Insignia*. 'Who is this?' she asked in her stiffest manner.

'That's my question,' said a rough flat voice.

Mira recognised the tone despite the time that had passed since she'd heard it. When the carabinere had chased her under Franco's orders, she had taken refuge on a hybrid biozoon named Sal. The captain, Jancz, had found and threatened to kill her. In the end he left her in Loisa with an agreement that she would forget their meeting. But she had not. 'What role have you taken in the destruction of my world, Captain Jancz?'

'Who are you?' His voice hoarsened. 'Tell me, or I'll have one of those carriers you're busy dancing around up there trash yer arse. Only reason yer still here is cos you're in a 'zoon.'

'My name is Mira Fedor. Baronessa Mira Fedor.'

The 'cast fell silent as Jancz grappled to place her name. He might not remember her at all, but his moud would. She tried to picture his face, but could only produce a vague image of a thin angular countenance, elongated limbs and unkempt, almost colourless hair.

'So, Baronessa,' he replied eventually. 'What brings you straight into the jaws of the enemy in the middle of a war?'

'I'm carrying an ailing Post-Species who requires assistance.'

'Post-Species, you say. What d'ya mean?'

'I mean one of the Host varieties, whose Host has perished. Its protective casing has been damaged. I believe the material it needs to regenerate is found on Araldis.'

'You don't say?'

Jancz's trite responses irritated her. 'I do, Captain Jancz. Or I would have kept quiet.'

'The Extros are taking over OLOSS. Won't be a planet left that doesn't answer to them.'

'It seems you chose the right side.' She kept her voice cool despite her rising agitation.

'You know your people are dead. All of them,' he added.

Acid rushed up into her gullet. She tasted its sourness and felt the burn.

Mama, the voice is trying to hurt you with its words. Nova's simple thought calmed her.

Si, Nova. This humanesque is cruel.

Are most like him?

Mira hesitated. *Some. You remember Thales?*

From my birthing place. Si.

He is not like that.

I'm glad.

'I'm here for the sake of the Post-Species. Will you help it?' she said into the comm.

This time it was Jancz who hesitated. 'Stand by.'

Mira waited, stroking Nova's back. *What is the status of the Geni-carriers?* she asked *Insignia.*

These are only a small portion of the ones we saw leave their system. The rest have been deployed.

Then he is not bluffing. Is there news of the OLOSS worlds?

No. The silence is most unnerving.

Unnerving? How unlike *Insignia* to use such an evocative word. The biozoon was largely pragmatic, and fatalistic. *Are the Pod safe?*

My link is very faint. But it is there.

Mira felt relieved. The notion of the Pod seemed almost as much 'home' to her as the world they now orbited.

'You are permitted onto Araldis,' said Jancz without preamble. 'We'll shortcast landing coordinates. Don't deviate from them, Baronessa – I'll be trackin' you.'

The 'cast terminated, and Mira indicated to Primo

that she wished to sit upright. The membrane moulded around her to bring her to a sitting position. She slid Nova down onto her knee.

The baby stared up at her. *Will it be safe where we are going, Mama?*

Mira sighed. *You are too young to concern yourself with risk and safety, Nova. That is my job.*

Nova kicked her little arms and legs in what appeared to be a mild protest. *I grew inside your womb. I understand danger.*

Did you . . . was there . . . a moment at which you gained clear thought? She tried to ask the question that had been burning her mind as delicately as possible.

Sí. I'm not sure how to explain it. Tasy-al was there. From the beginning. I could feel Tasy-al around me, around us. It was nice. Warm. Then it became difficult. You needed me, and I could no longer sleep and dream. Nova's thoughts were a little muddled.

When was that, little one?

On the Hub world.

Mira let out a breath. The Post-Species had altered her child, she was sure. *You helped me?* She repeated the thought despite already knowing it to be true. *Through the Hub wall and into the Bare World, and then again, when I would have fallen into the flood.*

It's all right, Mama. I will need you, too. Perhaps soon.

Nova?

What must be.

I don't understand.

I'm hungry now.

Mira sighed and put Nova to her breast.

I have the coordinates, Mira, Insignia said.

She leaned back more deeply into the Primo membrane. As the sensors reclaimed her skin, so an image of Araldis blossomed in her mind.

The image skewed, grew, shrank, then grew again. When the focus defined, she saw an enormous cylindrical object, mesurs wide, resting on the desert rock, its surface pitted from space travel. Hundreds – thousands – of Saqr crawled over it, their maws bent to the skin of the craft, as if either tending or feeding from it.

An AiV and numerous terrain vehicles were parked in a cluster near one edge, close to a wide opening in the ground. As she watched, a barge, like the one they had fled Ipo in, ground its way out of the mouth of the mine cut and along the rocky road towards the large craft.

I know this place.

Your familia called it the Juanita mine, said *Insignia.*

But what is that object covered with Saqr?

Nova paused in her suckling, her face upturned. *Wanton believes it to be* Medium.

You can speak with Wanton from a-a distance?

As I can with you, Mama. Wanton's energies are low, but it has listened to my description and recognises the craft.

Has . . . has Wanton told you what it is?

It's a carrier of what he calls n-non-c-corpo-real Post-Species. Unlike his own Host family. Nova stumbled over *Non-Corporeal,* having several tries at expressing the concept. Her difficulty was a small salve to Mira's anxiety. Perhaps there was yet some real child in the tiny body.

Does Wanton know what they are doing here? Mira asked.

Wanton says they need the same thing as him. A certain mineral.

'Quixite.' Mira said the word aloud. All the pieces of information she'd gathered since leaving Araldis began to arrange in a pattern. 'They destroyed my world for it. But why Araldis? There are other places in Orion where quixite can be found.'

Not like this, Insignia reminded her. *The alloy doesn't normally occur naturally; it has to be manufactured. I have a little of it in my substructure. It helps me configure my body to accommodate my symbiote, and handle res-shift.*

You've never told me that before.

It is very expensive. The Pod has had an agreement with a Post-Species supplier for many, many years.

Is that why you are permitted to trade with them when no other OLOSS members are?

Yes. That is part of it.

I don't understand. If the Post-Species can manufacture it, why would they need this supply?

Naturally occurring quixite has been proven to have certain properties that the manufactured material does not. I imagine the Post-Species have a need.

Nova, could you ask Wanton if it has any knowledge of this.

Insignia and Mira waited while Nova conferred with the injured Extro.

Wanton is unsure. It wonders if maybe it is to do with longevity, in the way your innate genetics offered better Host a-amal-g-am.

Nova stumbled over *amalgam*, as she had *Non-Corporeal*.

Thank Wanton for me, Nova. Tell it that I will do everything I can to secure what it needs.

Wanton knows that already, Nova thought to her gravely. And then, in a way that Mira knew was only for her, she added, *But you must be quick, Mama.*

Mira leaned back fully into Primo and let it subsume her.

Insignia, she thought. *Hurry.*

BALBAO

The guards took Ra away without warning. Not a bad
thing, Balbao thought, for the animosity between him
and Connit was making it all very unpleasant.

The tension dropped, and one by one the others
shared their stories. Balbao learned more about Sammy's
role in Consilience, and how she'd smuggled Tekton
and a young scholar named Thales Berniere aboard.
Hob shared his memories of the Stain Wars, which,
though interesting, went on a little.

Balbao found himself changing the subject by voicing
a question that had been burning his tongue.

'Miranda, what did Lasper Farr mean by thanking
you? What was the virus he mentioned?'

Miranda, who had begun to revive after several tubes
of water and some repose, visibly flagged; she looked
to Jise for support.

'We have long had a policy of not discussing our
personal projects for the Entity,' said Jise limply.

Balbao scowled. 'A moot point at this stage, tyro.
The Entity is gone, and sharing knowledge may be our
only means of survival.'

Sammy, Hob and Connit said nothing but watched
intently.

Eventually, Miranda cleared her throat. When she

spoke, it was only in a whisper. 'My brief from the Entity was "Show transformation."'

The others looked at each other, puzzled.

'That's all it said. From what Jise has told me and from what I can gather, it was the same for all of us. I interpreted within the only context I could – the medical model. Pathology is my special interest area, so I created a virus that changed – transformed – humanesque brain function. I'm embarrassed to say that Sole was not impressed, so I sold the virus on the open market. It was bought by an 'esque on Scolar. That's all I know.'

'What exactly did the virus do?'

She rubbed her chins self-consciously and sighed. 'It affects the orbito-frontal lobes, which manage decision-making. Potentially, it can change the process by which 'esques view the world. The brain has an unlimited capacity to learn. If you change one function, others are affected.'

'That sounds dangerous, in the wrong hands.' Balbao did not bother to keep the accusation from his tone.

She flushed. 'I'd used up my entire stipend and needed funds. They are ridiculously mean for what is required. How could I embark on another project without financial resources?'

Balbao reflected bitterly for a moment on the flaw in the whole tyro scheme. It was an upscale version of the pressure placed upon most academics in studiums. Funds meant professional survival – they became an end instead of a means. He understood Miranda's dilemma, but that didn't excuse her from selling something dangerous to the highest bidder.

His disdain of the tyros changed into something more deep-seated and unforgiving. It also triggered an uncomfortable notion. 'Labile, what was your project for Sole?'

Farr's biological son stared at his hands, taking his time to answer. 'My brief was "Show strength." I was designing a structure that could withstand force.'

'Jise?'

Jise was nodding to himself, as if working through an internal monologue. When it was time to speak, though, he dropped his head as if embarrassed. '"Show truth." And the truth of *that* is that I had not progressed far. I found it impossible to capture the concept. I know law and rules and evidence, but they are not relevant to the truth. The relativity of truth makes it elusive.'

Miranda stared at him. 'But you told me that—'

Jise gestured weakly. 'You were doing so well. I didn't want you pitying me, or trying to help.'

She lifted her hand and brushed his forehead lightly with her fingertips. 'I fear we've been incredibly foolish, spending our time pleasing a creature that cares little for anything.'

Balbao listened intently. There was more to this than they could see. 'Have you ever thought that the Entity had a purpose? Other than interacting with us? Other than learning about us?'

'Other than that?' echoed Jise. 'No. I thought that we were a novelty. Something it hadn't encountered before. I believed in its curiosity. Mirroring ours, I suppose.'

'My thoughts were similar,' said Miranda. She held Jise's hand again. They were like peas in a large pod, thought Balbao: both fleshy and indulgent with sharp self-centred minds.

Connit climbed off his bunk and moved to lean against the solid wall. 'I see what you mean, Balbao. But what use is that notion? We don't know what it asked the others for, and even if Ra tells us about his project – this device he speaks of – three of us have perished on Belle-Monde, and Tekton . . . Crux knows where the devious fellow is, or what he has done.'

Sammy and Hob, who had been silent throughout, watched Connit with clear fascination. Neither had known, Balbao guessed, that Commander Farr had offspring.

'You don't hold with your father's beliefs, then, young 'un?' blurted out Sammy.

Connit looked at her, confused and a little irritated. 'If you're speaking to me, my name is Labile or Connit. I'm not my father, nor do I wish to follow his path.'

'Where do yer figure about the scheme of things? You with OLOSS or Consilience?'

Connit looked momentarily flustered. His lean face flushed with emotion of some kind. 'That would be none of your business and irrelevant to our current conversation.'

'None of me business, maybe,' said Sammy, 'but pretty damn relevant, to my mind.'

'What do you mean?' asked Balbao.

Sammy looked at Hob, who nodded encouragingly.

'Well,' she began, in a voice so low that they craned forward to hear her. 'Things go like this . . .'

TRIN

Trin saw Djeserit before she saw him. She was using the moonlight to pick her way slowly over and around boulders.

'Djes,' he called softly, so as not to startle her.

'Trinder!' Her gasp of relief lifted him a little from his exhaustion. He had known she would look for him, but expected her to have followed his path, not anticipated it.

She scrambled quickly to reach him and threw her arms around his waist. He leaned against her, taking a moment to share his weight and feel her body against his.

'Juno has gone the other way, following the track he thought you would take.'

'And you chose to do the opposite.'

She looked up at him. Her skin had dried out and regained its papery texture now she was spending less time in the water, and he could see traces of blood and bruising.

'You've been injured?'

She leaned back from him. 'And you, Principe . . . your face and hair.' She reached up to touch the clotted mess. 'Did you fall?'

'I was pushed.' He couldn't keep the angry tremor from his voice.

'Innis?' she whispered.

He gripped her arms and pulled them both down onto a rock. 'How do you know that?'

'He came back to the caves some time after you left. He told us he'd gone out looking for food, and on his way back heard a noise and saw you fall. He said that your body was lost, that you were dead.'

She began to cry, soft noises and tiny, spare tears, as though her system could barely stand to lose the water.

'Did you believe him?'

'Juno was suspicious. He insisted that Innis show them.'

'And you came alone, the other way?'

'Not alone. Joe is with me. He went higher, to look for you there.' She pointed.

'Joe Scali is with you?' Trin's relief abated, and suspicion replaced it. He hated the thought of Joe alone with Djes again.

She felt the change in his manner, his stiffening.

'Trinder?'

He nearly told her how he felt – the jealousy born from seeing her with Joe on the beach that night – but pride and wariness stopped him. He was Principe.

'We must get back. Innis Mulravey will be called to answer. And I have news.'

'You found water?' Her voice lifted.

'Si. Water and something—' He broke off as little rocks began to tumble down from above.

'Joe,' Djes called out. 'I've found him! The Principe is here.'

They waited in silence as more rocks skittered past them, and Joe Scali slid and climbed his way down to where they sat.

'Over here,' Trin called him closer.

'Principe,' gasped Joe as he reached them. He threw his arms around Trin with relief. 'I knew he lied.'

Trin grasped Scali's shoulders briefly and then pushed him away. 'Let's hurry or the light will beat us.'

Djes stood and took his hand. 'Lean on me,' she said.

He dearly wanted to. Every part of his body hurt, but the worst was his head. With each movement, shocks of pain shot up from his neck and shoulders. Yet leaning on Djes was something he couldn't do. He must never do. As it was, too many of them saw her as his strength.

They reached the caves as Leah lightened the sky from a warm black to a heat-heavy grey. Tivi Scali was on sentry duty and shouted to all those settling for daytime sleep.

By the time Trinder, Djes and Joe had reached the shady protection of the overhang, everyone had assembled.

Trin interrupted exclamations and questions with an abruptly raised hand. 'Where is Innis Mulravey?' he demanded.

'He and Juno have not returned,' said Tivi.

'My brother said he saw you dead,' added Cass Mulravey. She pushed her way to the front of those gathered, Mira Fedor's 'bino in her arms. The baby had an unworldly look about him: overly thin, like the rest of them, with large serious eyes. Even now, with so many concerns on his mind, the 'bino made Trin uncomfortable.

'Your brother stole up behind me and pushed me from a rock,' Trin declared with vehemence.

'No!' The denial ripped from the woman in a way that sounded part apology.

Trin glared at her. 'At first dark the carabinere will look for them both.' He glanced at Tivi. 'Take the spears.'

'No—' This came from Cass Mulravey again, but another voice drowned out hers.

'Principe? What of Juno?' asked Josefia Genarro. She squeezed through the crowd to stand alongside Tivi. 'What if he is—'

'Juno can care for himself, Josefia,' said Trin firmly. They could do nothing about it during the light but hope that Juno was safe and had found shade.

'You can't jus' accuse Innis of tryin' to murder you,' said an angry voice.

Trin located the source of it, standing behind Cass Mulravey: the tall woman, Liesl, who'd been sleeping with Innis.

'He ain't even here to defend himself,' Liesl added.

Trin touched the crust of blood in his hair. 'And I was not able to defend *my*self when he pushed me from behind, hoping to murder me.'

'Don't say that about him!' she shouted.

Cass Mulravey grabbed her wrist, twisting it, urging quiet.

But even Mulravey's action didn't stop the wave of righteous anger that poured from Trin. 'I am Principe!' he roared back at Liesl. 'I do not lie!'

He'd never shown them such raw anger before, but this woman's bald accusation inflamed him beyond thought.

A tension overtook the group; wary eyes glanced around.

Djes put a calming hand on Trin's arm. 'We should all rest. The Principe is injured and hungry, and must be tended.'

Liesl looked as if she wanted to say more, but Cass Mulravey stepped in front of her. 'We'll bring some food in.'

Cass and Djes nodded to each other, and Trin felt a swell of misgiving – as if they indeed lead the survivors, not he. Their complicity worried him, and yet he was too exhausted to think more about it.

Instead, he walked stiffly into the cave, mollified by the fact that that at least the refugees parted respectfully to let him through. Inside the cave he turned and looked back at them. Most were watching him still, except Mulravey, who was looking at Josefia Genarro. 'I've found more water,' he said. 'We need no longer carry it up the mountain and risk the ligs.'

A small cheer rose.

Trin found his spot in the cave and sank gratefully onto the brush bed, knowing he had been right to give the news of the water last.

Djes followed him in with some berries and dried fish. As he ate, she tried to tend to his head wound, but he waved her away. He needed sleep first.

She woke him later by gripping his hand, her hot breath close to his ear. 'Trin.'

He rolled towards her, reaching to pull her closer.

She resisted, speaking again. 'Liesl's made trouble while you've been resting. A group of them are leaving.'

Trin struggled to sit up, his skin stinging and his head aching.

Djes handed him a shell of water, which he swallowed quickly to ease his sore throat. The cave was dimmer than when he'd laid down to sleep, and he could see the pinprick lights in the night sky through the opening.

'What's happening?' he asked her, to be sure.

'Innis is back. He and Liesl have persuaded some to leave with them and find another part of the island.'

'Juno?'

'Innis says they became separated.'

Fury coursed through Trin in an instant. 'Is Cass Mulravey siding with him?'

'No, not yet, but you should come now.'

Trin used the wall to help him to his feet. He felt hot and dizzy and his tongue seemed swollen. A fever?

'What is it?' whispered Djes.

He pushed away from the wall. 'Nothing.'

There was no one else in the cave. The whole group was outside, standing in a ragged circle.

As he drew closer, a wave of nausea beset Trin. He turned his head and swallowed the vomit that rose up his throat.

No one seemed to notice; they were too concerned with their argument.

'You can't take our food,' said one of the Pablo miners.

'We worked for it. We're entitled to some,' said Liesl. Trin could see Innis next to her, gaunt and belligerent and filthy. He held a spear in one hand and a club in the other.

The 'esque on his other side was one of theirs. Marrat was his name, Trin thought; he'd been a bullish type in earlier times. Now he was as lean and weak as the rest of them.

Several of the women stood behind Liesl, including Tina Galiotto, his mardre's servant. Just under a third of their females – too many to lose.

Kristo stood opposite Innis, with Cass Mulravey next to him.

'There's too few of us for this, Innis,' said Kristo. 'Use yer brains. We need each other to survive.'

'I'm sick of being kicked around,' Innis shot back.

'Lennie.' Cass used her pet name for him. 'Where've you been?'

'I've been thinkin' and lookin' around on my own. Not because I've bin *told* to do it. Crux, Kristo, ain't you had enough? Or've you gone soft on aristos, like you did with that high and mighty bitch Mira Fedor? I shoulda stitched her up proper back in Ipo. Then she wouldn't have gotten away and left the rest of us here to fr—'

Kristo launched himself at Innis, taking him full in the chest. They fell together, tumbling into Marrat and the women behind him.

Trin's madre, Jilda, screamed, and suddenly everyone was moving – pushing, shoving or shouting.

It's been coming. The thought hit Trin's consciousness as he stepped into the melee. *Now we've stopped running.*

'Tivi! Joe!' he bellowed. 'Arrest Innis Mulravey.'

Both men detached themselves from the melee and hastened into one of the caves. They reappeared within a few heartbeats, armed with spears and clubs of their own.

Making weapons was a mistake. Another glancing thought. *No*, he thought again. *This was coming.*

Someone knocked him forward to his knees. Josefia Genarro moaned and cursed in his ear, scrambling to get off him. Trin twisted and took her arm, helping them both up.

Liesl stood, glaring at them, fists half-raised. She kicked out at Josefia, catching her in the thigh. Before Trin could intervene, Josefia threw herself at the taller woman in much the same way as Kristo had at Innis.

Trin jerked his head around. Kristo had his hands around Innis's throat. Marrat was kicking Kristo.

Tivi and Joe ran across, shouting, readying their spears.

Trin looked back. The korm had intervened, pinning Liesl to the ground at Djeserit's instruction. Josefia was bleeding from the nose and mouth.

Trin gazed between the groups, caught by indecision. Then Juno Genarro burst back into the clearing.

'Principe! He tried to kill me! Innis tried to kill me.' Blood smeared his robe and his face.

Before Trin could respond, Tivi Scali's voice rose above the rest. 'Let go, Kristo,' he bellowed. 'Let go, so I can stick him.'

Kristo let go of Innis's throat and rolled away, but Innis responded by rolling after him, clawing at him.

Tivi Scali raised the spear. 'Let go of 'im, you bastard,' Tivi screamed.

Cass Mulravey's ragazzo bolted from behind his mother to throw himself across his uncle.

'Tivi!' roared Trin.

But it was too late. The young carabinere brought the spear down in a two-handed stab.

It pierced the child below his ribcage. Though the

ragazzo never uttered a noise, Cass Mulravey's scream pierced through every other sound.

'Caro!' she cried. She broke away from where she knelt over Liesl and ran down.

But the ragazzo lay limp across his tio, a thin bundle of bones with the life fading quickly from it.

Cass felt for his pulse and gave a pained moan. She wrenched the spear out and threw it away, and then she gently lifted him from where he lay atop Innis.

Silence fell over the group as they watched the distraught woman cradle her 'bino. She rocked back and forth on her knees, willing life back into him.

Tivi Scali fell down beside her and began sobbing apologies, but Cass didn't seem to hear him. Nor did she notice Innis crawl to her side and stare dully at the thin body.

A weight of despair and guilt settled on Trin. What had he set in motion by ordering them to make the spears? He should have dealt with Innis Mulravey differently, out of sight. Now what would happen?

He glanced around at the faces. Several of the women had hastened to Cass Mulravey's side, while others stood where they were, lit by the moon-glow. He saw tears or anger on their faces. Even Djes seemed lost, offering him neither counsel nor comfort.

Then a noise wrenched all of their attention to the light-studded sky above – an AiV flying low over the mountainside.

'Into the caves!' called Trin.

They all moved except Kristo, Cass Mulravey and Tivi Scali. Even Innis got shakily to his feet and staggered towards Liesl, who helped him inside.

Trin slid down the rocks to the others. 'We must get out of sight.'

But none of them responded.

The AiV sounded closer, circling back.

Trin grabbed Tivi's arm. 'It was an accident, Carabinere. Tragic, but just so. We must shelter now.'

Cass Mulravey stared at Tivi, ignoring Trin. She opened her mouth to speak but only an incoherent noise escaped.

'Get beneath the bushes.' Awkwardly, Trin grasped Cass Mulravey's shoulders and tried to pull her down towards cover. The woman stumbled, almost dropping the ragazzo's body.

Tivi Scali reacted by diving forward to catch the child.

Trin felt warm blood from the spear wound splatter across his face. Tivi and Cass were covered in it.

Then a light shot down from the belly of the hovering AiV, capturing them, and the dead 'bino, in its circle.

Jo-Jo Rasterovich

'Fuel cell's low,' said Randall. 'We need to turn back.'

'Just one sweep,' Jo-Jo urged. 'Otherwise the cell's been wasted. We'll have to come back again.'

Their search had taken them north-east over scattered islands, most of them flat and without vegetation. The most likely location turned out to be a largish tract of land at low tide that then diminished on the swell. They landed and explored it during the hour right after sunset. Though the island harboured no 'esques, they stretched out in the sand to sleep for a few hours.

Randall woke them well before light, and they continued on south to the other likely location. Just short of sunrise, Randall announced that they must turn back.

'No,' cried Jo-Jo, pointing out of his window. 'There.'

Randall grunted and held her line, taking them down lower.

A surge of hope livened Jo-Jo's tired body. This island was heavily vegetated and dominated by a small mountain.

'Looks better'n the last one, Capo,' remarked Catchut.

'Hope so,' said Randall. 'Most like we'll be stuck on here for ever. This cell's probably not gonna get us back.'

Jo-Jo saw them first: a scattered group of figures on the mountain crest, scrambling toward cave mouths.

'There!' He pointed again.

'I'll sweep back.' Randall dragged her finger around the screen, and the AiV obediently circled. This time, though, she brought them in to hover just above the crest of the peak, spotlights blazing.

Most of the figures had disappeared, leaving only a small group clustered together. One of them, a woman, huddled over the limp figure of a child. Three others, adult 'esques, stared up at the AiV.

'Looks like Cass Mulravey, Capo,' said Catchut.

'Think yer right, Cat. Don't know the others.'

'Bunch of skeletons, whoever they are.'

'Who is she?' asked Jo-Jo.

'Friend of Fedor's. They came into Ipo together. Tough woman. Not surprised she's still alive.'

A friend of Fedor's. That knowledge somehow fanned Jo-Jo's optimism. 'Let's land.'

'Cat,' said Randall, 'you stay on board.'

The light was approaching rapidly as Randall dropped the AiV onto a small cleared area just above Mulravey and the others. The vehicle thunked hard onto the uneven rock and teetered for a moment, as if it might topple.

Jo-Jo let go of a breath when it settled.

Unworried, Randall threw off her harness and slid the door back. 'Lemme go first. She'll know me.'

She jumped down lightly, despite the hours cooped up in the AiV, and stepped nimbly down the hill. 'Cass Mulravey.'

Jo-Jo climbed more slowly out of the passenger side.

He let his legs adjust to weight and movement before demanding anything from them. As he edged around the AiV to stand by Randall, he noticed something amiss. Blood. All over the woman and two of the men.

A thin, crimson-skinned 'esque with an aquiline nose that dominated his gaunt hawkish face stood up. 'Who are you?' he demanded.

Randall ignored him. 'Cass. Don't you know me?'

The woman slowly lifted her head. Her face was ravaged – dark brown and blistered with sun exposure – but her expression was the shocking thing: heart-broken and defeated. The child she held was dead.

She licked her lips and whispered, 'Rast Randall?'

'What's happened, Cass?' asked Randall softly.

'He's ... he's ...' She couldn't bring herself to say it.

'I'm Principe Trinder Pellegrini. Who are you that you wear Pellegrini fellalos?'

This time Randall directed her gaze to him. 'So Franco's pup did survive. Fedor was right.'

'You know Baronessa Fedor?'

Randall nodded to Jo-Jo, and back at Catchut in the AiV. 'We all do. She's the reason we're here. She told us about you.'

'Is she alive? Does she bring help?'

'Can't answer either of those questions. But maybe there're some others I can.'

The Principe glanced up into the sky. 'Then we should talk inside the cave. Sunrise is close.'

Randall gestured with her hand, indicating that she would follow him. She and Jo-Jo waited as they passed: Trin Pellegrini first, Cass, carrying her dead child, and then the two others who had been standing either side of her. The latter were still casting angry stares at each other.

Jo-Jo tried to work out what had happened. The way Randall's eyes were flickering around, she was too. She signalled for Catchut to follow them. The AiV would soon be too hot to stay inside without the engine to cool it.

They were greeted at the entrance to the caves by a ragged group of 'esques and one emaciated korm, who towered above them all.

The survivors huddled as close as they could to the growing light, curious about the newcomers. As Jo-Jo cast his gaze around the semicircle, one of them stood out from them in both appearance and manner. She was slim without being thin, and her facial skin was tight as a mask, flattening her nose and eyes. Not attractive, and yet something about her seemed . . . significant.

He knew he was right when Trin Pellegrini moved to stand close to her.

The girl looked him and Randall over, then immediately left Trin's side to go to the woman, Cass Mulravey, leading her away into the cave's darkness. Some of the other women followed, and the circle closed again.

'There was an accident,' Pellegrini explained.

Jo-Jo felt the weight of unsaid things in their tense manner; saw the complex mix of expressions on the watching faces. What had these people been through to survive?

'Do you have water?' asked Randall.

'Of course.' Trin nodded to one of the women. No one spoke until she returned with three shells of water.

Jo-Jo drank quickly. The liquid smelled of fish, just like the cave itself. The air burned despite the cave's shade, and he longed to be back in the sky, in the AiV's cooler cockpit.

'How did you find us?' said Pellegrini finally.

'Could take a while in the telling,' said Randall. 'Might be you want to sit down.'

Pellegrini hesitated, then agreed. 'We have a meal at this time. Before we sleep. Eat with us, and talk.'

It was not an invitation.

Randall nodded on behalf of all of them.

The group shuffled around until they were all seated close enough to the cave mouth to see.

'Not all of you have cooling robes. How can you stand it?' Jo-Jo asked, thinking it was time he spoke.

'If you keep out of the direct sun, it's bearable after a period of adjustment. We manage better than visitors who don't have our melatonin-rich skin,' said Pellegrini. 'Your name?'

To his surprise, Randall didn't jump in, but waited for him to answer.

'I'm Josef Rasterovich. Not a survivor from this terrible invasion, but a new arrival.'

A murmur went around the group which Pellegrini silenced with a word. The young Latino Principe spoke like a true leader.

'Before I tell you more, OLOSS does know what happened here,' Jo-Jo added.

'Tell us how you got here,' demanded Pellegrini.

Jo-Jo glanced at Randall. She'd folded her arms and

was leaning back against the rock wall. She seemed calm and attentive, but he knew she was cataloguing everything she could see. He had to give her time to gather information. Get the group members to reveal something about themselves.

'We were hired to escort your Baronessa Fedor to a place called Rho Junction. She was trying to make a deal to get you people rescued. OLOSS didn't want to do anything in a hurry, and she didn't want to wait, so she was using other means. Shit happened, and we ended up stranded on an Extro craft – fuckin' weird drum-shaped thing. Damn thing landed here a few days ago. We managed to get away. Found a flyer up on the mountain, and flew ourselves here. Fedor had said you'd head to the islands.'

'And Mira?' Pellegrini's voice rose.

'She got taken by Extros on Rho Junction.'

'She is dead?'

'No. At least we don't believe so.' He didn't tell them about the biozoon signature that they'd picked up with the com-cast or his feeling it was Fedor. Mira hadn't said much directly to him, but he knew she didn't hold Trin Pellegrini in high regard.

'She tried to find us help?' This came from Cass Mulravey. She and the girl Jo-Jo had noticed earlier had returned to the circle. Even in the dim light, Mulravey's face was distorted with anguish, though her voice sounded steady. She stepped to the front and sat down. 'I knew she wouldn't leave Vito. Or us.'

'Vito?' Jo-Jo glanced between Mulravey and Pellegrini.

'Her 'bino,' said Mulravey.

'Not her own,' corrected the young Principe. 'An adopted ragazzo.'

Randall made a slight jerking movement, as though someone had scraped a knife against her skin. Jo-Jo could just make out the tight outline of her jaw.

'And you?' Pellegrini asked Randall directly. 'What were you doing on Araldis?'

'Franco was expecting trouble. Brought us in to assess things.' She made a dry sound. 'Seems he left it too late.'

'My papa hired mercenaries?'

'Yep.'

'Are you saying he knew about the invasion? About the Saqr?'

'Nope.' She shook her head slowly. 'But he knew something was wrong. Maybe some deals he'd done had come back on him.'

The group fell silent as they digested this, particularly the young Principe, who seemed lost in thought for a few moments.

'How did you get off Araldis during the invasion?'

'Fedor. Someone gave her an AiV and sent her looking for your flagship.' She stared straight at Pellegrini. Jo-Jo didn't need to see her face clearly to read the hostility. 'She picked us up on the way. We were caught in a firefight out in the desert, with the Saqr. She could have left us for dead. But she didn't. That's not her way.'

'*You sent her!*' burst out Mulravey. She spoke to all of them, but her face turned towards Trin. 'She didn't abandon us. You sent her.'

'No,' said Pellegrini, seeking the attention of the girl next to Mulravey. 'Djes, that's not how it was.'

Jess? Jo-Jo's mind threw out an anchor. That was what Bethany had called her daughter. He scrambled to remember the girl's description and came up empty, other than the half-Miolaquan heritage. He wanted the girl to step closer to the light, so he could decide if the strangeness he'd noticed before fitted with being part fish.

'It's all she talked about, in fact,' added Randall. 'Finding a way to get back here to help you all.'

The survivors began to murmur among themselves again.

'Quiet!' Pellegrini ordered.

Jo-Jo clamped his lips together. The Principe applied his arrogant manner with ease, and mostly they seemed ready to accept it.

'You've seen the lights in the night sky? Tell us what is happening. Is it OLOSS?' the Principe asked.

Jo-Jo waited for Randall, but she didn't say anything. After a moment, he spoke. 'We got no way of really knowing, but we can guess. We think the Extros have made a move to invade the OLOSS worlds – the same way they did here.'

'So we're at war, like before. Does that mean there'll be no help?' said a woman from the back.

'Can't honestly answer that,' said Jo-Jo.

Randall suddenly spoke up. 'We flew over somethin' brewin' near one of the mines. The Saqr are all over it. Mebbe we can learn somethin' from there.'

'You're suggesting we go and spy on them?' asked the girl, Djes.

'Recon,' said Randall. 'Yeah. If OLOSS is at war with the Extros, then we need to do what we—'

'We're fortunate to be alive,' interjected Pellegrini. 'The toll to reach safety has been significant. We are not mercenaries. It would not serve us to antagonise our invaders; there are not enough of us to fight. I will not allow it.' He ground out the last of his words with grim authority.

'Seems mebbe the others might like a say in that.' Randall tone was sardonic.

'We have barely enough to eat. We are too weak to contemplate such a notion.'

'You want to starve to death or die of some disease while the rest of Orion fights?'

Randall was deliberately baiting him. They had no way to ferry any of the survivors back to the mines. The AiV would barely make one trip, let alone several. Yet Randall was seeding dissent.

'You should rest now,' said Pellegrini. 'We'll talk more when everyone has slept.' He stood up. 'Djes, find them beds.'

On his cue, the group dispersed; some disappeared past the narrow overhang into the next cave.

The girl, Djes, took them to an area on one side of the cave, a little way in from the entrance. An 'esque followed them with an armful of brush. 'We shake it out so there are no insects. You can sleep in peace,' she said, as the 'esque divided the brush into three piles.

Randall and Catchut dropped onto their piles, but Jo-Jo sidled close to the girl. 'Djes,' he said softly. 'Is your mother Bethany Ionil?'

She stiffened. He smelt a waft of something salty from her, as though she'd been shocked into exuding a scent. 'You know my mother?'

Jo-Jo took a deep breath to counteract a surge of emotion. Beth's daughter was alive. 'I do.'

'Then keep away from me.' She turned and walked deeper into the cave.

The emotion trickled out of him, and he sank onto the brush alongside Randall. What else could he have expected? Beth had abandoned her.

'Good job,' said Randall with quiet sarcasm. 'Didn't her mother dump her here?'

'How did you know that?' demanded Jo-Jo in a fierce whisper.

Randall rolled away from him without answering. He thought he heard her chuckle. Or it could have been a snore.

He lay on his back, ignoring the prickling of the brush. The cave harboured a confusion of smells, but unwashed bodies and the pungent odour of fish battled for highest honours. No doubt that was how they'd survived – on fish.

He thought about Bethany as people muttered and moved about him. Bethany had made him swear that he would find her daughter and tell her how her mother regretted what she'd done. When he'd agreed to that, he'd never for a moment thought that his path would actually cross with Bethany's daughter's. It seemed stranger than he could imagine, and too difficult to fathom how fate had brought him here.

But was it fate?

Some odd notion lurking in his subconscious thought

otherwise. A notion? Or a presence? Fatigue made it hard to tell, and despite the strange surroundings and the presence of half-starved strangers, tiredness won over everything else and soon he was asleep.

THALES

Thales woke in darkness, pain shooting up the side of his neck. 'Fariss.'

'Here,' she whispered.

He blinked and wiped his eyes, trying to clear his vision. It didn't help much. 'Where are you?'

'Up near the hatch. Found some lumps in the side of the catoplasma, like you said. Can get real close to the lid, but something heavy's on it.'

Thales levered himself upright and tried to rub the crick from his neck. He'd been sleeping, curled around, on the floor of the tank. 'I could get on your—'

'Sssh!' she said. 'C'n hear somethin'.'

Thales's heart pounded, sending a rush through his body. He bent down and rubbed circulation back into his legs. Had the Politics found them?

The hatch opened without preamble, and a light flashed down on them. He saw Fariss braced against the wall, ready to spring.

'Thales Berniere?' said someone from above.

He recognised the voice, vaguely. 'Who is it? I c-can't s-see you.'

The light moved, shining away from his eyes and onto a rope ladder which dropped into the space between him and Fariss.

'Climb, Thales. Hurry.'

The voice again. He knew it . . . 'Magdalen?'

'Yes.'

Thales grabbed the bottom of the rope ladder. 'Fariss. Come on.'

The soldier slid down from her vantage point and boosted him up several rungs. As he laboured up the moving ladder to the lip of the tank, she was behind him, nudging his feet.

Then suddenly they were both outside, breathing clear night air, peering into the dark. Magdalen had extinguished her light, and he could barely make out her outline in the moonless sky.

She took his hand. 'Follow, don't speak.'

He reached for Fariss and felt better when her hand engulfed his. They walked slowly, connected like this, along the side of the house and through the lanes to the edge of the settlement. Magdalen led them with little hesitation, as if she'd practised this dark walk many times.

Not a word passed between them until they belted themselves into a small AiV. Even then, as they lifted into the sky above the town, Thales could barely believe their escape.

Finally, Magdalen turned from the front seat to speak. Thales could see her face a little better now. She was still as slim and pale as he remembered: a similar build to Rene, a one-time friend of his wife's who had chosen a different philosophical path from them both.

'This is Linnea,' she said, indicating the female pilot. 'She was told that you asked for her in the town. She contacted me. Villon must have been watching over you, Thales. Your escape from the robes was more blessed than earned.'

'How can I thank you, Magdalen? This is Fariss O'Dea, my . . . companion.'

Magdalen raised an eyebrow at the soldier bent almost double so as to fit her tall frame into the cabin. 'Your tastes have changed, Thales.'

'Many things about me have changed, Magdalen. I've seen and heard much while I've been away from Scolar.'

Magdalen nodded. 'I have heard some of it. But you must tell me all.'

'How could you have heard?'

'We have some informants among the Sophos personal guard.'

'We?'

'It is not only you who has experienced change, Scholar Thales. Our world is—'

'Our world is being run by Sophos who are not capable.'

Magdalen made a dry sound. 'And you believe them to be infected by some virus.'

'I don't believe, I know. Villon . . . believed . . .'

'Villon? Villon is dead!' Magdalen exclaimed.

'Now he is, but not then.' Thales pressed his fingers against his eyes. 'Magdalen, there is so much I can – will – tell you, but the most important must take precedence. The Post-Species invasion is very real, and they'll destroy us if the shift sphere isn't disabled. You saw the 'casts.'

'The Eclectics believe the same thing,' she agreed.

'So how do we do it?' asked Fariss.

'Get to Scolar station,' said the pilot, Linnea.

They all stared at her. 'I worked as an IN tech for a while.' She shrugged. 'Moved on to essential services a little while ago. Pays more, and comes with transport. Means I get to spend time at home.'

Fariss grinned wide at that. 'An IN tech. Bonus.'

'You know how to shut down the sphere?' Thales asked Linnea.

'No,' the pilot replied. 'But I know how to get up there. Did the shuttle run more times than I could count.'

'Scolar station sounds good to me,' drawled Fariss.

Thales took her hand in a gesture of calm determination. He knew what he wanted to do: the same thing Villon had wanted. 'We will close down the sphere. And then deal with the Sophos.'

MIRA

Mira felt an odd pressure in her head. The beginnings of a headache perhaps, or an adjustment to having Nova's mind so close to hers. It left her quite detached as she climbed out of the egress scale into the sunset-soaked desert. Leah was below the horizon, but the ambient light was still bright and burning hot.

She took a moment to absorb the impact of the overwhelming heat, and the knowledge that she was home. *Insignia* had settled on a dune to the north of the Juanita mine, its scarred outer skin glistening darkly against the red sand.

Close by was another biozoon, a hybrid that Mira recognised by sense rather than sight. *Sal.*

To the south lay another huge, almost endless object, cylindrical in shape and half-buried in the sand. Mira's detachment faded a little as she recognised the creatures gathered in clusters across its hull.

What is it called? she asked *Insignia.*

Medium. *I docked with it when I was searching for you in Post-Species space. I should add that the other humanesques went aboard.*

Josef and Rast Randall? Her heart beat faster. Were they still there? Still alive? She would be pleased to see them.

Yes. Them, and the other two.

Mira paused, taking a moment to recall their names. Latourn and Catchut. So much had happened in between, she'd almost forgotten Randall's crew.

Mama, Wanton says the Non-Corporeal ship may be dangerous. Wanton cannot guarantee their reaction to you.

Mira felt inside the pocket of the new fellala she'd taken from *Insignia*'s storage. Wanton lay at the bottom of it, its normally slick casing grainy to the touch. It had subsumed its last bead of mycose before leaving the biozoon. Its present supply would only last hours. She'd washed the traces of mycose away with gloved hands before placing it in her robe.

Now she squeezed its casing gently in reassurance. 'Baronessa?'

The voice called from a terrain vehicle already parked in the shade of the biozoon. The figure inside was shrouded, but she knew it was Jancz.

She closed her hood. The TerV pulled in closer, and the passenger door opened.

Mira settled inside without a word.

They drove the dune-filled distance to the Post-Species ship. When Jancz stopped just short of the towering sides, Mira broke the silence.

'You remember me?' she asked.

'You made a deal with me. Safe passage to Loisa for forgetting that we'd met. You kept your word. 'Esques don't often do that; I'm impressed. That's part of the reason you're down here, not floating around in the mess of your detonated 'zoon.'

'Part of the reason?'

'The other part is not for me to say.'

Mira fought to keep the image of *Insignia* being annihilated from clouding her thoughts. 'The Post-Species
corporeal that I carry requires immediate assistance.
Why have you stopped here?'

He turned the TerV's cooler up to maximum and
dimmed the windows. 'Show me your face.'

Mira unsealed the hood and waited for him to do
the same. His face was less elongated than she remembered, but his eyes were still as cool and dispassionate.

'As you can see, I am the same person,' she said.

'My . . . it's been a while since I've seen a female
'esque.' His voice hoarsened.

'I imagine that is to be expected when you choose
as you have,' Mira returned.

'Are you judging me, Baronessa? I'd be careful of
doing that. You're the one aiding an injured Extro for
no good reason. My reasons are quite logical.'

She stared into his eyes. 'Then I hope they are
enough to wipe out the memory of the worlds being
destroyed on your account.'

'Not everyone views the new order of things as you
do.' His expression smoothed out and he pointed to a
spot in the apparently seamless hull. 'I'll take you there.
You're on your own then.'

'Why are the Post-Species here? Why is this supply
of quixite so important that they would send Saqr to
invade my world?' She thought to ask him about Josef
and the others, then changed her mind. It was possible
he didn't know of them, and in that case it would be
better if it remained that way.

Jancz's hands moved restlessly, and his glance strayed
to the marker pegs that signalled the opening to the

Juanita mine. 'They got plans. Their craft can't self-repair for as long as they'd like. It's a problem they need to fix.'

Mira thought of the Hub world. 'But they have self-maintaining technology. I – I've seen it.'

'Where there's oxygen, yeah. But out in the vac's a different thing.'

'Couldn't they have just *bought* the supply? Why such violence?'

Jancz's mouth kinked in a detached smile. 'So proper, Baronessa. So wedded to rules. They operate differently. Ain't you got that yet?'

Moments of past conversations with Wanton flashed through Mira's mind. Wanton had at certain times seemed kindred to her, and at others more different than she could comprehend. It had been upset when its cephalopod Host had died as they escaped the Hub, but she was not sure for what particular reason. The cephalopod had limited sentience. How attached did the Post-Species really become to a basic organism? Was it like a pet and its owner? Or something less?

And how different were the Non-Corporeal to the Hosts? she wondered. Did they value compassion? Did they experience emotion at all? 'What's inside there?' she asked.

He started the TerV and they moved slowly along the circumference of the enormous ship. 'That . . . you're about to find out.'

'But it's so large? Many times the size of a biozoon. If they are all Non-Corporeal then why would they need—'

'Shut your mouth, Baronessa. I ain't here to satisfy your curiosity.' He suddenly stopped the TerV and pointed out of the window to a mild blemish on the pitted metal. 'Get yourself over there and push against that spot.'

Despite the fellala, the heat was like a wave rising up to roll over her. The skin of the ship was burning hot, even through her gloves. She flinched and stepped back; the blemish was too high to reach.

'Get up on the front of the TerV,' Jancz called out. He waited while she climbed awkwardly onto the vehicle.

She hesitated before she touched the ship again. What would happen to her?

'Get on with it,' bellowed Jancz.

She pressed her hands against the hot skin. She had come here to do something and she would do it. Nova was safe in Primo, being tended by the membrane that would feed and clean her, and keep her muscles stimulated. Her babe could exist comfortably there for an indefinite time, if anything happened to Mira. *Insignia* would not leave Nova alone, though, without another humanesque. They had discussed that, and Mira knew that *Insignia* would find another innate to care for her child.

When the skin began to soften, Mira guessed what would happen next. The Hub world's wall had behaved in a similar manner when she and Wanton had escaped into the Bare World, sucking her through its semi-permeable membrane.

She didn't panic as she felt the pressure of being drawn in. This time she was not able to move her arms and legs, and had no sensation of her own movement. Matter pressed around her, changing and conforming as it pushed against her body. She felt neither breath nor the lack of it, only pressure, and Nova's curiosity prickling through her mind.

What's it like, Mama?

Shh, Nova. Not now.

Mira fell out and down, as if spat or propelled, onto a hard surface. She wiped her eyes and blinked. Ambient light glowed, but she couldn't determine its source. She tested her legs, climbing first to her knees, then to her feet. Though firm, the surface beneath her was springy, as if it might suddenly change consistency, or break. She stood, breathing softly, looking around. She was in a tunnel of sorts. With no other idea as to what to do, she followed its course.

It wound for a time, narrowing and then enlarging like the intestines of a large creature. The walls were semi-opaque and tinted amber, similar to the floor, and gave the impression that they were recently formed.

When the tunnel finally widened into a huge space Mira felt no wiser for the greater view. The near section – as far as she could see – was filled with a large slick object that pulsed with the regularity of a giant heart torn from a humanesque body. From where she stood, the object looked higher than *Insignia* and twice as wide. Silver tributaries of fluid streamed across it, encasing it in a silvery web.

Mama.

Nova, I told—

Mama, Wanton asks you to put him on the pupa.

Pupa?

That is what he says.

Mira stared at the throbbing slick mass before her. What could be encased in such a thing?

Wanton asks that you hurry.

Mira slipped her hand into her pocket and took out the little Extro.

Just step towards it, she told herself.

She reached up high, to place Wanton in a fold of the glistening wet skin, tucking it under the web of red vessels. In the time it took her to step away again, Wanton had disappeared, absorbed in the way Mira had been drawn through the craft's wall.

Nova? She waited for her daughter to reply.

Si, Mama. Wanton is healing. The pupa is full of the mineral amalgam that it needs.

Quixite? It's full of quixite?

There was another pause. *Si. Wanton says the quixite will seal the crack in its casing. It is not required to meld with the Non-Corporeals.*

I'm pleased.

Wanton says thank you. It will do what it can to help you.

What do you mean?

Nova's next thought sounded thin, almost frightened. *Mama, you must leave. Now.*

But Mira's feet had already begun to slide into the floor. She tried to lift them, to run back down the passage, but movement made it worse. She was stuck, and sinking.

JO-JO RASTEROVICH

The sound of a voice woke him, and he lay, confused, trying to remember where he was. *Cave. Island. Araldis. Survivors. Shit.*

<go now>

The voice was in his head. *Sole?*

<go now>

Go now, where? The Entity was so clear and loud that he wanted to plug his ears.

<*Medium* ship>

Back there? No way!

<now! go!> The imperative was so strong that he jerked upright.

Randall stirred and rolled over. Next to her, Catchut lay on his back, breathing evenly.

Jo-Jo barely had time to accustom his eyes to the darkness before the next imperative surged through him.

<now!>

Sole hadn't been so directly – so forcefully – in his mind since the Entity had driven him to the pseudo-world of Belle-Monde, back when he'd first encountered Tekton and wound up with a Hera contract on himself.

He'd tried disagreeing with Sole. Told him to go fuck himself, if he recalled correctly. But the concept had been meaningless to the Entity, and soon enough Jo-Jo had found himself sitting in the tyros' bar on Belle-Monde, doing exactly what Sole wanted him to do.

When he'd thought about it afterwards, he figured Sole's power over him was born from the mind reconfiguring that had saved his life.

Talk about strings attached! He couldn't believe that the tyros on Belle-Monde had actually *chosen* to have the process done to them. Shafting, they called it.

Unlike them, Jo-Jo had been an innocent bystander, quietly dying on the bridge of his ship after the environmentals had carked it. He hadn't been given a choice; Sole had just resurrected him.

And now, again, it seemed he was being robbed of choice.

His body took itself carefully through the cave, keeping to the narrow corridor between those still sleeping. He tried to pause at the mouth and take in the night-time vista, but his limbs climbed down directly toward the AiV.

An 'esque spoke to him, a sentry, but he didn't bother to reply.

By the time he'd climbed inside the flyer and had run his fingers over the com-sole, the sentry had alerted others. Jo-Jo thought he could see Trinder Pellegrini, and Bethany's girl, Djes; then Randall and Catchut. They scrambled from the cave towards him. Randall bellowed his name.

He wanted to stop and explain. She'd think he'd crossed her, and after the things they'd been through the notion pissed him off. He fought Sole's compulsion with everything he could: tried opening the door and throwing himself to the ground, but his hand wouldn't leave the com-sole, his feet wouldn't lift from the floor, and soon he was in the air, with the mountainside and the island diminishing into the deep dark.

The energy cell red-lined as he descended onto the beach near the chalet. Dawn was close, fuelling his sense of urgency. With quick, surprisingly efficient hands he transferred the cell from the other AiV into his, and was back in the air again before Leah broke the horizon.

Setting the auto, he dozed without really sleeping deeply. Since escaping *Medium* it had been that way, light, fearful sleep. And now here he was, on a course heading straight back to the object that had so terrified him. Restless half-dreams brought him images of Mira Fedor – stroking her skin – and arguments with Rast Randall, his hand to the mercenary's throat, her strong fists punching deep into his stomach.

He woke in pain, wanting to vomit. The AiV's locator told him that they had covered a large distance. He peered out. Even through the tinted windows, the brightness of the sun told him it was early afternoon. He searched through the emergency packs and found some protein biscuits and a tube of nutritional gel. They tasted better in his stomach than the raw fish and gritty roots he'd eaten the night before.

With food in his belly, his thoughts drifted to the surviviors. They were pitifully thin and worn, and their

Principe was everything Mira Fedor had said he was – arrogant, authoritative and, even after all he'd been through, filled with a sense of entitlement. And yet he'd kept thirty or so 'esques and a korm alive, a miracle of sorts.

Unlikeable bastard, thought Jo-Jo, *but tough. A little self-belief goes a long way.*

He stared outside, musing on Pellegrini, and soon enough fell into another doze. This time he was roused by a dull yellow light on the horizon. He checked the locator again. It was almost dark, and unless some external illumination had been rigged since they'd passed over, *Medium* appeared to be glowing.

As the AiV closed in on its target, his mind woke and questions began to fight each other for space. A sweaty fear engulfed him. Why did Sole want him to go to *Medium*? Why now? What were the Saqr doing there? How long would Sole's control over his body last?

Once again, he tried to reset the AiV's trajectory, but his hands still refused to obey his brain. He could think and make decisions, but none of them were translating to his physical self.

Fear turned to a raging frustration, and yet all the while his sense of urgency grew. He must hurry. Hurry! *Hurry!*

When the AiV began to descend toward the Extro ship, he got a close and terrifying view of hundreds and hundreds of Saqr crawling over the outer skin; lines of 'em, like ants toing and froing from their anthill to a good source of food, trailing off the sides and back in the direction of the mine. *They're taking quixite on board.*

As the AiV banked, something else caught his attention: two biozoons, side by side, wallowing in the sand dunes like impossibly large whale sharks. They were lit by the glow from *Medium* and the glittering satellites that were beginning to pop into existence as the sky darkened.

Sal! Jo-Jo knew his ship in an instant. The other one he recognised almost as quickly. *Insignia*. The fear and frustration tearing at him turned to a strange elation. *She's here! I knew it!*

Suddenly, he couldn't wait for the AiV to land. He sprang out of the pilot seat, down onto the sand, and tried to run in the direction of the 'zoons. But the Sole compulsion refused to comply, forcing him back towards *Medium*.

Hurry. Hurry. Over dunes. Staggering in sliding sand, until he found himself standing in front of the exact spot he and Randall and Catchut had been expelled from days before. He knew it from the dark burn-stain left by *Insignia* tearing away its coupling.

His hands lifted from his sides and pressed hard against *Medium*'s coarse outer skin. The blemish was higher than he could reach. *Too high!* He fell to the sand and frantically began to dig, creating a mound to one side. When it was high enough, he tried again. This time his palms just reached the bottom of the dark stain. He began to push and pinch, the way he had before, and moments later he was pulled in – sucked, almost like thick liquid through a straw.

The sensation was a terrifying as before and he found himself screaming through the transition.

Once inside, he felt as if he'd been wrung out: the pressure left him weak and headachy. Blinking, he looked around. The interior had completely changed; the chamber they'd been trapped in was no more. Instead, Jo-Jo found himself in a low-lit tunnel. The only likeness it had to his surroundings last time he was here was the amber tint of the walls and floor.

He wiped his face with his hands and got slowly to his feet. Where did the tunnel go? Why was it a tunnel and not a space? He moved forward cautiously, following the tunnel through a series of bends. *It's like the insides of a body. Ear canals or intestines.* The very notion made him want to run back to the scar in the wall and burrow out, but the compulsion wouldn't let him. He moved inexorably forward and deeper inside, his sense of urgency growing by the breath. *Hurry. Hurry.* He trailed his hands along the wall to keep his balance, and his pace quickened until he found himself running as fast as his condition-weakened legs could go.

Finally, he burst from the tunnel into a place that was wider and taller than he'd thought possible for *Medium* to harbour. At least, that was his fleeting hind-brain impression, for his conscious attention was drawn immediately to two things: a large slick organism filling nearly the entire space, and the small figure of a woman, standing before it – sinking.

Mira!

He leapt forward without thought for anything except to stop her disappearing beneath the liquefying amber floor. He grabbed her shoulders, and before she could even turn her head, pulled her back towards him. They fell together, her body cushioned by his. A moment later she began to fight him, writhing and slapping at his face.

'Baronessa,' he gasped hoarsely, gripping her fists. 'It's Josef Rasterovich. Jo-Jo.'

Her body went slack as his words penetrated, and he eased her onto her side so that they were lying face to face.

'Jo-sef!' A terrified whisper, broken by relief. 'Thank Crux.'

She gripped his arm as if she would never let it go, and a rush of elation made his body feel lighter and stronger. Jo-Jo had never experienced such pure pleasure. She was happy to see him.

'Don't move,' he managed to say. 'You'll break the surface tension.'

She gave the tiniest of nods. Their faces were so close that her breath mixed with his. She smelled of biozoon and something milky-sweet.

Without thinking, he slid a hand down her side to her stomach. Her flesh felt flat and loose beneath her robe. Not pregnant.

Her eyes narrowed. 'What – are – you – doing?'

'I – I – thought you were . . . I noticed . . . You were pregnant on Rho Junction. Weren't you? Did you lose it?'

She seemed startled for a moment, then collected herself. 'Si. It was not something I wanted to talk about then. And now the explanations could take some time. My baby survived, and is aboard *Insignia*.'

'You had a child?' He felt a well of endless questions opening inside. Who was the father?

'Si. A girl. Nova.'

Jo-Jo tried to work it out. How long had they been apart? It seemed longer than it was. She could not have borne a healthy child in that time.

'She was born early,' she said, as if guessing his thoughts. 'Tell me, do you know how to get out?'

He shook his head. 'Not really, except back through the tunnel. Same way I came in. Where we don't want to be is underneath this stuff we're lying on.'

'What do you mean?' She continued to stare straight into his eyes as he gave her a brief run-down of his time on *Medium* and his escape.

She didn't interrupt him, her eyes growing darker and more intense as he told his story. When he'd finished, they lay in silence for a while.

'And that will happen to us, if we move?' she asked.

'It might happen anyway. Seems they can make this stuff as liquid or as brittle as they like. Right now we'll stay on top if we don't move.'

'But you got out,' she whispered. 'So what are you doing back here?'

He paused before he answered. It seemed the right time for the truth, of sorts. If *Medium* engulfed him a second time, he might never see her again. There was no point keeping secrets. 'When the Entity saved me back near Mintaka, it changed my mind. You've heard of shafting?'

She nodded again, gently. 'The Entity alters the minds of its tyros so that it can better communicate with them.'

'Yeah. Well, it did the same to me when it resurrected me. See, I was dead out there. When it bought me back, it was able to talk directly into my head. I haven't heard it for a long while. But it started talking to me a day ago. Told me to hurry here. Thing is, when it's like that I can't do a damn thing to fight it. It wanted me to come here and find you.'

He watched her absorb what he'd said.

'Where were you when it ... it intervened?' she asked.

'With the survivors,' he said.

Her free hand shot out and gripped his shoulder again. Their lips were so close now that he had only to move his head a little, and—

'Who?' she whispered.

'Pellegrini and some others. About thirty of them. Maybe less.'

Her fingers clenched convulsively, pinching his skin. He didn't notice the discomfort, just that she was touching him. 'Was Cass Mulravey alive? Did she have a 'bino with her?'

'Mulravey? Yes, Randall knew her.' Then he hesitated. 'She did have a kid, but it died just as we got there. Killed in an accident. A fight between two of the men.'

'A boy?' she asked.

He nodded.

Her face went slack with shock, her hand dropping away from him and her whole body trembling. Though she shed no tears, her distress was like a knife twisting in his gut.

He slipped his arm across her and drew her as close as he could.

She didn't resist, nor did she respond.

They lay together for longer than Jo-Jo knew. As he

held her, he found himself caught in an inexplicable web of emotions, fear and sympathy overridden by a swell of protectiveness. His heart felt like it might explode with the volume of emotion pouring from it. He wanted to stay for ever with her in his arms, and yet he wanted to move. Get them out of there. See her happy again.

She stirred, leaning away from him.

Reluctantly he let her go.

'Why do you think the Extros are here?' she asked.

She seemed composed, though absent, as if only a part of her mind was with him and the rest was grieving.

'For the quixite,' he said. 'The Saqr are loadin' it into *Medium* like it's food for a long journey.'

'Not food,' she said. 'But a material that is versatile.' Her eyes lost some of their cloudiness as she visibly forced herself to think. 'I learned some things on the Post-Species world I was taken to. The Extros exist within two main divisions: those with Host bodies and those without. We call those without, 'Non-Corporeals'. The Non-Corporeals still need the corporeals to perform certain tasks for them.'

'Why?'

'Even with their ability to manipulate material at the atomic level, they cannot create everything they need. I think that somehow the quixite will help eliminate their dependency.'

Jo-Jo thought about what she said. He lifted his head carefully to inspect the object filling the huge space. 'Could this . . . thing . . . be part of their independence from the corporeals?'

She lifted her head as well. 'Si.'

'Then what in Crux is it?'

'I have an idea.'

'Tell me.'

'See . . . how it's growing?'

Jo-Jo considered the sticky mass. It did seem closer, but then he'd only glanced at it briefly before snatching Mira from the floor. Now he studied its organic contours. It was alive; he was convinced by the way it glistened, the faint sense of movement.

'Look.' She pointed to the ceiling where the mass appeared to touch the curve of the ship. 'See how the light is different up there.'

She was right. It was brighter there, but it wasn't direct light – more like the external skin of *Medium* had opened to the sky, yet the gap remained invisible to them, blocked by the mass within.

'Maybe that's where they're loading the quixite?'

She lowered her head to the floor gently. 'Si. I think so.'

He did the same, and their faces were close again. 'When I landed, I saw the Saqr trail to and from the mine. Knew they must be bringing the mineral on board.'

'Do you notice the scent? The sweetness?'

He nodded. 'That's them. The Saqr. I've smelt it before.'

'It's also the scent of ligs.'

Jo-Jo frowned, not understanding. 'What's ligs?'

'Ligs are one of the few insect species on Araldis. We use their pollen extract to scent our candles.' She ran her tongue over her teeth in a nervous gesture. He'd forgotten how crimson her skin was, and how deep the colour of her lips. 'Ligs are as much a part of Araldis as the dust and the rock. There is something in the ligs that the Post-Species need. The ligs and the quixite. I think it is enabling them to—'

But she stopped short as the object shifted.

'Josef,' she whispered. 'I think . . . we must get out.'

'If the tunnel stays there – there wasn't one before when I was here. All we saw of the ship was a small space. Then the floor liquefied, and we were trapped undern—'

A loud crackling noise stopped him. They both looked at the object again. It had split some of its skin, and a wet mound of tissue bulged out towards them. As they watched, the bulge grew, oozing through the fissure like thick liquid until it stopped only a short distance from their feet.

Jo-Jo felt the floor harden to accommodate the new weight.

'Now!' He scrambled to his feet, hauling Mira up with him.

They ran through the dim tunnel. Mira lifted the folds of her robe to make it easier, but she was still hampered by them. Jo-Jo caught her twice as she stumbled, but in truth he could barely manage her weight, his own strength diminishing rapidly.

The tunnel began to buckle and fold, the ceiling collapsing behind them as they moved.

By the time they reached the outer wall, only a short length of tunnel remained. Jo-Jo ran his hands over the blemish.

'What are you doing?' she panted.

'The 'zoon ripped its coupling here; it's still healing and there's a weakness.'

Her reply was a strangled noise, and her fingers tugged at his robe. Over his shoulder, Jo-Jo glimpsed the last of the passage disappearing. The object had spread right out to the ship's limits, and in a moment it would crush them.

'Shit!' Jo-Jo gouged at the roughened blemish. 'Scratch it, hit it. Anything!'

Mira roused herself and joined him, pinching and pushing at the skin. She cried a name he didn't recognise. 'Wanton!'

Another loud crack. Then the sound of something wet and heavy moving behind them. Jo-Jo felt pressure against his back and neck. This time he couldn't turn his head to see. He was pinned to the wall, his chest struggling to expand enough for him to breathe.

Next to him, Mira's eyes were closed, as if she were concentrating on something else. He clawed the wall with his fingers and dug his toes into it with the small room for movement he had left.

'Take my hand,' Mira said suddenly.

Her eyes were open, and clear. Strain showed on her face.

He reached down and felt her slim fingers grip his own. She squeezed his palm, giving comfort. Strength and calm flowed from her. His breathing steadied despite the crushing weight.

'It's going to expand again,' she said. 'Be ready.'

Jo-Jo had long fantasised about her voluntary touch, and the irony of it coming now angered him. He squeezed her hand and laboured over the words he had to say. 'I would've – come – anyway. Sole – didn't need – to – make me.'

He saw her brief surprise and something else, something he couldn't quite read.

Then the pressure began to build again, and his ribs felt like they were breaking. He tried to brace, tried to fight the compression, refusing to let go of Mira's hand even when her fingers went slack.

No. No!

Then the outer skin split, and he tumbled free.

MIRA

'Wanton!'

Mama? Are you all right?

The pressure against her was so great that Mira could barely breathe. *Nova, can you – speak to – Wanton? I'm in – trouble.*

Si, Mama. I will try. What should I say?

Unable to think in sentences, Mira shared images of her situation: of the object expanding so rapidly that it was pressing on their backs, and the weakness, the blemish that Josef had spoken of, where *Insignia* had torn away from the side.

Crushed, Nova. Wanton, help us.

Long moments passed, and the only things she was aware of were her battle to breathe and Josef holding her hand. With every increase of pressure against her body, his grip tightened as though he would never let go.

Jo-Jo

His fall to the dune below should have been soft, but the distance turned soft sand to rock. He lay, winded and paralysed by the agony of impact, unsure whether he'd broken anything.

Through sand-blurred eyes, he saw the glow emanating from *Medium*, and behind it a moonlit sky. Thank Crux it was still night. Then the outer skin of the ship ruptured above him, squirting fluid and a sticky wet mass into the hot air and spraying him with sweet fluid.

An intense rush of adrenaline got him upright. He searched frantically for Mira, and saw her in front of him, spreadeagled on her stomach. She'd been thrown further from the craft than he had, and he scrambled over to join her.

She moaned at his touch.

'Away!' he cried in her ear. 'We need to get further away.'

She struggled to her knees and collapsed, her moaning louder.

Jo-Jo swore at himself. He couldn't lift her. Randall's image sawed its way into his head. The damn merc would find strength from somewhere; he damn well would too. Bending down, he lifted Mira into his arms. She was light, but he was weak and hurting all over. Not just hurting, his body screamed at him. But he ignored it and began to stagger in the direction of the biozoons.

He only vaguely took in the headlights of the TerV that left the edge of the ship, heading towards the dark mouth of the mine. The activity of the Saqr, though, was more worrying. They seemed disorientated, some crawling in circles while others stopped to rear up on their hind legs. Their bodies made a weird shadow play against the still-glowing ship.

Jo-Jo set his jaw.

Can, he told himself.

Mira stirred in his arms. 'Let me walk,' she whispered.

He shook his head. 'You can't.'

The TerV lights had changed direction. It was labouring over the dunes towards them.

'Who's – in – that?' he asked her.

Mira pushed back the hood of her robe to see. 'His name is Jancz. He works for them. He led the invasion here. Brought the Saqr in.'

'What sort of 'esque would work for the Extros?'

'He told me it was logical that he did.'

'What's that mean?'

'I don't know. Maybe he formed a . . . relationship with them, as I did with Wanton.'

Wanton? The name she'd called out before they fell from the ship. 'Who's Wanton?' he said fiercely.

'Wanton is a corporeal. I brought it here, to save it. That's what I was doing in the ship. Wanton was dying. I brought it back so that it could integrate with the others.'

Jo-Jo took a couple of savage breaths that sent pains

shooting from his belly to the base of his neck. He gasped and staggered.

She hung onto his shoulders. 'Does your chest hurt?' she asked anxiously.

'No more than the rest of me,' he said, righting himself. 'Jancz stole my ship.'

'*Sal*? *Sal* is yours?'

He stared at her. 'You know *Salacious*?'

Mira nodded weakly. '*Sal* is a hybrid. We can communicate. Jancz hasn't treated it well.'

Jo-Jo set his jaw. 'You can save that story for another time. Right now, I'm going to get my 'zoon back.'

His staggering footsteps gained some strength and purpose. *Jancz framed me. The fucker stole my ship.* All the panic and fear and pain of being on board *Medium* again burned away on a surge of hot fury. Once before when Jo-Jo had thought he would die, as he floated free in space around Dowl station, anger had saved him, pulled him back from the brink of despair and defeat. It did the same thing now, channelling energy into his limbs, giving him a goal. His ship, *Salacious*, was the closer of the two biozoons.

Sal.

He reached the hybrid as the TerV climbed the dune closest to them. Though the 'zoon was half buried in the sand, its egress scale was too high to reach. He put Mira down on the sand, leaning her back against the 'zoon's skin, and turned to face the TerV.

He recognised both of the figures inside it: Jancz, who'd introduced himself in the station bar as Jud, and Ilke the Balol, who'd kept Jo-Jo busy in the bedroom while Jancz had stolen his ship.

He wasn't sure which one of them he'd kill first.

Jancz, he'd learned through a glimpse at Lasper Farr's Dynamic System Device, had been Randall's Capo during the Stain Wars. The 'esque was the worst type of mercenary, one who changed sides mid-conflict. Or maybe he'd been working for the Extros back then too.

The TerV grunted air from its brake jets, and settled to rest an arm's length away.

Mira moaned softly behind him, but he kept his focus on the mercs.

Ilke got out first. Then Jancz. Neither had changed as far as Jo-Jo could see through the film of their masks. Ilke's spikes were bunched together, her powerful body squashed into a cooling suit, but Jancz's suit had plenty of room. He looked as lightweight and unimpressive as he had in the bar. More so, in fact.

Both Jancz's and Ilke's eyes were on Mira.

'Hey,' said Jo-Jo, waving his hands. 'Remember me?' He loosened his hood, pushing it back far enough for them to see his face.

Ilke shrugged and moved to walk past him, but he blocked her way. She automatically pulled a pistol from the pocket of her suit and shoved it into his ear.

'Ilke!' barked Jancz.

She shifted the muzzle back a fraction. 'Yeah?' Her reptilian eyes glistened through the suit film at him. Then she blinked in recognition. She gave a belly laugh and glanced across at her partner. 'He's the one we took the 'zoon from.'

Ludjer Jancz didn't blink an eyelid. 'I know. Kill him.'

MIRA

I know you, Mira Fedor.

Mira felt a shiver run through the biozoon's outer skin. She sat up straighter. *Sal?*

You remember me.

Of course. You helped me.

I have communed with your mate, Tasy-al, who rests along-side me. What are you doing here, touching me?

Sal, can you let us come aboard? W-we cannot reach Insignia, *and we're in danger.*

I can see that.

Mira waited. She knew, from her brief encounter with the hybrid once before, that it was perverse and damaged.

I have news for you. I have a new captain, it said finally, almost jauntily, ignoring her plea.

Ludjer Jancz is not good for you, Sal. *There are others that would be kinder. He took you illegally.*

Not him, the hybrid scoffed. *Jancz is no longer my captain*. It made a sighing noise. *I have moved on.*

Would you ask your captain, if we might board?

I could.

Sal, *Jancz is dangerous. He'll hurt us. Please . . .*

Sal remained silent as Jancz and his Balol partner got out of the TerV and approached them.

Sal! Mira cried.

I don't need to concern myself with your problems, Mira Fedor.

The other one has a weapon. See . . . she will kill Josef.

Josef? The hybrid's tone sharpened. *Who is this 'esque that you call Josef?*

Josef is your true captain, your legal captain. Do you remember him?

The sound of a series of explosions froze them all, delaying the hybrid's reply. Across the dunes, *Medium* cracked open, its skin ripping apart like watery overripe fruit. The glow grew brighter as an enormous glittering carapace emerged, shivering and shaking bits of the ship's outer hull from itself.

Even Jancz and Ilke stopped and turned to watch.

'Josef!' called Mira, recovering first.

Josef, repeated *Sal*.

Mira's cry shook Jo-Jo from his trance, and he lunged for Jancz. The pair tumbled into the sand and wrestled.

Jo-Jo was the stronger of the two, but neither of them was a match for Ilke, who casually stepped forward and lifted them apart. She let go of Jancz, dropping him to his feet. Then, loosening her weapon again, she shoved it under Jo-Jo's jaw.

My Josef? exclaimed Sal.

Si. Jancz tricked Josef and stole you. He's been looking for you ever since.

The Post-Species stole me?

What do you mean, the Post-Species?

The corporeals, Ludjer Jancz and Ilke.

Jancz and Ilke are Post-Species?

Of course. Sal sounded perplexed and irritated by Mira's ignorance.

Then yes. The Post-Species stole you. And they've been cruel to you, binding your fins.

The hybrid emitted a sound somewhere between a screech and a squeal, and shifted in the sand; an impossibly large floundering whale, its tail pounding the dune and its gills venting odd noises.

Mira crawled away from its side.

'Crux!' shouted Jancz, backing away towards the TerV. 'Ilke!'

The 'zoon's cephalic fins began to strain against their cruel restraints. Each screech seemed to stretch them further, and sent more sand and rocks blasting out from underneath it.

'Ilke!' bellowed Jancz again. But the Balol was transfixed, glancing between the strange creature emerging from the discarded skeleton of the Extro craft and the thrashing squealing 'zoon before her.

When one of Sal's cephalic fins ripped free and wavered in the air though, Ilke began to run. She leapt into the TerV, and Jancz sent it skimming up over a dune.

But the 'zoon was quicker than them. It flicked its freed and powerful fin in an arc, and slammed the vehicle.

The TerV split apart, tossing Jancz and Ilke into the sand.

The fin lifted and pounded the bodies again and again, until there was nothing left of them but fin marks in the sand.

'Josef, look!' cried Mira, pointing. *Sal*'s egress scale had opened. '*Sal*'s letting us in.'

Jo-Jo got to his feet and took Mira's arm. They

hurried to a spot directly below the scale, and he laced his fingers together. 'I'll hoist you,' he said.

'But how will you get on board?'

'Just put your foot in my hands,' he shouted hoarsely.

Sal, we can't reach the egress scale.

Step away, Mira Fedor. Step away.

'Josef,' she said.

'Step up!' he screamed at her.

She made a fist and punched Jo-Jo in the side of the face.

He dropped his hands in shock.

'*Sal* wants us to move away. Quickly.'

She grabbed his hand and pulled him. Together, they climbed the closest dune. Halfway up, Mira began to tire. Jo-Jo's grip grew tighter, and their positions reversed. He was pulling her, urging her onward.

As they reached the peak, the sand began to vibrate. Behind them *Sal* was moving, rocking back and forth with gathering momentum. In front of them something else was happening. *Medium* glowed brighter than ever. The last of its outer skin sloughed away to allow a ghastly, glistening birthing.

Fluid sprayed forth in great bursts, sizzling as it touched the hot sand. A bulbous shape, the size of a dozen biozoons, had emerged. Then the shape split wide in another spray of fluid and a cavernous yawning hollow opened before them. Huge triangular-shaped objects glistened around the edges of the hollow. Teeth.

Jo-Jo fell to his knees, hands covering his face. 'No!'

Mira couldn't speak, couldn't do anything but watch the Extro craft transforming. Behind the maw another wad of skin unfolded, a body that seemed to expand until the scaly quivering length of it went further back into the dark than she could see.

An overpoweringly sweet scent assailed them; gusts of it had them both choking. Then the sand began to quake again.

Mira gripped Jo-Jo's shoulder and pointed back to the two biozoons. *Sal* had rocked itself until it had dug deep down into the sand. They could now reach the egress scale.

This time they helped each other, holding hands, pulling each other along. Josef had no more strength than she did, and tears poured down his face. Their only words to each other were encouragement or instructions, until they'd climbed in through the egress scale.

When the scale closed, they both collapsed onto the floor.

'Josef?' whispered Mira. 'Are you . . . ?'

He sat up suddenly, words tumbling from his mouth. 'We have to get out of here quickly. The survivors are on the islands to the west, like you said they'd be. We should go there.'

Mira pushed up onto an elbow. All her strength had gone, drained by the heat and the effort and the fear. 'Then I need to get to the buccal.'

Jo-Jo nodded. She saw he was still crying, a steady stream of tears of release that made him neither gasp nor sob, but which did not stop.

He tried to stand, but his legs buckled underneath him. His whole body trembled, but he got his knees underneath him and crawled to her. 'I – I, Mira, I c-can't carry you—' This time he sobbed. 'I'm sorry.'

Mira reached out and clasped his hand, letting him know that she understood. She'd thought him so rough and self-reliant, closed off, when they'd been together in *Insignia* before. Like Rast Randall, though more predictable and with a peculiar type of integrity. But this man who'd come to help her was altogether different, raw and open and unsure. When he'd pulled her from the liquefying floor of the Extro ship, she'd felt nothing but relief to see him. Now something else stirred. An emotion she'd not felt before.

He brought her fingers to his face and held them against his cheek. He was trembling, as if needing her close. She felt the hot wetness of his face against hers. Felt his exhaustion to match hers. He turned and pressed his lips into her palm.

Instead of pulling away, she welcomed his contact, letting her hand cup his jaw. They were alive.

'Baronessa?' A quiet and totally unexpected voice intruded into their space. 'Let me help you.'

Josef pulled away, and both of them turned in the direction of the voice.

A slim tight-skinned 'esque in a worn robe stepped around the bend of the stratum. 'My name is Tekton of Lostol.'

JO-JO

Tekton! A wave of shock passed through Jo-Jo's weakened body. 'What in Crux's name are you . . .' He trailed off, barely able to believe that Tekton was standing before him.

The tyro gave a strained smile. 'It would seem that fate has plans for us. Or should I say that Sole does.'

'You are the tyro from Belle-Monde. You knew Marchella Pellegrini,' said Mira. Like Jo-Jo, she forced herself to an upright position, her torso wavering as if she might collapse again.

Tekton went to her and lent his support. Slowly, carefully, he helped her to her feet. He was not much taller than her, or stronger, but he had energy where hers was spent.

'Marchella Pellegrini,' said Tekton. 'A name I had not thought to hear again. Perhaps, at another time, we can speak of her. But now there is some urgency, I believe, to leave this location.'

'Si,' she said. 'Help me to the buccal then come back for Josef.'

Tekton nodded his agreement, but Jo-Jo didn't trust the tricky Godhead.

As the tyro helped Mira Fedor around the stratum and out of his sight, Jo-Jo crawled after them. On hands and knees he made his way, painfully, towards the buccal. He knew this ship, remembered the contours and bends, the quicker ways. And the ship moud code.

'*Sal*,' he gasped as he put one hand in front of the next.

Josef? Josef Rasterovich? Salacious's reply rumbled through his mind as the longdormant moud reactivated.

Yes. I'm here.

You left me.

No. I was tricked and then put in prison on Dowl station. Jancz and Ilke stole you from me.

Oh. The hybrid seemed confused. *But I have a new captain now. Tekton.*

No. I am your captain. Still.

How can I know who it should be?

Serve me now, and I will release you to the Pod. End your tenure.

My contract?

It's in my name. I can legally rescind it.

I will be free.

Yes. If you help us to leave this world.

The hybrid's hesitation was as brief as Jo-Jo's next breath. *Welcome back aboard, my captain.*

Sole

Closer, Closer
Come To Me,
All Done Soon,
All Done.

MIRA

'I've heard of you, Godhead,' whispered Mira as they negotiated the obstacles along the rubbish-cluttered strata.

'And I, of you,' the Lostolian replied. 'Please . . . tell me what is happening outside.'

'The Post-Species are birthing something in the desert, a new craft from the old. It is spreading . . . growing as if the air feeds it. We must leave this area before we are damaged by its expansion.'

'A new craft from the old,' repeated Tekton. 'Fascinating. It must be the quixite.'

'Not fascinating,' she said, 'terrifying.'

As they reached the buccal, tears sprang to Mira's eyes; the walls of the hybrid's cheek were bleeding, and its flesh hung in unhealthy clumps.

She pointed to one of the nubs in the centre of the buccal. 'There, please, Tekton.'

Tekton helped her across to the unused Primo vein. The grey protective skin was thick and resistant to her touch. She hesitated to pierce it. She was already bonded to *Insignia;* if she used *Sal*'s vein-sink, what would happen? Would Sal's personality meld with hers? *Sal* was unhealthy, not sane in the way of other biozoons. Already she could feel its agitation.

Sal, *what's wrong*? she asked the hybrid.

Where are the other 'esques, Mira Fedor? Where are the corporeals? The Balol and Captain Jancz.

You killed them, Sal, Mira said gently.

It made a noise she thought to be mirth. *Yes, I did. It felt good, Mira Fedor.*

Were the corporeals cruel to you?

Cruel to be kind. Cruel to be kind. The hybrid sounded strained and odd, not incomprehensibly raving as Mira had heard it before, but distanced, remote.

Another sliver of fear stabbed her consciousness. Would she lose her mind to *Sal* if she used the Primo vein? Would she maintain her link with *Insignia*? And *Nova*?

Mama?

She ignored her daughter, lifting her finger to stab through the nano-membrane and begin the immersion process.

'Mira. No!' Jo-Jo Rasterovich stood swaying in the pucker of the buccal. 'This was – *is* my ship. I'll fly it. I know the island coordinates.'

He let go of the pucker and staggered across to the Autonomy nub.

Tekton made no move to help him or stop him.

Mira wavered with relief. *Sal? We wish to go somewhere where you can recover. Your fins will never be tied again, I promise.*

The buccal started to shake, and a noise vibrated along the hybrid's strata – part screech, part wail. Mira felt the creature's relief and anger, but underneath it all still mistrust.

'Josef,' Mira whispered. 'Be careful. Sal's damaged.'

He nodded. 'Then we're a good pair.'

Mira moved to another nub and watched Jo-Jo climb into Autonomy. The v-comm unfolded over his head, and his fingers moved slowly through the air in front of him, creating patterns.

'Tekton, sit.' She gestured to unused nubs. 'They will help protect you from the acceleration, but be careful not to pierce the outer layer of skin. The 'zoon is not . . . healthy enough to immerse in.'

The Godhead had not moved since Jo-Jo had entered the buccal, his brow drawn in concentration as though he was remembering or realising something important.

He shook his head slightly and stepped across to a nub. It responded to the pressure of his weight, folding around him. Mira sank carefully onto the surface of hers and let it do the same.

Another vibration spread through the buccal, a more familiar one. *Salacious* was moving. She glanced at Josef. He was concentrating, hands working, lips the same.

Finally she opened her mind to her biozoon. *Insignia?*

Dearest? The biozoon sounded anxious.

We're aboard the hybrid. Follow us to the islands. I will come back to you then. Nova—

I'm here, Mama. I am happy that you are with the hybrid. I was scared.

Nova, the Post-Species have created something terrible. We must get far away from it. Insignia, *it was so large . . . do you know what it was?*

I'm afraid so, Mira.

Insignia projected her own images to Mira's mind. They were moving. She saw the hybrid lifting high above *Insignia* and diving west towards the islands.

Then the dunes began to shrink as *Insignia* gathered height. A towering shadow fell across them, a shadow that *Insignia* must scale – so, so high and far, encroaching on the biozoon, threatening to engulf it.

How big is it? Mira wanted to know.

I can't say. It's still growing. Given time, it could cover much of the main continent. Perhaps more.

No!

It's possible while it has resources.

The quixite?

It would seem so.

As *Insignia* rose, the shadow seemed to chase them, while below the grisly object continued to expand.

Insignia, *you must get higher!*

But the shadow kept pace with them, blocking their view to the west. If *Insignia* faltered, the object would overtake them, suck them into its expanding mass like an exploding star gobbling a planet.

Hurry. Please. Save Nova.

Mira felt the surge of *Insignia*'s determination, the push of her energies as the biozoon dredged speed and energy from its dwindling supply of amino acids.

A tiny but pure beam of energy joined it, bolstering *Insignia*'s effort, and suddenly the biozoon was free, soaring above the object.

Nova.

Little one.

Look, Mama. Look, Tasy-al.

With altitude came more perspective, and something Mira could see but barely comprehend. *Crux! It's not a ship. It's a single Saqr.*

Insignia corrected her. *No, Mira. It is both.*

THALES

Thales looked around the group of Swestr gathered in Magdalen's home: thirty or more women who'd arrived during the evening in twos and threes, now occupying every available space in Magdalen's living room. He recognised a few faces, Eclectics from the candlelight vigil at the statue of Exterus, where he'd last seen Magdalen. One woman he knew separately, an academic from the Motokiyo Aesthetics stream. *Ling-Ma*. She was a descendant of the famous Ma dynasty who owned the Heka system. What would her family think of her membership of the Swestr? Ling-Ma nodded at him but made no further attempt to reacquaint.

The atmosphere in the room was furtive, as though at any moment their gathering might be discovered. Thales glanced nervously at the large bay window, now shuttered, that he knew gave a splendid view of the leafy Place de Liebniz. He remembered having been in this room once before with Rene, a bohemian dinner party where they'd eaten with their fingers, and he'd drunk too much piska wine. Rene had been annoyed with him, and displeased by having to use her fingers.

They did the same now, though more for expedience, passing around slabs of hot cheese dough and carafes of juice. The dough, though tasty, sat heavily in his stomach, and he was forced to eat it slowly. Fariss had no such problem, demolishing a panful by herself. The Swestr watched her with approval while Magdalen talked.

'We need a way to the shift station,' she said. 'Who can help?'

'The Sophos are monitoring all traffic. Politics are searching shuttles,' said a heavyset women with long white hair.

'What about private craft?' asked Magdalen.

'It's impossible to get clearance. The uplift zone is chaotic.'

'I can get us clearance,' said Linnea. 'If you can get transport.'

'I have a space-worthy,' said Ling-Ma quietly.

More looks of approval. Most of them knew, Thales judged, but had been waiting for her to speak.

'Thank you, Ling-Ma,' said Magdalen. 'Now, once on the station we'll meet resistance. We need to bring as many of the Feohte as you can fit. What's your capacity?'

'Twenty. Thirty if we don't have to shift.'

'What's a Feohte?' asked Fariss with interest. She'd stopped eating, and now picked dough from her teeth. Her large body sprawled across the floor, taking up the space of three women.

'*Feohte* are the Swestr's combatants. The Swestr doesn't advocate violence, but they recognise the need for protection.'

'And we are that protection,' said a woman from the back of the room.

Thales – and everyone – turned to look at her. Though not as tall or broad as Fariss, she stood with the ease of someone who was comfortable with her physicality. Her arms appeared muscular beneath her short-sleeved tunic.

'Janne,' said Magdalen in acknowledgement. 'You're late.'

Thales knew the uniform. Janne was a free-hand, one of Scolar's manual workers who'd chosen labour as the way to enlightenment.

'The Politics are active all over the city. This meeting is being monitored. I saw them in the street. Best we appear to be carousing.'

Magdalen threaded her fingers together and twisted her hands. 'I'll bring in some bottles of piska. Everyone must drink a little before leaving. How much did you hear of our conversation, Janne?'

'Enough. How many of the Feohte can you take, Ling-Ma?'

The Hekarian looked to Magdalen. 'Who else will it be?'

'Thales and Fariss. You, me and Linnea. That leaves space for fifteen Feohte.'

Janne made a dissatisfied face. 'Twenty would be better.'

But Magdalen didn't agree. 'We don't know what will happen up there. It's possible we may have to shift to survive. I won't risk more than I need.'

'Fifteen Feohte against squadrons of politics . . .' Janne trailed off and crossed her arms.

'We aren't seeking conflict, Janne. Simply shielding. We have one ambition only, to close the shift sphere.'

Janne narrowed her eyes. 'That is what I'm talking about.'

Ling-Ma's craft would be luxurious as the ship, the *Last Aesthetic*, which they'd taken from Rho Junction to Edo station, though Thales could only recall the cabin Tekton had rented for them, having been too sick to venture out into the ship.

He ran his fingers over the roughened texture of his cheek. The scars had finally healed thanks to the biozoon, but they would never fade, and nor would his bitter memories of Lasper Farr. The hero of the Stain Wars was a terrifying and immoral man who wielded too much power.

After they boarded Thales lay for a while in one of Ling-Ma's guest cabins, but was roused by Farris what seemed to him almost immediately after he'd fallen asleep.

'Nope, it's been hours,' Fariss told him. 'We'll be docking at Scolar station soon.'

Thales stretched and sat up. 'What have you been doing?'

'Gettin' acquainted with Janne and the Feohte.' She grinned.

Fariss was happy. Things were happening. How could she ever be that way with him, living an ordinary life on Scolar? If they succeeded in closing the shift sphere, that's what she would face.

'You know, when we shut the sphere you'll be trapped here,' he said.

Her smile faded. 'Can't say I like that idea much. But could be it's the only way to stay alive. If so, then you're gonna have to keep me entertained.'

Her answer was light, but Thales saw the slight tightening of her jaw. Fariss was a free spirit, not a person to be tied to one place. But their choices were limited. The Extros had seen to that.

'I'll do everything I can,' he promised.

'Make sure of it.' She leaned over and kissed him deeply, stirring his desire.

He washed, then followed her out of the cabin to the low-lit lounge area. Janne and half the Feohte were there with Magdalen and Linnea. All of them were watching a map in the centre of the room.

Linnea glanced across at them and pointed at the diagram. 'This is the area around station Shift Command, where the res-shift controls are. There're two ways in – either through the front door, or by busting a hole through from the information node which backs on to it. IN is the best option, in my opinion. Other than the technicians, there's usually only a small entry guard. Whereas Shift Command's got a series of checkpoints.'

'We've brought cutting tools,' said Janne. 'Are the walls titanium?'

The galley supervisor and former IN tech nodded. 'Behind the actual node is steel. The outer walls are titanium.'

'Ling-Ma will stay with her craft,' said Magdalen. 'Linnea will lead us to the IN.'

'And then?' asked Janne.

'Then I call the tune,' said Fariss.

Thales held his breath, waiting for objections. But no one spoke, not even Janne. Strangely, the Feohte leader seemed satisfied. As they all did.

At some point in the short time they'd been together, an implicit agreement had been reached among the Swestr. Fariss knew danger better than anyone.

BALBAO

'We're station side,' said Jelly Hob. 'C'n feel it.'

Balbao roused from his doze and sat up. He sensed nothing different to the previous days they'd spent in their prison. 'How can you tell?'

'C'n hear it,' said Hob.

The others joined them in paying attention. The old woman, Samuelle, nodded her head. 'Yeah. You're right. They haven't vacced us yet, Jeremiah. So now what?'

Balbao was wondering the same. Days had passed with no contact from Farr, or anyone save the guards. Ra had not returned, which, though a relief in some ways, had made him speculate over what had befallen the arrogant Godhead. Was Ra assisting Farr is some way? Or was he dead? Somehow, he felt it might be the former.

'That would be Scolar res station?' asked Lawmon Jise.

He and Miranda Seeward had spent much of the time over the last few days huddled together, whispering and petting. Their fellow prisoners had tried ignoring them, but the pair seemed almost childishly unaware, or uncaring, of their exhibitionism.

'Less Lasper decided something else, I'd say so,' said Sammy. 'You know, the Swestr are strong here,' she added under her breath to Jelly Hob.

Balbao wanted to ask her what Swestr were, but Connit jumped up off his bunk and smacked the wall.

'Why did he come here? It's suicidal!'

Commander Farr's son appeared to have inherited none of his father's unnatural calm. In fact, Balbao was starting to fear for the young 'esque's sanity. In sleep, Connit had moaned and ground his teeth, and during waking moments he was singularly withdrawn.

His dour mood infected them all, and they fell glumly silent in the wake of his statement.

Even later, when they ate together, conversation didn't improve, and Balbao went to sleep feeling disconsolate and helpless.

He was woken by a hand across his mouth and a warning in his ear. 'It's Sammy. We wanna talk to you, nice and quiet now, over at our bunk.'

Balbao fought his instinct to swing at the person who'd brought him abruptly from sleep, and nodded.

She took her hand away and disappeared back across the dark cell.

Balbao gave himself a few moments to wake before sitting up. Jise, Miranda and Connit all appeared to be asleep. He trod carefully over to Sammy and Hob's section of the prison cell.

Sammy reached out and pulled him down onto the bunk between them. The two old 'esques crowded uncomfortably close, their faces almost touching his.

'We're thinkin' they might come for you soon,' she whispered. 'We're thinkin' that Lasper weren't out looking for his son near Mintaka; he was wantin' to find that Lostol fella.'

'Ra?' whispered back Balbao.

Hob took up the thread. 'Yeah. See, Tekkie stole his future predictin' device. We thinkin' mebbe he wants Ra to build him another one. That's why we're here.'

Balbao let Hob's theory sink in. 'Lasper wants to re-create the device here?'

'Well, somethin'. Scolar station's got an information node. Probably the only one left, now everyone else's closed their spheres or been wiped out,' said Sammy. 'Lasper's no fool. He wouldn't be riskin' comin' here for no good reason.'

Balbao waited, still not sure what they wanted.

'We're thinkin' scientists like you might be thin on the ground on Scolar. We're thinkin' Lasper might need you, so you gettin' out of here might be our only chance.'

'Only chance to do what?'

'To get rid of Lasper Farr. Consilience needs a new leader, someone who ain't crazy. And she's here, aboard this ship. Name's Bethany Ionil – Lasper's sister. We want you to get a message to an 'esque named Petalu Mau. Tell him Sammy said, "Now's the time." That's all you gotta do.'

'"Now's the time"? What does that mean?'

'That means Bethany's supporters take over the ship; we get outta here and away from Scolar. You and the others go where you want. That's gotta be better than sitting in this cell waiting for the Extros to come.'

Balbao's frill stiffened. A mutiny.

He'd been an academic for his entire adult life, but at the mention of a revolt his carefully constructed civility began to peel away. He would die here soon if he didn't grasp the opportunity. Though he had no way of knowing the full implications of Sammy's plan, or even if what she sought would be better or worse for them all, he did know he had no wish to remain Lasper Farr's prisoner.

'How will I find this Petalu Mau?'

'He'll be with Lasper, bein' his bodyguard. Big, wide teranu who likes to eat. Can't mistake him. No one else looks like him.'

'Farr's bodyguard?'

'Bethany's as well. Beth treats him a lot better.'

'But what about Farr's soldiers?'

'We been laying the groundwork for years. Won't take more than a word and a show of strength; most of them will come over. They ain't loyal to Lasper. They just get paid.'

The idea of treachery made Balbao's thick skin sting. Farr would be betrayed by his personal bodyguard and his own soldiers. What did that say for these two old fiends? Should he trust them at all? 'You think they'll come for me?'

'Mebbe. Mebbe not,' said Hob. 'Sure as hell they won't come for us, 'cept to spit us into the black.'

'What about the others? They all have their expertise. It might be one of them. Labile is a geneer.'

'You said you was chief scientist?'

Balbao nodded.

Sammy gave a quiet, satisfied grunt. 'He'll need you.'

TRIN

Trin watched the mercenary closely. Two, nearly three days had passed since one of the arrivals had stolen the AiV in which they'd come. Randall had been fit to murder when she'd seen Rasterovich go, swearing all kinds of revenge.

Trin told Juno and Tivi to watch her too. He sensed her volatility and suspected that only the solemnity of the burial they gave Cass Mulravey's child kept her anger from spilling out. Respect for the dead. And the mother.

Mulravey herself seemed broken. Though she still fed and tended to Vito, the child Mira Fedor had left behind, her manner was reflexive. Her physical body had become a shell that housed no spirit.

Trin almost missed the antagonist he'd become accustomed to fending off. Despite her disruptive manner, Mulravey had been a clear and quick thinker, a person worthy of notice. Trin felt the need for good opinions.

Innis had disappeared again. His woman, Liesl, was feeding him, slipping extra food in her robe and stealing away in the darkness to meet him. Trin thought to send Tivi and Juno after her, to bring Innis to account, but for now he needed them close by, watching Randall and her man Catchut.

He didn't think that the survivors could tolerate a

sentencing at this moment. The group had come so close to splitting. Only the arrival of the strangers had halted that, yet still he felt it could happen at any time, with Innis hiding and Liesl agitating the others.

'Principe, food is prepared,' Djes called out to him.

Trin turned back from where he stood at the edge of their camp, staring at the bright objects in the night sky, and walked back to the dinner circle.

Spirits were low; he saw it in the dispirited postures and lack of conversation. Randall and Catchut sat apart from the rest, with Kristo.

Despite Djes's catch of bass and squid, and the sweet paste that Tina Galiotto had made from berries and water, Trin felt as despondent as the rest.

The arrival of the AiV had resurrected thoughts of rescue in all of them, and now its loss and the accidental death of Mulravey's boy deepened their collective misery. For the first time since they'd begun their flight through the Pablo tunnels, Trin had nothing to give them. No hope. No direction.

He sat next to Djes and ate in silence. What would become of them? Would they gradually kill each other off with surprise attacks, such as the one Innis had attempted? Or would they simply die of disease when their HealthWatch ran out? And what about Djes? Did she prefer Joe Scali's company to his?

The howling noise in the distance took some time to register in his consciousness, so deep was he in despair.

Djes nudged him. 'Trinder? What's that?'

He stood up. From the east came the sound of rushing wind.

Other heads lifted; bodies stiffened.

Trin craned his neck skyward, searching for the source. Fear spiked through him. 'Take cover!'

The survivors picked up their food shells and hastened to their caves, staying close to the mouths so they could still see out.

'There!' Joe Scali pointed east, just above the tree-line.

Trin saw the shadows in the sky, like giant moths given dim outline by Tiesha's glow and the backdrop carpet of satellites.

'AiVs,' said someone.

'No!' Randall laughed and walked out into the open. Trin couldn't see her face, but her voice was filled with sudden energy. 'Biozoons. Crux-damned biozoons.'

The shadows passed over the mountain crest and swept on out to sea.

'They've missed us!' Josefia Genarro exclaimed.

Others joined in her cry of disappointment.

'No.' Randall again. This time she turned and walked straight back up to Trin. 'They'll have to land down on the beach, in the water. You got someone who can show me the quickest way down?'

Trin hesitated. 'Who would be in the biozoons? Why would they come here?'

'Not sure who the second is, but one of them's got to be Fedor. We picked up a 'cast back on Pell, her 'zoon's signature from orbit. Not sure how the hell she made it down here without getting banged up, but I warrant it's her, and that she's come for us.'

Trin stared back into the sky with disbelief. *Mira Fedor*.

MIRA

Mira started awake as a hand touched her shoulder. Tekton had disengaged from his nub and was standing next to her.

'Baronessa, I would speak with you privately,' he whispered.

She blinked and looked around the buccal. Josef was still in Autonomy, eyes closed and flickering with dreamsleep. Tapping the nub to release her, she got to her feet. Sleep had refreshed her enough that she was now hungry. 'Would there be food?'

'I have hoarded some in my cabin. If you would accompany me there, I have something of the utmost importance to show you.'

Mira regarded the man. She'd heard little of Tekton of Lostol that would recommend him as trustworthy, and yet right at this moment he seemed as sincere as any 'esque could be.

'What is the nature of the thing you would show me?' she asked.

'It is . . . without meaning to sound grandiose . . . a matter of our survival.'

She nodded.

As they made their way along the strata to Tekton's cabin, Mira was again pained by what she saw – the piles of rubbish and the unhealthy smell of rot. The corporeals, Jancz and Ilke, had not cared for the hybrid at all.

Not surprising, she thought, given what they were. Wanton had been correct when it had said that Hosts could be humanesque, and yet she had not quite believed the little Extro.

'The biozoon is sick,' she said.

'Yes.' Tekton stopped in front of a ridged door and pressed the pucker. It opened sluggishly.

Inside, the room was similar to *Insignia*'s cabins, save for the grey tinge to the walls and small pools of biozoon secretion in the corners. There were no furnishings other than the bed, on which lay a small dark box.

Mira paused just inside the pucker and waited for Tekton to speak.

He pointed at the box. 'Do you know what that is, Baronessa?'

She regarded the innocuous object, wondering why the sight of it filled her with dread. Finally, she shook her head.

'I . . . borrowed it from Lasper Farr after he tried to have me murdered. At the time I thought it would be both a fine revenge and a useful appendage. That's all. But now, having spent many hours between Intel station and here learning its nuances, I'm not sure that my choice was the most judicious.'

Mira's eyes widened a little. 'You stole something from Commander Farr?'

'Yes. While you were making your pronouncements of impending doom on Intel, I was busy ransacking his cabin. But that is far from the point I would make. Do you know what this does?'

She shook her head again.

'It is called a bifurcation or Dynamic System Device, a fascinating object that has only, until this was created, been theorised about.'

Mira frowned, recalling the encounter with Commander Farr at the trade faire. Josef Rasterovich had fallen into a deep trance-like state and then collapsed on the floor of the tent after immersion in Farr's virtual world. He'd spoken little of his experience to them, other than to curse the Commander.

'I have heard something of such theories. The idea is to predict things,' she said.

'That is a most simplistic explanation of its capabilities. It's fed by information, collected and delivered to the device's astounding – unbelievable – processing capability. Skilled interaction with the DSD will enable you to view possible outcomes of events, but it will also allow the user to locate optimum points at which changes might be made to affect those outcomes.'

'To change life?'

'More precisely, to create new outcomes. Acting at those points is essential to the change. Attempting to make alterations at a less than optimum point will amount to nothing more than a clustering and local disturbance. The outcomes will remain the same.'

He picked up a juice container and sipped from it. Then he rummaged in a crate on the bedside table and produced another one, which he offered to Mira.

She saw that the seal was intact and took it. The sweet tepid liquid eased her dry throat.

'Here.' He passed her a small carton of dry biscuits and sank onto the bed next to the box. 'After spending much time observing Orion's future with the device, I have learned that there are few outcomes from the Post-Species invasion of OLOSS that don't end in the destruction of all the humanesque and alien species.' He sagged further until his body appeared almost folded upon itself. 'In fact, Baronessa, there is only one.'

She waited again, nibbling the biscuits as he sought to convey what he knew.

'Excuse my bluntness, but time is a factor. You see, the optimum point for averting the destruction of our species, Baronessa, is nearly upon us, and involves you.'

'Me?' Mira stepped back against the pucker.

'You and your newborn child, who I believe is aboard your biozoon, and the man piloting this ship.'

'Josef?'

'Yes. Josef Rasterovich.' Tekton's face crumpled into a kind of disgust. 'I've seen the point of change, and the three of you must be there.'

'W-what must w-we do?'

'It is unclear to me exactly what you should do, only that you must be there. It would be best if I showed you. Have you heard of the Sole Entity?'

'Si.'

'You know then that I was one of its tyros?'

'Si.'

'The device has shown me that the Entity has left the space around Belle-Monde, and has been travelling throughout Orion to the areas of destruction.'

'What is it doing?'

'I could not be sure. But I am not convinced, now, that its purpose is entirely benign. I do however think that it has a curious way about it. It has given us a

chance to manage our own affairs by giving us this gift.'
He held out his hand. 'Come, Baronessa, and see what
I mean.'

Mira hesitated, unsure that she liked the desperate
light in the Godhead's eyes. He seemed a little . . .
disturbed, though lucid enough with it.

Mama?

Si, Nova.

You must listen to him, and see.

Why do you say that?

You must trust me, Mama. Even if you don't trust him.

Mira took a deep breath. 'Where would you have
me stand? And how do I watch?'

Tekton smiled and patted the bed. 'No need to
stand, Baronessa. In fact, best not to.'

Mira's immersion was intense, but not painful like her
early days of bonding with *Insignia* had been. She let
Tekton's voice guide her through the streams of images.
His narration became an anchor in a sea of horror and
destruction.

Her connection to the Post-Species invasion was more
vivid and visceral than anything she'd seen on farcast.
The dust of imploded worlds seemed to coat her, the
screams of the dying twisted her stomach, and the
dryness of the solar winds parched her mouth. She was
there, witnessing the end of family dynasties, the disfig-
uration of whole planetary systems, the sudden and
profound snuffing out of billions and billions of lives.

The scale of annihilation became incomprehen-
sible, and yet among it she saw faint shafts of hope.
Many systems had closed their shift spheres. Some

might never reopen, while others would do so to find Geni-carriers still waiting. Non-Corporeal Post-Species had no age, no limit on patience, no need to find other distractions. They would wait, and they would kill.

'They must never reopen their shift spheres,' she whispered.

'There is another way,' said Tekton. 'Come.'

He guided her in deeper. She saw images of herself, scenes that had already played out: sitting at a table with Bethany Ionil and Josef at the trade faire on Edo, riding in the taxi with Thales, the markets on Rho Junction, being enveloped by a crowd of siphonophores ...

'Now we move forward,' said Tekton. 'Commands can be given sub-vocally or using micro-expressions, the same way most virtuals interact.'

Mira tried using a combination of both to slow the image flow. After several tries she became accustomed to it. It was much clumsier than her mind bond with *Insignia*, but effective enough.

All the while, she followed Tekton's crisp monologue on how to follow the pathways of projected futures, making great leaps in time like an all-powerful god.

She saw many different paths leading to one result: the rise of the Post-Species consciousness and the end of humanesque- and alien-kind.

'Did Commander Farr know this?' she asked Tekton.

'I expect so.'

'How far forward can the device forecast? Is it infinite?'

'I've explored that question a little, and strangely it is not. There is a point at which the information stops

propagating. Not an end but more like an invisible wall
– a barrier between us and what comes next.'

Mira might have found Tekton's answer fanciful at
any other time, but not now, not with what she had
seen. The device itself was remarkable – and fright-
eningly powerful.

Suddenly, she wanted to disengage from it. Get away.
Toss it into the void. No person should have such potential at their beck and call, least of all a selfish academic
or a mercenary leader. Neither Farr nor Tekton, nor
even she, was safe with its powers. She wanted to tell
Tekton how she felt, but he kept on talking.

'If we take a different perspective on the information streams, you can see the potential change nodes,
the points at which optimum change can be effected,
the point at which *you* must be present.'

Her virtual landscape changed to the impression of
a chaotic spinning knot. She could hardly breathe,
wondering what it represented.

'Shall we look, Baronessa?'

Mama. You must. Nova had been quiet throughout,
but now she sent another urgent thought. With it, her
child sent her a sense of confidence and inevitability.

'I must,' said Mira. 'I must.'

BALBAO

They came for him sooner than even Hob or Sammy could have guessed. The lights flared, disturbing their slumber, and guards dragged him from his bunk soon after he'd returned to it.

Miranda and Jise roused enough to make a faint protest, but Sammy and Hob simply watched. Connit never stirred.

They marched him through the convoluted corridors of the ship to the transport lock. Farr was waiting on the station side of the hatch, speaking with a harassed official. Ra was with him, and a huge teranu with a fleshy face and broad shoulders that he had to compress to fit in the narrow tube. Petalu Mau.

'Balbao.' The Godhead nodded.

'What am I doing here?' snarled Balbao.

'I need your assistance,' said Ra.

'For what?'

Ra ignored him, focusing back on Farr's conversation with the official. As Sammy had guessed, the Commander was trying to get access to the station information node.

'Our IN's in lockdown, Commander,' said the 'esque. 'The Sophos have restricted access.'

'Mau,' said Farr.

The huge teranu grabbed the 'esque by the tunic and lifted him off his feet, shaking him.

Farr folded his arms. 'Unrestrict it.'

The official paled and nodded.

Petalu Mau dropped him to the floor and gave him a shove.

The terrified official hurried forward. Mau followed him with Farr striding on Mau's heels. He didn't bother to acknowledge Balbao's presence, and his soldiers nudged Ra and Balbao along quickly to keep up.

The station was chaotic and at capacity, bodies crowding every standing space. It seemed to Balbao that everyone there was either arguing or pleading with someone else.

Getting to the information node became a nightmare of mini-confrontations between Petalu Mau and Farr's soldiers, and those in their way. The red robes of the Scolar police punctuated the milling throng, but even they only seemed to be able to contain pockets of the confusion.

Scolar station was close to anarchy. Balbao saw it in the aggressive stares; felt it in the undercurrent of panic. Everyone wanted off, but the planet-transit ships were backlogged, and the sphere itself could only process at a certain speed. Farr must have used extreme coercion to get docking permission.

The IN entrance was guarded by a contingent of four tired station security guards. Farr ordered several his of soldiers to stay with them and the rest to accompany him inside.

Balbao followed Ra and the others into the darkened chamber. The smell of sweat and the whirr of fans assailed his senses, twenty or more data dispersal technicians working on top of each other.

'Ra?' Farr's calmness unnerved Balbao.

Ra pointed to a workstation on the other side of the chamber.

Petalu Mau advanced on the person using it and cleared her with a clout of one large hand. The IN supervisor stormed across but Farr's soldiers backed him up against the wall at gunpoint. Soon all the technicians and scientists were next to him.

Balbao guessed the same was happening to the guards outside the door.

Ra sat himself at the chosen station and began to generate, as far as Balbao could tell, pseudo-code.

'Balbao,' Ra tapped the desktop. 'Come over here. I need you to breed a Henon map.'

Balbao felt something hard thrust up under his armpit into the soft part of his skin in line with his heart.

'Now,' Farr said in his ear.

Balbao pulled away stiffly and threaded through the other workstations to join Ra. His own face, he was sure, matched the angry fearful stares from the techs herded against the exterior wall behind them.

'What do you want?' he growled as he sat down.

'An orbital diagram,' said Ra.

'What for? What did you build on Belle-Monde?'

'A bifurcation device,' Ra answered absently.

'That's not possible.'

Ra took a brief moment to give Balbao a deprecating stare before turning back to his workstation. 'What did you think we were learning on Belle-Monde, Balbao? How to culture fungi?'

With a tremor in his hands, Balbao reached for the interaction pads. Ra's sarcasm had jolted him. He'd taken the tyros far too lightly, concerned as he'd been with collecting empirical data about the Entity. But a bifurcation device – a device that can predict futures – surely not! 'So you're trying to re-create the same thing? Here?'

'That's not possible without the Entity's assistance. And as you may have noticed, Sole seems to have deserted us,' Ra replied softly.

'Then what in Crux's name are you doing?'

'I'm searching for a repeller, something to destabilise the dynamic system of the universe.'

Balbao's frill stiffened to the point of pain. 'What?'

'A repeller will disrupt whatever changes Tekton has set in place with the DSD.'

Tekton? Balbao sucked in a deep noisy breath. 'If this bifurcation device really exists, then a repeller – in theory – risks causing a dysfunction that could have any number of catastrophic results. You would do that simply to thwart your cousin?'

Ra gave a small and wholly unpleasant smile. 'No more catastrophic than what we currently face. It may even disrupt the final outcome of the invasion.'

'May? But you don't *know* that.'

Ra turned his multi-faceted eyes on Balbao. His thin skin concertinaed into a frown. 'If you say that any louder, I will kill you myself.' He slid a thin knife from inside his robe and rested it on his knee.

Balbao felt a surge of uncontrolled fury. He glanced over at Lasper Farr. The commander watched their whispered conversation, as he watched everything, with suspicion. Ra had convinced the Commander that he could somehow deter the Extros' invasion. That was why Farr had bought them here.

Balbao looked for Petalu Mau, who'd taken up a position near the lab hostages. He wanted to deliver Sammy's message to him, but something other than the knife on Ra's knee held him back. *Not yet*, he thought, *not quite yet*.

Instead he clenched his teeth, slapped the I-pads on his neck and entered the virtual patterner.

THALES

'The commander's here,' whispered Fariss.

She brushed past Thales and crouched close to Janne and Magdalen. Getting this far had been harder than they'd anticipated; the station was frenzied. They'd travelled in small groups so as not to attract the attention of the red robes, who were scattered among the crowds. Linnea knew the way to the information node and had given precise instructions to the Feohte.

Now they'd reassembled a corridor away from the IN and Fariss had just scouted the last stretch. The news she had to give was the last that Thales expected to hear. He joined their huddle, anxious to know exactly what she'd seen.

'There're a bunch of soldiers at the door. Some mercs have got station sec baled up against the wall. I've seen the mercs before. For some Crux-damned reason, Commander Lasper Farr's in the IN.'

Magdalen and Janne stared at her.

'Commander Farr,' said Magdalen. 'Of the—'

'Stain Wars. Yeah.' Fariss turned to Thales. 'Ideas?'

Thales shook his head. He couldn't imagine what had bought Lasper Farr here at this time. What could be so important that he would risk his ship by coming to Scolar station?

'We could go through the front door,' said Janne.

Fariss shook her head. 'They'll have more Robes at Shift Command than anywhere else. It's this way or none. We've got surprise on our side. Don't imagine the Commander's expectin' to see us either.'

'Will the mercs know you?' asked Thales.

She thought about it for a moment. 'Yeah, but that might not be a bad thing. A little reputation, you know . . .'

Thales's stomach clenched even tighter. 'Fariss, please—'

She ignored him and spoke directly to Janne. 'I'll get close enough to deal with two or three. When I make that move you need to get down the corridor quick. Take the mercs first. Station sec won't know what the fuck is going on. My guess is they'll run.'

Janne nodded.

Both women were bright in a way that brought a bitter taste to Thales's mouth, but he set his jaw and swallowed. His idea had brought them here.

Fariss's large hand descended on his shoulder. 'You stay behind Janne and the Feohte with Magdalen and Linnea. Got it? Sammy might be inside there – don't let any of the Feohte shoot her.'

'Fariss?' He wanted to thank her for this – it was his world not hers – but the words dried up in his mouth.

She didn't wait for him to free his tongue. Slipping her weapon into her belt, she sauntered straight out into the IN corridor.

Janne and the Feohte crouched closer to the bend. Thales couldn't see past them, or hear anything until the first shout. Then suddenly the Feohte were gone, a dozen women swarming up the passage.

Magdalen put a restraining hand on him. 'We'll just give them more to worry about. When the hatch is clear, we go.'

Thales waited in an agony of dread while Linnea crept forward and peered after the Feohte. A moment later she flattened herself back against the wall. Instinctively Thales did the same but Magdalen was slower to react.

The station sec guards bolted past them, one of them colliding with the slight woman, knocking her against the rough conduit. The guard picked himself up and kept running but Magdalen lay still.

Linnea went to her and felt over her head. 'She's out.'

'Can you get her back to Ling-Ma's ship by yourself?' asked Thales.

Linnea nodded. 'Should do. She weighs less than a bag of beans. Now, remember that the common wall is the one behind the node. You cut through the wrong one and you'll be floating – permanently.'

Thales gave a grim nod. 'May Villon protect you, Linnea.'

She gave him a strange look. 'That's what Mira Fedor said too.'

He watched the brawny woman lift Magdalen into her arms and leave. When she'd gone he walked into the IN passage.

Farris was crouched at the hatch. A mess of tangled bodies lay before her on the floor, throats cut. Most of the dead were Farr's mercs but not all. Two Feohtes were being shifted aside from the mercs and covered out of respect.

As Thales drew closer he saw the surviving Feohte sheathing curved bloody swords in their belts alongside their soft-projectile guns. He wanted to force his way past them to Fariss's side and touch her for reassurance, but he wouldn't get that chance again, not until this was over.

She glanced over her shoulder and saw him. A quick frown creased her blood-dirtied face. 'Where are they?'

'Magdalen was knocked out by a station guard. Linnea's taking her back to Ling-Ma.'

She pressed her lips together, unimpressed. 'Janne, you got that cutting gear? Could get messy in here, depending on how many Lasper's got with him. I'm bettin' on not too many.'

Janne tossed her the sack. 'Sounds like a good bet.'

BALBAO

Balbao didn't register the intruders at first. He was deep in a sea of virtual images: Lorenz attractors, Tangent and Rossler maps and Listovich equations, the elegance and mystery of which had transported him far from the fraught IN chamber. Ra had shown him things he'd never dreamed to know, reconstructing a chaotic beauty and symmetry from an ancient humanesque theorem.

We've had the key to read our futures all this time, said virtual Balbao. *But we've not known which way to turn it.*

Frustrating and amusing, said virtual Ra.

And now?

And now to perturb the stability of the system.

Virtual Ra flew at the ocean of fractals with fierce active hands. As he worked, their symmetries faltered and began to change, so that they became a chain of staggered links. Ra stabbed at the breaks in their flow, prising them apart. Then he began picking at them like a carrion bird, searching through them for . . . what?

Aaah. There. Virtual Ra disappeared, funnelling down into the break in the fractal like water draining through a low point.

Virtual Balbao felt the pull as well, the attraction of the break that Ra had manufactured. His perspective began to alter, the diagrammatic vanished and he found his mind-self immersed in a spinning well of images –

fleeting, overwhelming rushes of information that Balbao couldn't possibly process.

Ra was ahead of him diving in and out of information accumulations, ripping and tearing and flinging segments about.

What in Crux is he searching for? Balbao fretted. *What is he doing?*

That's when he heard the fracas.

He ripped the pad from his neck and blinked into a nightmare: gunfire and screams as plain-garbed women – insurgents of some kind – swarmed over Farr's soldiers with scimitars and soft-projectile guns. The soldiers replied with their own weapons.

The coralled technicians dropped to the floor on instinct, spreading out in all directions, and over against the far wall a large figure was crouched over a glowing cutting tool. Another woman, not quite as big but with equal purpose about her, held anyone who might interfere with the cutting at bay with her gun.

'Stop them!' Farr screamed at Petalu Mau.

Mau moved across the IN towards the two women.

The armed one cocked her weapon.

'Stay back!' she yelled.

'Petalu Mau. It's Thales, Bethany's friend. We have to close the shift sphere; otherwise the Post-Species will annihilate the planet.' This shrill shout came from the hatchway of the IN where a lean young 'esque stood.

Balbao knew the face, the scar and the fine features, the cultured voice; this 'esque had spoken at the summit meeting on Intel station.

Mau stopped, momentarily confused.

'Thales Berniere. What in—' Lasper Farr didn't bother to finish. He snatched a gun from one of his soldiers and fired across the room. It took the armed woman in the shoulder and she went down.

'Janne!' Thales Berniere started into the IN.

At the same time Balbao became aware of Ra. The Godhead had removed his pads and was standing, fists clenched.

Balbao rose automatically. 'What?'

'It's him,' muttered Ra. '*He's* the disruption.'

'Who? What do you mean?'

But Ra moved without answering, lunging towards Thales Berniere.

His movement snapped Balbao from his daze and he made a quick and unalterable decision.

'Petalu Mau!' he roared in full Balol battle voice. 'Sammy says the time is now! THE TIME IS NOW!' The huge bodyguard jerked his head towards Balbao, who nodded vigourously. 'I've been in the ship's containment with her.'

As the meaning of the message seeped in, Mau changed direction. He swung at Lasper Farr as the Commander raised his weapon to shoot the woman cutting through the wall. The teranu threw out a powerful jaw-breaking sideswipe that sent Farr down without a sound. He seized the scimitar from Janne's bleeding hand and hacked into the Commander's neck. Violent chopping motions splintered his backbone in a gush of blood.

Balbao wrenched his horrified attention back to Ra. The Godhead was advancing on Thales Berniere. Though not much bigger or heavier than Thales, Ra had a burning intensity about him, a feverish unholy energy. He waved a knife with eager but inexpert hands.

Thales stepped behind a workstation and stumbled over a body.

'We're in!' roared the woman with the cutting tools. She kicked in the wall panel, calling the insurgents with her. Mau followed as well.

The knot of technicians lying on the floor scrambled to their feet and ran for the hatch.

Suddenly, only three people were left alive and on their feet in the IN: Thales, Ra and Balbao.

'Ra!' bellowed the Balol chief. 'Stop!'

Thales

Lasper Farr is dead. The notion stunned Thales. As did the sight of the Commander's savaged body.

'We're in!' shouted Fariss.

Her voice delivered Thales from his shock. He saw the Feohte and Mau follow her through the wall panel, and the comm technicians rush for the hatch.

Then he was alone with the dead and two 'esques he'd never seen before: a Balol who stood behind his workstation as if rooted there and a Lostolian with strange multi-faceted eyes. The latter advanced on Thales with a knife in his hand.

Thales backed towards the direction the technicians had fled, but the Lostolian cut him off from the hatch so he crouched down and looked around for something to defend himself. He spotted a gun partially covered by a body.

'Ra!' bellowed the Balol. 'Stop!'

Ra? The name meant something, but fear prevented him from being able to remember.

'*He's* the disruption. *His* death will be the repeller,' hissed the Lostolian. He moved closer as he spoke, stopping just short of stabbing distance from Thales.

'*Him.* Why is *he* important?' said the Balol.

'He's not. It's his connection to others. How his death will affect their actions.'

'You're being insane, Ra. You can't possibly believe—'

The Balol broke off as Thales grabbed the gun and raised it.

With one tiny movement of his thumb, Thales knew he could end the Lostolian's life, but he baulked.

Thoughts cartwheeled through his mind, and emotions deluged his body. He felt as if the whole point of his existence hinged on what he did right now. He'd left Scolar as a naive young man who, for a time, deserted his Jainist principles. But now he'd returned, knowing much more of himself. He wished Villon was here to tell.

Then, just as quickly as he'd become paralysed and confused, the right choice became clear. He would not kill anyone. Not even to defend his life.

He threw the gun away and stared at Ra.

The Lostolian, surprised by his action, hesitated.

And as he did, the Balol made a choice of his own. He pushed aside the workstation and leapt forward. With nearly as much force as Petalu Mau had used on Lasper Farr, the Balol punched Ra in the back of the head.

Ra fell.

Thales watched the Balol dive forward, teeth bared and face contorted. Heaving his body at the Lostolian, the Balol impaled Ra with the spikes of his stiffened frill.

Ra made one short gurgling sound of pain then fell still.

Immediately, the Balol withdrew his frill and wiped the spikes clean on Ra's robe. When he stood up again, his teeth were still bared but his face was composed.

'He wanted to change the course of events,' the Balol told him, as if Thales should understand.

But Thales shook his head in bewilderment.

The Balol gave a rough laugh. 'My name is Balbao, formerly Chief Astronomein of Belle-Monde. That was Ra of Lostol, one of the tyros. The rest of it will take a while in the telling.'

'Thales!'

Farriss was back, covered in blood. 'It's done!' Her eyes narrowed and she looked between him and the Balol.

'What's done?' asked Balbao.

Thales stared at Balbao. 'We've started the sequence to close the shift sphere. In a few days no one will be able to leave Scolar station.'

'And now we have to get out of here,' said Fariss with feeling. 'Every red robe on the station is coming our way.'

'Commander Farr's ship is close,' said Balbao.

Fariss looked to Thales and nodded. 'Let's go.'

TRIN

They reached the beach before dawn when the darkness became a pearly grey. As Randall had predicted, two enormous biozoons were set deep in the wet sand of the shallows. The survivors waited in the treeline, watching as three figures emerged from inside one of the creatures. The three climbed down the roughened side of their craft and stepped into the shallows. One of them waded across to the other biozoon while the other two headed up onto the beach.

Even from a distance Trin recognised the two approaching the shore: Randall's man Josef had returned and – Trin's heart contracted into a tight fist – Mira Fedor.

'Mira,' croaked Cass Mulravey. The woman broke from shelter and ran down to the beach, arms outstretched.

'It's Mira!' This came from Djeserit, at his side.

'Wait!' said Trin.

But, like Mulravey, Djes was already moving.

Along the line of watchers, calls went out to each other.

'The Baronessa is back.'

'She's come for us!' cried Josefia Genarro.

'It's her! Mira Fedor is here!'

Trin wanted them all to stop, wanted to take control, wanted to speak to Mira before anyone else, but their excitement wasn't to be contained, even by him.

They spilled down onto the beach, leaving Trin alone with the two mercenaries, Randall and Catchut.

Both stared keenly at the new arrivals.

'It's Rasterovich, Capo,' said Catchut.

'I got eyes, Cat.' Randall turned to Trin. 'Don't seem as thrilled as the rest, Pellegrini?' Even in the dull light he could see her expression hardening. 'Don't you wanna be saved today? You maybe enjoyin' this cock-o'-the-walk thing you got goin' here.'

Mira Fedor. His saviour? The idea was repugnant. He'd sent her away in the hope that she would find help from OLOSS. He had not expected she would come back herself. And where was the baby he'd impreg-nated her with? He saw no signs of pregnancy in her thin straight physique. Had she lost the babe? Miscarried it? Or had it removed? Eccentric as her morals were, surely she would not have aborted her own child.

Panic streaked through him. He must speak with her alone before she said things that might damage the balance of things here, things that could undermine his authority.

He started forward but Randall tripped him.

He fell flat and a weight descended on his back, pinning him there. Thighs gripped his head, pushing his face into the sand. 'Not so quick, Pellegrini. I'm thinkin' your flock might need to have a confab with the Baronessa without you breathin' down their necks.'

Randall shifted around on top of him as if making herself comfortable. 'We'll just wait a little before we go and join them. Have a bit of a confab ourselves. What you say to that?'

MIRA

Mira saw Cass first, heard the hoarse call and recognised the thin ragged shape running down to meet them. Her heart leapt in her chest and she let go of Josef's hand to wade out of the water.

They met in the sand above the water line in a tight and emotional embrace. No words came immediately, just relief and heartfelt joy.

'He said you'd run out on us. I knew it was a lie,' whispered Cass after a moment.

Mira stiffened for an instant. 'Trinder?'

Cass stepped back so she could look at her. 'We need to talk, you and I, alone. But not now. Not in front of the rest.'

Mira nodded. 'There's not much time. I have to go soon. We'll leave one of the biozoons for you.'

'Go?'

'Something important I have to do. Cass, the Post-Species are controlling the Saqr. And now they're overrunning Orion.'

'We feared something like that,' said Cass. 'Mira, if you have to leave, take Vito.'

Mira gripped her arm. 'Vito's alive?'

Cass nodded, tears beginning to fall without check. 'I fed him what I could, but we've had little enough to eat.'

Mira faced the rest of the advancing survivors. She picked out Josefia Genarro among them, who carried a small thin 'bino. 'But Josef . . .' Mira swung back to Josef, who had stopped behind her. 'You said he'd died!'

He looked confused. 'I saw a boy killed with a spear. Happened as we got here.'

Cass's fist went to her lips. She ground her knuckles against her teeth before replying. 'Not your 'bino, Mira. Mine. Both gone now. Both of them.'

'Chanee? And your ragazzo?' Mira saw the pain on Cass's face. She wasn't just starved and exhausted, her spirit was in tatters.

Mira hugged her again, more fiercely this time, not knowing how else to give comfort.

They stood together as the survivors surrounded them. But at the sight of Josefia with Vito, Mira let her go of Cass and reached for her adopted child. She lifted him into her arms. To her distress, he didn't feel much heavier than Nova. Nor did he seem to know her.

'Vito.'

He blinked his solemn eyes at the sound of her voice.

She leaned forward and gently kissed his forehead, aware of the tension in the little body.

He reached out for Cass Mulravey, who shook her head. 'Mama, Vito. This is your mama.'

The survivors watched silently.

'Vito.' Mira said his name again and traced her finger down his bare legs. 'Mira. It's Mira.'

There was some jostling in the group and the korm pushed its way through. It whistled to her and bowed its tall frame, until its head was close to hers. 'M'ra.'

'Korm!' The tears she had kept at bay while comforting Cass Mulravey sprang freely to her eyes. The alien ragazzo was a scarecrow, barely recognisable save for its size and fur.

She reached up and fondled its crest. It chittered softly.

Copying Mira's action, Vito lifted his thin arm and put his fingers to Mira's cheek.

She turned her head and kissed his fingers, hardly daring to breathe.

Suddenly Vito smiled and brought his other hand up to link around her neck. 'M'ra.'

Mira hugged him to her. 'He's speaking,' she said ecstatically.

'A few words only. Not much for us to say to each other these last months,' said Cass.

A ripple of emotion passed through the group.

Mira felt it keenly, just as she felt her own elation, and relief, and despair. She should have been quicker with help. They were barely alive. And where was Trin Pellegrini?

Before she could ask Cass about the young Principe, the silence broke.

'What's happening out there?' asked someone.

'Have you come for us?' Another 'esque.

Questions flew at her and voices rose to such a pitch that she could barely hear one from the other.

'Quiet!' Josef stepped in front of her, arms outstretched.

Surprisingly, they responded to his firm order.

'Back up,' he said to the first line of people.

They complied, creating room around Mira and Cass.

Though Josef was much thinner than Mira remembered him, he looked strong and capable alongside the starved survivors.

'Yes, we've come for you. And yes, we'll tell you everything we know. But it's only a short time until daylight,' he said. 'We will need to take cover.'

'It's too far back to the caves,' said Cass Mulravey. 'We'll rest in the bushes above the beach.'

Jo-Jo nodded and looked to the lightening night sky. 'Then we should get there now.'

As the group began to move back up the beach, Mira noticed a slight figure standing off to one side under the waning moonlight. 'Djes?' she called softly. 'Djes?'

The young girl she had rescued from the ruins of Villa Fedor came towards her hesitantly.

As she got closer, Mira held out her hand to her, and suddenly Djes was in her arms as Cass Mulravey had been, clinging to her with relief and disbelief.

'Mira.'

Djes's body felt muscular and lean and tense with emotion, and she smelt of the sea. As Josef hustled them along, she threaded her arm through Mira's and they walked together behind the rest.

'Why did you leave so suddenly? Trin said that you'd deserted us but I didn't want to think that.'

'Trinder bends the truth, Djes,' said Mira bluntly. 'He told me to leave. When I refused, his carabinere forced me.'

'Forced you? I don't understand? But perhaps his decision was for the best? You've come back for us now.'

'His decision was selfish. Djes, I have birthed a 'bino

while I have been searching for help, a babe, born early, sired by Trin Pellegrini the night he sent me away. I was the last crown aristo alive. He feared that his bloodline would die out, so he raped me and forced me to leave. To protect his progeny.'

'No!' Djes pulled away from her. 'That's not true!'

Mira wished there was more time to explain gently, but she must leave again within a few hours. It was important that Djes knew the truth. 'My baby is aboard *Insignia*, my biozoon. Her name is Nova.'

Djes stopped and took several steps away from Mira. Then she turned and ran down the beach.

Josef dropped back to speak with Mira. 'Bad news?'

Mira sighed. 'The truth. I've hurt her, but she must know what he is.'

'Rast Randall told me some of it. I worked the rest out for myself. He's Nova's father.'

'Her sire, not her father,' Mira corrected.

Josef stopped her. 'I will try speaking to Djes. I promised Bethany I would.'

Mira hesitated then nodded. She moved forward to catch up with the rest of the group.

As they reached the crest of the beach, the survivors halted and divided. In front of the stunted trees stood Rast Randall, her man Catchut and Trin Pellegrini.

The gratification Mira felt on seeing Randall alive diminished at the sight of the Principe. From his tense, wary expression, she knew he'd seen Djeserit leave.

Suddenly Mira wished that Josef had stayed with her. Wished she could reach for the comfort of his hand. But he was not. And this she had to face alone.

She stepped forward.

JO-JO RASTEROVICH

He caught up with her as she was about to dive into the sea.

'Jess. Wait!' Deliberately he used Bethany's pronounciation of her name.

It stopped her short. 'What do you want?' She'd been crying, he thought.

Jo-Jo sank onto the wet sand above the waterline. 'To talk. To tell you things. Please.'

She didn't come any closer to him, nor did she move.

He took that as consent, so he told her what he knew of her mother – how she'd tried to follow her daughter to Araldis but had been put in detention on Dowl station.

He told her about their escape from Dowl and how brave and smart and resourceful Bethany was, and how she'd saved him.

When Djes didn't respond, he talked more, about Lasper Farr and how Bethany had feared him; the power that Farr wielded and Bethany's desire to distance herself from her brother's fanaticism. And finally how her mother had helped Mira.

Only when the sun came close to cresting the horizon did he stop.

'Come back,' he said. 'Some things need to be faced. Mira tells the truth.'

He got up and walked up the beach to the closest

tree cover and waited. She stood facing the ocean as the light grew more intense, and he began to fear that she'd choose neither the sea nor returning, but simply perish right there in the sunlight.

Then, in an oddly final gesture, she scooped water in her hands and splashed it over her face.

TRIN

Mira had changed little, save for new age lines which he didn't see until she came closer and her calm expression. With each step she took towards him Trin felt the pain of his past decisions and the weight of his future. What had she said to Djes? What would she say to his people?

He waited, more fearful of her than the Saqr. And the 'bino . . . there was no sign of pregnancy? What had gone wrong?

'Fedor.' The mercenary next to him strode forward and lifted the Baronessa from her feet to embrace her. Just as quickly, she set Mira down and stepped aside. 'Never figured to see you alive again,' she drawled. 'Never figured to be so pleased to see you alive again. Looks like I'll be owin' you again.'

Mira seemed flustered, her composure deserting her for a moment. 'I would say the same thing to you, Rast Randall. We are both fortunate, it seems.'

Trin saw his opportunity; the mercenary's unexpected greeting had rattled her. 'Mira Fedor,' he said loudly, 'your biozoons are a welcome sight.'

His rebuke, couched in an innocent greeting, didn't slip past her though, and as quickly as she'd become ruffled, her face regained its mask. 'As are your people.'

The moment hung between them, filled with tension and anger. She'd gained confidence, he thought.

Despite her fragile appearance, her will projected fiercely upon him.

'I have little time before I must leave again and there is much to tell.' She looked around the group. 'Please sit, all of you, and I will begin.'

Many of them glanced to the Principe, who nodded.

Once they had settled Mira told them of the Post-Species invasion across OLOSS.

'The satellites in the skies?' asked Cass.

'Geni-carriers, which are gradually being dispersed all over Orion. Millions have been murdered. Systems reduced to dust.'

'How many are there?' asked Juno Genarro. 'The lights have diminished over recent nights.'

'Thousands,' said Mira. 'Perhaps more.'

The survivors moaned with one voice.

'There is something I can do to arrest the destruction of our species but it is complicated to tell and not a certainty. I will be going at dusk, but will leave you the hybrid biozoon. It is space-worthy, though it needs some days bathing in sea minerals to replenish its amino acids. It has been treated cruelly.'

'But where would we go?' this came from Jilda.

'Principessa,' Mira acknowledged Trin's mother with a tiny bow of her head. 'The Post-Species are preparing to leave here. They've transformed their ship into an organic lifeform, a gigantic Saqr which continues to grow as we sit here. Its genesis is inexplicable. I cannot tell you how it happened, other than it grew from within the old ship. And it smelled of ligs.'

Ligs. Mira's story jolted Trin. 'There are ligs on this island, huge ligs that attacked us near the spring.'

'You believe the giant ligs are linked to the Saqr, Principe?' said Juno frowning.

'When I searched for water alone, I found a grove of trees. Bigger, stronger, more developed than these.' He waved his hands at the stunted bushes under which they'd taken cover. 'I rested there and broke off a branch to help me walk. The ligs came in while I was there, swarming after the sap. It's the sap, I think, that has made them grow so large. Perhaps the Post-Species have used the same sap to grow their organic ship?'

'Possibly the sap is in other places,' said Mira thoughtfully. 'Or they have harvested the ligs themselves. In which case, the quixite is only their fortification, the external protection against space travel. The ligs have been used to grow the Saqr. If so, then Araldis had everything they needed.'

'Dandy!' interceded Randall. 'But how does that change anything? I say we go load up the hybrid and I'll take us the hell out of here.'

'I will be the one to make that decision,' said Trin. 'And I believe it safer to stay here until the Post-Species have left.' He glared at Randall until the moment was broken by another voice.

'Neither of you'll decide for anyone else.'

Heads turned to see Djes and the third mercenary, Josef Rasterovich, in the bushes behind them.

The pair crawled forward to the front of the circle.

'The hybrid is mine by law, and I have given it to Djeserit Ionil. She'll choose her pilot, her route and when she'll leave. Those who don't like this arrangement can, as your Principe suggests, stay right here.'

Trin's heart, which had contracted into a tight fist,

relaxed. Djes would never leave him. 'At dark we should return to the caves for food—'

'I will leave in three nights,' said Djeserit, cutting across him. 'Long enough for the biozoon to replenish and for those to who wish to, to return to the caves and collect berries and roots.'

'Djes—' But Trin was cut off again.

'Where will you go?' asked Cass.

'To the Biozoon Pod. I'll ask for their protection.' She crawled out of the circle and moved to a thick bush at the side. 'I'll speak now with those who want to come with me.'

After a moment of silence, most of the survivors moved over to be near her, including Cass Mulravey, Joe and Tivi Scali, and Jilda.

'Madre,' said Trin hoarsely.

Jilda clutched at Cass Mulravey's arm. 'She has been kind to me.'

Only Juno Genarro, Josefia and Tina Galiotto stayed near Trin. Innis Mulravey's woman, Liesl, crawled away into the bushes.

Trin suppressed a moan. Everything he'd tried to preserve for the renewal of his world had just disintegrated before him.

'It's decided,' said Mira Fedor, with open satisfaction. 'I wish you all to be safe.'

Djeserit left him before dark, when Leah had dipped and left only her indirect glow to light the beach. Mira Fedor and Josef Rasterovich had gone before her, taking the 'bino, Vito.

Trin and Mira had not said goodbye.

Djes came to him though, for a brief moment. He wanted to hold her in his arms and prevent her leaving but Rast Randall hovered close.

'It's not as Mira told you,' said Trin.

'You raped her,' said Djes.

'It was my right to sire a bambino. It has always been the way among our people.'

'Then your way is wrong,' she said simply.

He fell silent, unable to find the right words to defend himself. 'I love you,' he said softly.

Her mouth softened as if she was weakening, but then she spun on her bare feet and walked away.

As he watched her go, he became aware of Tina Galiotto's presence at his elbow.

'She does not understand our ways, Principe,' said Tina.

Trin's sore heart eased a little, and he took solace in the truth. Djes wasn't one of his kind; she didn't truly understand his beliefs. Tina was right. But there were still those with him that did.

Perhaps that was enough.

MIRA

Mira carried Vito along *Insignia*'s strata to the buccal, myriad things playing on her mind.

'Trust me. Nourish the biozoon. Clean it. Then it will carry you away from here,' she'd told Djeserit as she left.

'What do you have to do?' Djes had asked.

'Something no one else can.'

Vito didn't look back when she and Josef left the island to go aboard *Insignia*.

Now, as she entered the buccal, she kissed the 'bino again, and felt him cling closer to her. To her relief, Nova lay in Primo, just as she'd left her, nourished and peaceful.

You have my fratella. Nova opened her eyes and smiled at her mother and Vito. *We must go now.*

Mira sat Vito on the edge of the vein and scooped Nova into her arms. She held them close, inhaling their scent and revelling in the touch of their skin. She could not remember ever feeling such aching joy. She would not leave her baby, or Vito, again.

Ever.

'What's her name?' asked Josef Rasterovich as he came in behind her.

'Nova,' said Mira.

Josef moved closer, his face flushed. 'She's beautiful.'

Nova reached out and caught his finger. *He is sweet, Mama, can I go with him? Secondo vein will care for us, and you can carry Vito.*

Mira laughed. 'She likes you. You should hold her for a while.'

Jo-Jo took Nova carefully from her, as if the child might disintegrate under his touch. 'Where are we going?'

'To Semantic.'

'The bigger moon?'

Mira nodded. 'Nova told me that she would like to travel there with you – in the Secondo vein.'

His mouth fell open. 'She told you that?'

'Si,' said Mira as she lay herself and Vito down in Primo. 'Nova knows what she likes.'

'Thales!'

Thales stared at the person entering the command brief chamber on Lasper Farr's ship. Bethany Ionil looked exhausted, but her embrace was fierce and full of relief.

Behind her, Thales saw Samuelle and the old fellow that Thales had met on Edo, Jelly Hob. Three other 'esques followed them in, and they gravitated straight over to Balbao.

With Petalu Mau, the Feohte injured leader and several of Lasper's mutinous soldiers, the chamber was suddenly full. One of the soldiers passed around rehyd-tubes and some jerky.

After they'd drunk and eaten a little, Bethany sent the soldiers out. She identified each remaining person for the benefit of them all and told everyone to sit. Then she took up a position in the centre and encompassed them all with her gaze.

Thales thought she looked older, more worn, but there was a tautness to her body, a resolution that comes with assuming responsibility. He'd seen it before in Lasper Farr, and the mercenary Rast Randall. And now he saw it in Bethany Ionil.

'You've closed the sphere?' she said to Fariss and Thales.

'Yeah,' said Farris. 'And you've taken command of the ship.'

Samuelle moved next to her. 'Not just the ship. Consilience too. Some of our ships have survived. We'll rendezvous with them soon.'

'My brother was a brilliant man but he risked too much for personal ambition,' said Beth wearily, and that was all.

Thales could see how close she was to tears but she kept them at bay. 'We're prepping to leave, an hour at most. Word's out that the sphere is closing. Things will get worse. Will you come with us?'

Thales couldn't bear to look at Farris as he shook his head. 'I'll stay here. The virus has spread among the Sophos. I must find a way to right things.'

'With the sphere shut you'll be cut off from the rest of Orion. Possibly for ever,' said Beth.

Before Thales could respond, Balbao spoke up. 'Would this be a virus that affects humanesque behaviour? One that alters the processes in the orbito-frontal lobe?'

Thales stared at him, astonished. 'You know of it?'

Balbao's thick-skinned face became unreadable. 'Not only do I know of it, but I can introduce you to the person who developed it and can, no doubt, negate its affects.' He gestured at the female tyro.

'You!' exclaimed Bethany. 'Do you realise what misery you've caused?'

Thales touched his scarred skin.

The tyro, a fleshy female with trembling lips who'd identified herself as Miranda Seeward, opened her mouth and shut it again. 'I needed lucre for my research, so I sold it,' she said finally. 'I never expected it to . . . You must understand that what we were doing was very important. I needed funds.'

Bethany's face set in a grim expression reminiscent of her dead brother. 'If your intention was not malicious then you'll have no qualms accompanying Thales back to Scolar to reverse what you've done. Janne will . . . escort you.'

The injured Feohte leader shifted closer to Miranda.

Seeward grasped the hand of the male tyro next to her and nodded mutely.

Bethany looked to Jelly Hob. 'Jeremiah, can you go to helm? I would be happier if you were there. Leaving here will be fraught.'

Jelly Hob's old face lit with pleasure. Before he left he shook hands with Thales and then Balbao. 'Farewell,' he said with feeling, and left.

Bethany surveyed the rest of them. 'Those of you staying on Scolar must leave now. Petalu Mau will show you off-ship.'

The teranu waved his arm meaning that they should move. Janne, Miranda Seeward and Jise went first. But the other tyro held back. He looked at Bethany almost shyly, Thales thought.

'I would stay if I could, Captain Ionil.'

She regarded him with curious eyes. 'Why would you do that? We will be on the run.'

Labile Connit licked his lips.

'Cos he's your nephew, Beth. Mebbe he thinks some family's better than none,' piped up Samuelle.

Bethany stared at him in shock. 'You're Lasper's son? I never believed the rumours.'

Connit couldn't meet her gaze. 'I never knew him, but I am genetically his son. That is all,' he added quietly. He waited then as if fearing a death sentence.

But Bethany was not, and would never be, her brother. She held out her hand. 'You are welcome on my ship, Labile Connit.'

Relief smoothed the distress from his expression.

'Sammy, find him a cabin and report back to helm,' said Bethany.

'Aye, Captain,' said the old woman with a bright-eyed gleam.

And then only Thales, Bethany and Fariss were left.

Bethany broke the silence by embracing Thales again. 'I will miss you.'

This time he returned her hug fully – for what they'd shared and what she'd done for him.

'Goodbye, dear Thales,' she whispered.

As he followed Fariss to the docking tube, neither of them spoke.

When they reached it, the last of the Feohte were disembarking. They waited for them on station-side with the tyros and Janne.

'Thales!' Janne called. 'We must get back to Ling-Ma.'

Thales waved a hand to acknowledge her and finally lifted his gaze to Fariss. She returned it steadily, her expression infused with conflicting emotions.

'You'll stay with the ship,' he said.

She nodded. 'And you'll stay with your world.'

Thales felt his heart tear into pieces. He'd not known

what she would choose, not until now, when he'd seen her face.

'I'd cause trouble for you down here, Thales. You'd grow to hate that.'

He didn't know what to say. So he let her kiss him one last time, a lingering, deep, breath-robbing kiss.

'When we've beaten the Post-Species, I'll be back to see you,' she said.

He nodded, believing her. 'I'll be waiting.'

MIRA

Mira?

Primo vein's attention to Vito's nutritional deficiencies had engrossed Mira as they left Araldis, but the biozoon's anxious tone dragged her attention back to their task. *What's wrong?*

See – this.

An image slowly bloomed in her mind, an object seemingly half as large as Tiesha or Semantic, burning its way out of Araldis's ionosphere.

The Post-Species Saqr ship.

It pursues us.

Insignia . . .

What do you want from me, dearest?

The Entity is out beyond Tiesha. I've seen it in Lasper Farr's device. I must reach it. The Saqr mustn't stop me. Mira put all her desperate need into her thought.

I am not equipped to combat the creature that pursues us. I'm not even sure what it is.

It is fast?

Yes. I'm at full propulsion and it gains on us easily.

Mira felt Insignia's desolate certainty.

How much longer?

Moments only.

No!

'No!'

Mira's cry was echoed by Tekton, who had settled in the Autonomy nub. Only Josef, cradling a peaceful Nova in the Secondo vein, seemed unaware.

'Mira?' he called softly as he rocked the baby. 'What is it?'

But Mira was transfixed by the image of the approaching Saqr. How enormous it had grown. As she watched it through Insignia's corduroy perspective, she saw a crack appear in the forward section of its body. It began as a large fissure in the gleaming carapace, which elongated and widened until the split was wider and longer than *Insignia*.

The Saqr ship was so close now that she could see inside the split to a frightening and immense mass. At first she thought it to be some type of vegetation, grown within the Saqr's body, but as it closed on them, she realised it was something else – a jungle of coiled flesh that rippled as though underwater.

What is it? she asked Insignia.

A section of the flesh shifted, an eruption of the mass, and something began to unravel. It was longer than anything she'd ever seen, and sinewy.

It reached out for them across space and she felt *Insignia*'s searing pain as the gigantic stamen caught and burrowed into the biozoon's ventral.

Insignia!

Mama! Tasy-al is hurting.

Nova. What can we do? The creature has attached itself to us.

They wish to reach the Entity before us.

Mira's stomach contracted into a tight fist. *How do you know of the Entity, Nova? Or what the Saqr intend?*

Wanton told me.

You are speaking to Wanton? Now?

Wanton says the Non-Corporeals are trying to extract its essence. Wanton said I should tell you that the Post-Species wish to destroy the Entity, so that they may control their own evolution. They fear a more evolved being than themselves.

Mira thought wildly about the point of change that the device had shown them. The Saqr were not there. Not in the images she and Tekton had seen. 'Tekton!'

The Godhead didn't reply, entranced by his immersion in the DSD.

Insignia moaned. *Dearest, I am dying.*

Wanton! shrieked Mira to her daughter. *Wanton must help us, Nova. Help* Insignia.

Nova gave a little cry. *Wanton.*

'Mira!' exclaimed Jo-Jo. 'Nova is ... she's ... convulsing. Mira!'

But Mira could see what Nova was doing, in a way that Jo-Jo could not.

Her daughter projected a wave of electromagnetic rebuke that crossed the space between *Insignia* and the Saqr, and slammed the Post-Species ship.

The shock caused the Saqr to withdraw its stamen from *Insignia*, and a myriad of other fissures spread across its surface.

Insignia shuddered at the release, but already the Saqr was self-repairing, the cracks disappearing almost as quickly as they'd appeared.

The biozoon strained to gain distance as the Saqr's maw opened again, this time unfurling countless stamens and sending them snaking across space, hunting them.

Nova repelled the attack with another EM wave, but she was not strong enough to sustain it and as the wave began to diminish, the hungry stamens pursued them again.

Nova! Wanton! Mira screamed with frustration and powerlessness.

'Mira. Help her!' Jo-Jo again.

'Just hold her, Josef. Let her do what she must,' cried Mira.

Nova sent another wave out, but her strength had gone and the stamens broke through. Yet this time, as they touched *Insignia*'s skin, the Saqr ship itself began to buckle.

The stamens retracted from *Insignia*'s ventral, lashing empty space, convulsing like the legs of an intolerably large spider. Then, slowly, they collapsed back into the Saqr's maw in a tangled, wilted confusion.

The Saqr ship appeared to lose control of its trajectory, an object the size of a small moon whirling out of control.

But as *Insignia* gained distance from it, the ship ceased its uncontrolled spin and changed course directly towards Leah's burning intensity.

Nova?

Wanton says goodbye, Mama. And thank you. Her daughter sounded heartbroken.

What has Wanton done?

Wanton said that I should tell you that it does not wish you to lose your 'poda', as Wanton did.

Mira watched the Saqr ship's trajectory. Leah would envelop it soon; there would be no escape. She was overcome with relief and sadness and loss.

As *Insignia* took them out past Tiesha, she dwelt on those emotions, let them swamp her.

Mira. Do you see it? Do you see it there?

But Mira had felt it before *Insignia* spoke. Its presence entered her mind like a shaft rammed along her backbone, a painful, stiffening jolt and a sense of invasion. She'd expected to feel fear as well, but the only thing beneath the pain was a sense of utter inevitability.

<who? who seeks me>

I am no one. But this no one would tell you that you must stop what you have started, Mira replied.

<must?>

Your device has predicted the destruction of my species. You have brought this upon us.

<device told you?>

The device has shown me outcomes and your hand in their making.

<hand. so corporeal. so tiny>

Anger surged through Mira. The Entity was more obtuse than Insignia. *You have given extraordinary powers to your tyros, encouraged them to venture in certain directions. One has infected our greatest thinkers with a virus that impairs their decision-making, another has used your device to his own gain, passing it to a man who would cause further division between Post-Species and OLOSS under the guise of keeping peace.*

<little problems, little things, little one>

No, she shouted. *Not little problems. You've given us the tools to create our destruction and we've followed your intentions perfectly. You play a cruel game.*

Mira felt its indifference, felt its withdrawal from her mind, the shaft softening in her back.

No! Wait. You must listen to me.

<never must>

Mama, said Nova. *Let me.*

The Entity's withdrawal halted and a sense of curiosity seeped through Mira's being. Sole's curiosity.

I am Nova, said her daughter. *You seem alone. Is that why you have made these things happen?*

<lonely? strange little?>

Like this . . . Nova projected a grave melancholia, a vast emptiness without end that made Mira want to weep.

<you know this? little one?>

We all know. Do you feel it too?

A cold tingle shot through Mira as though she'd been injected with a drug.

<come. show>

Come, Mama.

Mira fell into a dizzying whirlpool of consciousness; was consumed by it and carried an immense, unfathomable distance to a place of dust and dust between galaxies. A place of cold mystery. A place of dark energy. Many Entities. Countless. Roving in their dark playground.

Yet only one of them asked a question. Only one of them cared to know. *Sole.*

<where do we come from?>

You've come to us looking for your origins? Nova was gentle, soft persistence. No anger.

Mira felt the rightness of Nova's statement. The rightness of Sole's accord. *You believe your origins are with us?* she asked.

The sense of rightness came again.

I am young and don't understand. How do our deaths serve you? Nova, so sweet and simple.

Mira imagined that at the corporeal level she was holding her breath, clenching her hands, waiting for Sole's answer. Yet she felt nothing of her body.

Then understanding began to wash through her in little waves, like an incoming tide of knowledge that she could only truly grasp when it was high enough to drown her.

<in death there is life>

And she saw it, the life energy from billions and billions of dead sentients released into space, combining with all matter, colliding and transforming into dark energy.

You wanted to prove that you came from us, from our destruction?

Rightness. Complete and utter.

The idea numbed Mira. She revisited it, toyed with it, tried to read all its sides. *You believe this has happened before?*

Rightness.

She continued to think around it. *But you are matter as well. Which means, if you are correct, that we are you and you are us. And if you are considered God then God is . . .*

Si, Mama, Nova said. *God is us. Or that is what Sole wishes to prove.*

You would have billions of sentients die to know . . . that?
<what other way?>

Rightness without remorse.

Mira sank under Sole's answer, was overwhelmed by the sheer magnitude of its callousness. She floundered to stay afloat in the present, her daughter's voice her only lifeline.

Look to the future for your answer, not the past, her infant told the Entity. *Let me come with you, help you.*

Hesitation. Interest. <little? come?>

I give you willing energy, not stolen. I give you company. <little give answer?>

We'll find the answer together. Without destruction.

Nova! You cannot! Mira panicked.

Mama, it is how it will be. Sole must have company. Nova was definite.

Then let it be me. She felt the Entity's focus on her like a pouring of molten metal.

But Nova addressed the Entity again, ignoring her. *In exchange for my company, you will make amends to our kind. Or at least . . . halt our extinction.*

<possible>

Now! insisted Nova.

Nova, I forbid—

But the encompassing warmth of Nova's love and affection silenced Mira, choking her words and dissolving her protest, softening and comforting her fear.

And before she could further protest, she found herself propelled away from the vast spaces, back into the whirlpool, spinning slower and slower until, eventually, she opened her eyes.

'Mira!' Josef's voice was hoarse and brimming with emotion. He sat on the edge of Secondo, rocking back and forth, holding Nova's body in his arms. 'Something's wrong. I can feel it. Her energy is . . .'

You cannot let her die. Insignia's words crushed Mira.

She climbed from Primo, leaving Vito in cushioned sleep. 'The Entity is here, Josef, close to us. It believes our extinction will offer proof of its origins. Nova has

convinced it to consider another way. She's bargained
her companionship – her life – for ours. For all of Orion.
I must get back to them.'

'Sole promised Nova?'

Mira nodded, distraught.

Josef's face hardened. 'Take her.'

With surprising tenderness he kissed Nova's forehead and handed her over, then he lay back down in
Secondo.

'What are you doing?' Mira started forward.

He took her hand and buried his face in it the way
he had on Araldis. His lips burned against her palm in
a devoted and passionate kiss that told her the depth
of his feelings for her. Then slowly his grip faded and
the pressure of his lips slackened.

Jo-Jo Rasterovich

Jo-Jo had never tried to reach out to the Entity before; it had always sought him. He wasn't sure how to draw its attention, other than to demand.

Sole! Fuck you, Sole!

But Sole did not respond.

Desperate, he cast back to the occasions that Sole had spoken directly to him and tried to re-create the same division in his mind. He'd thought of it like sliced fruit, a kind of soft and slightly messy process. But this time he tried something different; this time he forcibly shrank his emotional centre into a tight and unreachable orb, leaving only the logic side of his brain functioning.

Sole entered the accessible side like a thrown spear.

<need?>

You cannot take this child.

<explain>

The reason came to Jo-Jo with startlingly simplistic clarity: *Nova has been altered by the Post-Species. They oppose your existence. Their changes to her will damage you. It was always their intent to use her against you. And her mother.*

The Entity withdrew a little while it considered his declaration. Perhaps it was running its own type of bifurcation analysis – performing a prognosis of its own future.

Jo-Jo's dislocation from time and place was so

complete he wasn't sure how long he waited, nor did he care. What mattered was that Sole knew the veracity of his statement and left Nova and Mira alone.

<possible>

Probable, he countered.

<probable>

I am the one you should take.

<explain>

My life is yours anyway. You resurrected me. And you've altered my mind for your expediency. Perhaps I was the always the one you would take. Perhaps you knew that at the beginning.

<perhaps> Amusement and mimicry.

Jo-Jo kept the ball of his emotions fiercely contracted not letting anything escape that might shake his resolve.

Agreed then?

<agreed. come>

MIRA

'Crux!' exclaimed Tekton from Autonomy, where Lasper Farr's device rested on his legs like an innocent seemingly benign object. 'There are 'casts coming in from Scolar. Oh . . . my . . .'

'*Insignia*,' said Mira. 'Show us.'

A projection appeared above Primo filled with a vision of the Scolar shift sphere, where a Geni-carrier hung at the centre.

'They've tried to close the sphere but it hasn't completed its shutdown sequence. The Geni-carrier will destroy the whole system,' said Tekton.

'Thales!' cried Mira.

But as they watched the rings of the sphere brightened and began to shrink. The closing sequence appeared to accelerate and the Geni-carrier was caught in the vibration well. In the space of several heartbeats, it disintegrated under the pressure.

Tekton quivered in his seat as the image faded out, his hands fluttering. 'The Scolar 'cast is gone but other feeds are coming in. Reports of Geni-carriers imploding across Orion.'

'Imploding?'

'Self-destructing. The Saqr craft has been engulfed by Leah. It must have affected the commands sent to all the Geni-carriers. They're self-immolating. The

DSD was correct, Baronessa. There was a way.' The Lostolian waved his fist in victory.

Nova stared up at her with solemn eyes. *Josef has saved us, Mama.*

'Si, Nova,' she said, bending down to kiss Jo-Jo's lifeless lips gently. 'Si.'

Sole

Luscious, luscious
Together

extras

orbit

www.orbitbooks.net

about the author

Marianne de Pierres is the author of the multi award-nominated Parrish Plessis and Sentients of Orion science fiction series. The Parrish Plessis series has been translated into eight languages and adapted into a D20 Role Playing Game. 2011 will see the release of her new young adult dark fantasy duology. She is also the author of a humorous crime series, written under the pseudonym Marianne Delacourt. Marianne is an active supporter of genre fiction and has mentored many writers. She lives in Brisbane, Australia, with her husband, three sons and three galahs. Visit her websites at www.tarasharp.com and www.mariannedepierres.com

Find out more about Marianne de Pierres and other Orbit authors by registering for the free monthly newsletter at www.orbitbooks.net

if you enjoyed
TRANSFORMATION SPACE

look out for

SEEDS OF EARTH

book one of Humanity's Fire

by

Michael Cobley

PROLOGUE

DARIEN INSTITUTE: HYPERION DATA
RECOVERY PROJECT

Cluster Location – Subsidiary Hardmem Substrate (Deck
9 quarters)
Tranche – 298
Decryption Status – 9th pass, 26 video files recovered

File 15 – The Battle of Mars (Swarm War)
Veracity – Virtual Re-enactment
Original Time Log – 16:09:24, 23 November 2126

>>>>>>   <<<<<<

FADE IN:
CAPTION:

MARS
THE CRATER PLAIN: OLYMPUS MONS
19 MARCH 2126

The Sergeant was on the carrier's command deck,
checking and rechecking the engineering console's mod-
ifications, when voices began clamouring over his
helmet comm.

'Marine force stragglers incoming with enemy units in pursuit . . .'

'. . . eight, nine Swarmers, maybe ten . . .'

The Sergeant cursed, grabbed his heavy carbine and left the command deck as quickly as his combat armour would allow. The clatter of his boots echoed down the vessel's spinal corridor while he issued a string of terse orders. By the time he reached the wrecked and gaping doors of the rear deployment hold, the stragglers had arrived. Five wounded and unconscious, all from the Indonesia regiment, going by their helmet flashes. As the last was being carried up the ramp, the leading Swarmers came into view over the brow of a rocky ridge about 80 metres away.

A first glimpse revealed a nightmare jumble of claws, spikes and gleaming black eye-clusters. Swarm biology had many reptilian similarities yet their appearance was unavoidably insectoid. With six, eight, ten or more limbs, they could be as small as a pony or as big as a whale, depending on their specialisation. These were bull-sized skirmishers, eleven black-and-green monsters that were unlimbering tine-snouted weapons as they rushed down towards the crippled carrier.

'Hold your fire,' the Sergeant said, glancing at the six marines crouched behind the improvised barricade of ammo cases and deck plating. These were all that were left to him after the Colonel and the rest had left in the hovermags a few hours ago, heading for the caldera and the Swarm's main hive. One of them hunched his shoulders a little, head tilting to aim down his carbine's sights . . .

'I said wait,' said the Sergeant, gauging the diminishing distance. 'Ready aft turrets . . . acquire targets . . . fire!'

Streams of heavy-calibre shells converged on the leading Swarmers, knocking them off their spidery legs. Then the Sergeant cursed when he saw them right themselves, protected by the bio-armour which had confounded Earth's military ever since the beginning of the invasion two years ago.

'Pulse rounds,' the Sergeant shouted. 'Now!'

Bright bolts began to pound the Swarmers, dense knots of energised matter designed to simultaneously heat and corrode their armour. The enemy returned fire, their weapons delivering repeating arcs of long, thin black rounds, but as the turret jockeys focused their targeting the Swarmers broke off and scattered. The Sergeant then ordered his men to open up, joining in with his own carbine, and the withering crossfire tore into the weakened, confused enemies. In less than a minute, nothing was left alive or in one piece out on the rocky slope.

The defending marines exchanged laughs and grins, and knocked gauntleted knuckles together. The Sergeant barely had time to draw breath and reload his carbine when the consoleman's urgent voice came over the comm:

'Sergeant! – airborne contact, three klicks and closing!'

Immediately, he swung round and made for the starboard companionway, shouldering his carbine as he climbed. 'What's their profile, soldier?'

'Hard to tell – half the sensor suite is junk . . .'

'Get me something and quick!'

He then ordered all four turrets to target the approaching craft and was clambering out of the carrier's topside hatch when the consoleman came back to him.

'IFF confirms it's a friendly, Sergeant – it's a vorti-wing, and the pilot is asking for you.'

'Patch him through.'

One of his helmet's miniscreens blinked suddenly and showed the vortiwing pilot. He was possibly German, going by the instructions on the bulkhead behind him.

'Sergeant, I've not much time,' the pilot said in accented English. 'I'm to evacuate you and your men up to orbit . . .'

'Sorry, Lieutenant, but . . . my commanding officer is down in that caldera, engaging in combat! Look, the brink of the caldera is less than half a klick away – you could airlift me and my men over there before returning to—'

'Request denied. My orders are specific. Besides, every unit that made it down there has been over-whelmed and destroyed, whole regiments and brigades, Sergeant. I'm sorry . . .' The pilot reached up to adjust controls. 'ETD in less than five minutes, Sergeant. Please have your men ready.'

The miniscreen went dead. The Sergeant leaned on the topside rail and stared bitterly at the kilometre-long furrow which the carrier had gouged in the sloping flank of Olympus Mons. Then he gave the order to abandon ship.

In the shroud-like Martian sky overhead, the vorti-wing transport grew from a speck to a broad-built craft descending on four gimbal-mounted spinjets. Landing struts found purchase on the carrier's upper hull, and amid the howling blast of the engines the walking wounded and the stretcher cases were lifted into the transport's belly hold. The turret jockeys, the consoleman and his half-dozen marines were following suit when the German pilot's voice spoke suddenly.

'Large number of flying Swarmers heading our way, Sergeant. Suggest you get aboard fast.'

As the last of his men climbed up into the vortiwing, the Sergeant turned to face the caldera of Olympus Mons. Through a haze of windblown dust and the thin black fumes of battle, he saw a dense cloud of dark motes rising just a few klicks away. It took only a moment to realise how quickly they would be here, and for him to decide what to do.

'Best you button up and get going, Lieutenant,' he said as he leaped back into the carrier and sealed the hatch behind him. 'I can keep them busy with our turrets, give you time to make orbit.'

'*Nein*! Sergeant, I order you—'

'Apologies, sir, but you'd never get away otherwise, so my task is clear.'

He cut the link as he rushed back along to the command deck, closing hatches as he went. True, the Colonel's science officer had slaved all four of the turrets to the engineering console, but that wasn't the only modification he had carried out . . .

The roar of the vortiwing's spinjets grew to a shriek, landing struts loosened their grip and the transport lurched free. Moments later, the fourfold angled thrust was driving it upwards on a steep trajectory. Some of the Swarm outriders were already leading the flying host on an intercept course, until the carrier's turrets opened fire upon them. Yet they would still have kept on after the ascending prey, had not the carrier itself now shifted like a great wounded beast and risen slowly from the long gouge it had made in the ground. Curtains of dust and grit fell from its underside, along with shattered fragments of hull plating and exterior sensors, and when the carrier turned its battered prow towards the centre of the caldera the Swarm host altered its course.

On the command deck, the Sergeant sweated and swore as he struggled to coax every last erg from protesting engines. Damage sustained during the atmospheric descent had left the carrier unable to make a safe landing on the caldera floor, hence the Colonel's decision to continue in the hovermags. However, a safe landing was not what the Sergeant had in mind.

As the ship headed into the caldera, steadily gaining height, the groan of overloaded substructures came up through the deck. Even as he glanced at the glowing panels, red telltales started to flicker, warnings that some of the port suspensors were close to operational tolerance. But most of his attention was focused on the host of Swarmers now converging on the Earth vessel.

Suddenly the carrier was enfolded in a swirling cloud of the creatures, some of which landed on the hull, scrabbling for hold points, seeking entrance. Almost at the same time, two suspensors failed and the ship listed to port. The Sergeant boosted power to the port burners, ignoring the beeping alarms and the crashing, hammering sounds coming from somewhere amidships. The carrier straightened up as it reached the zenith of its trajectory, a huge missile that the Sergeant was aiming directly at the Swarm Hive.

Ten seconds into the dive the clangorous hammering came nearer, perhaps a hatch or two away from the command deck.

Twenty seconds into the dive, with the pitted, grey-brown spires of the Hive looming in the louvred viewport, the starboard aft burner blew. The Sergeant cut power to the port aft engine and boosted the starboard for'ard into the red.

Thirty seconds into the dive, amid the deafening cacophony of metallic hammering and the roar of the engines, the hatch to the command deck finally burst open. A grotesque creature that was half-wasp, half-alligator, struggled to squeeze through the gap. It froze for a second when it saw the structures of the Hive rushing up to meet the carrier head-on, then frantically reversed direction and was gone. The Sergeant tossed a thermite grenade after it and turned to face the viewport, arms spread wide, laughing . . .

CUT TO:

VIEW OF OLYMPUS MONS FROM ORBIT

Visible within its attendant cloud of Swarmers, the brigade carrier leaves a trail of leaking gases and fluids in its wake as it plummets towards the Hive complex. The perspective suddenly zooms out, showing much of the wreckage-strewn, battle-scarred caldera as the carrier impacts. For a moment there is only an outburst of debris from the collision, then three bright explosions in quick succession obscure the outlines of the hive . . .

VOICE OVER:
In the first phase of the Battle of Mars, a number of purpose-built heavy boosters were used to send a flotilla of

asteroids against the Swarm Armada, thus drawing key vessels away from Mars orbit. The main battle, and ground offensive, cost Earth over 400,000 dead and the loss of seventy-nine major warships as well as scores of support craft. This act of sacrifice did not destroy all the Overminds of the Swarm or deter them from their purpose. Yet vast stores of bioweapons, like the missiles that devastated cities in China, Europe and America, were destroyed along with several hatching chambers, thus halting the production of fresh Swarm warriors and delaying the expected assault on Earth.

That battle brought grief and sorrow to all of Humanity, yet it also bought us a breathing space, five crucial months during which the construction of three interstellar colony ships was completed, three out of the original fifteen. The last of them, the *Tenebrosa*, was launched from the high-orbit Poseidon Docks just four days ago, following its sister ships, the *Hyperion* and the *Forrestal*, on a trajectory away from the enemy's main forces. All three vessels are fitted with a revolutionary new translight drive, allowing them to cross vast distances via the strange subreality of hyperspace. First to make the translight jump was the *Hyperion*, then two days later the *Forrestal*, and the *Tenebrosa* will be the last. Their journeys will be determined by custodian AIs programmed to evade pursuit with random course changes, and thereafter to search for Earthlike worlds suitable for colonisation.

And so they depart, three arks bearing Humanity's hope for survival, three seeds of Earth flying out into the vast and starry night. Now we must turn our attention and all our strength to the onslaught that will soon be upon us. In twelve days, spearhead formations of the Swarm will land on the Moon and at once attack our civilian and military outposts there. We know what to expect. The Swarm's strategy of slaughter and obliterate has never wavered, so we know that there will be no pity, no mercy and no quarter when, at last, they enter the skies above Earth.

Yet for all that the Swarm soldiers are regimented drones, their leaders, the Overminds, must themselves be sentient and able to learn, otherwise they would not have developed space travel. So if the Overminds can learn, let us be their teachers – let us teach them what it means to attack the cradle of Humanity . . .

>>>>>> <<<<<<

END OF FILE . . .

1

GREG

Dusk was creeping in over the sea from the east as Greg Cameron walked Chel down to the zep station. The great mass of Giant's Shoulder loomed on the right side of the path, its shadowy darkness speckled with the tiny blue glows of *ineka* beetles, while a fenced-off sheer drop fell away to the left. The sky was cloudless, laying bare the starmist which swirled for ever through the upper atmosphere of Darien. Tonight it was a soft purple tinged with threads of roseate, a restful, slow-shifting ghost sky.

But Greg knew that his companion was anything but restful. In the light of the pathway lamps, the Uvovo stalked along with head down and bony, four-fingered hands gripping the chest straps of his harness. They were a slender, diminutive race with a bony frame, and large amber eyes set in a small face. Glancing at him, Greg smiled.

'Chel, don't worry – you'll be fine.'

The Uvovo looked up and seemed to think for a moment before his finely furred features broke into a wide smile.

'Friend-Gregori,' came his hollow, fluty voice.

'Whether I ride in a dirigible or make the shuttle journey to our blessed Segrana, I am always amazed to discover myself alive at the end!'

They laughed together as they continued down the side of Giant's Shoulder. It was a cool, clammy night and Greg wished he had worn something heavier than just a work shirt.

'And you've still no idea why they're holding this *zinsilu* at Ibsenskog?' Greg said. For the Uvovo, a *zinsilu* was part life evaluation, part meditation. 'I mean, the Listeners do have access to the government comnet if they need to contact any of the seeders and scholars . . .' Then something occurred to him. 'Here, they're not going to reassign ye, are they? Chel, I won't be able to manage both the dig and the daughter-forest reports on my own! – I really need your help.'

'Do not worry, friend-Gregori,' said the Uvovo. 'Listener Weynl has always let it be known that my role here is considered very important. Once this *zinsilu* is concluded, I am sure that I will be returning without delay.'

I hope you're right, Greg thought. *The Institute isna very forgiving when it comes to shortcomings and unachieved goals.*

'After all,' Chel went on, 'your Founders' Victory celebrations are only a few days away and I want to be here to observe all your ceremonies and rituals.'

Greg gave a wry half-grin. 'Aye . . . well, some of our "rituals" can get a bit boisterous . . .'

By now the gravel path was levelling off as they approached the zep station and overhead Greg could hear the faint peeps of *umisk* lizards calling to each other from their little lairs scattered across the sheer face of Giant's Shoulder. The station was little more than a buttressed platform with a couple of buildings and a five-yard-long covered gantry jutting straight out. A government dirigible was moored there, a gently swaying 50-footer consisting of two cylindrical gasbags lashed together with taut webbing and an enclosed gondola hanging beneath. The skin of the inflatable sections was made from a tough composite fabric, but exposure to the elements and a number of patch repairs gave it a ramshackle appearance, in common with most of the workaday government zeplins. A light glowed in the cockpit of the boatlike gondola, and the rear-facing, three-bladed propeller turned lazily in the steady breeze coming in from the sea.

Fredriksen, the station manager, waved from the waiting-room door while a man in a green and grey jumpsuit emerged from the gantry to meet them.

'Good day, good day,' he said, regarding first Greg then the Uvovo. 'I am Pilot Yakov. If either of you is Scholar Cheluvahar, I am ready to depart.'

'I am Scholar Cheluvahar,' Chel said.

'Most excellent. I shall start the engine.' He nodded at Greg then went back to the gantry, ducking as he entered.

'Mind to send a message when you reach Ibsenskog,' Greg told Chel. 'And don't worry about the flight – it'll be over before you know it . . .'

'Ah, friend-Gregori – I am of the Warrior Uvovo. Such tests are breath and life itself!'

Then with a smile he turned and hurried after the pilot. A pure electric whine came from the gondola's aft section, rising in pitch as the prop spun faster. Greg heard the solid knock of wooden gears as the station manager cranked in the gantry then triggered the mooring cable releases. Suddenly free upon the air, the dirigible swayed as it began drifting away, picking up speed and banking away from the sheer face of Giant's Shoulder. The trip down to Port Gagarin was only a half-hour hop, after which Chel would catch a commercial lifter bound for the Eastern Towns and the daughter-forest Ibsenskog. Greg could not see his friend at any of the gondola's opaque portholes but he waved anyway for about a minute, then just stood watching the zeplin's descent into the deepening dusk. Feeling a chill in the air, he fastened some of his shirt buttons while continuing to enjoy the peace. The zep station was nearly 50 feet below the main dig site but it was still some 300 feet above sea level. Giant's Shoulder itself was an imposing spur jutting eastwards from a towering massif known as the Kentigern Mountains, a raw wilderness largely avoided by trappers and hunters, although the Uvovo claimed to have explored a good deal of it.

As the zeplin's running lamps receded, Greg took in the panorama before him, the coastal plain stretching several miles east to the darkening expanse of the Korzybski Sea and the lights of towns scattered all around its long western shore. Far off to the south was the bright glitterglow of Hammergard, sitting astride a land bridge separating Loch Morwen from the sea; beyond the city, hidden by the misty murk of evening, was a ragged coastline of sealochs and fjords where the Eastern Towns nestled. South of them were hills and a high valley cloaked by the daughter-forest Ibsenskog. Before his standpoint were the jewelled clusters of Port Gagarin, slightly to the south, High Lochiel a few miles northwest, and Landfall, where the cannibalised hulk of the old colonyship, the *Hyperion*, lay in the sad tranquillity of Membrance Vale. Then further north were New Kelso, Engerhold, Laika, and the logging and farmer settlements scattering north and west, while off past the northeast horizon was Trond.

His mood darkened. Trond was the city he had left just two short months ago, fleeing the trap of his disastrous cohabitance with Inga, a mistake whose wounds were still raw. But before his thoughts could begin circling the pain of it, he stood straighter and breathed in the cold air, determined not to dwell on bitterness and regret. Instead, he turned his gaze southwards to see the moonrise.

A curve of blue-green was gradually emerging from behind the jagged peaks of the Hrothgar Range which lined the horizon: Nivyesta, Darien's lush arboreal moon, brimming with life and mystery, and home to the Uvovo, wardens of the girdling forest they called Segrana. Once, millennia ago, the greater part of their arboreal civilisation had inhabited Darien, which they called Umara, but some indeterminate catastrophe had wiped out the planetary population, leaving those on the moon alive but stranded.

On a clear night like this, the starmist in Darien's upper atmosphere wreathed Nivyesta in a gauzy halo of mingling colours like some fabulous eye staring down on the little niche that humans had made for themselves on this alien world. It was a sight that never failed to raise his spirits. But the night was growing chilly now, so he buttoned his shirt to the neck and began retracing his steps. He was halfway up the path when his comm chimed. Digging it out of his shirt pocket he saw that it was his elder brother and decided to answer.

'Hi, Ian – how're ye doing?' he said, walking on.

'Not so bad. Just back from manoeuvres and looking forward to FV Day, chance to get a wee bit of R&R. Yourself?'

Greg smiled. Ian was a part-time soldier with the Darien Volunteer Corps and was never happier than when he was marching across miles of sodden bog or scaling basalt cliffs in the Hrothgars, apart from when he was home with his wife and daughter.

'I'm settling in pretty well,' he said. 'Getting to grips with all the details of the job, making sure that the various teams file their reports on something like a regular schedule, that sort of thing.'

'But are you happy staying at the temple site, Greg? – because you know that we've plenty of room here and I know that you loved living in Hammergard, before the whole Inga episode . . .'

Greg grinned.

'Honest, Ian, I'm fine right here. I love my work, the surroundings are peaceful and the view is fantastic! I appreciate the offer, big brother, but I'm where I want to be.'

'S'okay, laddie, just making sure. Have you heard from Ned since you got back, by the way?'

'Just a brief letter, which is okay. He's a busy doctor these days . . .'

Ned, the third and youngest brother, was very poor at

keeping in touch, much to Ian's annoyance, which often prompted Greg to defend him.

'*Aye, right, busy. So – when are we likely to see ye next? Can ye not come down for the celebrations?*'

'Sorry, Ian, I'm needed here, but I do have a meeting scheduled at the Uminsky Institute in a fortnight – shall we get together then?'

'*That sounds great. Let me know nearer the time and I'll make arrangements.*'

They both said farewell and hung up. Greg strolled leisurely on, smiling expectantly, keeping the comm in his hand. As he walked he thought about the dig site up on Giant's Shoulder, the many hours he'd spent painstakingly uncovering this carven stela or that section of intricately tiled floor, not to mention the countless days devoted to cataloguing, dating, sample analysis and correlation matching. Sometimes – well, a lot of the time – it was a frustrating process, as there was nothing to guide them in comprehending the meaning of the site's layout and function. Even the Uvovo scholars were at a loss, explaining that the working of stone was a skill lost at the time of the War of the Long Night, one of the darker episodes in Uvovo folklore.

Ten minutes later he was near the top of the path when his comm chimed again, and without looking at the display he brought it up and said:

'Hi, Mum.'

'*Gregory, son, are you well?*'

'Mum, I'm fine, feeling okay and happy too, really . . .'

'*Yes, now that you're out of her clutches! But are you not lonely up there amongst those cold stones and only the little Uvovo to talk to?*'

Greg held back the urge to sigh. In a way, she was right – it was a secluded existence, living pretty much on his own in one of the site cabins. There was a three-man team of researchers from the university working on the site's carvings, but they were all Russian and mostly kept to themselves, as did the Uvovo teams who came in from the outlying stations now and then. Some of the Uvovo scholars he knew by name but only Chel had become a friend.

'A bit of solitude is just what I need right now, Mum. Beside, there's always people coming and going up here.'

'*Mm-hmm. There were always people coming and going here at the house when your father was a councilman, but most of them I did not care for, as you might recall.*'

'Oh, I remember, all right.'

Greg also remembered which ones stayed loyal when his father fell ill with the tumour that eventually killed him.

'*As a matter of fact, I was discussing both you and your father with your Uncle Theodor, who came by this afternoon.*'

Greg raised his eyebrows. Theodor Karlsson was his mother's oldest brother and had earned himself a certain notoriety and the nickname 'Black Theo' for his role in the abortive Winter Coup twenty years ago. As a punishment he had been kept under house arrest on New Kelso for twelve years, during which he fished, studied military history and wrote, although on his release the Hammergard government informed him that he was forbidden to publish anything, fact or fiction, on pain of bail suspension. For the last eight years he had tried his hand at a variety of jobs, while keeping in occasional contact with his sister, and Greg vaguely recalled that he had somehow got involved with the Hyperion Data Project . . .

'So what's Uncle Theo been saying?'

'Well, he has heard some news that will amaze you – I can still scarcely believe it myself. It is going to change everyone's life.'

'Don't tell me that he wants to overthrow the government again.'

'Please, Gregori, that is not even slightly funny . . .'

'Sorry, Mum, sorry. Please, what did he say?'

From where he stood at the head of the path he had a clear view of the dig, the square central building looking bleached and grey in the glare of the nightlamps. As Greg listened his expression went from puzzled to astonished, and he let out an elated laugh as he looked up at the stars. Then he got his mother to tell him again.

'Mum, you've got to be kidding me! . . .'